S.R. CLARK

Dangerously Kept

McDermott Empire Book Two

First edition

ISBN: 979-8-218-37397-9

Editing by S.R. Clark
Editing by Jaquelyn Vale
Cover art by S.R. Clark

This book was professionally typeset on Reedsy.
Find out more at reedsy.com

To all the women who are afraid to ask for what they want in bed
. . . Be the boss bitch and the dirty little slut I know you are, own
that shit, and . . .
Make. Him. Beg. For. It.
You go girl.

"Don't underestimate the allure of
darkness. Even the purest hearts are
drawn to it."

-Niklaus Mikaelson

Preface

Welcome back! I'm so glad you're here. This is Part Two in the McDermott Empire duet with Harper and her guys. To understand this book, it's important you read book one, *Dangerously Safe*, first. Have fun!

Warning
Content and trigger warnings include: kidnapping, mentions of rape, homophobia (not the main character), torture, mentions of forced marriage and pregnancy, starvation, murder, gun violence, fire, explicit sex scenes, group sex scenes, mfmm, degradation, breath play, light bondage, and spanking.
If none of this is for you or if any of this triggers you, please do not continue. You're mental health matters.

PS: Seeing as none of you listened to me the last time . . . If you are an immediate member of my family or know me personally in any way, proceed with caution. But if you do read it, don't say I didn't warn you!
PS: Grandma P, this one's still not for you.

DANGEROUSLY *Kept*

1

Ronan

She looks like a fucking goddess, a queen on her throne. Lucky me, because my dick is that throne. Harper's tits bounce in front of my face as she rides me like it's her damn job. I look up at her, head tipped back in ecstasy, just in time to hear a deep moan spill past her pretty pink lips. "That's it, Baby. Ride me, milk my fucking cock."

Her back bows even further, and I can feel her chocolate curls dust the tops of my thighs. "Yes! God, Ronan."

"That's right. I am your God. Don't you ever forget it."

I can't help myself; I slide my hand around her waist and grip the locks that are tickling the tops of my thighs, pulling her head tight as I lean forward and take one of her nipples into my mouth, clamping down on it with my teeth and give it a sharp tug.

"Fuck!" Harper yells, still bouncing up and down on my dick. I grin wickedly around the tight bud.

I fucking love it when she curses.

Harper's pussy starts to tighten around me, her orgasm's like a ticking time bomb, right on the cusp of exploding. I'm about ten seconds from blowing inside her, so we need to get this show on the road. I let go of her hair so she can look down at me. "Tell me what you need, Baby."

Her big emerald eyes meet mine, trying to relay precisely what she wants without having to say it out loud. But I know. I know what my girl needs. The sadistic side of me just needs to hear her say it out loud. You'd think after months of living with and fucking the three leaders of the Irish mafia, she'd be a little more brazen by now. Not our little bookworm. When she climbed on my lap in the middle of the movie we were watching, I was more than happy to let her be in control, or at least think she was. I've been gentle, letting her lead the show, but we both know what she wants, what she needs from me. To own her. To ravage her entirely.

"Say it, Harper."

She hesitates only a second more before saying, "More, Ronan. I need more."

I slide my hand up her stomach, between the valley of her perfect breasts, and along the column of her neck until it meets her jaw. I firmly grasp it in my hands, squeezing just hard enough that her eyes widen. "You want me to be rough with you, Baby? You want me to own this sweet ass?"

She pulls her bottom lip into her mouth, still sitting on my lap with my cock buried inside her. I reach my thumb up and pull her lip from between her teeth, resisting the urge to take it between my own.

"Yes," she whispers breathlessly.

I cock a brow and fold my lips in, trying to hide my smart-ass smirk. "I thought you wanted to be in charge?"

She gives me the most dramatic eye roll. There's my girl.

"I thought so, too."

Before she can blink, I lift her off of me and roll us over so she's lying on her back on the couch with me nestled between her hips. Her beautiful hair is fanned out across the couch cushion as she looks up at me, her chest heaving as she takes in each breath.

Scooting down the couch, I run my lips up the inside of one of her thick thighs, savoring the way her body still reacts to mine. I'll never get sick of it. Never. But what I want to do to her can't be done on this couch. I want her on my bed, tied up and at my mercy. I sit back on my knees, and she pinches her brows in confusion.

I give her my most sinister smile. "Run, Baby."

A wide grin takes over her face, and she doesn't waste a second before taking off down the hallway toward my room. I give her a few-second head start before taking off after her. As I move across the living room, I feel something soaking the bottoms of my feet. I look down to find myself standing in a deep crimson pool of blood. A sinking feeling immediately settles in my gut, and I sprint towards my room. Towards Harper. Only when I slam the door open, she's nowhere to be found.

Panic claws at my chest as I throw open every other door, calling out her name. "Harper! Harper, Baby . . . Where are you?! Harper!!!"

Where the fuck is she?

Who's blood is that?

Where's my Baby?

Just as I'm about to check my office, I feel drops of blood trickle down the side of my face. I reach up to touch the sudden throb at my hairline, wincing when I make contact with a giant open gash. "What the fuck?"

I don't remember getting hit.

I feel myself getting lightheaded now. Everything around me is spinning. But I have to focus. I need to find Harper. I need to make sure she's safe. I dig around the leather couch cushions to find the phone I discarded when Harper climbed on top of me. Once I find it, I pull up Mac's contact number. He can help me. He'll be able to find her.

My finger shakes as I move to unlock my phone. I can't seem to focus long enough to put in my passcode.

Come on, Ronan. Call Mac. Find Harper. Keep her safe.

I repeat this to myself as if it will somehow push away the blackness taking over my vision.

I drop to my knees, unable to hold the weight of my own body any longer. My phone falls from my grip as I hit the ground. Suddenly, my eyes feel heavy—so, so heavy. Tipping over onto my side, I fight with everything in me to keep my eyes open.

I can't sleep.

I have to find her.

I have to find Harper.

But, it's no use. I can't fight against it.

Just as darkness takes over, I hear it. I hear her voice. It sounds so weak. So sad. She calls out to me, "Baby."

2

Mac

"Tell me, boy. How does Harper like her new security detail?" Declan's menacing threat rings through Finn's otherwise silent Audi Q2. I look over from my spot behind the wheel just as Declan hangs up the phone, and it falls into Finn's lap. I've been running through every light and breaking every speed limit to get through the streets of New York and back to the apartment as fast as possible since we got into the car. I've been trying to get ahold of Ronan since Declan called Finn's phone, but he isn't picking up. And now . . . now I *know* something is wrong. Declan's words are like a razor blade to my skin. He's done something. And if the look on Finn's pale face is any indication, he knows it too.

My hands grip the steering wheel impossibly tight as I swerve through the busy streets. I can feel it start to settle in my gut. I can see it crowd the edges of my vision and hear it ringing in my ears—the killer, the animal inside of me gearing up to destroy anything in its wake.

"Not yet," I whisper to myself. I can't lose control yet. Not until I know what we're dealing with.

Get a fucking grip, Mac.

Finn's voice brings me back. But he doesn't sound like himself. My strong and steady best friend sounds unsettled— he sounds *terrified.* "Mac, what if she's *gone*? What if he—"

"Don't." I cut him off before he even dares to speak the words that would be the end of my life as I knew it. "She can't be dead, Finn. She's not fucking dead." I know I'm trying to convince him as much as I am myself, but we can't think about any of that right now. We can't think about the fact that she might be gone, that right now, she might be in unspeakable pain. We can't think about what happened to my brother. We can't think about the fact that they both might be dead. The only thing we can do right now is get back to the apartment.

Finally, our building comes into view as I round the last corner. The second we get past the security in the parking garage, I throw the car in park, not even bothering to pull into a stall or turn it off, and Finn and I sprint to the elevator. The moment the doors close, we draw our handguns from where they're tucked in the waistband of our pants. Ready and willing to kill anyone that gets in our way.

As we begin climbing the highrise, I feel my pulse pick up, my breathing becoming more rapid by the second as I stare at myself in the reflection of the elevator doors. The side of me I fight every day to keep locked away, begging to be released.

Finn's hand squeezes my shoulder, and I snap my face

toward his. Slowly shaking his head, he says softly, mimicking my words from the car. "Not yet. Not yet, brother."

His hand remains on my shoulder the rest of the way up as if he's grounding himself to me and me to him. Once the elevator reaches the floor below ours, the two of us share a look in our reflection on the doors and take a deep breath, silently preparing ourselves for whatever we're about to find. The door dings and the elevator stops, along with my heart in my chest when the door opens and I see Tanner, dead, lying in a pile of his blood, with his throat cut open ear to ear. Neither Finn nor I take the time to deal with Tanner. Stepping over him, we race through the kitchen to find Ronan unconscious on the floor at the mouth of the hallway. I drop to my knees beside him and wave Finn on. "Go! Go find Harper." Without arguing, he moves toward Ronan's room, gun at the ready.

Looking down at my brother, I notice a small pool of blood on the ground beneath his head, coming from the decent-sized cut on his forehead. My breathing slows slightly at the sight of his chest rising and falling with each shallow breath. *He's alive.*

I reach for his neck, relieved to feel his pulse beating strong. There isn't enough for him to have passed out from blood loss, so his unconsciousness is likely due to a pretty decent concussion. Whatever happened with Logan, he got the drop on Ronan, and I know he will never forgive himself.

I have to wake him up. We don't have time for this shit.

"Sorry, brother." I rear back and slap him across the face, not hard enough to worsen whatever injury he has but enough to wake him up.

The second my hand meets his cheek, his eyes snap open, immediately meeting mine. It's then that I know. I watch

Finn slowly walk down the hallway, and before he even says anything, I know she's not here. The sadness and anger swimming in my big brother's eyes is unlike a look I've ever seen on his face before.

She's gone.

They took her.

They took Harper.

I look up at Finn from where I sit on the floor next to Ronan. He stares at me momentarily before dropping his chin and offering me a slight nod.

Now, Mac.

Just like that, I welcome *him* in.

I will burn the world down around me and leave a trail of bodies in my wake. Anyone who touches a hair on her head or so much as breathes in her direction will wish they were never born. I will stop at nothing until my Princess is back in my arms.

They better make friends with the Devil because they're about to spend eternity in Hell.

3

Harper

The first thing I notice as I come to is the overwhelming smell of cologne. It doesn't smell like any of the guys, and it's so strong it burns my nostrils. A sudden jolt causes me to hit my head on the floor, and I groan in pain, only worsening my pounding headache.

What the hell was that?

"Well, well, well. Good morning, Sunshine." A deep, raspy voice drums in my ears. It sounds so familiar, but I can't put my finger on it. My head feels so fuzzy, my body exhausted. I can't even get myself to think straight.

What is going on?

Finally, I muster up the energy to open my eyes to find myself in the back of a van. A surge of panic races through me as I move to sit up, only to find that my hands are tied behind my back. The strange voice chuckles from the front seat, and I snap my head toward it. The second my eyes land on the driver of the van, everything comes crashing back to me in rapid succession.

Logan.

He took me.

Drugged me.

Tanner couldn't stop him.

Ronan couldn't stop him, either.

He . . . he *killed* Ronan.

The image of Ronan lying lifeless on the floor in a pool of blood dripping from his head floods my memory, and I can't stop the pained sob that slides past my lips.

"Baby . . ." I whisper to myself. Silently hoping that, by some miracle, my whispering it will bring him back to me. But when it doesn't, I scoot myself against the van wall, biting the inside of my cheek, forcing the tears to stop falling. I notice Ronan's signet ring, the one I slid on when I woke up to find him, still on my finger and begin spinning it around with my thumb, using it to center me. I can't fall apart. I have to focus. I have to make it long enough for Mac and Finn to find me.

"Why?" I ask in the strongest voice I can manage.

"Why do you think? Declan."

That name cuts through me like a knife. I should have fucking known. After everything he's done, killing his daughter and teaming up with Liam McDermott, I should have known he would have found another way to get to me. I just never would have thought he would have found someone this close.

"Played my part well, didn't I? It really wasn't that hard. You all made it too easy. You were all so focused on Liam and protecting you from randoms on the street that you never thought to take another look at me. I just had to bide my time." Logan's voice now has a thick Irish accent, making it clear he was covering it up before.

"Keep him talking, Baby." I hear Ronan's voice in my head, telling me what to do. Logan's in the mood to chat might as well make the most of it.

"H–how?"

He scoffs as if I'm the biggest idiot on the planet, but little to my surprise, he babbles on. "As soon as Liam figured out those three idiots were falling for you, he told Declan. Declan knew it wouldn't be long until they hired security for you. They have too much shit going on to all be around you 24/7. And wouldn't you know, he was right? He had one of his guys hack the system of the security company the McDermotts use. They put in a fake file, and all we had to do was wait until Ronan made the request. Badabing, Badaboom, I was your new security detail."

"There's more, Harper. Keep pushing."

"What's Delcan have on you? Why are you doing this?" Logan's face falls briefly, but I see it before he has a chance to cover it up. *Got it.* "What did you do?"

I watch in the rearview mirror as his face twists in anger. "I fucked up. This is how I'm fixing it," he bites out.

Before I can ask what he did, he slows and pulls off to the side of the road. My breathing speeds up as I take in our surroundings. There are no windows back here, but all I see out the windshield is the dark and vast expanse of wilderness. *Shit.* If he takes me out there, they'll never be able to find me.

"Fight, Baby. Fight."

Logan unclicks his seatbelt, climbs out, and rounds the

front of the van to slide open the door. The second he reaches his hand out to grab me, I kick and fight with everything in me.

"Would you calm the fuck down!"

I scream at the top of my lungs, but even I know it's useless. We're in the middle of nowhere. Nobody is going to hear me. I try my hardest to kick him away, but he's twice my size, and my hands are still tied behind my back. He grabs me by the ankle and pulls me across the van floor towards him. "Get the fuck off of me!" I'm dressed in nothing but the shirt I threw on before he took me—Ronan's shirt. It rides up as he pulls me across the floor, leaving me completely exposed. I can practically feel his eyes burning holes into my body.

My eyes widen as he pulls another syringe out of his coat pocket. He slides my legs over the edge of the van and pins them between his own. His giant fist grabs the front of my shirt and pulls me so I'm sitting in front of him. His eyes look down at me, making me beyond pissed at myself that I ignored my instincts when it came to him. Because I can see it clear as day now—he's crazy. A disturbing grin spreads across his face as he brings it closer to mine, but, much to my dismay, not close enough for me to headbutt him. "As much as I love hearing you scream, we have to keep moving. Declan has plans for you, and the trip will be much easier if you're unconscious."

"What trip?" I practically snarl at him.

"Forgot to tell you, Declan is coming to get us in Pennsylvania in a couple of weeks. We're staying at one of his cabins until then. Congratulations, you get to meet Grandpa."

Shit. Shit, shit, *shit!* I don't get a chance to protest, though, as he plunges another needle into my neck.

That's going to get real old real quick.

The last thing I hear before darkness consumes me once again is Logan's whisper in my ear, "But until then, Princess, it's just you and me . . . all alone."

Princess.

No. I'm Mac's Princess.

Mac.

Help me. Find me.

4

Ronan

It's been five hours. Five agonizing hours since she was taken from us. Five hours since I failed her. She could be anywhere by now, going through God knows what, and it's all my fucking fault. She's never going to forgive me for this, hell, I'll never be able to forgive myself. Regardless, we have to find her. I'd rather live in a world where she's alive and hates me than one where she isn't in it at all.

The minute I was conscious, I threw on some clothes, and Mac, Finn, and I got to work. I explained to them every detail that had happened since Harper and I got home, purposefully leaving out the fact that Harper whispered "I love you" in her sleep. I could barely handle thinking of the memory without feeling like I was going to die, let alone speaking it out loud.

What if that was the only time I would ever get to hear her say it?

We had our men sweep the entire building to ensure she wasn't still here. I knew she wouldn't be, but I wasn't going to take any chances. We also made sure Tanner's body was taken care of properly and had him sent to a top-of-the-line mortician. I don't know what all went down between Tanner and Logan, and I probably never will, but what I do know is that he died protecting my girl. And because of that, I will ensure his body, when the time comes, is laid to rest with the utmost respect. But I can't think of any of that right now. Right now, all of my focus needs to be on finding Harper and murdering every single person who had a hand in taking her from me.

Because I *will* find her, and I *will* kill them all.

I will *not* fail her again.

The three of us wasted no time pulling up security footage from the building and surrounding traffic cameras, trying to get a lead on the direction they may be heading. We got access to all those cameras just a few weeks after I took over for Liam. A couple of officers I have on my payroll in the local precincts set everything up for me, and I've been able to monitor the streets of New York ever since. But no matter how hard or how far into the city we look, we can't find a fucking thing. Not even footage of them leaving our apartment or getting into a vehicle in the parking garage. Nothing. It's like the two of them vanished off the face of the planet.

I can feel the all-consuming rage crushing me from the inside out. I feel like a dying star wanting to destroy everything in my path. Until I get my Baby back, that's exactly what I'll be—dead.

Destroying the world around me.

"Motherfuckers!" Finn slams his fists on the table where he's set everything up. He hasn't moved from his chair in hours; meanwhile, I can't sit the fuck still. Mac left shortly after I woke up, and I just know he's been burning down the streets of New York around him, but he's more useful out there than he is here. "This doesn't make any sense, Ronan. They didn't just disappear. Declan has to have some sort of computer genius working for him. Someone who could access all of the footage and alter it." Finn is pretty well-versed when it comes to computers. But even I know his need to solve any problem, and his computer skills aren't enough right now.

"We need help, Ronan." The desperation in Finn's voice is deafening. Still pacing, I run my hands through my hair, ignoring the sharp sting from the cut on my hairline. I wouldn't let Mac or Finn stitch me up when they found me. As long as Harper's out there somewhere suffering and in pain, then I will be, too. I don't deserve to feel better. I didn't keep her safe.

I failed her.

I will *not* fail her again.

"I know," I murmur as I finally stop moving about the apartment. Pulling out my phone, I call the only person I know that has more resources than I do and would be willing to help us without trying to fuck me over in return.

"Buongiorno," Pascal's voice rings through the speaker-phone. "Your mother is fine, boys. We're sitting on my patio watching the sunset and drinking wine as we speak." I hear the faint sound of Mum's giggle in the background. If I weren't a shell of a man right now, the sound would make me smile.

"Pascal, we need your help." The urgency in my voice must spring him into action because I hear him excuse himself, and a few moments later, the sound of a door closing.

"What happened? Your father?"

With everything that has happened in the last six hours, it feels like killing our father happened a lifetime ago when, in all actuality, it hasn't even been a day. "No. He's been taken care of and is no longer a problem. It's Harper."

"The girl?" Pascal asks inquisitively.

"They took her, Pascal. Declan managed to get one of his men on our security team. He ambushed me while Mac and Finn were still at the docks. He knocked me out and took her. We've been up all night searching cameras, and we can't find a fucking thing. We have no idea which direction they're headed or if they're even still in the country. She's been gone over five hours already. We can't fucking find her." The last sentence causes my voice to crack and tears well at the back of my eyes, a feeling of such sorrow I've ever only experienced in regards to her I clench my fist at my sides, willing myself to keep it together.

"Don't fall apart now, boy," his voice is stern. "Here's what's going to happen. My son, Luca, lives in New York. He runs all of my business' over there when I'm not in town. He's well versed in dealing with those who *betray* us." I don't miss the underlying meaning of his words. I'm not one who ever asks for help. I take great pride in being able to run this empire on my own with the help of Mac and Finn. I'm a prideful man who has grown accustomed to having the weight of the world on his shoulders. But right now, for Harper, I will take all of the help I can get. And if it's someone Pascal trusts, then so do I. "He has a team that can help you with anything you need. I'm going to hang up the phone and call Luca. Expect him and his team in thirty minutes."

"Okay."

"You keep it together, alright? She needs you."

"I'm trying, and—"

"Don't you even worry, son." Pascal cuts me off, already knowing what I'm going to say. "I will protect her as if she were my own."

"Thank you. Tell her we love her."

"I will."   I hang up the phone without another word, unwilling to waste any more time.

The elevator dings, and Finn and I watch Mac storm in, not at all surprised by what we see. Mac's practically dripping in blood from head to toe. I don't ask who's it is, nor do I really fucking care, because judging by the look on his face, they didn't tell him what he wanted to hear.

"Anything?" I ask him, even though I already know the answer.

He looks at me with a blank expression before shaking his head. If it weren't for the crimson stains covering his body, you would think Mac is the calmest of us right now. But I know better. I see the war inside of him—the chaos. Right now, he's nothing more than a killer, trained to make even the devil himself drop to his knees in fear, and that's what we need. It's what Harper needs to bring her home. I just hope that when we finally get her back, she's strong enough to pull Mac out, and I hope he's strong enough to let her.

He sits on a dining room chair across from Finn, not even bothering to change his clothes, likely succumbing to the fact that this will be his permanent state until we get her back.

"I called Pascal. His son, Luca, and his team will be here soon to help us."

"We will find her. We have to." I don't know if Finn's trying to convince Mac, me, or himself, but either way, I nod my head in agreement. Mac looks up at me, and for a brief moment, I can see the unrelenting sadness in his eyes. Water pools in the corners before he quickly blinks it away and breaks eye contact with me, moving his gaze toward the large windows across the room. My eyes follow his, taking in the sight of the city, waking up and preparing for another day, utterly oblivious to the war that's taking place.

We will not fail her again.

5

Harper

We're still driving. I've been awake for a while now, but I've kept as quiet as possible, not wanting to be stabbed in the neck and rendered unconscious . . . *again*. We've been in this van since last night, and the sun is starting to rise. I don't know how often we've stopped while I was out, but it can't be that much further to wherever he is taking me. Even Lake Erie is only a good eight hours from the city, which is about as far in Pennsylvania as he can go. I know we're not on a major highway anymore. Our speed has slowed by quite a bit, and the roads are getting bumpy.

Just as the thought crosses my mind, the van slows to almost a crawl as Logan turns onto what sounds like a gravel road. My chest tightens at the thought of us getting to our destination; at least with him driving and me in the back of the van, I'm out of his reach.

"Just a few more minutes, Princess. You can stop pretending to be asleep now." *Shit.*

"Where are we?" I ask while nervously thumbing at Ronan's ring, hoping this idiot will be dumb enough to tell me exactly where we are. Maybe if I can get away and call Mac and Finn, they can come get me.

"None of your damn business," he bites back—*double shit.*

"Stay calm, Baby. Save your energy for when it's important."

Ronan's voice in my head makes me feel like I'm dying. How will I survive without him? A piece of my soul now lies within each of them, pieces I will never get back. And now that he's gone, he took that piece with him. I can never be whole again.

The overwhelming urge to give up rears its ugly head at the memory of him. To lay lifeless in the back of this van for the rest of time and just live in the memory of him. The feel of his rings on my skin as his touch explores my body, the smell of whiskey and smoke invading my senses whenever he was near, and the way he acted like he couldn't be bothered to feel for anyone or anything when in all actuality he cared and loved deeper than anyone I've ever known.

I don't want to live without him. Every minute that passes without his heart beating chips away at my soul. How long will it be until there's nothing left?

I have to fight, though. I have to be strong for Mac and Finn. They already lost their brother because of me, and I will *not* let them lose me, too. I have to make it back to them. I have to be strong . . . *for them.*

The van comes to a stop before Logan gets out and slides open the back door. "You can get out yourself, or I can make you." The look on his face tells me he'd be more than happy to go with the second option. Based on my fight with him earlier, I know that fighting him right now wouldn't be much use, so I slowly scoot across the van, hands still tied behind my back, and climb out on my own. I make sure I take my time, though, looking at my surroundings as much as possible. A small cabin that doesn't look to be more than a thousand square feet stands in front of me. The cabin is made of dark-stained wood, and all the windows are framed with black shutters. The front porch sags a bit on one side, and the roof is covered in moss. But other than that, it looks like it's in fairly decent shape. At least he didn't take me to a total shithole.

Count your blessings where you can, Harp.

"Home sweet home," Logan says from beside me, and I give him the most sinister look I can manage. However, I bite my tongue and decide it's best not to say anything smart. I don't know his plans for me yet, but I know he's not afraid to put his hands on me. "Stay here. I have to go turn the water on."

I wouldn't run anyway. I still feel tired from whatever he injected me with, and I know I wouldn't make it far, especially since it looks like we are surrounded by nothing but never-ending trees. What I need is to find a way to get the keys and drive away in the van.

"Patience, Baby."

"I know, I know," I whisper under my breath.

I watch Logan as he moves about the property. He's tall, not quite as tall as the guys, but at least a few inches taller than me, and his body is packed with muscle. His dusty blond hair is shaved close at the neck and is curly at the top, held in place by an exorbitant amount of gel. I don't think a tsunami could mess up his hair. If I'm being frank, he's a relatively good-looking guy, which, considering his dickhead personality, I'm sure is how he's gotten this far in life. His chiseled cheekbones match his square jaw, which looks sharp enough to cut diamonds, and he has a nose that's the perfect size for his face, minus the small crook on the bridge, probably from taking a punch to the face.

Fucking dick. He'll have to worry about more than a punch to the face when Mac and Finn get their hands on him.

But as he makes his way back to me and I look into his dark brown eyes, all I can see is every menacing thought rattling around in his brain, reminding me of who I'm in the presence of.

"Let's go, Princess." I fight the urge to kick him right in the balls whenever he calls me that.

Grabbing me by the elbow, he pulls me, more forceful than necessary, toward the cabin, leaves and sticks crunching under my bare feet. Once we get inside, I'm overwhelmed by the stench of mothballs and dust mixed with Logan's obnoxious cologne. Clearly, no one has been here in a long time. Logan stops to let me use the bathroom at the front of the house. I don't even have any goddamn panties on, so I sit on the toilet as he stands there staring at me. I don't miss the way his eyes linger on my exposed skin.

Once we're done in the bathroom, he pulls me through the rest of the house. I try to memorize the small layout as much as possible. Everything from where each window and door is to the location of the knife set on the counter by the fridge. As we move down the hallway, passing two more bedrooms and another bathroom, I see the small room open at the end. Inside, there is nothing besides a metal bed frame with a thin mattress. There's not even a window in this room. My heart stops when I look at the bed closer, a rope with a leather cuff is attached to each leg of the bed. Logan shoves me past the door and into the room. I feel his large frame behind me before his hot breath skates across the side of my face. It's enough to make me want to vomit.

"This has got to go," he says as he grips the back of my shirt.

"Wait, wha—" But before I can finish my thought, he yanks at the back of the shirt, ripping it open at the front and sending buttons flying across the room. He cuts the sleeves with his pocket knife, and the shirt falls to the floor. Leaving me completely naked with my hands tied in the middle of the room. I force myself to take a deep breath, holding back the bile working its way up my throat.

"Fuck. I get it now." Logan walks around to stand in front of me, eyeing me up from head to toe.

"Get what?" I snap, looking him dead in the eye.

"How you had the three of them worshiping the ground you walked on." He grabs my jaw and runs his thumb across my bottom lip. I try to rip my face from his grasp, but he only grips it harder. "The things I could fucking do to this body."

Before he moves his hand, I take his thumb between my lips and bite down as hard as possible. Howling out in pain, Logan rips his hand away before using it to backhand me across the face. The hit knocks me to the floor, and I immediately know he hit me hard enough to break the skin. I feel the blood drip down my cheek. I don't have a chance to get back up before Logan grabs me by the hair and drags me up onto the bed. "You fucking bitch." I fight with everything in me to stop myself from yelling out in pain. He doesn't deserve the satisfaction. "You can't play nice, can you?"

He throws me onto the bed and climbs on top of me so he's straddling my ankles, making it impossible for me to kick my way out of his hold as he carefully unties my hands from behind my back and ties them to the frame of the bed instead. "Do as I say, and I can make your last few days on this earth far more enjoyable."

"Fuck. You." I spit as he manages to attach my ankles to the foot of the bed.

"Oh, I plan to, Princess." Logan trails his hand from my ankle up my leg and over my exposed pussy. "But, whether you enjoy it or not . . ." His hand doesn't stop as he continues to make his way up my stomach and over my breasts before stopping once he's firmly gripping my throat. I feel my eyes widen as he grabs my throat hard enough to stop my breath. "Well, that's up to you."

"They–They're going to k–kill you." My body fights for air underneath his hold.

"They can try." I watch his eyes peruse my body again before he lets me go. "But we'll be long gone before they ever even find out where we are." He spins on his heels and walks towards the door. "Get some rest, Princess. I've got a lot planned for us while we're here." I listen as he closes the door and latches what sounds like several locks. As his footsteps retreat toward the other end of the house, I finally let my tears fall.

6

Finn

I feel like I can't fucking breathe. From the moment I answered my phone at the docks, my chest felt like it was locked in a vice, and the only person with the key is Harper—my Angel.

I don't understand how we fucking missed this. I mean, we knew that Declan would show his hand sooner rather than later. As a man with as many resources as he has, there was no way Liam McDermott was the only plan he had in motion. But never in a million years did I think it was Logan. Someone we had in our home. Someone *we* hired to protect her. Someone *we* trusted with her life. And I can't help but feel like this is all my fault. It's my job to read people, to figure out who they are, to sniff out the liars and the bastards who are out to do us wrong. Yet, somehow, I missed this. I let him get close to her, and I fucking missed it.

Everything went so wrong so fast. Hell, I was about to rush home to tell her I loved her, and now she's just *gone*.

I've been sitting at these god-forsaken computers for hours, trying to find any sign of where Logan may have taken her, but I can't find a fucking thing. I know my way around a computer. I made it a point to learn as much as I could years ago. Just another way to make myself valuable to Liam. Another way for me to solve any problem he threw at me. For the most part, everything I have learned is self-taught, meaning there are limits to what I can do, and whoever Delcan has scrubbing all of this footage has made me reach my limit. My eyes burn from staring at the screens, and my fingers ache from flying across the keyboards, but I won't stop.

Mac got back about twenty minutes ago, and I wasn't the least bit surprised when he walked through the elevator doors. Him being covered in someone's blood is nothing new, but what is new is the look on his face—or lack thereof. My brother isn't in there, and I know he won't be until we get her back. Neither Ronan nor I bothered to ask Mac to whom he paid a visit. Even in this state, we both trust him enough to know he wouldn't lay a hand on someone who didn't deserve it. So, even if he didn't get the answers we needed, at the very least, Mac rid the world of one more asshole.

I continue to work at the dining room table, while we wait for Pascal's son and his team to arrive. I glance at Mac and Ronan across the table, ensuring they're not completely falling apart. Mac still hasn't showered and has barely spoken a word. I know it killed Ronan not to go out with Mac earlier, but we all knew he needed to be here. He did what he does best and took control—directing everyone where they needed to be and what they needed to be doing. The time will come when he can get his hands bloody, and when he does, I will be more than happy to join him. But for now, while we wait for the others to get here, he's sitting next to Mac, unloading and reloading every weapon he could get his hands on. Every click of him chambering a round or sliding the magazine in and out sets my teeth on edge, yet I keep it to myself because I know that's what he needs right now. Ronan needs something to keep himself busy, or he will go mad, and the only person allowed to do that now is Mac.

"Where the fuck are they?" he snarls. "Every minute we sit here is another minute we don't know where the fuck she is!" Tears pool in his eyes, and I know that he, just like Mac and myself, is hanging on by a thread.

"It's only been twenty minutes, Ronan," I answer in the calmest voice I can manage, even though I only want to scream right along with him. "They'll be here any minute. You need to stay calm." He runs his fingers through his dark hair and pulls on the ends, wincing in pain as it tugs at the cut on his head. The stubborn ass wouldn't even let us stitch him up.

"Fuck, Finn . . ." He hangs his head, trying to hide his emotions from me, but not before I watch a tear drop onto the table. It's then I know just how deep he's in, how deep we're all in. Because I have never, in all of my life, seen Ronan McDermott shed a single tear. Shit, we just murdered his father, and he hardly even batted an eye. "He can't have our girl, Finn. Declan can't have her. We have to—"

I reach across the table and firmly squeeze his forearm, drawing his attention to me and letting me see how deeply he's hurting. "We will, Ronan. We will get our girl back."

If you had asked me before that night in Hayes' Bookstore about the prospect of "our girl" being a phrase I would use, I would have told you that you were batshit crazy. But now, sharing Harper with the two most important people in my life feels like it was how all this was supposed to play out. Harper deserves everything she wants in this life and more. If the three of us can give that to her, I'm not selfish enough to want to take that away. Because she is *ours,* and when we get her back, we'll give her the world.

I look at Mac, who, with the same distraught look as his brother, is nodding in agreement. I don't miss the tears that roll down his cheek either, leaving a trail in the blood splattered across his face.

As if the universe knew I couldn't string together any more words, the intercom buzzes before Ralph's voice rings through the speaker located on the wall by the elevator. "Excuse the interruption, gentleman, but Mr. Luca Vittori and three of his friends are here to see you."

Ronan abruptly stands from his chair and sprints over to the intercom. "Send them up, Ralph. Thank you."

"Do I need to send them through security first, sir?" Ralph, who is now the building's "doorman," is a retired Navy SEAL we hired to work the front door of the building. Regardless of his age, he's more than competent when it comes to hand-to-hand combat and can hold his own against just about anyone. He knows who we are and what we do and is a trusted friend who keeps the coming and going of all of our visitors on the down low and is compensated well for it. He works with the security we have placed throughout the building, ensuring nobody enters our apartment without our approval, as well as the safety of everyone else in the building. The three of us aren't naive enough to think that someone wouldn't use one of the other residents against us.

"No. They're alright, Ralph," Ronan answers anxiously.

"Okay, sending them up now, sir."

I nod at Mac, and he and I make our way over to Ronan, ready to meet our guests. A few moments later, the elevator door opens and we're met with a team that looks as formidable as our own.

"Gentleman." Luca Vitorri, Pascal's son—damn near twin—exits the elevator first, shaking each of our hands upon arrival, not even batting an eyelash at Mac's horrifying appearance. Anyone who's anyone knows Pascal's reputation. He's a ruthless businessman who does whatever it takes to protect everything he's built and those he loves. However, much like us, he abides by a particular code of ethics, making him more than a trustworthy companion if you're on his good side. Lucky for us, we are. Considering everything we know about Pascal, it's safe to say he raised his son, Luca, to be the same way. If he didn't, Pascal would have never sent him our way to help—son or not. Because of this, my brothers and I trust him and his team immediately. No questions asked. And, if they can help us find Harper, we will be forever in their debt.

"Thank you for coming on such short notice," Ronan greets him, shoving his hands in the pockets of his joggers, anxiously shifting on the balls of his feet, more than ready to get this fucking show on the road and find our girl.

"Not a problem at all. Any friend of Dad's is a friend of ours." If my world weren't crumbling around me, I would be amazed at how much Luca looks and sounds like Pascal. His voice has a deep timber, but his accent isn't nearly as thick, indicating he's spent far more time in the States than his father. He has the same square jaw covered in dark stubble and the same perfectly styled midnight-black hair, albeit Luca's a lot less gray. He stands about the same height as Ronan and me, around six-foot-five, but is slightly leaner. However, judging by how his body fills out his black cargo pants and Henley, his body is packed with muscle. He has the same eyes as Pascal's too, such a dark brown they're almost black yet shine bright with mischievousness; but if you look close enough, much like his father's, you can see the torment seething inside of him.

"Just tell us what you need, and we'll help anyway we can," says the man standing directly off his right shoulder. The three of us look to Luca, waiting for him to introduce us to the rest of his team formally. We've heard about the four of them but have never officially met, but based on appearances alone, I can probably figure out who is who, regardless of their matching outfits.

It's all in the eyes.

"My apologies," Luca sweeps his hand towards the man beside him. "I'm sure you've seen him around. This is Enzo Santoro, my best friend and business partner."

"Sorry, we had to meet under these circumstances," Enzo nods.

Luca steps to the side to reveal the man behind him, as if we couldn't see his giant body already. "This is our muscle, Dante DeLuca." Dante does nothing but drop his chin in acknowledgment, standing perfectly still with his arms across his chest. "And this is Sebastian Moore. He can find just about anyone and anything using a computer. He's a fucking genius."

A look passes between Sebastian and Luca that's hard to miss, something more profound than friendly adoration, but I choose not to analyze it further. Now isn't the time. I reach out to shake Sebastian's hand, immediately recognizing he's a bit shyer than the other three. "Nice to meet you, man."

"You too."

"Alright, now that introductions are out of the way, can we get a fucking move on," Ronan clips.

Luca smiles softly. "Lead the way, amico."

* * *

An hour later, the seven of us have split up and are doing everything we can to dig up some sort of lead as to where Declan has Logan and Harper hidden.

Mac took Dante with him across town to pay a visit to some of our Russian friends, not to murder anyone per se, but just to see if they happened to strike up some sort of deal with Declan. I doubt it, as most of them would rather die than work with any of us—us being the Irish mafia—but we can't be too sure. Ronan, Luca, and Enzo are sitting in the den calling anyone and everyone we know, just hoping someone may have heard or seen something—anything—while Sebastian and I are camped out in front of the computers at the dining room table. Sebastian managed to get into Declan's bank records, and I am currently combing through every single one of his transactions, hoping there's something that can give us a clue as to where she is. Sebastian also installed some sort of program onto our computers.

With it, he says he should be able to find the IP address of the person who hacked into all the security and street cameras and altered the footage. He tried explaining everything to me, but honestly, the entire thing is so far beyond my fucking pay grade it isn't even funny. All I know is that his fingers are quite literally going a mile a minute trying to find her, and I couldn't be more grateful.

I hear Ronan cuss somebody out in Gaelic before throwing his phone across the room. I watch as it hits the wall and shatters into pieces. It's not the first time that wall has met Ronan's wrath, and it won't be the last.

"Seb!" Luca yells before patting Ronan on the shoulder and squeezing it firmly.

Sebastian simply walks across the room and moves to pull something out of the many duffle bags they brought with them. He walks back over to his computer with what I now see as a phone in his hand. He bends over the back of the chair he was just sitting in and begins typing. After just a few moments, the phone in his hand lights up, and he walks it over to Luca, who has his hand outstretched over the back of the couch. "Same number," Sebastian says as he places the phone in Luca's hand, letting the tips of his fingers linger on Luca's just a moment longer than necessary.

Luca puts the phone in Ronan's hand. "Next person, amico."

Ronan's shoulders rise slowly as he takes a deep breath, trying to recenter himself. He unlocks his new phone and calls the next person on his list without saying a word.

7

Harper

I've been gone for two days now.

Correction: Logan has had me tied naked to this bed in the middle of the woods for two days now.

Two days since I've seen them.

Two days since I saw Ronan lying on the kitchen floor.

Two days since they took a piece of me.

Mac and Finn have to be close to finding me. There's no way they've stopped looking for me since I've been gone. With the amount of resources they have at their disposal, they have to be close. *Right?*

Logan left this morning to run and get supplies while we're here. I've barely slept the entire time we've been here. I didn't trust that he wouldn't do anything to me while I was unconscious. He hasn't done much since he first brought me here, but I'm not naive enough to know he doesn't want to. So, when he left this morning, I used the time to try and get some much-needed rest, as best as I could anyway, considering my arms and legs are still tied to the bed, and I'm fucking freezing. But any sleep is good sleep. I need to keep my strength up as much as I can.

Speaking of which, I wince as my stomach cramps from being so hungry. He hasn't fed me a damn thing since we got here. The only provisions he's given me are a few glasses of water and to let me get up a few times to use the bathroom. If I have any chance of getting out of here, I need to convince him to give me some food.

I didn't even bother trying to escape once Logan left. I know I'm desperate, but I'm also not stupid. Logan took the van, and I had no chance of making it through the deep Pennsylvania wilderness with no clothes, shoes, or food. I lived in New York City my entire life; for Christ's sake, I know nothing about how to survive in the woods. I just have to wait for the right opportunity.

"Patience, Baby."

I hear the crunch of tires as the van pulls back up the drive, and I steel myself for Logan to come in here. Spinning Ronan's ring around with my fingers, I listen as he makes a few trips from the van to the cabin, unloading everything he bought while he was out. The monotonous sounds of him putting everything away in the kitchen reminds me of Finn. A faint smile graces my lips for the first time in days as I remember watching him tidy up the kitchen after every meal. Making sure everything was exactly where it was supposed to be. My smile fades as quickly as it appears as I hear Logan's footsteps draw closer to my door.

I try to twist my body in various directions, hoping to hide some of my most private areas from him, but it's no use. Not that it matters anyway. He's seen it all already. He unlocks the numerous locks on the door before strolling in with a cocky look on his face, like he's God's gift to man.

I really can't wait to deck him.

I relax into the mattress slightly once I see he's holding what looks like an oversized T-shirt. "I'm going to untie you so you can go to the bathroom and put this shirt on. If you behave, I'll get you something to eat."

Oh, thank God.

I don't speak, just nod. I've barely talked to him since we got here. Mostly because I don't trust myself not to give him attitude, and I don't entirely want to find out what the repercussions will be, but also because he does a lot of talking on his own. I've noticed the less I say, the more he feels the need to fill the silence with his endless blabbering. Eventually, he's going to slip up and tell me something useful.

Logan leads me into the bathroom, where he towers over me, yet again, while I do my business. Of course, he waits until after to give me the shirt to put on. It's nothing fancy, but at least it covers my boobs and is long enough to hang below my ass. Regardless, Logan's eyes linger when he notices my nipples poking out beneath the white cotton.

To my surprise, he doesn't take me back into the bathroom but into the kitchen. He pulls me onto a stool, "Sit there and don't move."

My eyes immediately dart toward the countertop by the fridge, looking for the knife set I saw when he brought me in a couple of days ago. Of course, he doesn't miss it and chuckles darkly. "Nice try, Princess. Hid them when I got back."

"Figures," I mumble under my breath as he walks toward the stove. Logan sets a small pot onto the lit burner and dumps out a ninety-nine-cent can of chicken noodle soup. What I wouldn't give for one of Mac's meals right about now.

A few minutes later, Logan plops a bowl of lukewarm soup down in front of me, along with some saltine crackers and a glass of water. At least he bothered to warm it up a little. Beggars can't be choosers, I guess.

I quickly eat the shitty chicken noodle soup while listening to Logan talk about how annoying he thought Tanner was. "He was such a fucking stick-in-the-mud." I feel a pang in my chest at the thought of Tanner. Logan killed him simply because he was protecting me.

He probably had a family, but I wouldn't even know because I never even thought to ask him. I was too busy avoiding them because Logan's stare always made me so uncomfortable. Hell, now that I think of it, I don't even know what his last name was.

I take the last bite of soup and dramatically drop my spoon into the bowl, letting Logan know I'm finished. The sooner he takes me back into my room, away from him, the better.

Logan rounds the kitchen island and pulls me out of my stool so I'm standing in front of him, flush against his body. "You gonna keep up the silent routine, Princess? Because I gotta tell ya, I liked it better when you were yelling."

I still don't say a word and instead roll my eyes.

"That's fine," he drops his head so it's right next to my ear, and I flinch as his lips touch my earlobe. "I can think of a few other ways to make you scream."

Yeah, fuck this.

I square my shoulders and look him dead in the eye. "One,

you've probably never made a girl scream out in pleasure in your miserable life. Two, any time you are anywhere near me, all I want to do is vomit. And three," I manage a maniacal smile, "you'll be the one screaming once they come for me."

Logan squeezes my arm harder, but I make sure not to react. His breath is coming out in hard pants. Clearly, I struck a nerve.

"What's the matter? Not used to women fighting back? Gotta make sure they're drugged up enough to let you into their pants?"

"*Baby . . .*"

This isn't smart. I know it's not. But I'm not the type of woman who's just going to stand by while someone continues to threaten her. Never have been, never will be.

"You don't know what the fuck you're talking about."

"Oh, I don't, huh? Tell me, Logan. When's the last time a woman willingly slept with you." His eyes immediately dart away from mine—interesting. "A man?"

The minute the words leave my mouth his head snaps back toward mine, his dark brown eyes filled with anger. "I am not fucking gay."

"Then why are you so offended, Logan?"

"You better shut the fuck up right now."

"Is that what happened? Declan found out you were fucking someone you weren't supposed to?" I watch regret take over his face momentarily, but then he blinks, and it's gone. "I was wondering why you haven't made good on your threats since we've been here. That's why, isn't it? Pussy doesn't do it for ya?"

Holy shit. That's it.

"Who was it?" I ask, poking the bear even further. Instead

of answering, he drags me across the room and toward the hallway. "There's no reason to be ashamed, Logan. I like a good dick, too."

In a split second, I'm being thrown across the room and into the wall, knocking the wind right out of me. "Shut the fuck up! You stupid bitch! You don't know what the hell you're talking about!"

I manage to catch my breath and sit up against the wall. If I can get him to just come a little bit closer, I can drive my fist right into his tiny package, grab the keys he stupidly left sitting right on the counter, and get the hell out of here. "You top or bottom, Logan?"

In two long strides, he's right in front of me. I don't miss a beat, rearing my fist back and slamming it into his crotch with every bit of strength I can manage. Hitting my target, Logan drops like a bag of rocks.

"Run, Baby."

I get to my feet as fast as possible and sprint towards the keys on the counter. Grabbing them, I run for the front door, stopping dead in my tracks when I see the giant deadbolt and padlock keeping me in.

Fuck.

I spin around to assess my options. The back door is on the other side of the kitchen, right where Logan is lying, groaning like a baby. My only option is a window. I run toward the window next to the large stone fireplace and try to open it. It won't budge. I reach down to pick up a log from the stack next to the fireplace to smash it open, but just as my fingers wrap around the bark, Logan's strong hand grabs a fistful of my hair.

Without hesitation, he throws me, yet again, this time

causing me to crash into the solid wood coffee table in the middle of the living room. My head smacks the edge of it, and immediate pain courses through me. The room spins around me, rendering me unable to get up from the floor. I feel the back of my head growing wet with blood where I hit it.

"Get up, Harper. You have to run."

I try to get up, but the second my head lifts off the ground, the dizziness knocks me right back down. Before I get the chance to move again, Logan grabs another fistful of my hair and begins dragging me across the floor. I reach up with both hands to grab his wrist, trying to lessen the pressure on the cut, but it's no use. The pain is excruciating. "Let me go!"

Logan pulls me down the hall and into the room, all while I'm kicking and fighting with everything I have. He throws me onto the bed, and I immediately try to sit up. I see it before it happens, though. His hand curled into a fist as it flies toward me, hitting me right on the side of the head. I crash back onto the bed with a cry, and his fist lands another blow on my side. A crack of my ribs rings through the cabin.

I lay on the bed crying out in pain, unable to move, as he ties me back onto the bed. "You dumb fucking whore. I was being nice to you, you know? I was taking it easy on you because I know what Declan has planned once he gets his hands on you."

"Just let me go, please. They'll kill you when they find us. Just let me go, and you can live," I plead between struggled breaths. He definitely broke a rib, and I can feel the pillow growing wet with blood from the back of my head.

He tightens the last cuff around my leg. "I can't. If I fail Declan, what he'll do to me is much worse."

Logan grabs my face, forcing me to look at him, except my eyes can't focus because there are currently four of him. "You try that shit again, and I will fucking kill you."

He throws my face to the side before storming out of the room without another word, locking the door behind him.

I almost fucking had it. I was right there.

I let out a yell loud enough it could shake the foundation of this shitty cabin. Not that it matters. There's no one around to hear me.

I can feel sleep try to take hold of me as I continue to sob into the empty room, likely passing out from a concussion or blood loss. I don't fight sleep for the first time since we got here. I know now that Logan won't touch me anymore. The only reason he was doing it before was to make me uncomfortable, and it fucking worked. Instead, I let sleep wash over me. At least when I'm asleep, I can dream about them. I can dream about the way I felt safe when I was in their arms. I can dream about the way I loved them.

"Just wait, Harp. Get some rest and wait. I just have to hold out until they come for me. They'll find me. They'll find me, and I'll be safe. Declan won't get to keep me." I repeat it over and over, spinning Ronan's ring as I do until I finally drift off to sleep.

8

Mac

Two Weeks Later

Red.

That's all I see every day, all day long. Since they took Harper, it's been nothing but red.

Red from the uncontrollable fury coursing through my veins. Red from watching my brothers, my best friends, unravel right along with me. Red from the blood of every person who has gotten in my way. But I can't let myself feel any of it. If I do, I'll collapse into nothing. Because that's what I am without her.

Nothing.

Today, we finally got a lead. After fifteen agonizing days, Finn and Sebastian finally found something, and just for a moment, the red started to fade. Now it's back in full force, though, as I listen to the sound of Dante's fist split open this motherfucker's nose.

Early this morning, Sebastian and Finn were finally able to

track one of Declan's bank transactions to a low-level gang that works out of Mott Haven in The Bronx, one of the most dangerous neighborhoods in the city. Sebastian was able to figure out where the guy, Tony, lived in a matter of minutes. In no time at all, the six of us, with Sebastian staying back at the apartment to monitor surrounding security cameras and keep an eye out for any facial recognition on Harper, were out in front of Tony's run-down house. Ronan, Finn, Luca, and Enzo are posted in surrounding buildings, ensuring no other gang members or police officers interrupt our mission. Dante and I had no idea how many people were in the building, and to be honest, we didn't give a fuck. Between the two of us, we knew we could handle whatever was going on inside.

Over the last two weeks, Dante has more than proven himself. He can handle any weapon you put in his hands, and the guy is built like a brick shithouse. He also doesn't say much, which is more than okay with me right now. The last thing I need is someone constantly checking in with me and asking if I'm okay. Because I am not fucking okay, and if I talk about it for even a minute, I'll fall apart.

Thankfully, only five people were inside the house: Tony and four of his men. It only took a couple of minutes for Dante and I to round them up and move them to the kitchen, where they were all sitting on the floor. Correction, four of them are dead, lying in pools of their blood, and Tony is sitting on the floor crying like a little bitch next to them. For someone who "runs" a gang, all it took was a couple of hits to the face before he started crying.

Pathetic.

Once we had them all confined to the kitchen, we sent Sebastian pictures of their faces so he could run facial recognition. It only took him a few moments to figure out who they were, each of their rap sheets a mile long. As soon as I found out that none of them had any family or children that would need our help, it was lights out.

Dante rears his gigantic boot back and kicks Tony right in the stomach.

"Please, just tell me what the fuck you want!" Tony screams, tears, snot, and blood running down his face.

Usually, I am far more patient with the people we interrogate, waiting until Ronan or Finn gives me the go-ahead to use my specific set of skills. However, I think it's safe to say we've all been feeling a little less generous lately.

Dante looks at me, waiting to see if I'm finally ready to ask Tony what I want to. I nod, and he takes a step back as I take a step forward. I squat down and grab a fistful of Tony's hair, forcing him to look at me. "You know who I am?"

"Y–yes. I know who you are."

"Good, then you know that if you don't answer my next three questions very carefully, I will not hesitate to end your miserable excuse of a life."

I let go of his hair as he nods his head frantically. "I'll tell you anything you want to know."

"One," I hold up my pointer finger. "Do you know who this is?" I hold up Logan's picture on my phone.

"Yeah, L–Logan, right?" I nod. "I only met him once. Like three weeks ago."

"Two," I tuck my phone back into my pocket and hold up another finger. "What did you meet him for?"

Tony looks down at the floor. I don't hesitate to grab him by the hair again, this time much, much harder. "Shit. Fuck! Okay, okay . . . He got my number from someone. Called and told me he needed to buy s-something from me."

"What did he need to buy, Tony?" I growl. My voice is practically unrecognizable.

"He needed roofies."

"Rohypnol?" I fist his hair tighter, feeling strands break free from his scalp.

"B-but he said he needed to be able to inject it. So I sold him a few doses and some needles."

I take a deep breath through my nose before asking my final question and holding up a third finger. "Three, did you know Logan worked for us?"

"No! No, man, I swear, he said his boss was some guy in Ireland! I never would have met him if I knew he had anything to do with you guys. I swear on my fucking life, man!"

I let go of him and move back toward Dante. "You guys hear that?" I ask into the coms, hoping Ronan and Finn heard what he just said.

"Yeah, we fucking heard," Ronan snarls.

"You guys think he knows anything else?" Enzo asks.

I look over my shoulder to see Tony curled into a ball. "No. I think he's just a low-level piece of trash. He sold Logan the drugs used to knock Harper out. That's it."

Heavy sighs fill the coms. "I agree," says Finn, "But that still doesn't explain how Declan found out about Harper in the first place, what exactly he plans on doing with her, or where the fuck she is!" Finn's voice grows louder with each word. I know it's becoming harder and harder for him to keep it together. Every day we can't find her, we all seem to be slipping further and further into the darkness. I listen as he takes another deep breath.

"I mean, the more that I think about it, if he just wanted her dead, why didn't he have Logan do it? Why take her and hide her away? Just so he can come here and kill her himself? I know Patrick said he wants her dead, but the way Declan's going about it doesn't make any sense."

"You're right, it doesn't," Luca agrees. "There's something that we're missing."

"Mac, get that shit taken care of and meet us back at the cars. We'll regroup at the apartment. I think we need to give Patrick another call."

I slide back the barrel of my handgun and load one last round, pointing it directly at Tony's ugly fucking face. "I told you everything you wanted to know! P–please, please, please! Don't kill me!"

I crouch down again so I'm right in front of him. I want to be able to see the light leave his eyes. "You helped them take her. My Pretty Girl is gone, and you're partially responsible. For that and that alone . . ." I press the barrel between his eyes, "you die."

The bullet leaves the barrel before Tony even has a chance to blink. And just like I wanted, I watch as the last bit of life leaves his eyes.

Dante and I leave all five bodies exactly as they are, walk out of the house without a backward glance, and make our way through the shitty neighborhood back to our cars, where the rest of the guys are waiting for us. Ronan, Finn, and I climb in one car, and Luca and his guys get in the other. The three of us don't say another word, surely all trying to figure out what the hell we're missing because Finn's right. This doesn't make any damn sense.

Sure, we got answers from Tony, but none of them were

overly helpful. All we did was confirm that Declan hired Logan, and Logan drugged Harper to get her out of the apartment. But those weren't the answers we've been dying to get. And I mean it, I feel like I'm literally dying.

Without Harper, I. Am. Dying. Lost in all the red.

9

Ronan

Once we return to the apartment, Finn immediately joins Sebastian at the computers, and Dante and Mac get cleaned up. Luca calls to update Pascal—who has offered more than once to come back to the States to help us, to which I immediately told him to stay put and keep our mother safe—and Enzo calls to order us some dinner. None of us have had a home-cooked meal in weeks, as the only one of us who can cook worth a damn is Mac, and I know my brother doesn't have the energy for such a menial task. Hell, he is barely eating as it is.

I snuck off to my office, needing a few minutes to myself before we gave Patrick a call. The weight on my shoulders is unbearable. I've spent my entire life taking care of everything and everyone. Trying to live up to the impossible expectations Liam set for me, taking over the empire he built and turning it into something better than he could have ever even imagined, keeping Mac safe from the world—our father, and at times, himself—ensuring Finn has a place, and protecting our mother. All of it was already more than one person should ever have to handle. Then Harper came into our life, and the weight doubled with the uncontrollable urge to keep her safe. Now she's gone.

She's gone, and I have to get her back. For her. For myself. And for my brothers.

And that weight, it's almost more than I can bear.

But I have to bear it. There is no other choice.

I will *not* fail her again.

It's the same mantra I've been repeating to myself over the last two weeks. Yet, as each day passes, each hour, each minute, each second, I'm terrified it's becoming less and less true.

I spend a few more minutes sitting at my desk, trying to regain the slightest bit of composure. But the longer I stare at the dark wood, the more I become flooded with memories of her—my Baby. Of the time I pinned her against the wall by the door, all the times she stormed in and out of this room after chewing me a new asshole, of the night I finally gave in and let myself have her right here on this desk. My eyes begin to sting, and in the safety of my solitude, I let a lone tear roll down my cheek over the memories of her. That can't be all there is. I have room for so many more memories to be had with her, my brothers, and the life we could build together.

I let out a deep yell, reach my arm out, and swipe the contents of my desk onto the floor for what I'm sure is the tenth time in the last two weeks.

Luca barges into the room, not bothering to knock, to find

me heaving in my desk chair. He sits in the chair on the other side of my desk, resting his elbows on his knees while boring holes into my head with his eyes, waiting for me to speak.

He and I are alike in more ways than I care to admit. Which is how I know he is currently reading every thought rattling around in my head. So, instead of sitting in stifling silence, I lift my head to meet his stare head-on. I don't know how he does it, but every bit of armor I have falls to pieces around me, and I let out a sob. "I can't fucking do this, Luca. Every day that passes, every dead end, every moment without her, every time I look into Mac and Finn's eyes, knowing we're no closer than we were yesterday feels like it's killing me." More tears roll down my cheeks, but I don't bother hiding them. Because, like me, Luca knows how rare it is for me to be this transparent with my emotions. And, like me, he knows I wouldn't want anyone to see me like this. Fragile. Weak.

He doesn't placate me. He doesn't tell me that "everything will be okay." Because he and I know better than most that there's a very real possibility it might not be. I will do everything I can until my dying breath brings her back to me, but sometimes, in this life, even your dying breath isn't enough. So, Luca says nothing. He just sits there and lets me fall apart.

Once the tears finally stop falling, I wipe my face with the backs of my hands. I'm about to stand up when his voice stops me. "You're wrong, you know."

I pinch my brows in confusion. "Wrong about what?"

"Being no closer than we were yesterday."

"And how exactly is that? Because from where I'm fucking sitting, we still have no idea where the hell she is or if she's still even alive." My voice cracks over my last words, physically paining me even to say.

"No. We don't." I throw my hands up in the air, resisting the urge to reach over the desk and punch him in the face. How is this helpful? "But what we do know is where she isn't. Every lead we come up with empty-handed is just another we can check off the list. We're getting closer, Ronan. We just have to keep looking. Never stop looking."

I sit up straighter, taking slight comfort in his words. Nodding in agreement, I take a deep breath. "I'll never stop looking for her. Until I'm dead, I'll never stop looking for her."

The corners of his lips turn up slightly. "That's what I like to hear." Luca stands up from the chair and looks around the room. "Now, let's clean this shit up and eat some food before we call Patrick."

Luca and I move about the room, silently picking up everything I knocked onto the floor and putting it back in its rightful place on my desk. Before we walk out of the office, I grab his arm. His eyes meet mine, and we exchange a silent conversation.

Will they be able to tell?

He dips his chin slightly, letting me know that any trace of my meltdown is long gone. I stand up straight, and we go to the dining room table, where the rest of the guys are already digging into the takeout.

My eyes find Finn's, who's giving me an apologetic look. I'm momentarily confused until I look at the food spread out on the table that Enzo ordered. Then, I recognize the takeout containers from the Thai restaurant down the street.

Fuck me.

* * *

After we all ate dinner, actually after Luca and his guys ate while Mac, Finn, and I pushed our damn Thai food around our plates while giving one another somber glances, we gathered in the den, glasses of whiskey in hand for some and red wine for others. Everyone except for Enzo, that is, he always opts for sparkling water, and I know enough about personal demons not to ask him why. If he wanted to tell us, he would.

My phone sits on the coffee table as we all anxiously stare at it, willing it to ring. I shot a message to Patrick a few minutes ago, letting him know we urgently needed to speak with him. With any luck, he was able to sneak away and will call us back any minute now.

"You think he lied to you when you first spoke to him?" Enzo asks.

"No," Finn and I both answer in unison.

"He has no reason to harm Harper," Finn explains, "All he wants is Declan gone so he can take over and fix everything Declan has fucked up. He seems to take pride in their organization and wants to restore it to what it once was."

"But . . ." Sebastian cuts in warily. I've studied him enough over the last two weeks to recognize that he's not overly confident when he isn't behind his computers. He tends to keep to himself and only speaks when he's spoken to. Sebastian shakes his head, cutting himself off before he can finish.

I know what it's like to constantly be filled with self-doubt, so I urge him to continue. "Please, what were you going to say?"

Sebastian's eyes meet Luca's for reassurance, and I don't miss the way Luca's light up for a moment at the gesture before giving Sebastian a nod to continue. "You probably already thought of this, but wouldn't Patrick want Harper out of the picture, too? I mean, if she's the only other living Whelan, she could take over, right?"

"You're right," I answer, watching Sebastian sit up a little straighter in confidence. "But we thought of that already and we discussed it with Harper and with Patrick. He offered to step down if she wanted to take over. Patrick truly just wants what's best for his people. Harper wholeheartedly declined the invitation. She wanted to stay here . . . with us." I look over at my brothers, likely feeling the sting of my words just as much as I am. "He agreed to help us take down both Liam and Declan. All four of us believed him to be a hundred percent genuine."

Sebastian looks down at his lap. "Oh, okay. Sorry."

"Don't be sorry, man. It was a valid thought." Sebastian gives me a soft smile.

My phone suddenly rings from its spot on the table. Luca reaches down to answer it, putting it on speakerphone.

"I got your message," Patrick greets, skipping the formalities. "What's going on?"

"Harper's gone." Those words burn my mouth just as much as they did the day she was taken.

"Was it Liam?" I forgot for a moment that we haven't spoken to Patrick since our original plan was set in place.

"No. Liam's dead." Mac answers without an ounce of regret.

"Who then? Declan hasn't left Ireland, and he called off all the hits on her weeks ago."

"Exactly why we're so confused. He planted a man within our security company, one we hired to watch Harper. Two weeks ago, he ambushed me and Harper in the apartment. Killed our second guard, knocked me unconscious, drugged Harper, and took off. We have no idea where he took her or what their plans with Harper are." The line momentarily goes silent.

"I had nothing to do with this Ronan. I swear to you. I am not a good man, but I would never stoop as low as to hurt an innocent woman."

"We know, Patrick," Finn answers, "We were just calling to see if you had any other ideas."

"Ideas?" he asks in confusion.

"None of this is making sense," I deadpan. "If Declan wanted Harper dead, why didn't Logan just kill her that night? Why take her—"

"What did you just say?" Patrick asks as he cuts me off. All of us look at one another in confusion.

"If Declan wanted Harper dead—"

"No," he interrupts me again. "The name. What was the name of the guard?" The urgency in his voice is unmistakable.

"Logan," I bite out, his name like venom on my tongue. "The guard's name is Logan."

"Holy fucking shit." I immediately hear the surprise in Patrick's voice.

"What?" Finn asks, standing from his spot on the couch next to me. "What is it, Patrick?"

"What did he look like?"

"Uh . . . tall, dark blonde hair, dark eyes, crooked nose."

The line goes quiet again, and I can't fucking handle the

anticipation. "Patrick!"

"They're not going to kill her," he finally answers wearily.

"What do you mean? What are you talking about? Who is Logan?" My questions become more and more frantic.

"Logan is Declan's protege. Don't ask me why, but Declan took him in years ago when Logan was only eleven or twelve. He was an orphan Declan found on the streets. Since then, Declan has been turning Logan into a copy of himself, and Logan did anything and everything Declan asked him to. Wherever Declan was, Logan wasn't too far behind. Until a couple of months ago."

"What happened?" I ask.

"Nobody knew. All of a sudden, Logan was just gone. Whenever someone asked Delcan where Logan disappeared, all he would say was that he 'Had to go away.' All of us thought the whole thing was strange. It didn't make sense, until a couple of weeks ago, one of Declan's cronies let it slip."

"Patrick..." I snap. I understand he's trying to help, but he could really speed it the fuck up. "What. The hell. Happened?"

"Declan caught Logan fucking some guy. Apparently, Declan freaked out, saying how much of a disgrace it was that a man he took in as his own turned out to be a fag." I don't miss the way everyone in the room flinches at the term. We're a lot of things, but being judgemental of anyone's sexual preferences is not one of them. "Everyone else thought Declan killed him."

"But not you?"

"No. That is too good of an opportunity for Declan to miss. Logan worships the ground Declan walks on. And if he really did fuck up that badly, he would do anything to get back into

Declan's good graces. Anything . . . "

"Like get sent here to infiltrate the McDermott's syndicate and kidnap Harper," Luca interjects.

Patrick doesn't question the unfamiliar voice in the room; it's not important. "But that still doesn't answer my question. Why not just kill her? Why kidnap her?"

"Like I said, Declan has spent years brainwashing Logan. He's a carbon copy of the man he thinks saved him. Declan is terrified that I will undo everything he's done once he's no longer in power. *Which I will.* The only reason he hasn't gotten rid of me is that I've garnered the trust of his entire syndicate now that I'm basically running everything. He will lose them all if he kills me. But what he can do is ensure that the next in line takes over and keeps everything he's built in place."

"But Harper wants nothing to do with any of it. She said so herself." Clearly, I'm still not getting the fucking message.

"Ronan . . ." Luca looks at me, concern etched all over his face. "Patrick said Logan would do anything to get back in Declan's good graces. *Anything.*"

The room is quiet, and so is Patrick on the other end of the phone. In rapid succession, like everyone in the room is reading Luca's mind, their faces change. First in understanding, then into panic. My little brother follows suit, and for the first time in two weeks, I watch his entire demeanor change from being filled with uncontrollable rage to undeniable sadness. "Brother . . ." he says in nothing more than a whisper.

And just like that it dawns on me.

Holy fuck.

"He's going to make Logan marry her." The second the

words are out of my mouth, it feels like a bomb went off.

"I–I think so." Patrick's voice is filled with regret. "I think he's going to make Logan marry Harper; that way, Logan can take over without me pushing him to step down. Declan will control Logan behind the scenes; nobody will ever find out that the man Declan raised as his own likes to sleep with men. Logan and Harper will have children–another generation of Whelan's, and what's worse, I won't be able to do a damn thing about it. Blood comes first."

"And Harper?" Mac's voice cracks as he says her name.

"She will have Logan's children and be locked within the walls of that house. You will never see her again. You will never be able to step foot in Ireland, let alone get close enough to save her. If we are right, Ronan," another heavy sigh rings through the phone. "Listen to me and listen to me right now. I don't know where Logan took her, but I do know that you have to find her. You have to find her *now*. If you don't, and they make it to Ireland, they're not going to kill her, Ronan, but she's going to wish they had."

10

Harper

I don't know how many days it's been. I lost track after the day I tried to escape, constantly drifting in and out of consciousness, as any time I've so much as looked at Logan wrong, he's beaten me. I might be able to push through his kicks and punches if he weren't also starving me. Since that day in the kitchen, he's given me nothing more than a couple of glasses of water a day and a bowl of soup every few days with a handful of saltines. It's like that day unlocked something inside of him. Gone is the composed, albeit somewhat charming, man that took me. Instead, I'm left with a monster, clearly battling some deep demons of his own.

If this were any other normal situation and he was any other normal person, I might feel bad for him. It's obvious that he is going through something that has caused him immense pain and regret. But this isn't any other normal situation, and he isn't any other normal person. Having a shitty life is no excuse to treat someone with such disregard for life. He's kidnapped, stripped, and beaten me regularly, and for that, regardless of his trauma, he deserves to die a slow and torturous death.

Judging by how my stomach is writhing in pain from hunger, I should be due for another bowl of soup today. Maybe if I do everything right, he won't lay another hand on me today. Maybe he'll give me a little extra to eat. I'm just so hungry, so thirsty. I didn't realize how all-consuming the thought of food could be, but apparently, it's something I've taken for granted. I'm getting to the point where I would do just about anything for a decent meal, that and a shower. I haven't had one since the night Logan took me. I know I smell disgusting, and I feel even worse. In a way, I'm glad Logan hasn't offered to let me bathe because I know he'd stand in the bathroom the entire time, ensuring that I don't have an ounce of privacy or make another move to escape.

Not that I could, anyway.

I'm beyond exhausted physically and mentally. If the blood and bruises, constant hunger, and rapid weight loss weren't enough, I feel completely broken on the inside. Broken by the man who has held me hostage for days on end, broken by the man whose blood runs in my veins, the man who has made it his life's mission to ruin mine, and broken by the fact that *they* haven't found me yet.

Day in and day out, I fight the spiraling thoughts inside my head.

What if Declan got to them, too?

What if Mac and Finn are dead, just like Ronan?

What if they gave up looking for me? Maybe they just cut their losses and moved on with their life.

What if . . . what if I never see them again? Never feel Mac's strong arms around me. Never inhale the scent of fresh linen as I bury my face in Finn's chest.

If they're dead, too, I might as well let Declan kill me. Because if they're gone, I'd never survive it.

But I don't know any of that for sure, and until I do, I can't stop fighting.

"Never stop fighting, Baby."

Ronan's voice in my head causes tears to roll down my face, much like they have every. Single. Day. But, I let them fall, not that I could wipe them away anyway, considering my hands are still tied to this damn bed. I let them fall because I want to feel every ounce of pain. Pain means I'm still alive, I'm still fighting.

"I'll never stop fighting, Ronan," I whisper into the empty room.

When I hear Logan's steps moving throughout the cabin I will my tears to stop falling and brace myself against the mattress, thankfully still covered in the oversized T-shirt. I will *not* let him see me crumble.

Only when his footsteps stop a few feet from my door do I hear another voice. I only heard one set of footsteps, so he must be speaking to someone on the phone. He probably still thinks I'm passed out from his earlier beating. I told him I needed to go to the bathroom, and he kicked me so hard in the stomach I threw up. Then I got backhanded across the face because I made a mess from throwing up. *Fucking ridiculous.* I use this to my advantage, though, and listen in on the phone call as best as I can.

"You can't make me do this." Logan's voice pleads to whoever is on the other end of the line.

"You can and you will, boy." The thick Irish accent could only be one person, Declan.

"You told me I just had to find a way to get the girl. 'Get Harper and bring her to the cabin.' That's what you said." Logan is clearly doing his best to mind his tone, but I can tell he's fuming.

"Yes, that is what I said." Delcan's voice, unlike Logan's, remains eerily calm. "But that's not the plan. I'm not coming there. You *will* bring her here. You *will* keep her alive. You *will* do as you are told." What? They're taking me to Ireland? What the hell for?

"Declan, please—"

"End of discussion, Logan. You have embarrassed me for the first and last time. This is your only option. Do you understand me?"

There's a moment of silence before Logan sighs loud enough to hear through the thick wood door. "Yes sir, I understand."

"There will be a plane ready for you at Erie International in two days. You will both get on it. Once you arrive here, we will move forward with the plan."

Without another word, the line goes dead. Just when I thought Logan would come storming in here, his footsteps retreat to the other side of the cabin. Only when I hear the front door slam and the sound of tires speeding down the gravel drive do I let my body relax, yet my mind begins reeling.

This whole time, I thought Declan just wanted me dead. I thought he was going to kill me, just like he did my parents.

I thought all he wanted to do was keep me from taking over his empire, even though I have explicitly said *several times* that I want nothing to do with any of it.

However, now that I think about it, it doesn't make much sense that Logan didn't just kill me that night at the apartment. This whole time, I thought it was just so Declan could come here and take care of me himself, like the sadistic bastard he is. Obviously, that's what Logan thought, too. That doesn't seem to be the case, though. So, why in the flying fuck does he want Logan to take me to Ireland?

Regardless of the answer, I can't wait for Mac and Finn to save me any longer. I have to find a way out of here myself. Because even though I don't know what awaits me in Ireland, I know it's nothing good. I also know that as soon as they get me there, I'll never see Mac and Finn again. And that's a risk I'm not willing to take.

I have to get out of here.

11

Finn

"Holy shit. Finn! I think I got it!" Sebastian's yelling causes me to spit out my toothpaste before I've even finished brushing my teeth. I don't even bother putting on a shirt before sprinting down the hall toward the dining room table where Sebastian's sitting.

"What? What did you find?" His eyes move over my naked chest, and if I wasn't so concerned with whatever the hell he found, I might take the time to question him on it.

He must catch himself doing it, too, because he abruptly jerks his head back toward the direction of his monitors and clears his throat. "I was going back over Declan's bank transactions but decided to go back as far as six months ago. Nothing really stuck out until I saw this here." He points at the screen, where I see not an outgoing payment but an incoming one from *One Five One Tower.*

"What the fuck? Why did Declan receive a payment from our building?"

"It's not just a payment," Sebastian clicks on an attached document. "It's a paycheck."

"A paycheck?"

"Yeah, for someone named Paul Smith."

I give him an unimpressed look. "Wow, that's original."

"Tell me about it. Anyway, I got into the building's employee database, and they hired him to work the night shift as a valet about five months ago. I pulled up his personnel file, and surprise, surprise, the name's a fake. Lucky me, though, they scanned his fake driver's license, so I ran facial recognition on his picture."

I wait with bated breath as Logan pulls up a different image of the same man, and I read the name below his picture. "Thomas O'Connor."

"Yup. And guess who Thomas O'Connor is known to work for?"

"Declan Whelan?"

"Declan Whelan. And guess who I found getting in from a flight with JFK just a few days before he got hired in this building?"

A genuine smile spreads across my face for the first time in days. "Thomas O'Connor." I firmly squeeze Sebastian's shoulders in excitement, watching as he pulls up a plethora of other files on the screens.

"I quickly combed security footage from the nights Thomas was working. It looks like he was making copies of keys and using residents' vehicles after hours to tail you three throughout the city."

"We never noticed because he was always in a different

vehicle." It's not a question but a fact.

"Right. It looks like he followed you to Hayes' Bookstore on more than one occasion. My best guess is Declan was using him to figure out where you all were keeping your money. Until this night right here."

Sebastian pulls up security footage. I take a look at the date and realize it was only a few nights before Liam originally came to us about bringing Harper here. I watch her head of chocolate brown curls as she locks the door to the shop and begins walking down the street. I watch as Thomas follows her to her apartment. And I watch as his car sits outside her apartment for hours, taking pictures of her through her windows. "He's the one who told Declan about Harper. That's how he found out she existed, where she lived."

"Thomas was probably going to use her as a way to get into the store, but once he sent the pictures to Declan, well, everything changed from there."

"Where is he?" I ask urgently, my fingers immediately itching to wrap around his neck.

"Obviously, the address on the paystub was fake, and the bank account was Declan's and not his. Asshole can't even let his guys keep the money they make. Anyway, I was able to follow him on traffic cameras the last night he worked at this address. It's just a small apartment only a few blocks from here. It doesn't look like he's left the building since the night before Harper was taken."

"This whole time, the answers to where she is were only a few blocks away?"

"Yeah, man, I think this is it."

"Call everyone and tell them to meet me there. You stay here and watch the cameras around that building. Make sure he doesn't leave."

Everyone else left this morning before the sun came up. Luca, Enzo, and Dante had some business to catch up with at their office, and Ronan and Mac went to check on Kings and some product that got delivered down at the docks last night. As much as we hate to admit it, there are still things that need to be taken care of while we look for Harper. We can't let everything fall apart around us. She has to have something to come back to. Sebastian, of course, offered to stay here and keep digging. It was evident by the look on Luca's face that he didn't feel comfortable leaving Sebastian alone and unprotected, so I offered to stay here with him.

It only takes me minutes to change, grab my gun, and quickly call down to Ralph. "Yes, sir?" Ralph answers his phone on the first ring.

"I'm on my way out; my friend Sebastian is upstairs. I need you to place two guards on our floor. No one goes near him."

"Right away." He hangs up the phone, not wasting any time following my instructions.

Once I'm in the elevator and on my way down to the garage, I dial Ronan's number. "Yeah?"

"Ronan ," My voice hopeful.

I hear him calling to Mac and moving through the club, likely already on his way to his car. "Tell me, Finn."

As quickly as possible, I fill him in on everything Sebastian found. Once I reach my Audi Q2, I put the phone on speaker and set it on top of the car while I grab a handful of weapons I have stashed in the trunk. It's not likely I'm going to need any of this. Thomas is probably just holed up by himself, and judging by the looks of him on the security footage, any one of us could knock him out with one well-placed punch, but the faster we scare him into spilling everything, the faster we can find Harper.

Climbing into the driver's seat, I start the car and speed out of the garage. "I'm sending you the address right now. It's just a few blocks from me. Should be there in ten minutes."

I hear Ronan's phone switch to Bluetooth, letting me know he and Mac are already headed my way. "We'll meet you there. Mac just called Luca, they should be there before us. He said they'll wait at the back entrance of the building."

"Finn," I hear the desperation in Mac's voice. He's barely spoken since the night Harper was taken, and the way he sounds right now almost knocks the air from my chest. "Is this it?"

"He knows where she is, Mac. I can feel it." I don't know what it is, call it a sixth sense or whatever the fuck you want, but I can feel it in my bones. Thomas knows where she is.

"Me too." He answers softly. However, his voice isn't nearly as hopeful as my own. I don't blame him, though. I know how much he's struggling to block it all out. He won't let himself feel until he sees her again.

"See you there, brother." Ronan ends the call as I speed towards Thomas' apartment.

Minutes later, I race around the corner into the alleyway behind the apartment complex to find Luca, Enzo, and Dante dressed in their usual gear. I grab my weapons from the passenger seat next to me and climb out of the car. As I approach them, I watch Luca instantly tense when he doesn't see Sebastian behind me. "He's back at the apartment."

Luca's brow pinches in frustration, and I hold up my hand as he opens his mouth to speak. "Security is posted at the apartment, and I instructed Ralph not to let anyone near him.

He's safe." All three of them, Luca, most of all, visibly relax.

Enzo nods over my shoulder as Ronan's tires peel into the alley. He and Mac rush out the second the car is in park. Like me, the two of them have been trained to guard their emotions during the worst of times, not to allow people to read what's going on inside their heads, but, also like me, it's nearly impossible when Harper's involved. Because with one look at each of them, I can read exactly what is running through their mind. Ronan's body is coiled tight in anticipation, his jaw is set with nerves, and his finger is twitching on the trigger of the gun already in his hand. Mac, on the other hand, all I can see is the absolute fury of a man who has lost the only woman he has or will ever love. The fury of a man who knows that the one upstairs knows where she is. The fury of a man who isn't leaving here without getting what he wants.

"There's no security in this building, so we should be able to slip in unnoticed through the stairwell," Dante says as soon as Ronan and Mac make it to us. Ronan gives my shoulder a firm squeeze before focusing his attention back on Dante. "He's on the third floor at the end."

"Dante's big ass will kick the door down," the corners of Enzo's lips curve up as he points his thumb toward their gigantic bodyguard, "and we'll move in. I'm assuming you want us all to go in, correct?" he asks as he looks at Ronan.

"Fuck yeah. Everyone got weapons?" We all nod. "Good, get 'em out. Chances are we won't need to get a single shot off, but the show of force will get him to open up. I want us on our way to Harper within the hour."

"Alright," Luca says, squaring his shoulders. "Let's move."

The six of us move in a single-file line up the flight of stairs to the third floor, with Dante in the front and Mac at the rear. Once we reach Thomas's door, Dante looks behind me, ensuring we're ready. After Ronan nods, Dante rears his foot back, kicking down the door in one go. Thomas startles from his spot on the couch and immediately cowers, trying to disappear into the cushions. None of us hesitate. We form a circle around him, each pointing a weapon at his face, which is already covered in snot and tears.

Pussy.

Ronan crouches down on his haunches right in front of Thomas. "I'm going to ask you this once and one time only." Ronan's voice is cool and calm, and if it were anyone else, I would think that's exactly the way he felt. But he's not anyone else, and I know he's doing everything he can to prevent his control from breaking. Not that any of us give a flying fuck if this bastard lives or dies. "Where is she?"

"Where is wh—"

The sound of a gunshot rings through the apartment. I look over to Mac, who just shot Thomas in the knee. He gives me nothing more than a shrug, and I have to fight to hold back my smile. So much for not using our guns.

"Okay, okay!" Thomas shouts between screams of pain. "Logan took her to Declan's cabin until he could get a flight into Erie International. They're supposed to leave in two days."

"All it took was one bullet to the knee, and he folded like a fucking lawn chair," Luca laughs.

Enzo snorts, "Fucking pathetic."

"Where's the cabin, Thomas?" Ronan asks, still maintaining his icy tone.

"I don't—"

Another shot goes off, hitting Thomas in the opposite knee. "Ahhh! Fuck!" He screams, "Please, he–he'll kill me."

"You're as good as dead anyway," Mac states matter-of-factly. "It's up to you whether it's a fast or slow death." He bends down so his face is level with his older brothers. "And I promise you, there are a lot of other places I can shoot you before you bleed out."

I watch as the resignation of what he's done and his situation wash over Thomas' face. He's been in this life long enough to know the consequences of getting caught up in something like this. He also knows how excruciatingly painful we can make his death, not that we want to. We all want to get out of here as fast as possible and on the road to wherever she is. His breathing slows as he sits up straighter on the couch, seemingly forgetting about the two bullet holes in his legs, apparently coming to terms with his fate. "Hand me that pen and paper," he points at the small table behind Enzo.

Enzo grabs the small pad of paper and pen and hands it back to Thomas, who shakily writes down an address. "It's a small cabin in Pennsylvania, about an hour outside Erie. Logan and the girl should be the only ones there. If you leave now, you should get there this evening."

Ronan snatches the paper from Thomas' hand and stands up from his crouched position. "Thank you, Thomas."

In a split second, Ronan raises his gun and puts a bullet between Thomas' eyes.

None of us so much as flinch.

The faint sound of sirens sounds outside the window. "Someone in the building probably called the cops. We've got to move," Luca states.

We make our way down the stairwell in the formation we came up in. Once we get into the alley, the sound of sirens grows louder. "Finn, give me your keys." I toss Luca my keys to my Audi as I move towards Ronan's Lexus. "Dante and Enzo will follow you all there in case you need backup. I'll go back to the apartment and stay with Sebastian."

"We'll call you once we get on the road to figure out a plan," Ronan says to Enzo as he gets in the driver's seat. Mac climbs into the passenger seat next to his brother. I move to get in the back before Luca's voice stops me. "Hey!"

"Yeah?"

A small smile pulls at his lips. "Go get your girl."

12

Harper

The slam of the front door breaks me from my thoughts.

This is it, Harp.

I just have to get him to let me into the bathroom alone. I thought about using the excuse that I have my period because, quite frankly, most men are terrified of the thought. But, he'd be able to see that I don't have any blood between my legs, seeing as I still have no fucking panties on.

So I thought of the next best thing.

Logan opens the locks on my door, and before he can make it even a foot inside, I speak up, making sure my voice sounds panicked. "Thank God you're back. I need to use the bathroom. Like now."

"I haven't given you any water since last night. There's no way you need to use the bathroom again." I can tell he's already gearing up to punish me in some way for asking for such a simple request.

Fucking asshole.

"No. You don't understand. I need to use the bathroom, *like right now.*" I widen my eyes, hoping he will pick up what I'm putting down, but his dumbstruck face tells me he's still not getting it. "Look, unless you want to add cleaning up diarrhea to your list of duties, I suggest you untie me so I can use the bathroom."

His face curls in disgust before he stomps over to the bed. "Jesus fucking Christ." He begins untying my hands and feet, more aggressively than necessary, of course, and pushes me down the hall and into the bathroom.

I stop and look over my shoulder when he doesn't follow me. "You're not coming in?" I try to keep the excitement out of my voice.

"No, I'm not fucking coming in. Just do what you've gotta do and hurry the hell up." I move to close the door when he stops it with his foot. "I will be right here, though, so don't even think of trying anything."

Outside of the bathroom is better than in it.

He moves his boot, and I calmly close the door when I hear him yell, "And turn the fucking fan on!"

I flip the switch for the fan and lean against the sink, mentally preparing myself for what I'm about to do. "You can do this, Harp. You *have* to do this. You have to get out," I whisper to myself, talking low enough so that he can't hear me over the roar of the fan. I take a deep breath before pushing off the counter and moving toward the towel rack on the opposite wall.

Pulling the towel off, I wrap it around my arm just above

my elbow. I know that as soon as I do this, the noise will be loud enough that he'll come busting in here. I have to get it on the first try.

I summon every last bit of strength I have in my body before bringing my arm up and crashing it into the wooden bar, using the towel to help cushion the blow against my arm. The wood breaks free of the wall from the force of my hit and falls to the ground. In rapid succession, I pick up the largest piece as Logan bursts through the door. I don't hesitate, I don't waste a single second, I don't doubt myself for a moment. As Logan lunges at me, I drive the piece of wood right into the center of his abdomen. Blood begins rapidly staining his shirt around the wound. Logan hits the floor, both hands wrapped around the piece of wood lodged inside him. I don't wait to see if he dies. I can't risk it. I have to move.

Lunging over him, I run toward the kitchen, looking for the van keys. When I can't immediately find him, I don't stop. At this rate, risking the wilderness is a far better option than whatever they have planned for me. The door is still locked, and I have no idea where the keys are. I grab a log of the stack of wood by the fireplace and bust open the window next to it, just like I intended to do all those nights ago.

The glass shatters, and I use the log to knock off the pieces left around the frame. I hear Logan's gurgled groans as I crawl out the window and run straight toward the treeline. I can't risk running along the road on the off chance that Logan gets up and climbs in his van. My best bet is to run through the woods a few hundred yards from the road and pray I don't get hopelessly lost in the endless abyss of Pennsylvania wilderness.

I pump my legs as fast as I possibly can, trying to ignore

how utterly exhausted my body feels. I can feel the sticks and stones tearing away at the skin at the bottom of my feet, the branches cutting my bare arms and legs, the way my stomach cramps from being so incredibly hungry, but I ignore it all. I have to keep moving and get as far away from here as possible.

I have to keep moving.

"Run, Baby. Run."

13

Mac

"Right down here," I point to the left, directing Mac to where there's nothing but a small gravel drive. We've been driving as fast as physically possible, breaking every speed limit and only stopping once for gas, but it's still taken us five hours to get here. However, as the miles grew between us and the city, the undeniable feeling in my gut has only grown—she's here.

I know it.

I look in the side mirror as Enzo and Dante make the same turn behind us. "The house should be just up here," I instruct my big brother. Where most people would drive cautiously down the gravel drive, Ronan doesn't let off the gas—speeding and kicking up rocks as we go.

"If you kick a rock up at their car, Dante will kill you," Finn pipes up from the back seat.

"I'll buy them a new one," Ronan grumbles in annoyance. Even though we all know Finn means nothing by it. He's just nervous, we all are. "Hell, if we find Harper, I'll buy them each a new one."

"I heard that, and I'm gonna hold you to it," Enzo's voice echoes through our car.

"There it is!" I point at the small cabin just appearing just around the trees. Ronan slams on the brakes, not bothering to drive up to the house. Enzo skids to a stop behind us, and with no time to spare, we're all out of the cars and ready to move. We had a plan to stealthily move into the cabin, but judging by the way Ronan's sprinting toward the cabin, that plan is out the window. Not that I blame him anyway.

We run to catch up to Ronan, only for him to stop about ten feet in front of the deck. A trail of blood leads out of the still-open front door to a smaller puddle where we're standing, where a set of read marks lead back down the gravel trail we came from.

Ronan looks from the ground up at me, white as a ghost with tears in his eyes. I'm right there with him, but I shove the worry and fear deep down like I have been the last two weeks. "We don't know if that's hers, brother."

Like he's shaking himself out of a stupor, Ronan shakes his head and blinks back the tears that were about to fall. Clearing his voice, he looks at all of us. "Enzo and Dante, scan the area and see if you can find anything. You two," he looks at Finn and me, "with me."

The three of us hesitantly move into the cabin, terrified of what we may, or may not, find. As soon as we enter, we follow the trail of blood to a bathroom in the hallway, where a much bigger pile awaits. I look around the small space to find a busted towel rack. A large piece of it, coated in blood, lays in the sink along with several blood-soaked towels.

"We don't know if that's hers," I repeat my words from outside. Trying to convince them and myself. "We don't stop until we find her."

"We have to clear the rest of the house." Ronan commands. We move down the hallway, and my heart stops when I see the room at the end. It's nothing more than an empty bed with a rope and cuff attached to each corner. Small traces of blood are scattered across the mattress, some darker than others, indicating how long they've been there.

"Holy fuck," Finn mumbles behind me.

The three of us stand there, staring at what has likely been her prison for the last two weeks. My fists clench at my sides, and I let out a shaky breath as a tear rolls down my cheek. All I see is red.

And what's worse, this time, it's Harper's.

I managed to tear my eyes away from the room, and we quickly looked through the rest of the small cabin, only to come up empty. I'm about to take after my big brother and throw something at the closest fucking wall when Enzo's voice calls from outside, "Guys, come here!"

We sprint outside towards the treeline where Enzo and Dante are standing. "Look." Enzo points to a patch of mud where a small footprint lies—Harper's footprint.

"Finn, call Sebastian," Ronan demands.

Sebastian picks up on the second ring. "Did you guys find her?"

"No, she's not here, but we found her footprints. I need you to pull up satellite images of the area. Is there anything else around here? Anywhere she would go?"

I can hear Sebastian clicking away in the background, and after a few beats, he answers regretfully, "No, Ronan. There's nothing. Just woods."

"Fuck!"

"Ronan," our eyes snap towards Dante, who is now crouched by the small puddle of blood in the driveway. "These small drops leading from inside are still wet. They can't be more than thirty minutes old. Any longer than that, and they would have been dry." I give him a curious glance from over Ronan's shoulder. "Trust me on this. I have a lot of *experience* tracking people."

"He knows what he's talking about, Ronan." Luca's voice rings through the speakerphone, filled with nothing but confidence in his friend's abilities.

Ronan nods in agreement before returning to face Finn and me, still standing at the treeline by Harper's footprints. "Alright. We don't know for sure whose blood that was, but considering that the blood stops by the tire tracks and not over here by her footprints, I think it's safe to say it isn't hers."

"Right," Finn agrees, "And taking into account the fact that she's barefoot and judging by the blood on that mattress," I swallow hard at the thought of her spilling even the smallest drop of blood, "and how dense these woods are, she couldn't have gotten that far."

"Are you guys sure she's out there? We can have Seb try to find the make and model of the vehicle that fled from there using traffic cameras?"

"No." I cut Ronan off before he can answer, even though I'm pretty sure he would agree with what I'm about to say. "That'll be no use. There will be no traffic cameras he can use this far out. I don't care about Logan right now. We can worry about him later. Right now, we just need to find Harper. She's out there. Mo Grá is out there. I can feel it."

"Sebastian and Luca, keep running facial recognition on Logan. Dante and Enzo, you guys stay here in case she comes back." He looks at Finn and me and nods. "Let's move."

14

Harper

I know I haven't been running that long. The sun was just setting when I fled the cabin, and a sliver of daylight is still left. But it feels like I've been running for hours. My feet hurt, I'm thirsty, and my side keeps cramping; whether that's from exhaustion or hunger, I'm not sure. If that wasn't enough, the sharp pain radiating down my side and across my chest, screams in agony with every movement and breath. I know it's only a couple of broken ribs, but it feels as if my chest collapsing in on itself.

"Keep going, Baby. Don't stop."

I listen to Ronan's voice in my head and keep moving through the dense forest. I've heard a handful of cars go by, so I know I've been running in somewhat of a straight line and am still close to the road. Maybe if I run far enough away from the cabin, I can flag down a car on the side of the road.

"Shit!" I yell as my ankle catches a downed tree branch, and I drop to the forest floor, landing hard on my knees. "Goddamn, motherfucking, son of a bitch!" I roar as I repeatedly kick the stupid branch. I don't think I've ever used that many expletives in a row, but I'm just so . . . so . . . so mad. Mad at the situation I'm currently in, mad at Logan for killing Ronan, mad at Declan for trying to ruin my life, and mad at this stupid branch for busting up my ankle!

I take a beat, sitting on the cold ground, to try and regain a modicum of composure before standing up. I wince in pain as soon as I put pressure on my foot. Surely, I've given myself a decent sprain. I take a few slow steps when I hear a branch crack behind me.

Snap.

I stop dead in my tracks, hoping it was just some random squirrel.

Snap.

Another branch snaps, closer this time. It definitely sounded heavier than a squirrel. I hold my breath, hoping that maybe if I'm still enough, whatever it is won't find me.

What if it's Logan? I didn't wait to see if he was dead. What if he followed me out here? He probably just heard my meltdown and is on his way here.

Way to go, Harp. You couldn't wait to freak the fuck out.

I stay still as humanly possible.

Crunch, crunch, crunch.

Those were definitely footsteps.

Fuck.

I take off in a sprint, as fast as I can manage, ignoring the sharp pain in my ankle. As beat up and exhausted as I am, I did stab him in the stomach. There's no way he can outrun me. I dodge and weave through tree after tree while trying to keep an eye on the ground below me. I can't afford to fall again.

I quickly look over my left shoulder to make sure I can't see anyone behind me. When I don't see anyone, I spin my head back, only to run right into a solid wall of muscle.

15

Finn

I stumble backward and wrap my arms around the curly head of brown hair that just slammed into me to prevent us both from falling on our asses as she struggles against me. "Harper?"

I'm looking right at her, but until she speaks, I won't let myself believe it's really her, that I really have her in my arms. But she doesn't just talk. No, she continues to thrash in my arms, growing more and more panicked by the second. "No! Get off of me!"

"Harper, calm down." I try to keep my voice as even as possible as she beats at my chest with her fists.

"No, no, no! Let me go!"

I grab her face between my hands, forcing her to look me in the eyes. "Harper, it's me. Look at me, Angel."

The second the nickname leaves my lips her eyes snap up

to mine. I've never been so happy to see those deep emerald eyes, even if they are filled with tears. Her shaking hands grip onto my wrists. "Finn?"

"Yeah, Angel. It's me."

A strangled sob leaves her lips, and her legs give out from under her. "Oh my God. You found me."

I quickly scoop her up in my arms. "Always. I'm so sorry it took us so long." She buries her head in my chest as sobs continue to wrack her body. I place a soft kiss on the crown of her head before moving back through the trees as fast as possible. She's wearing next to nothing, and it's only going to get colder out. There will be time to hold her in my arms later.

"I've got her," I say out loud. Knowing everyone just heard what happened through the coms in my ear that each of us put in before we broke off into the woods. I feel a burn behind my eyes as I speak the words, words I wasn't sure I would ever get to say.

"You-you have her?" I hear the crack in Ronan's voice.

"Yeah. I've got our girl."

"Where are you? I'm coming to you now." The urgency in Ronan's voice is evident.

"No. It'll take too long for you to find us, and it's getting cold out. Meet us back at the cabin. Grab some clothes and the first aid kit out of the trunk of your car."

Mac's panicked voice sounds through the coms. "First aid kit? Clothes?"

"How bad is she, Finn?" Ronan asks.

I look down at my sweet girl, wearing nothing but a tattered shirt and covered in cuts and bruises of various colors. One of her ankles is black and blue, she has pretty decent abrasions around her wrists and ankles from being tied to that fucking bed, and her feet have a generous amount of scrapes on them from running through the woods barefoot. And those are just the injuries I can see at first glance. Who knows what lies beneath the surface? "She's alive, but . . . she's pretty beat up."

There's a beat of silence before Ronan speaks again. "We'll meet you there."

I continue to carry Harper through the woods as she cries into my chest, repeating over and over again, "You found me, you found me, you found me."

I walk toward the house as fast as possible, minding my step as I go. The last thing I need is for me to trip and drop her. Finally spotting the treeline a few yards ahead, I place another firm kiss on the top of her head. "We're almost there, Angel."

As we break through the trees, I see Enzo and Dante leaning against the front of their car, first aid kit and clothes in hand, while Mac and Ronan pace around the driveway. As soon as Ronan spots Harper in my arms, he moves toward us.

"Baby . . ." Ronan chokes out. I can already see the tears pooling in his eyes. There have only been a few times I've seen this man shed tears, and every single time, they've had to do with the woman in my arms.

It must take Harper a moment to register who is talking to her, but when she does, she rips her head from my chest. "Ronan?" She says his name as if she didn't think she would ever see him in front of her again. "You're–You're a–alive?"

Then it hits me. She probably thought he was dead. She saw Ronan lying unconscious on our kitchen floor, blood flowing from his head. This entire time, she thought he was dead.

"I'm here, Harper." Two strides later, Ronan is in front of me, ripping Harper from my arms, and I gladly let her go. Her legs wrap around his waist as he holds her tight against him, one arm around her waist and one hand threaded in her hair.

"I can't believe you're alive," she cries into his neck.

"There isn't a world that exists without you and me together, Baby."

Ronan peppers kisses across the side of Harper's face as he holds her in his arms. I let them have a few minutes before stepping up behind her, unable to resist the urge to have my hands on her again. I wrap my arms around her, leaving her sandwiched between us. Once her cries begin to slow, she pulls her face from Ronan's neck. "Where's Mac?"

I look over their shoulders to find Mac still as a statue a few feet behind Ronan. Ronan shoots me a worried glance because we both know exactly what's happening. This Mac, the one that we've known for the last two weeks, isn't the Mac that she knows. This Mac hasn't let himself feel a single emotion besides rage. This Mac, it's the darkest part of him. We all knew that the only person who could pull him out of the monster he became that night would be her.

We just have to hope that she's up to the task.

Harper must spot Mac behind Ronan, and like the incredible woman she is, immediately senses how desperately he needs her. "Ronan, put me down."

"You're feet, Baby."

She gently caresses the side of his face. "I'm okay. Put me down. Let me go to him."

Briefly hesitating, he gently sets her down. She winces

when her feet hit the gravel but waves Ronan away when he reaches for her again. She takes a few steps forward, only to stop when she sees Enzo and Dante out of the corner of her eye.

"It's okay, Angel. They're with us." She nods and slowly walks over to Mac, with Ronan and I following close behind her.

Once she's close enough, Harper reaches out to grab his hand, only for him to flinch away.

"Mac . . ." she says his name as softly as possible, but there's a raspiness to it that's oddly relaxing. Mac's face remains entirely unreadable. "It's okay, Honey. I'm okay." She takes another step toward him.

"You're okay?" He asks her like he can't believe she's standing before him. Honestly, part of me still really can't either.

Harper nods. "I'm okay." She reaches her hand out again, only for him to pull away again. "Cormac, please. I missed you so much. Let me touch you."

Mac shakes his head.

"You won't hurt me, Mac." There it is. We should have known she'd know exactly what was going on without us even having to tell her. She knows us better than we know ourselves. "I need you." Her voice is nothing more than a whisper now.

I see the moment that what she's saying registers in his brain. "I won't hurt you."

Harper holds out her hand. "You won't hurt me."

Mac's face softens, and his shoulders relax. He inhales a deep breath, then, ignoring her outstretched hand entirely, crashes into her. Mac drops to his knees with her in his arms in the middle of the gravel driveway. Her bare legs wrap around him as she strokes the back of his head, and the two of them sob in one another's arms. I look over at Ronan, who swallows hard at the sight of his brother falling apart in front of him. But his expression isn't one of worry. It's of relief. Relief that we found her, relief that she's okay—or at least she will be—and relief over the fact that we didn't lose Mac, too.

Harper lifts her head and looks over her shoulder at where we're still standing behind her, eyes red and puffy. "Take me home."

Home.

"Alright, Angel. Let's go home."

16

Harper

They found me.

They really found me.

Ronan's alive. I can't believe he's alive. I can't believe we're all together again.

I woke up a few minutes ago from what felt like the deepest sleep I've had in my entire life. I'm curled up on my side in my bed, which, after two weeks of sleeping like a starfish on my back feels like heaven, by the way.

My bed.

I wasn't sure I'd ever be back here again. I mean, I hoped, but I wasn't sure.

After the guys got me dressed in the extra sweats they had in the back of their car and bandaged up any obvious cuts that were still bleeding, they loaded me into Ronan's car, and we came straight home.

They asked if I wanted to go inside and shower before we left. Enzo and Dante offered to clean up the blood from Logan before I went back in, but I told them I couldn't bear to step foot back in that cabin ever again. I was worried about stinking up the car on the way home, but none of them said a word about it. I just laid in the back seat, my head on Mac's lap while he stroked my hair, and slept the entire way home.

I knew they all wanted to be in the back by me, but I could tell that, at that moment, Mac was the one who needed me most. I knew that having his hands on me would ground him in some way.

We got back to the apartment in the early hours of the morning. I thanked Dante and Enzo, who left when we arrived, saying they needed to meet with the rest of their team, who apparently left before we got back. I made a quick mental note to thank them properly later for helping save my life.

Not more than five minutes after we got up to the apartment, a doctor was brought upstairs to examine me from head to toe. Only two of my cuts needed stitches, one on my foot and the one on the back of my head from the first night I tried to escape that has refused to close on its own. On top of being severely malnourished and dehydrated, I have two broken ribs, a fractured cheekbone, and a sprained ankle. After Finn got me into a bath and cleaned up, he dressed me in the warmest clothes he could find. Once he got me into bed, the doctor hooked me up to an IV and gave the guys a plethora of vitamins I'm supposed to take for the next couple of weeks to get all of my levels back where they should be. Besides that, he gave me a referral to his wife, who's a therapist who specializes in trauma, and told me to get plenty of rest, which is exactly what I've been doing.

I slept most of the day, only waking up here and there. Yet every time I woke up, at least one of them was in the room watching me. Never asleep, just watching. Like if they took their eyes off me for even a moment, I would simply disappear.

The last time I woke up, I ate some pancakes that Mac made for me because he knows breakfast for dinner is my favorite, and drank a cup of warm tea to help soothe my throat from all of the crying. When I laid down to go back to sleep, the sun was just starting to set, and now, judging by the warm glow peeking through the curtains, it's just beginning to come up. Which means I slept all night, I haven't been able to do that in weeks.

None of them filled me in on all the details of how exactly they found me or what Declan's plans for me were. I knew it was because they didn't want to cause me panic when I was already in such a fragile state. But they told me Logan was gone when they got there and had no idea where he was. It burns me to know that he's still out there somewhere, conspiring with Delcan to get me back. However, I'm not ashamed to admit I've got a sick sense of pride knowing he's at least in pain. Pain that I caused. Just like the pain he inflicted on me.

Over the last two weeks, I honestly wondered If I would ever see Mac and Finn again, let alone Ronan. I wasn't sure I would ever have the chance to escape.

But I did.

I got out.

And now I'm here . . . with them.

I'm dying to know what exactly Declan wants with me, and

I know they'll tell me when I ask them to. But, for now, I want to bask in the ignorance that everything feels okay. I'm back with them; my wounds will heal, and everyone is safe.

I roll over to my other side to see which one of them is in my room, and I find Ronan sitting on my chaise, watching over me, wearing nothing but a pair of black sweatpants. The scruff on his face is longer than he usually keeps it, his black curly hair looks disheveled like it does when I run my fingers through it, and his eyes, now the color of the deepest seas, look utterly exhausted.

"Hmmm. Good morning. How long have you been in here?" I ask him.

"Most of the night. I told Mac and Finn to get some rest. They didn't like it, but they did it." The corners of his lips turn up, but I can tell it's not genuine.

"They could have stayed in here with me."

"We didn't want to risk climbing in bed and scaring you." I know what the underlying meaning of that statement is. Besides when they found me and when Finn bathed me, none of them have touched me. I know why.

"You could never scare me." I mean that with every fiber of my being.

He looks away from me, and I watch as he swallows hard, curling his hands into fists as they rest on his thighs. I pull back the comforter on the side of the bed closest to him, opposite where the IV pole stands. "Come here, Ronan." He looks back at me as if he's confused by my demand. "Come lay with me."

Slowly, he stands from his spot on the chaise and climbs into bed, laying down so he's facing me, but not touching me. I pull the covers over him and drape my leg over his, letting him know that I'm okay with him touching me.

Thankfully, he accepts the invitation and scoots closer. I lift my head up slightly so he can slide one arm underneath it while he caresses my cheek with the opposite hand. We lay there like that for a while, staring at one another, his thumb moving in slow circles across my cheekbone.

I can tell by the way he's clenching and unclenching his jaw that there's something he wants to ask me, and I know exactly what it is. They weren't in the room when the doctor did my full exam. The doctor figured I would be comfortable giving him all the details if the guys weren't hovering over me. When he asked me if I was raped, I let out a thankful sob before telling him 'no' because I know I easily could have been. And I don't know how I would have come back from that.

I'm just about to put Ronan out of his misery when his deep Irish accent finally breaks the silence, "I'm so, so sorry, Baby."

"You have nothing to be sorry for, Ronan. None of this is your fault." I mean that wholeheartedly. The three of them didn't cause this. That heinous man who calls himself my grandfather is the only one responsible—well, Logan, too.

"I–I let him take you. He took you, and I couldn't stop him. And t-then we couldn't find you, and you were gone for such a long time." A lone tear rolls down the apple of Ronan's cheek, and I swipe it away with my thumb, careful not to let anything catch the IV still attached to the top of my hand. Granted, I haven't known Ronan long, but in the time I have, he's become a part of my soul. Just like I'm part of his. I know when he's hurting, and right now, even though I'm back and in his arms, his hurt is more evident than ever. "I swear to you, Harper, I will kill all of them. Anyone that had a hand in taking you from me, *from us*, will die."

Now it's I who lets a tear fall, which feels like all I've been doing since they found me in the woods. I should be startled at the violence of his words, but I'm not. Because, as twisted and messed up as it makes me, I want that. I want them to face Ronan, Mac, and Finn's wrath for taking me. So all I do is nod and whisper, "Okay."

"He–he hurt you." It's not a question but more of a statement. I know this is killing them, but I won't shy away from it, from telling them what happened to me.

"He did."

Ronan's hand falls from my face as he moves it down my arm, letting it rest on my hip, where he continues rubbing his thumb in small circles. "He touched you."

I nod again, and more tears pool in his eyes, and when he blinks, another falls. He hasn't even tried to stop them, and knowing he's willing to show me this broken side of him mends a little piece of my heart. I brush his wayward onyx hair from his forehead. "Ronan, Baby."

"Did he–did he touch *all* of you?" His chin trembles at the question.

"No," I whisper. "Remember what you said? I belong to you. I am yours. I am yours and Mac's and Finn's. I am yours, and you are mine. No one else gets to have me."

A desperate sob leaves Ronan's mouth before he buries his head in my chest. The vulnerability is such a stark contrast from the man who fought me tooth and nail when I first got here. From the moment I met him, I saw that he had the weight of the world on his shoulders. He's felt the responsibility to care for everyone and everything, trying to be the leader everyone expects him to be, unable and unwilling to lean on anyone. But that's not the man who's wrapped in my arms. The man in my arms is someone who felt like the world fell out from under his feet. Like he would never be able to fix a problem that would destroy him and his brothers. The man in my arms is one who is at his breaking point, unable to hold in his heartache for another moment.

And yes, I was the one who went through a terrible ordeal, but so did they. They lost me just as I lost them. I have all three of them to lean on, to be vulnerable with, and to pick me up when I fall apart. So I need to do that for them. Which is why I'll lay here and hold him for as long as he needs. I'll be the one to pick up the pieces of his heart.

"I'm so sorry, Baby. I will never let anyone hurt you again. Please forgive me," Ronan says as he continues to cry into my chest.

I hold him tighter. "It's not your fault, Ronan. There's nothing to forgive."

He lifts his head as his cries begin to slow, and his blue eyes meet mine. "I love you, Harper."

I can't help it—my breathing stalls.

"I think I've loved you since the night I walked into your bookstore. That's why I fought this thing between us so hard. I knew that if I let myself feel what I feel for you and it was taken away from me, it would break me—and it did. I know how it feels to love you and not get the chance to tell you. I will never let that happen again. I love you, Harper Hayes."

I won't waste another second. "I love you too, Ronan."

He chuckles, and I swear the sound of his laugh heals another little piece. "I know."

I playfully slap him on his bare chest, loving the way his bare skin feels under my hand. "What do you mean you know?" I give him a suspicious grin.

A soft smile plays at his lips. "I heard you that night, Baby. You said it in your sleep."

"Shit." I laugh. "I forgot about that. Can we pretend this was the first time I told you?"

"Nope. Not happening. You said it first, and I'll never let you live it down."

I laugh louder this time before placing a featherlight kiss on his lips. "That's fine because I love you. I love you so much, Ronan McDermott."

He softly kisses me. "You've probably made smarter decisions in your life."

"Probably."

17

Ronan

My phone vibrating against the chaise behind me wakes me from my sleep. Harper and I must have dozed off for a while. I'm not complaining; I needed the rest, and I know she did too. She'll be lucky if we let her leave this bed at all over the next couple of days.

The buzzing causes her to stir, and I quickly but smoothly slide out of bed to grab it, not wanting to wake her. I pick it up and see Luca's name on the screen, but before I answer it, I take a moment to stare at Harper's sleeping form. Her chocolate curls spread out against the white pillowcase, her soft pink lips parted slightly, and the color is starting to come back to her stunning face. I know that's all I did last night, sit here and stare at her, but it all feels different now. Lighter somehow. Regardless of what lies ahead, knowing that she loves me and I love her makes everything else feel insignificant.

I slip out of her room to answer the phone call in the hallway. "Hey, man."

"Hey. Sorry to bother you. I just wanted to check in to see how she was doing. How you *all* were doing."

I take a moment to pause, thankful for Luca and his guys. I'm not sure we would have found Harper if it hadn't been for them. I don't think I've ever been able to lean on anyone besides Mac and Finn like I have with their team the last few weeks. And for that, I will be eternally grateful.

"She's doing good. She's still getting some rest. She's taking all this better than I ever could have imagined."

"And you three?" he drawls, fully aware I ignored that part of his question.

I huff an exasperated laugh, "We're as good as can be expected. Mac and Finn got some much-needed rest, and I spent the night with Harper. We talked this morning when she woke up." I don't feel the need to explain to him exactly what we talked about because surely he knows. He's all too familiar with the weight that I carry day in and day out.

"Good. And Mac? Is he coming around?"

Luca had never met Mac before Harper was taken, so for all he knew, my brother was just some raging psychopath who was killing anyone he could get his hands on. Not that Luca would judge him for his actions, but I could tell he was wary of Mac. So, one day, I pulled him aside and explained Mac's past and exactly what was going on with him. From that moment on, Luca kept an extra eye on my brother, ensuring he didn't get too lost inside himself.

"It's hard to say, honestly. He let his guard down when we found her at the cabin and held her in his arms all the way home. But there's still that vacant look in his eyes, you know? I just hope her being back is enough."

"It will be. Just give him some time. He was in a really dark place, and it's going to be hard to just snap out of it." I know Luca's right. It's just hard to see my brother without that light in his eyes. "You guys have any idea what your next move against Declan will be?"

I scrub my hand down my face. "No. We haven't got a chance to talk about it yet."

"Alright, when you do, we're here for whatever you need."

"I appreciate that. Is Sebastian still running facial recognition on Logan?"

"Yeah. If he shows up on camera, we will find him. I'll let you know the second we do."

"Thanks, man. For everything. I mean it."

Luca scoffs on the other end of the line, like what he's done for us over the last couple of weeks has been no big deal. "Don't even mention it."

"I'll call you in a few days when we come up with a plan?"

"Sounds good. Hey, tell Harper I'm sorry I was gone before I got a chance to meet her, not that she really would have been up for it anyway. Sebastian and I had some *things* to take care of, and we knew you were all safe and on your way back."

I've been so hung up on everything happening that I haven't gotten a chance to pry into this. Looks like now is as good a time as any. "Hey, speaking of you and Sebastian. Want to tell me what's going on there?" I don't even bother fighting the sly grin on my face.

There's a beat of silence on the other end of the phone before Luca answers, "Nope," he says, making sure to pop the

P.

"Oh, don't be such a prude, Luca. We all see it." I decide to dig even further, "I mean, you're a hot piece of ass. He'd be crazy not to jump on that."

"Shut the fuck up, Ronan." I let out a deep belly laugh, the first one since before we killed Liam.

"If you guys ever want to double date, just let me know."

"I'm hanging up now," his tone sounding beyond annoyed, and I don't even care. I just keep laughing. "Call me in a couple of days."

The line goes dead, and I slide my phone into the pocket of my sweats. Slipping back into Harper's room, I walk over to her side of the bed, noticing her empty IV bag. Doc said once this one was gone she should be good to remove the IV from her hand. Bending over, I tuck some hair behind her ears, trying to gently rouse her from her sleep. She stirs a little before slowly blinking and smiling up at me.

And *fuck* if that sleepy little smile doesn't hit me square in the chest.

I still can't believe she's here, back in her bed where she's safe. And safe is what she will be for the rest of her life. Because I, no, we, intend on keeping her.

"Hey, Baby."

She stretches her arms over her head, pushing out her chest, causing her nipples to poke through the fabric of the sweater she has on. I *try* not to stare at them, but I'm only human after all, and damn, do they look good, even underneath the heavy cotton. She follows my line of sight and just lets out a soft giggle. "My eyes are up here, *sir*."

My eyes snap to hers, and I can't help the groan that slips past my lips. "I almost forgot how good it sounded when you called me that."

"I almost forgot how good it felt to say it."

Fuck me.

It takes every ounce of my restraint not to climb on this bed and sink into her. But, I can't—not yet. Not until she's fully healed. Tipping my head back, I close my eyes tight, willing myself not to get a hard-on. "Harper, you can't say things like that to me right now."

I don't have to see her face to know she's sporting a devious grin. "Why not?"

I look down at her and give her the most serious face I can manage, which isn't saying much. "You know exactly why. Now stop."

Her lips curl as she holds back a laugh. "Yes . . . sir." If I didn't love her already for everything she is, that smile right there, that would be enough.

Leaning down, I put my face right above hers as she tries to pull the cover up over her mouth so I can't see that she's still fighting a laugh. "Go ahead, keep it up. Because I distinctly remember promising not too long ago that I wouldn't hesitate to punish you for disobeying me, and the day will come when all your wounds are healed." I lower my face ever so slightly, my lips dusting against hers now. "And I fully intend on making good on that promise."

I chuckle as her eyes widen and give her a light kiss on the lips, stopping myself from taking this moment any further. Standing up straight, I hold out my hand. "Come on, I have to take your IV out. Can you sit up for me?"

She takes my hand, using it to help her sit up straight. I clench my teeth as she winces in pain as she moves. I cannot wait to get my hands on Logan. What he did to Harper will be nothing in comparison to the pain we will inflict upon him. He will be begging for death long before we're finished with him.

Harper, like always, notices my sudden rise in temper. "I'm alright, Ronan. Just a little sore. I'll heal."

I give her a smile that I know doesn't reach my ears. "I know, Baby." I pull back the covers before asking, "Can you swing your legs over for me?"

She does as I ask, so I get down on my haunches in front of her. Grabbing her hand I set it flat on her thigh, noticing how thin her leg feels. I make a mental note to talk to Mac about her diet over the next few days. Hopefully, with the vitamins Doc gave her and a proper diet, we can put back all the weight she lost.

Suddenly a flash of silver on her thumb catches my eye. I don't know how I hadn't noticed it yet; I was probably too focused on her myriad of wounds. Taking a closer look, I see it's my silver signet ring. I run my thumb over the metal. "Where did you get this?" I ask as I lift my eyes to meet hers.

"I woke up that night to come and find you after I realized what I said in my sleep. I wanted to say it to your face." Her eyes immediately get glassy at the memory of that night. "I went to your dresser to grab one of your dress shirts to put on because I knew Tanner and Logan were in the apartment, and when I did, I saw your pile of rings on top of it. Don't ask me why, but" she shrugs her shoulders, "I grabbed this one and slid it on my thumb. It was always my favorite."

"You've had it this whole time?"

She pulls her bottom lip between her teeth and nods. "It–it helped me, you know. The entire time I was in that cabin, it helped me. Whenever I touched it, I thought of you and how strong you would want me to be. I heard your voice in my head, telling me what to do. It helped me remember you when I thought you were . . ."

She can't even say the word, and I don't ask her to. Instead, I just look at her in absolute awe. This amazing, brave, and incredibly strong woman has been through more heartbreak in her life and has survived more trauma than any person should have to bear. And I'm lucky enough to call her mine.

She shakes her head as if trying to shake away the memory. "Anyway, I forgot I even had it on." She moves her opposite hand to grab the ring I'm still stroking with my thumb. "You can have it back."

"No." I grab her hand. "You keep it. It's yours now. It's going to be your last initial before long anyway." I don't doubt that for even a second.

She doesn't offer a smart remark; she barely even reacts. The only response I get is a soft smile and an "Okay."

Whether she's saying okay to keeping my ring or to taking my last name, I'm not sure. But, I'm going to take it as an okay to both.

She looks down at our joined hands and pinches her brows in confusion. "Where are the rest of your rings?"

Now it's my turn to shrug. "I haven't worn any of them since that night."

Tilting her head, she asks, "Why not?"

"I knew you liked them. Whenever I looked at them sitting on my dresser, all I could think about was how you would shiver when they touched your skin. The thought of putting them on was just . . . it felt like too much."

"I do really like them," she answers softly, cupping my face now.

"I'll put them back on today," I say as I turn and kiss the palm of her hand. "Come on, let's get this IV out."

I move to take the tape off the IV on top of her hand, still resting on her thigh, when she stops me. "Ummm, do you know what you're doing?"

"Doc showed me what to do before he left. I won't hurt you, I promise." Leaning down, I place a soft kiss on top of her hand. Her jade-green eyes meet mine and she nods. I do exactly as Doc showed me, removing the IV carefully. A small drop of blood pools where I pull it out, and instead of moving for a band-aid, I lean down and place my mouth back on top of her hand—this time, dragging my tongue across the drop of blood. I gaze up at Harper just in time to see her eyes glaze over with lust.

Removing my mouth and standing up straight, I hold out both my hands for her to grab onto and pull her up slowly. "Teasing isn't nice," she says, looking up at me with flushed cheeks. I swear, I've never been so happy to see her blush.

"I don't know what you're talking about," I reply before shooting her a wink. "Why don't you go soak in a hot bath, and I'll go see Mac about making us some food. How's that sound?"

She hits me with another megawatt smile. "That sounds like the best idea you've had all day."

"Can you walk to the bathroom, or do you need me to carry you?" I know she has no severe injuries, but I also know she's probably still feeling pretty sore and exhausted.

"I can walk. Can you just help me?"

"Of course, Baby." I help walk her to the bathroom with her hands firmly gripping my arm. Once we get in there, I run her a hot bath with a generous amount of Epsom salt and a lavender bubble bath. I pull her curls up into a haphazard bun on top of her head, and as I help get her undressed, I mentally catalog every single cut and bruise. I didn't see them all when Doc examined her as he shooed us all from the room, much to my annoyance. I swear, if I didn't cry already this morning, I would now at the sight of her. Not because she isn't beautiful but because she looks so broken. But I know she isn't. My girl is anything but broken. She's stronger than all of us combined.

After Harper slowly sinks below the bubbles, sighing in relief as she goes, I roll up a bath towel and place it on the ledge behind her head. She leans her head back and looks up at me, nothing but adoration shining in her eyes. I drop my head down and kiss her firmly on the forehead. "You relax. I'll come get you when breakfast is ready."

"Hmmm, okay." She says as she lets out a content sigh.

"I'm going to leave the doors open. Yell if you need anything, okay?"

"Okay." I turn around to leave the bathroom when she grabs me by the wrist. "Hey."

"Yeah, Baby?"

She squeezes my wrist a little harder before saying softly, "I love you."

I could never ask for anything for the rest of my life as long as I hear those three words from her lips every day until the day I die. "I love you, Harper Hayes."

18

Mac

I've been awake for a while now, just sitting in the den, staring out the window, watching the city streets below. Ronan sent Finn and I to our rooms last night to rest. We all wanted to crawl under the covers with her, but we didn't know how she would react if she woke up and we were in her bed. Finn and I didn't want to leave her, but Ronan gave us a stern look, telling us not to argue. And honestly, I'm glad he did. That's the first night I've slept more than three hours at a time since she was taken, and my body needed the rest, especially after the emotional roller coaster of us reuniting at the cabin.

I'm not going to lie and say I wasn't terrified at the thought of Harper being unable to pull me out of my darkness. All those days ago, I sank into that space to be what she needed me to get her back. But, even more so, I let the red swallow me so I wouldn't have to *feel it*. If I had allowed myself to feel all of the pain, sorrow, and despair that was coursing through every fiber of my being, I would have been a shell of a person. I was, anyway, in some ways, but at least I was still strong. And that's what Harper needed me to be—strong.

I froze when I saw her in Finn's arms coming out of that tree line. I wanted, more than anything, to run to her. To have her in my arms and tell her how much I loved her. But I couldn't get myself to move. I was terrified that she would be afraid of the monster I had become, I was terrified that she would no longer want the person that was in front of her, and most of all, I was terrified that I would hurt her. I had been swimming in endless seas of pain and violence since she was taken from us—endless seas of red. I was so afraid that the other side of me, who longs to care for and protect the people I love, would never return.

But with just four words, *"You won't hurt me,"* all of my armor came crashing down around me. All of the red disappeared, and in its place was Harper's light—my light.

Because she is *mine.*

She isn't a light we need to keep away from our darkness. She's the light we need to let live inside of it. She is woven into every fiber of my being, and I will die before I ever let someone take my light from me again.

The noise of Ronan running the bath in Harper's room pulls me from my thoughts, so I head to the kitchen to put on a pot of coffee. For the past couple of weeks, none of us have eaten anything that hasn't come in a takeout container, which means our kitchen was in desperate need of a grocery store run. Finn went out yesterday to grab everything we would need, including all of Harper's favorite snacks and coffee must-haves.We all know how much our girl likes, more like needs, a good cup of coffee.

It felt good to be back in the kitchen yesterday, cooking for the people I love. I'm by no means a chef, but I like to think I'm pretty good at it. It's clearly better than anything Ronan or Finn can make. I just haven't had the mental capacity to do it lately, for obvious reasons. But yesterday, I made Harper her favorite breakfast for dinner, and the smile that spread on her face when she took her first bite of pancakes was exactly what I needed.

Just as the coffee begins percolating, Ronan comes strolling down the hall with the biggest grin on his face. And fuck if that doesn't make me happy. "You look like a lovestruck moron," I jab as he enters the kitchen, and fuck if picking on him doesn't make me even happier.

Judging by the look on his face, he's just as happy to hear it, not that he'll ever admit it to me. "That's because I am, brother."

I raise my brows at his confession. "Oh yeah?"

He slides onto one of the chairs at the island. "Yeah." Before I can crack another smart remark, he points at me. "Don't even fucking start." I tip my head back and let out a roar of a laugh. The sound slightly shocks us both. "It's good to hear you laugh."

"It feels good to laugh," I answer.

Turning around, I grab four coffee mugs from the cabinet and set them on the island. I nod toward the hall, "She taking a bath?"

"Yeah. I told her to yell when she was done so I could help her out."

I can't help the tightness that coils in my chest at the thought of her not even being able to get out of the tub by herself. "How is she this morning?"

Ronan scrubs his hand across the dark stubble on his face. Actually, it's more of a beard now. The scrub hasn't trimmed it in days. Not that I'm one to talk, my usually longer hair is looking extra shaggy lately. "Honestly, man, she's better than any of us could have hoped. Physically, she's still pretty sore. But mentally, she's a lot stronger than any of us give her credit for."

A smile pulls at my lips. "That's my girl."

"I still think we should make sure she sees Doc's wife, though."

"I agree," Finn says as he emerges from the hall, blonde hair disheveled, looking as well rested as I am.

"Well, well, well. Good morning, sleeping beauty," I poke as he slides into a chair beside Ronan.

He scoffs, "Nice to see you're feeling better."

I laugh as I turn around to grab the now-full pot of coffee, pouring each of us a glass and leaving a decent amount for Harper.

"Hey, I gotta talk to you about something," Ronan says as he reaches for his mug.

"What's up?"

"I saw her for the first time before I put her into the tub—really saw her. She's so thin, you guys." I swallow hard. "I didn't ask, but it's obvious he starved her. I know Doc gave her vitamins, but I think it's important we pay close attention to what she's eating over the next couple of days."

I nod adamantly, willing to do whatever we need to to get our girl healthy again. "I'll make sure I use a lot of full-fat foods and red meats over the next few days."

"Okay, good," Ronan answers.

Finn and I share a look, silently begging one another to ask

Ronan the question we're both too terrified to ask Harper. Being the know-it-all he is, my brother must pick up on our looks. "Just ask me what you want to ask me."

I look at Finn, pleading for him to be the one to spit the words out. Finally, he lets out a heavy sigh, "Did he rape her?" He spits out the question as if the words taste like poison on his tongue. In a way, I'm sure they do.

Ronan pauses for a beat, and I swear to God, it's the longest second of my life. "No." Finn and I both let out a harsh breath. "She said he didn't touch her like that. He beat her," he draws his hands into fists, "but he didn't touch her."

"Thank God," Finn says as he drops his head into his hands.

"I know," Ronan replies. "I mean, we know that Declan sent Logan here because he caught him with a guy, but I just wasn't sure. Declan doesn't seem to have a lot of limits, so I wasn't sure Logan would have any, either. Thankfully, I was wrong."

Finn and I both nod in agreement. I lean down, placing my forearms on the cool marble. "Speaking of Declan and Logan, what are we going to do?"

"I think we should give it a few days," Finn answers. "She's safe here."

Ronan immediately hangs his head in regret, surely beating himself up over the fact that she was taken from the apartment in the first place. But the truth of the matter is, it's not his fault. It's none of ours. Logan had a solid background check by a company we regularly use, and he put on a damn good show. None of us blamed Ronan for what happened, and we never will.

Finn pats Ronan on the back. "She is safe here, Ronan. None of us plan on leaving over the next few days. The groceries are all taken care of, and if Harper needs to see Doc for any reason, he can come here. I already spoke to Ralph last night. He pulled extra security and has them posted throughout the building. His team is filled with nothing but men he's known since he was a SEAL. We still don't know where Logan is anyway, and Declan can't get to us here. Plus, we *all* could use the rest."

"We should have used Ralph and his guys in the first place," Ronan mutters.

"We probably should have," answers Finn. "But our first instinct was to rely on the same company we've been using since Liam was in charge. Now we know. We can't change what happened, Ronan. The best we can do is learn from it."

"Finn's right, brother. The most important thing we can do now is move on so we can keep her safe." Ronan's eyes lift to meet mine. "I agree with Finn. I think we all need to take a breather for a few days. Try to get Harper back in good health and rest up."

Ronan knocks his knuckles on the countertop. "Yeah, you guys are right."

Finn bumps him on the shoulder. "Let us help you make some of these decisions, man. You don't need to do it all on your own."

Reluctantly, Ronan nods, "I know, I know."

"Ronan, I'm done." Harper's voice sings-songs through the apartment, and Ronan's face instantly lights up.

"Be right there, Baby," he yells back with a dopey smile.

I can't help the laugh that bubbles out of me. Finn does the same. *"Be right there, Baby,"* Finn and I both mock him at the same time.

"You know what," Ronan shoves out of his chair while

flipping each of us off, "I don't even care." Finn and I laugh louder as he makes his way back towards Harper's room, calling over his shoulder as he goes, "And make us some breakfast, asshole!"

I'm laughing so hard now I'm crying, and I don't even try to stop it.

19

Harper

"Ronan, I can brush my own teeth, " I laugh while simultaneously trying to swat his hand away. After he came in and got me out of the tub, he helped me get dressed in a pair of sweats and my favorite Led Zeppelin T-shirt; he then sat me down on a chair he grabbed from somewhere else in the apartment, where he applied all of my skincare products and is now trying to brush my teeth. He continues trying to come at me with my toothbrush when I grab his wrist, stopping him in his tracks. "Ronan, I love you, but I am perfectly capable of brushing my teeth. I promise."

He sighs before reluctantly handing over the toothbrush. "Yeah. That's probably a bit much, right?"

I softly grin at him, not wanting him to feel guilty about helping me. "I know you're trying to help, but if you end up sliding that toothbrush down my throat, I'll gag, and I might accidentally punch you. That would just be bad for everyone involved."

He laughs, "Trust me, Baby, I know your gag reflex is better than that." He shoots me a panty-melting wink before handing over the toothbrush. Once I'm done with my teeth, I fix the bun Ronan attempted before my bath and throw on some chapstick, knowing this is as good as it's going to get for the day. But I'm anxious to see Mac and Finn and spend the day with all three of them, so I don't mind.

I stand from my chair, and Ronan bends to pick me up. Stopping him, I say, "Ronan, Baby, I can walk. I just need you to help me."

"You sure?" He asks, his voice full of concern.

I stand on my toes and place a soft kiss against his plush lips. "I'm sure. I promise I'll tell you if I'm in any pain, okay?"

"Okay."

"Come on, I want to go see them," I say as I wrap my hands around his outstretched arm. "Plus, it smells like Mac made cinnamon rolls and I. Am. Salivating." Ronan's shoulders shake with laughter as he leads me out of my room and down the hallway. The smell of frosting and cinnamon assaults my nose, and my stomach immediately growls with hunger. After eating next to nothing for two weeks, I am more than ready to fill up on Mac's cooking.

As Ronan and I walk out of the hallway, I see Mac whipping up a bowl of frosting for the rolls that are cooking away in the oven. Finn's standing at the sink behind him doing dishes. The two of them are lost in conversation, and I stop to stare at them, tears stinging my eyes. This is the first time I've *really* seen them since that day in the woods, the first time I've really been able to *look* at them. I know I've done nothing but cry since they found me, but I don't try to stop them. Because, unlike my time with Logan, these tears are that of happiness. Happiness that I'm back where I belong, happiness that all four of us are together, happiness that I get to see the smile on their faces, taste Mac's cooking again, watch Finn meticulously clean the apartment, and once again be the subject of Ronan's watchful eye.

Just like that, another piece of me feels like it's healed.

Finn must see us out of the corner of his eye because he drops whatever he's washing and hits me with a face-splitting grin. "Angel . . ."

In just a few long strides, he moves across the kitchen, wearing black sweatpants and a white v-neck, his blond hair unkempt, and is wrapping me in his arms, one around my back and one around the back of my head, pressing my face into his chest. My broken ribs cause me to wince in pain as he holds me tight to him. But I don't stop his embrace. Because the pain means I'm alive. I'm alive and in his arms.

He holds me for a minute before whispering in my ear, "You have no idea how happy I am to see you looking so much better." He stands up straight and cups my face in his hands, tears pooling in his eyes. Like Ronan, Finn isn't one to show much emotion. He keeps most of his feelings pushed down for reasons I'm fully aware of. So, knowing that he's incapable of holding back his tears only further proves how deeply he feels for me.

"Don't you ever leave me again, okay?" His voice is nothing more than a whisper now. Bending down, he places a brief but fierce kiss on my lips before resting his forehead on mine.

"I have never felt so empty," *kiss*, "So alone," *kiss*, "So irrevocably broken as I did when you were gone." *Kiss*. "Do not ever do that to me again, okay?" A small tear escapes his left eye, and I watch as it drops to the floor between us.

I nod, my forehead still pressed against his. "Never again, Love. I'll be here, always."

Those three unspoken words are on the tip of my tongue, and judging by the look in his eyes, Finn feels it too. But when I open my mouth to speak, he silences me with a harsh kiss. I don't hesitate to open for him, letting his tongue brush up against mine and savoring the way his beard feels against my skin. The kiss is over all too soon, and when he pulls his lips from mine, he says, "Later, Angel. I want to be able to tell you properly, without those two idiots eavesdropping on my every word."

Finally, I look past our bubble to find Ronan in the kitchen leaning against the counter next to his brother, matching shit-eating grins and cups of coffee in hand. I look back at Finn; I know how private he is and how much he likes to keep his emotions close to his chest, so I nod in agreement. "Is that a date, Mr. Donovan?"

"It's a promise, Miss Hayes."

Finn leads me into the kitchen, where I try to move toward Mac; instead, he pushes me toward one of the chairs. When I look at him to ask what he's doing, he says, "You've been standing long enough."

His stern voice lets me know there's no room to argue, so when he leans down to give me one last kiss, I whisper against his lips, quiet enough for only him to hear, "Yes, Daddy."

He lets out a harsh breath, and when his lips meet mine, he gently bites my bottom lip between his teeth. I instantly feel my panties growing wet.

It's good to know the last couple of weeks hasn't completely killed my sex drive. Not that anyone could resist these three.

Finn moves back around the counter to continue washing

the dishes, but not before hitting me with a look so full of heat I could practically combust. Ronan takes his usual spot to my right, and I feel Mac come up behind me.

Reaching over my shoulder, he places a steaming cup of coffee on the counter in front of me, fixed just how I like it. I'm about to spin my chair around so I can hug him too, but instead, he wraps his arms around me from behind and drops his head to my shoulder.

He begins peppering kisses along the skin of my neck, and I can't help the shiver that rolls through my body. "You have no idea how much I missed you, Princess."

My entire body immediately goes stiff at the name. Flashes of every time Logan mocked me and called me Princess while he beat me run through my memory in rapid succession as I suck in harsh breaths, the all too familiar feeling of a panic attack working its way through my body.

"Harper," Ronan says as he places his large hand on top of my shaking one. "Baby, what's wrong? Are you in pain?" The concern and panic in his voice was clear as day.

Mac climbs into the chair on my left, spins me to face him, and takes my opposite hand, putting it on the center of his chest, just like he did all those weeks ago. "Breathe, Harper." He takes a deep breath, and I feel his chest rise and fall beneath my hand. "Breathe with me. Remember?" I nod frantically, trying to force my body to match his breaths. After a few moments, I can feel my harsh breaths begin to even out. "Good girl," he says as he squeezes my hand. His thumb starts stroking the back of my hand, and when he sees me breathing normally again, he picks my hand up and kisses my palm softly. I finally pull my gaze from the center of his chest up to his eyes. "Tell me what happened?"

My chin trembles. I hate that Logan took this from us. "You–you can't call me that." The hurt on Mac's face is evident. "He called me that." I don't have to say who *he* is—they know. "I–I'm sorry, Mac. I didn't think it would bother me. But then you said it, and it took me right back to that cabin. He took that from us. I'm so, so sorry." I choke on a sob as I look down at my lap, unable to stomach the look on his face.

"Harper," he hooks his finger under my chin. "Look at me." He lifts my chin, and I'm fully expecting to see anger and frustration when I look into his steel-gray eyes. Instead, all I see is complete understanding. "You have nothing to be sorry for, absolutely nothing. Do you understand me?"

"But—"

Mac shakes his head. "But, nothing. It's just a word. Consider it eliminated from my vocabulary."

"I loved being your Princess," I whisper, my voice laced with regret.

"I know you did, but you are so much more than that."

"I am?"

"You are. You are our queen, Harper. Only a queen could have been strong enough to make it through all of that. Only a queen could have escaped and made their way back to us. Only a queen could have brought me out of the darkness I was swimming in. Only a queen could have washed away all the red." Mac's voice cracks, and I push one of his long strands out of his face. He immediately leans into my hand and whispers, "Is tú Mo Grá."

He's called me Mo Grá before, but I've never asked him what it means. I tilt my head in confusion, and he exhales heavily before giving me the sweetest smile, quickly glancing between Ronan and Finn, who I can see out of the corner of my eye are trying their best to pretend like they are not listening. I get the feeling that this is a conversation Mac would rather have had in private, but it's too late now.

"It means . . ." he grabs my hand from where it's still resting on the side of his face and kisses the top of it before resting it back on his chest, this time over his rapidly beating heart. "It means, 'You are my love.'"

All the air is immediately sucked from my lungs, not because I don't love him, but because after the way he looked at me when I came out of the woods, I wasn't sure I would ever hear these words from him. As soon as I saw him, I knew what was happening with my sweet, gentle giant. Nobody had to explain it to me. I could see the torment in his eyes clear as day. I thought my Mac was gone for a moment, but then he looked into my eyes, and I knew he was in there somewhere. I just had to let him know I trusted him enough to come back to me. I know who Mac is, *all* of him, even the parts of him he despises. I know he tries with everything in him to hide that part of himself, to keep it as separate as he can from the man he wants to be. But he doesn't see what I see... what we see. We see a Mac that's strong enough to embrace every single part of him because that makes him who he is, and who he is, is perfect. I just hope he can see that he's strong enough one day. He's strong enough to face his demons and be the man he *wants* to be to live and the man he *has* to be to survive.

"Honey," I release a harsh breath.

He closes his eyes briefly, and when he opens again, all I see is an unconditional and all-consuming love. He shakes his head and lets out a light chuckle, "I *really* didn't want to do this in front of these two," he nods toward Ronan and Finn, who, when I glance back at them, are practically trying to be invisible while simultaneously folding their lips in trying to hold in their laughs. I roll my eyes and give them a stern look, silently warning them not to be dickheads, before looking back at Mac.

"But I do, Mo Grá, I love you. You stole my breath away the day we met you; ever since, it's been yours. Because I cannot breathe when you are not near, Harper. My reason for living is now wrapped up in you." He scoots towards the edge of his chair, drops his forehead to rest it against mine, and whispers, "Thank you for bringing me back."

"Always, Cormac." He doesn't even flinch at the use of his full name. I know it's not his favorite, but for some reason, it just felt right. "I will always bring you back. I'm not afraid. Just as I'm safe with you, you are safe with me. I love you too."

Mac's lips crash into mine, kissing me so hard it literally feels like I am breathing for him. Mac continues to kiss me deeper, and I can't help but tug at his bottom lip with my teeth. A rough groan falls from his mouth when I do. He kisses me softly before pulling his lips away, keeping his forehead firmly pressed against mine. "I love you, Harper. You're my whole heart, my Queen, my Pretty Girl—Mo Grá."

"Now I'm the one that's going to cry," Ronan laughs behind me.

Mac lets out an exasperated sigh. "I knew he was going to ruin it."

I laugh as Mac sits up straight and grabs the back of my chair, spinning me to face the counter again. Finn's still standing at the sink, but his hand is now covering his mouth, trying to hide what I'm sure is a shit-eating grin.

The oven timer goes off, signaling Mac's delicious cinnamon rolls are done. He makes his way around the kitchen, and I jokingly reach out my right hand and backhand Ronan in the chest. His jaw drops with feigned shock, and he dramatically grabs at his chest where I tapped him. "You always take his side!"

"Because you're usually the one giving him shit."

Mac looks over his shoulder and winks. "Still my hero."

Unable to hold it back any longer, Finn drops his hand and lets out a roar of a laugh.

"Not cool, Baby. Not cool." I'd maybe take him seriously if he didn't have a practically devious look on his face.

The guys continue poking jabs at one another but not picking on Mac any further about the fact that he just told me he loved me for the first time in front of them. I know they're nothing but happy for their brother, and as obnoxious as it sounds, even happier for me.

Mac plates cinnamon rolls that are easily as big as my head, topping each with a generous amount of cream cheese frosting and roasted walnuts. He gives us each a side of mixed berries, and I don't miss that he adds an extra spoonful to my plate. I inhale the roll and side of fruit in minutes, and they all smile big when I ask for seconds. I know they're worried about how thin I got while I was gone, and quite frankly, I am too. I miss my curves and want them back.

Once we have all finished eating, I clear my throat, drawing their attention toward me. "Sooo, what's the plan? What are we going to do about Declan and Logan? Does anyone even know where Logan is?"

They share quick glances among one another before Ronan speaks, "Luca still has Sebastian running facial recognition on Logan. So far, he's stayed under the radar, but Sebastian will find him if he shows up anywhere with a camera."

"If he's still alive," Finn says, now sitting at a stool next to Mac at the end of the island. "Judging by the amount of blood in that bathroom, you got him good." He winks at me, and I feel the puff of pride in my chest as I sit up a little straighter and turn back to Ronan.

"He must have gotten a hold of Declan after you escaped because the plane he was supposed to send to Erie International never showed up. Logan hasn't been seen at a single hospital or any other airport. If he is alive, he's hunkered down somewhere, probably waiting on further instruction from Declan and trying to heal whatever nasty wound you gave him."

"Okay, but you didn't answer the first half of my question. What's our plan?"

"Mo Grá," Mac says gently from my left as he reaches up and twirls a stray curl that slipped from my bun in his fingers, "We talked about it while you were in the bath."

"Okay?"

"We think it's best to wait before making our next move. None of us have any reason to leave the apartment for at least a few days. Finn has already spoken to Ralph, and he has placed extra security throughout the building. We don't believe Logan is of any threat to anyone at the moment, I bet he can barely walk, and Declan is all the way in Ireland, likely running around like a chicken with his head cut off, trying to figure out what to do next."

"Shouldn't that be why we do something *now*? Strike while he doesn't have a plan."

"We could, Baby. But it would only end badly."

"What? Why?" I don't understand why they're not ready to jump into action right now. I would have thought they wouldn't want to rest another minute until they had both Logan's and Declan's blood on their hands.

"Because none of us are mentally capable of dealing with that right now," Mac answers.

"You almost died, Harper." Ronan lowers his tattooed hand and wraps it around my thigh. I smile when I see he has all of his rings back on. "You were gone for fifteen days. They took you from our home, and *you almost died.*"

Finn leans forward and rests his forearms on the counter, "You are nowhere near healed enough to leave this apartment, and we are nowhere near ready to let you out of our sights. You need to rest, and quite frankly, so do we. What's best is for all of us to take the rest of the week, and then we will go from there. Okay?"

The stern look on Finn's face lets me know he's not asking. None of them are. On one hand, I want to disagree; I want all of this behind us as soon as possible. I want the threats over our heads gone so we can focus on building a life, the four of us, together. I know that, without a doubt, there will always be people in the shadows waiting for the perfect opportunity to destroy the empire the three of them have built. An empire to which I am now unequivocally connected. But right now, this feels bigger. Like once it's gone, we will all be able to breathe. On the other hand, though, I know they're right. I barely had the energy to pull myself out of bed this morning, let alone join them on some revenge mission. One of them will want to stay here with me, weakening us even further, and I know that if I'm here and they're out there, their heads won't be in it. Someone will get hurt, or worse, killed. My heart can't handle losing one of them dying. Not again. I know Ronan's alive, but it was all too real for a while. I'll never be able to forgive myself if I put them in that position.

This is why, without any argument, I nod and say, "Okay."

"I hope you're ready for some serious cuddles," Mac says as he leans forward and drops a messy kiss on my cheek.

"Aweee, I'd love to cuddle with you, little bro." I reach to my right to smack Ronan in the chest again, but this time, he grabs my wrist to stop me. Instead, he lifts my hand and gently kisses my thumb where his ring still resides. Goosebumps skate over my skin at the sentimental gesture.

Mac gets up from his chair, walks behind me, and while Ronan still has his eyes locked on mine, smacks his brother across the back of the head. "You always have to say something smart."

Ronan grabs at the back of his head. This time I think in real pain. "Ouch, you fucker. That hurt."

Mac doesn't acknowledge his whining as he sets about putting the leftover rolls in the fridge, and I look over at Finn, who is again rolling his eyes at his best friend's antics. His warm, brown eyes meet mine as his lips curl up, and he winks, his entire demeanor radiating happiness and belonging.

We haven't had a chance to talk about what happened that night down at the docks, but I know Ronan and Mac have zero regrets when it comes to killing Liam. He was a danger not only to me but to their mother and everything the three of them were trying to build. And judging by the way Finn looks at his best friends, he finally feels like he truly has a place here, even though he always did, rather than feeling like it was his duty to be here.

That's what I want for him, for them, for all of us. To have a place where we can belong—a place where, regardless of all the darkness, there's a tiny pocket of light.

20

Finn

We've spent the majority of the last two days sleeping and snuggling together while watching movies in Harper's bed. All four of us. *Together.* I'd be lying if I said I hadn't loved every minute of it, even if it did include an ungodly amount of time in bed with my two best friends. But I guess, if we're going to do this, like *really do this*, we better get used to it.

It was clear that Harper was still utterly exhausted and pretty sore, so rather than camping out in the den, we decided to hole up in her room and spend the days watching movies. She made us watch every *Harry Potter* movie, and not one of us cared because the smile on her face the entire time was worth it.

I've been most impressed with Ronan and his complete willingness to drop everything to sit around the apartment and do nothing. I haven't even seen him so much as pick up his phone to answer one business email. As someone who has been running at a hundred miles per hour, 24/7, for the last three years, I know this is exactly what he needs, but that doesn't make it any less surprising. We have all of our bases covered at Kings and with all of our underground dealings throughout the city. Sebastian still hasn't seen Logan pop up anywhere, and Luca is keeping an eye out for Declan. With any luck, no one should need us until next week; for now, we're all more than happy to hang out in our bubble.

Mac's in the kitchen, cooking what smells like Chicken Parmesan, and Ronan is currently in the shower, his shower, to be specific. When Harper told him he could just use her shower, he quickly looked at me before dropping a light kiss on her lips and saying he didn't want to bring all his bathroom stuff in here. Harper was none the wiser, but both Ronan and I knew that was bullshit, likely for the same reason I had to go shower in my own bathroom this morning. Being pressed up against Harper's body for the past two days and not being able to do anything about it is its own personal brand of torture. None of us have so much as made the slightest move on her because we know that's the absolute last thing she needs or likely wants right now. We aren't willing to set her recovery back because we can't keep our dicks in our pants. So, jacking off in the shower for the foreseeable future it is.

We finished the last *Harry Potter* movie a couple of hours ago, and now I'm stuck watching two brothers named Stefan and Damon attend high school so they can pine after the same girl. They're like five-hundred-year-old vampires, by the way.

I think I'd rather watch the teenage wizards, if I'm being honest.

But I won't complain because I'm propped up against the headboard with Harper curled into my side. I'm sliding my fingers through her curls while she moves her thumb in soft circles against the top of my thigh. Her vanilla and caramel scent invades my senses every time I take a deep breath, and I don't think I've ever been more content doing absolutely nothing.

"You guys were right," she says as she nuzzles deeper into my side.

"Hmmm?" I answer, still mindlessly playing with her hair.

"We needed this. The time to ourselves. The quiet." She tilts her head up, emerald eyes covered in her black-rimmed glasses, meeting mine. It's only been two days, and she's already looking so much better. Her eyes have a brightness to them, her cheeks no longer appear hollow, the deep purple bruises that cover her body are starting to turn yellow, and her sprained ankle is far less swollen. Never underestimate the power of a few good day's rest. She's even stopped dressing in sweats from head to toe, saying she no longer feels cold all of the time. Now she's lying under the covers in nothing but one of our T-shirts and a pair of cotton panties.

Like I said, a special kind of torture.

I tip my head forward and place a kiss against her forehead. "I'm so glad you're feeling better, Angel."

"And you, how are you feeling? With everything that is . . ."

I know what she's referring to. With everything that happened immediately after, I've never spoken to her about that night down at the docks with Liam. I honestly haven't felt the need to. What Mac said to me that night helped more than he will ever know. I'm their brother, and Liam and his cruel words can't take that away from me. "I'm okay, I promise."

"You'll tell me if you're ever not okay, okay?"

"Okay." My perfect, beautiful Angel. After everything she's been through, she still has it in her to worry about us and how we're feeling. Fucking hell, do I love her.

Now's as good a time as any, I guess.

Sliding my hand free of her hair, I cup her cheeks so she remains looking at me, "Harper, I–"

"I love you, Finn," she yells, cutting me off. I can't help the small laugh that slips out as her eyes widen. "I'm sorry. I didn't want to waste another second not telling you that I love you." She slowly sits up and straddles me, gently pushing her fingers through my hair. "I love that you make me brave. I love that you taught me how to let go when I thrive on being in control. I love the man that you are, for me and for everyone around you." A small tear escapes her eye, but I quickly slide her glasses over her head and brush it away with my thumb. "Most of all, I love that you dance in the dark with me." She pulls one hand from my hair and pushes it through the hair covering my jaw. "I love you, Finn."

Her glassy eyes dart between mine as I try to remember how to breathe. I don't think I've ever been struck so speechless. I was totally prepared to tell her how I felt, but for some reason, I wasn't the slightest bit ready for what she would say. Because, *fuck,* that was everything I could have hoped for and more. Harper loves me. She really loves me. For all that I am.

"Angel . . ."

"Now is the part where you say it back, you know?" she laughs.

"I love you." Leaning forward, I kiss her fiercely, trying not to pay attention to the fact that my cock is growing hard the longer she sits on my lap. "I love you, I love you, I love you," I repeat over and over again between each kiss. "Never in my wildest dreams did I think I would get lucky enough to have a woman like you in my life, but here you are—my Angel on earth. You are the strongest person I've ever known, and I can't wait to spend the rest of my life being the man you deserve."

"You already are, Finn Donovan." Her mouth crashes into mine again, and this time, I don't hesitate to slide my tongue into her mouth, swallowing and savoring every moan that slips past her lips as I do. It's not long before she wraps her arms tighter around my neck, bringing her chest tight against mine. Even through both of our cotton shirts, I can feel her tight nipples pressing against my chest.

It's when she slowly moves her hips above my straining erection that I tear my mouth away from hers, "Fuck, Harper. We can't." Her eyes flash with disappointment and rejection. "It's not because I don't want to, because fuck do I want to. But, you're not healed enough, Angel, you'll get hurt."

She slowly rolls her hips forward again, a devious look on her face, and I swear to God it takes every ounce of self-control I have not to flip us over and drive my cock deep inside her. I can't, though. I will not be the reason she gets hurt again. So, I firmly grab her hips and stall her movements. "Harper, don't test me," my voice stern now, "Just because I told you I loved you doesn't mean I won't punish you for disobeying me."

"You know, you all keep saying you're going to punish me, and yet," she leans forward so her lips are featherlight against mine, "it has yet to happen."

"Just you wait. The day will come, naughty girl."

"Looking forward to it, *Daddy*."

Fuck my life.

My cock twitches beneath my sweatpants at the word, and judging by the smile on her face, she knows exactly what she just did. "Harper, enough," I growl.

She tilts her head back and laughs before putting her hands up in mock surrender, "Okay, okay. I'm done."

Moving slowly, she sets her glasses on the nightstand and stands from the bed; holding her hand out, she asks, "You wanna come take a bath with me? My muscles could use a good soak."

Shit, I don't know why none of us have thought of this before, "How does a soak in the hot tub on the roof sound?"

Her jaw drops so dramatically, I swear it hits the floor, "You have a hot tub?"

Standing up, I lead Harper down the hall and toward the elevator. "Yeah, we have a private hot tub and a pool on the roof. We're the only ones that have access to it, but we never use it because we're always too busy doing other shit. Kind of forgot it was there, to be honest." As we approach the kitchen, I notice Mac is nowhere to be found, and the Chicken Parm is already in the oven. If he's been feeling anything like Ronan and me, I'm sure he's in his room taking a "shower." His absence gives me an idea, so I quickly sidestep to grab the key to the rooftop door out of the junk drawer and shoot a text to Ronan and Mac, letting them know where Harper and I will be.

"Oh my God, to be so rich, you forget you have a private rooftop pool." I don't look at her, but I can practically feel her eyes rolling. "Wait! Let me go get my suit!" She yells in excitement, trying to turn back toward her room.

I stop and stare at her deadpan. "Harper, did you miss the part where I said it was private?"

"No, but . . ."

I cock an eyebrow at her, "Just because I won't fuck you doesn't mean I don't want to stare at you naked, given the opportunity. No suits allowed."

She steps toward me and runs her hand up my chest before wrapping it around my neck, playing with the hair at the nape. "Hmmm," she says as she taps her lips with the opposite hand, "sitting in a private hot tub with one of my hot boyfriends— naked. Don't have to ask me twice."

Mockingly, I bite at the tip of her finger, but I don't miss the way her eyes heat as I suck the tip of it into my mouth. "If I didn't love the three of you before, I sure do now."

"The private rooftop pool and hot tub is all it would have taken, huh?"

"Well, duh," she answers, giving me her best dumbfounded look.

"Come on, naughty girl," I say with a chuckle before pulling her into the elevator and hitting the button for the rooftop. Hearing my phone dinging repeatedly in my pocket, I pull it out to see what I'm sure are messages from Ronan and Mac.

Me: Taking Harper up to the roof to soak in the hot tub.

Ronan: Fucking hell, how did I not think of that.

Mac: Because you barely even took ten minutes out of your day to take a piss, let alone go up to the pool.

Ronan: I'll be up to join you in ten. Mac, shut the fuck up and finish making us dinner.

Mac: Piss off. I want to come too.

The elevator dings, signaling we've arrived at the roof, the door opens, and as soon as I see it, I'm honestly a little more pissed at myself that we've never brought her up here. There are a few cabanas and lounge chairs spread across the rooftop, a fully stocked bar, a small pool just big enough to swim laps in, and a hot tub large enough to seat six people comfortably. The glass railing that wraps around the building's edge allows for an unobstructed view of the city, and the outdoor string lights make for the perfect atmosphere.

"Wow, Finn," Harper looks at me, the string lights reflecting in her green eyes, and I swear, it takes my fucking breath away for a moment.

"Yeah, wow is right." A bright red blush spreads across her cheeks, fully aware I'm not talking about the rooftop. My phone sounds again in my hand.

Mac: Dinner's warm and in the oven. We can have it after the hot tub.

Ronan: Finn, why won't the elevator come back down? Where's the key to the door?

Harper laughs as she reads the messages along with me. Clarifying, I tell her, "I pulled the emergency stop button so they can't call it back down to the apartment, aaaand I took the key that opens the door to the roof before we left."

"You don't want them to join us?" she asks, brows pinched in confusion.

"Maybe a different time. But right now, I want it just to be you and me. Just for tonight."

Harper stands on her tiptoes and slants her lips over mine before whispering against me, "That sounds perfect."

"Why don't you go grab some towels. I'll turn the hot tub on."

She spins to walk toward the stack of towels near the bar, and I don't miss the opportunity to give her a firm pat on the ass as she walks away.

Before I silence my phone, I send the guys one last message.

Me: Because you're not coming up here. If I have the opportunity to have a naked Harper in the hot tub by myself for an hour, I'm taking it.

Me: Feel free to have dinner without us. Consider it brotherly bonding time.

Me: Don't be pissed just because I thought of it first.

Their responses immediately roll in.

Ronan: What do you mean she's naked?!

Mac: I don't want to spend time with Ronan. I've been doing it all my life. Send the elevator back down, Finn.

Ronan: Finn, I swear to God. I'm going to murder you. Send the elevator back down.

Mac: We deserve to see a naked Harper, too.

Mac: Finn???

Ronan: FINN DONOVAN!!!!

I roar a laugh before silencing my phone and throwing it down on the nearest lounge chair. I know they're going to be pissed, but they'll get over it. I'll deal with them later.

Turning the jets to the hot tub on, I watch as Harper makes her way toward the steamy water. Her eyes meet mine over her shoulder as she reaches down and slides her panties down her legs. I wait with bated breath as she grabs the hem of her t-shirt and pulls it over her head.

Scrubbing my hand down my face, I just stand there for a moment, admiring her beautiful body and all that she is. Because, right now, I don't see the bruises or the cuts. I don't see the way her curves aren't filled out like they used to be from being starved for two weeks. I only see this incredibly strong woman, a woman who was brave enough to escape her own personal hell to make it back to us—a woman who is strong enough to handle all three of us and the life that we lead.

All I see is a woman that loves me.

Harper Hayes loves me.

Harper climbs into the water and sinks down just so the swell of her breasts is above the water, her hair floating around her. Meanwhile, I'm still fucking frozen. She cocks her head to the side and smiles."You coming?"

"Oh, I think I just did, Angel."

She roars out a laugh, and it's music to my ears. Following

her lead, I quickly remove all my clothes and climb in with her. I make sure to sit on the stone bench that wraps around the inside of the hot tub as far from her as possible. She's naked and wet and looks so fucking pretty underneath these lights, and I only have so much willpower. She takes a step to move towards me, and I raise my hand from the water, pointing a finger at her. "You stay all the way over there, Angel."

She gives me a knowing grin, "Yes, Da—"

"Don't, Harper. Just, don't." I swear on all that is holy, if she says that word one more time tonight, it will be my breaking point.

She laughs at me again before settling back in her spot. I watch in rapt attention as she leans her head back onto the ledge and stares at the stars. Her toes brush against the inside of my calf every so often, sending waves of pleasure through my body with every touch. But I don't move. I sit there and stare at her as her muscles relax further and further into the steaming water. We spend an hour sitting under the New York night sky, just like that.

And every second that passes, I fall deeper and deeper.

21

Harper

It's been seven whole days of sitting inside the walls of this apartment, and I can't do it anymore.

As excited and grateful as I was that the guys wanted to spend all this uninterrupted time with me, resting, recovering, and relaxing, I just can't do it. I started to feel much better a couple of days ago. The constant achiness is gone for the most part, minus the pain in my ribs, the swelling in my ankle has all but disappeared, the couple stitches on my foot fell out this morning, and with any luck, the ones on the back of my head should any day now, and I'm starting to feel like I have all of my energy back.

While the physical recovery has been relatively easy, the mental recovery may be a little trickier than I thought. The guys told me they were genuinely shocked at how well I was handling the trauma I was going through and were worried that I might be repressing my feelings. Turns out they were right.

I've had appointments with Doc's wife, Lisa, the past few days. While I went into the first one on my high horse, thinking it would be a total waste of time, I was quickly knocked down a peg. The moment I wasn't around Ronan, Mac, or Finn and stopped feeling like I had to be strong for them, even though I don't, nor are they asking me to be, it was like a damn broke open and I couldn't get it to stop.

My first session with her was utterly exhausting, and I was physically and mentally drained for most of the day afterward. While the next few days weren't much better, this morning's felt *bearable*. I only shed a few tears and was able to make it through the entire session without feeling like the walls were closing in on me. Lisa informed me that we would move our sessions to once a week as long as I felt comfortable. She also prescribed me some anxiety medication, which I was briefly hesitant about taking. But then she said, "Harper, that wound on the back of your head needed stitches, right? Without those stitches, the wound would never have healed. That's what this medication is for. It's meant to help you heal."

It's safe to say that struck a chord with me.

Hopefully, down the road, I won't need the medication anymore, but for now, I'm willing to accept all of the help I can get.

Once I started feeling better, I convinced the guys to crawl out of the hole that was my bedroom and move the party into the den, where episodes of my favorite vampire brothers have been playing on repeat.

I know the three of them hate it, and quite frankly, I'd be more than willing to change it. But seeing as they are willfully catering to my every need, I might as well watch it while I can get away with it.

I'm not stupid, after all.

However, as much as I love the Mystic Falls crew, I can feel myself starting to go certifiable. If I have to hear Ronan spin the ice in his tumbler, Finn scratch at his beard, or sit and watch Mac make one more meal, I might honestly kill us all—regardless of how much I love them.

I know they're feeling it, too. Ronan has been dying to hide in his office for a few hours and catch up on emails. Finn has asked about Kings several times in the last few days, and Mac is just downright antsy.

Yet none of them will leave or let me leave the house. I don't know if it's because they don't really believe I'm feeling better, if they don't want to pop the little bubble we're in, or if they're worried about letting me out of their sight.

Honestly, it's probably a bit of all three.

Fidgeting out of boredom on my spot on the leather couch, Mac starts mindlessly running his hand up and down my thigh underneath my blanket. Ronan's in his usual spot in the armchair next to Mac, and Finn's sitting on the other end of the couch with his arm draped over the back. Every so often, he'll twirl a strand of my hair, which sends butterflies to my stomach, just like Mac's hand is doing now or Ronan's eyes whenever I catch him staring at me.

That's another thing! Besides a deep kiss, gently wrapping me in their arms while we sleep or snuggle on the couch, none of them have touched me. And it's kind of starting to piss me off.

I'm a little bruised, not dead.

For the first few days, I was grateful for it. I could hardly function, let alone climb any of them like a tree. But now, now I'm just horny.

Mac's hand absentmindedly moves a little higher up my thigh at the exact time Finn lightly squeezes the back of my neck. My eyes snap towards Ronan, who's still staring at me like he's either afraid I'll disappear or like he wants to devour me—maybe a bit of both. I clench my thighs together underneath my blanket, trying to relieve the pressure, effectively pinching Mac's hand between them. Slightly turning his head to the side he gives me a cheeky wink before drawing his eyes back to the TV. He knows exactly what he's doing.

Smart-ass. Two can play this game. Let's see who will cave first, shall we?

Throwing my blanket off me, I hop off the couch at lightning speed and spin so I'm facing the three of them.

I dramatically point my finger down at Mac, who still has a shit-eating grin. "You. Shirt off."

Ronan slowly stands from his chair and crosses his arms over his chest. "Harper, you're still healing. That's not—"

"I wasn't talking to you, *sir,*" I cut him off and turn to face him. He fights but fails as the corners of his lips turn up. If this were any other time, he would put me in my place so fast my head would spin—before fucking me silly, that is. I miss that, and I want it back.

But I know who I'm dealing with here. Finn and Ronan are stone walls of stubbornness. Mac, however, my sweet teddy bear, the one who will give me exactly what I want without even having to ask, I can break him. I know it.

Ronan sweeps his hand out dramatically, gesturing for me to continue. Turning back to Mac, I cock a hip, put my hands on my waist, and puff out my chest, thoroughly aware of my nipples poking through the cotton shirt. I watch Mac's eyes land on my chest before quickly darting back to my face.

Atta girl, Harp.

"As much as I love the bad boy hair and the nose ring, you're starting to look like Pete Wentz circa 2005." Finn snorts a laugh before he has a chance to cover it up. "It's not a good look, Honey. Time for a haircut."

Mac mimics his brother and crosses his arms over his broad chest, his biceps bulging against his black T-shirt. "And who's going to give me said haircut?"

"Me, duh." I hold my hand out for him to take, urging him off the couch. He takes it but doesn't use any of my body weight to lift his massive frame. Once he's standing in front of me, I gently pat the center of his chest and stand on my tiptoes to kiss the side of his face. "Now, take your shirt off and sit on one of the chairs in the kitchen."

He laughs and kisses the top of my head. "Yes, ma'am."

As he's about to walk away, I give him a firm pat on the ass. "Good boy."

His head whips around so fast I'm sure he pulled a muscle. His eyes are wide and dark, and his breathing has stilled. A lust-filled moment passes between us before he shakes his head and walks toward the kitchen, ripping his shirt off and throwing it on the floor on his way.

Hmmm, interesting. Filing that away for later.

Looking between Ronan and Finn, I ask, "Clippers and scissors?"

"There's some under my bathroom sink," answers Finn. "Left side, in the drawer between the one with the extra toothbrushes and the one with your hair ties and clips." I smile at the fact that he knew exactly where they were and went out of his way to keep some of my things in his bathroom.

Making my way to him, I softly kiss his lips. "Thank you, Love."

Before I can walk away, he stands and grabs my wrist. "Don't think I don't know what you're up to, Angel."

"I have no idea what you're talking about."

His mouth may display a smile, but his narrowed eyes tell me he's serious as he whispers, "Just be careful."

He lets go, and as I move toward the hall, I hear him tell Ronan, "Might as well grab ourselves a drink and get comfortable. This is about to be quite a show."

"What do you mean?" Ronan asks, but I don't stop to hear Finn's answer or what I'm sure will be a lecture from the boss man.

I'm a woman on a mission.

Once I find the clippers and scissors exactly where Finn said they'd be, I head back into the kitchen to find Ronan and Finn sitting in the den with drinks in their hand, Finn looking more than amused with the situation that's about to unfold while Ronan looks, well, I can't quite put my finger on it.

Worried.

Annoyed.

Sexually frustrated.

Slightly amused.

Pick one.

But the fact that neither of them are trying to stop me, while Mac is still completely oblivious, means that they trust me. As much as it grinds on Ronan's nerves, he trusts me to know I'm healing. That I'm ready. And I think they know, much like I do, that Mac is the perfect one to test the waters with. He's both gentle and assertive in all the right ways. His soft touches and whispered praise are what I need.

I also don't miss the fact that, while they could have easily slipped away toward their rooms, they decided to stay out here and watch. I'm sure to both watch the show and make sure I'm okay. Not that I mind. The thought of them watching only spurs me on further.

Mac's sitting on a stool with his shirt off as instructed. Stopping in front of him, I let my eyes roam over his naked torso. I lick my lips as my eyes trace over each of his tattoos until I find the dark trail of hair that disappears into his low-hanging jeans with the button undone, making it perfectly clear that, as usual, he has no briefs on.

This man sitting shirtless in a kitchen, barefoot and in unbuttoned jeans, black nose ring shining in the light, with his steel blue eyes burrowing into my skin is every woman's fantasy, and I'm the lucky bitch that gets to have him.

"You gonna stand there and eye-fuck me all day, or you going to cut my hair?"

"I honestly can't decide."

I set everything out on the counter and start cleaning up the edges around his hairline, ensuring that I run my fingers over his shoulders and back every so often. Every time my skin touches his, I watch as his entire body stiffens, knowing good and well it's not because he's uncomfortable.

After using a longer guard on the clippers to do the backs and sides of his head, I set them down on the counter. Grabbing the scissors next, I move to stand in front of him. Mac shifts in his seat, and I look down to see a very prominent bulge underneath the crotch of his jeans. Curling my lips in, trying not to make my smile obvious, I start combing his black hair forward so I have a better idea of how much I need to cut off.

As I bring the scissors toward his head to make the first cut, he stops me. "You know what you're doing, right? I mean, I know I go for the whole messy and undone look, but I'd really appreciate it if you didn't fuck up my hair."

"Honey, I've been trimming my own hair for years. I know what I'm doing." I don't mention the fact that my idea of trimming my hair is snipping off the ends of a stray curl that doesn't lay right, but that's neither here nor there.

He inhales a ragged breath as I listen to Finn and Ronan chuckle from their spots in the den, the ice in their drinks rattling against the glass.

As I start making headway on Mac's hair, easily cutting a good inch off, I move toward the crown of his head. However, instead of walking behind him, I pat the tops of his knees, signaling for him to move his feet from the bar on the bottom of the chair onto the floor, "Feet down, please."

Doing as he's told, I'm able to scoot closer and straddle one of his thighs with both my feet still firmly on the ground, but bringing my panty-covered pussy right against the top of his thigh. I can feel his hot breath against my neck as I look over the top of his head and begin cutting the hair at the crown. Every so often, I shift my weight from one foot to the other, rubbing myself against his jeans.

After only a couple of minutes, I feel his large palms wrap around the backs of my thighs. Pretending I don't notice them, I finish up the top of his head. As I move to take a step back to work on his bangs, his hands grip me harder, holding me steady right where I'm at. Giggling softly, I sit myself down on his thigh so I can lean back and take a look. As I begin clipping away at his bangs with the scissors, I watch as some of the hair falls onto his cheek. Leaning forward, I softly blow the hair out of his face. His whole body shivers beneath me.

"You okay?"

"Yep, fine. Just tickled."

When I'm almost finished with his bangs, I feel his hands move slowly from their spot on my thighs, past my cotton underwear, and under my shirt before reaching my waist. He grips me tightly, sending a rush of heat straight to my core, causing me to grind myself against his leg. Just as I finish with the last strand of hair, his right hand moves up even further, brushing against the underside of my breast. My breath stills as he swipes his thumb over my nipple. "Mac . . ." his name is nothing more than a prayer on my lips.

His thumb brushes against my nipple again, and I grind even harder against him, surely causing a wet spot on his jeans. A deep rumble sounds from his chest before his hand slides out from my shirt and grabs my leg, pulling it from between his and around the other side of him. Dropping the scissors and comb onto the floor behind him, I plant both hands on his shoulders. His skin burning beneath my touch.

Now that I'm straddling him, I can feel just how hard he is beneath his jeans. He wants this just as bad as I do, and damn it if I'm not going to get it.

I need this.

I need this to feel whole again.

I need this to heal a piece of me.

The piece that wants nothing more than to have the men she loves love her back with everything they have.

Fully straddling his hips, I rock against him, loving the way his cock feels against me. Both of his hands find my waist again, stopping my movements in their tracks. "Harper."

My eyes meet his, and I see they're full of concern. "Please, Mac."

He gently shakes his head. "This isn't a good idea. You're still healing."

Sweeping his now much more manageable hair out of his face, I drop my forehead to his. "Do you not want this? Do you not want me?"

"Mo Grá, I want this more than you know. Ever since you came to me at that cabin, I've wanted to have you back—in every way possible. I just, I don't want you to do something you're not ready for. I don't want to hurt you. I'd never forgive myself."

"I'm okay, Mac. I need this. I need *you.*"

He doesn't say anything as his eyes cast down to where I'm sitting on his lap, and his hands loosen and tighten their hold on my waist repeatedly. I can practically see all of the gears turning in his head, mentally trying to decide whether he trusts himself with me or not.

"Mac, look at me." His eyes meet mine, our foreheads still connected. "I trust you. If I didn't, I wouldn't be doing this. I trust you with every fiber of my being. With my mind, my body, and my heart. But just as I trust you, you have to trust me. Know that I'm ready for this. Trust me and trust them." I pull my head from Mac's so we can look at Ronan and Finn, who are still watching intently from the den. "Trust that whether or not you trust yourself, they would never let you do anything to hurt me, and they'd never let me do anything to hurt myself."

Mac grips my shirt and begins bringing it up my body. Following his lead, I raise my arms and let him slide it over my head before discarding it on the floor. His eyes rake over my body, cataloging every faint yellow bruise that still lingers on my skin, the biggest of which sits over my broken ribs.

He lightly brushes his fingertips against the large spot, "You'll tell me if it's too much."

I nod as his fingers continue to graze over my body. I can't help but close my eyes, reveling in how his touch feels against my skin. "Please, Honey. I need to feel this again. Let me feel it with you."

"I won't hurt you."

It's not a question but a statement, yet I answer anyway. "You won't hurt me."

And just like it did the day they found me, those four words unlock something inside of him. Mac's lips crash into mine, and I immediately let out the most satisfied moan, letting him swallow the sound.

His hand threads into my curls, careful to avoid the hair around my stitches, while the opposite hand grips my hips, urging me to continue moving against him. I know this isn't going to be slow and steady; both of us are entirely too keyed up, too desperate to have one another again to make this last long.

I grind my hips against him faster, harder, getting off on the noises he makes with every pass. Bending forward, Mac takes one of my nipples into his mouth, and I swear, if I weren't so desperate to have him inside of me, I would come right now.

"Yes, Mac," I moan as he tugs it with his teeth.

"Fuck, Harper. I missed hearing the way you moan my name."

"Don't stop then. Keep going." My head tilts back as he kisses across my chest, taking the opposite nipple into his mouth.

"I'll never stop," he mumbles against my skin. "For the rest of my life, I'll never stop."

Tears sting behind my closed eyes because I know the sincerity of his words. I know that this man, this gentle yet savage man, will give me everything I need for as long as we live.

When his mouth leaves my breast, I tip my head forward to look at him, pausing the movement of my hips when I do. His gray eyes filled with unshed tears, likely just as moved by this moment as I am. Cupping his face, I wipe away a tear that falls with my thumb before he can blink it away.

I'm not sure if it's five seconds or five minutes, but we sit like that, staring at one another before he speaks, "I love you."

"I love you." The four of us have been saying it to one another all week, but at this moment, it feels different. Like he and I are cracking each other's chests open and taking the other's heart as our own.

"You sure about this?" he asks.

"More than sure," I whisper as I slant my mouth over his again.

"Lift up a little for me," he says against my mouth. I stretch my long legs out so my toes touch the floor and lift off of his lap slightly, allowing him to free his throbbing cock from his jeans.

Eyes locked on one another, I raise ever so slightly with one hand firmly placed on his shoulder for balance. Mac fists the front of my cotton panties and, with one firm tug, rips them clean off my body. I wrap the other hand around the base of his dick. He lets out a hiss and tips back his head. Taking the opportunity, I run my tongue along the column of his neck. I notch the head of his cock at my entrance and sink down slowly, inch by delicious inch. I'm so wet and ready for him that there's not a bit of resistance. Once I'm fully seated with his hands still firmly cupping my ass, I grab the sides of his face, bringing his eye back to me. As we stare at one another, I revel in the feeling of him being inside of me. This feels like literal heaven after all these weeks of not having any of them.

"God, I fucking missed you," his voice sounds almost pained. I know he's talking about so much more than sex.

"I'm right here, Mac. I'm right here."

"Move, Pretty Girl. Ride me. Take what you need."

Out of the corner of my eye, I spot Ronan and Finn, who are now leaning forward, both with their elbows on their knees, fully engrossed in the scene before them. Their intense stares cause me to clench around Mac's length, but I turn away, focusing on the beautiful man beneath me—the one who trusts me enough to trust himself.

Rhythmically, I start moving my hips back and forth while Mac's hands roam my entire body. As one hand runs the length of my spine, a shiver runs through me, and my pussy clenches around him. "Fuck, Harper."

Gripping the back of his hair tightly with both hands, I lean forward and bury my head in his neck, breathing in his smell: Cedarwood and ginger. God, I missed him.

Mimicking me, Mac buries his face and gently bites and kisses the skin along my neck. Baring down, I focus on the way he feels beneath me, inside of me, around me. My hips start moving faster, all while my clit rubs against his pubic bone at just the right pace.

"You feel so good, Harper. This pussy was made for me. I never want to be without it again," he begs, face still buried in my neck.

"Never, Mac," I mumble against his skin. One hand moves around the globe of my ass, squeezing so hard I know there will be a bruise there tomorrow. But I don't care. In fact, I love it. These are the kinds of bruises I will gladly wear for the rest of my life.

"Yessss. Again."

His hand squeezes my ass even harder as the other wraps around the back of my neck, pulling my face away from his shoulder so I'm face-to-face with him again. Using his hold on me, he slams my face into his, kissing me with more passion than I've ever experienced from another person in my life. Mac swallows every single moan and whimper that leaves my mouth as if he's trying to keep every noise I make buried deep inside of him.

Mac shifts his hips forward slightly on the chair, changing the angle of him inside of me, and on the next roll of my hips, the head of cock hits just the right spot. I try to pull my lips off his to call out his name, but his hand on my neck holds me still, not allowing my lips to stray even an inch.

I bite down on his bottom lip, causing him to let out a deep moan. I do it harder while pulling the strands of his hair so hard I can feel them break loose in my grip, and I'm pretty sure I can taste a droplet of blood against my tongue, but he doesn't beg me to stop. In fact, his moans grow more desperate for release.

I'm rocking against him so hard I'm worried the chair is about to tip over, but I can't find it in me to care. I *have* to keep going. I need this more than I need my next breath.

Mac gives my ass another painful squeeze at the same time I press my clit hard into his pubic bone, all while his cock continuously rubs against my G-spot.

The feeling I've missed with every fiber of my being suddenly crashes into me in an all-consuming wave. My entire body shakes against Mac's, but he doesn't let my hips stop moving. Finally removing his hold from the back of my neck, he grabs both of my hips with his hands and continues rocking me back and forth. I tear my mouth from his and scream so loud I'm surprised the windows don't shatter. Mac doesn't stop moving me on top of him. My vision starts to black out as hot spasms of pleasure continue to wreak havoc over every inch of my body. Tears fill my eyes as I desperately gasp for breath. I've never felt an orgasm consume my entire being quite like this.

"Mac! Oh my God!" I pull at his hair even harder, not knowing what else to do with all of the pleasure coursing through me.

Mac hisses out in pain before tightening his grip on my hips. "Fuck, Harper. Harder."

His words surprise me for only a moment, but I do what he says and pull harder, the waves of my orgasm still washing over me. I pull his hair hard with one hand, tilting his head back while bringing my other hand around to rest on his chest. Mac moves one hand between us and begins rubbing at my clit with his thumb, causing me to scream out again.

It's not a new orgasm, but the same one coming back at full force and hitting me like a damn brick wall. He continues rubbing feverishly while I pull at his hair and dig my nails into the skin on his chest. Quickly looking down, I notice droplets of blood beneath my nails, but neither of us stops.

To lost in each other's pleasure.

Suddenly it all feels like too much, my orgasm still has a hold on my body, and with Mac rubbing at my overly sensitive clit, it won't let go. "Mac, I can't. It's too much."

"Keep going, Mo Grá. Milk my fucking cock. Take me with you."

He pinches my clit, and I rock forward once, twice, three more times before Mac's body stills beneath me. My name roars from his lips as he spills inside of me. Much like mine, his orgasm is long and drawn out, filling me so deeply I can feel it leaking out and onto his lap beneath me.

My body falls against his chest as my orgasm finally starts to come down. Yet, every few seconds, my pussy clenches around his still-hard cock. Like my body is subconsciously trying to make the most of this moment as possible.

Mac wraps his arms around me tightly and begins softly stroking the back of my head. I nuzzle into his chest, wanting to stay here for as long as he lets me.

Tilting my head to look at him through my lashes, I whisper, "Thank you."

He kisses the top of my head. "No need to thank me. You know I'll always give you what you need. From now until forever."

I smile softly up at him, my chest filling with warmth because I know he means that with his whole heart. "Me too, you know? I want to be everything that you need."

"I know, and you already are."

"I love you, Cormac."

"I love you too, Pretty Girl."

We sit there for a moment, just holding one another, when I hear Ronan and Finn's footsteps come up behind me.

A set of fingers caress my cheek, and I instantly know they're Ronan's as I feel the warm metal of his rings against my skin. Not caring that I'm in Mac's arms or that his dick is still inside of me, he bends down and kisses my cheek. "How do you feel, Baby?"

I lift my eyes, expecting to find a hint of jealousy that I took this step with his brother and not him, but instead, I am met with a look of absolute love and adoration. I smile and nuzzle against Mac's warm chest. "So much better."

"I'm so proud of you." Ronan crooks his head so he can reach my lips and gives me a gentle kiss. "I love you."

"And I love you." Most people might think it's weird that he's expressing how proud of me he is, considering I just fucked his brother. But I know exactly what he means and why he's proud of me. I didn't let Logan or what he did to me at the cabin take this away from me, either. I took the time to care for myself properly and listened to my body. I was strong. Strong enough to take this back for myself. And for them.

For us.

Ronan brushes a couple of curls behind my ear and straightens. Finn's hand runs up my back as he says, "Come on, Angel. Let's go get you cleaned up."

I unwrap my arm from around Mac and hold it out behind me. In one swift move, Finn grabs it, and I'm being cradled in his arms. Mac stands from the chair and begins tucking himself back into his jeans.

I look at his hair, smiling. Surprisingly, I did a pretty good job. But I'll keep that shock to myself.

Looking between the three of them, I ask, "Group shower?"

Smiles light up all three of their faces, and Ronan answers,

"Group shower. But shower only." He points his finger at me and gives me a look I know all too well. One that means there's no room for argument. "You've had enough for one night."

Wiggling in Finn's hold, I realize he's right. I can already feel my body growing tired. "Alright. Shower, then cuddle."

Finn kisses my forehead as he chuckles. "Shower then cuddle, Angel."

As Finn walks me toward my room, I feel it settle in my chest. Another little piece of me has been put back together. I don't know how many pieces are left or how long it will take. Maybe I'll never be fully healed. But I know one thing is certain: as long as I have the three of them helping pull me back together, I'll be okay.

22

Harper

The morning light peeking through a crack in the curtains wakes me from a deep sleep. My entire body is damp with sweat, and I feel like I'm sleeping inside of a furnace. Eyes still closed, I roll to my side only to realize a tattooed arm is pinning me down across my abdomen on one side and a set of muscular legs entangled with mine from the other. Well, that explains why I'm so warm.

After screwing Mac senseless in the kitchen after his haircut, the guys took me back to my room to shower. I stood there while the three of them scrubbed and lathered every inch of my body. I didn't have to lift a finger. I'd be lying if I said I didn't love it. Once we got out of the shower, they left me to my nighttime routine, where I applied a plethora of skin care products and curl creams.

I leave the bathroom to find them curled up in my bed with

the TV on. Mac was already passed out on the edge of the bed, his soft snores filling the room. Ronan and Finn were sitting against the headboard, stark-ass naked, and waiting for me to climb in between them. The moment I did, they wound their arms around me, kissed me goodnight, and the three of us quietly drifted off to sleep.

A couple of days after I got back, Ronan had a new mattress and bedframe delivered to the apartment that would comfortably fit all four of us. After carefully searching the two men who delivered everything, the guys watched them like hawks the entire time they were taking apart my old bed and setting up the new one. When I asked Ronan why he got me a new bed instead of one of them, he simply shrugged and said, "We wanted to be in your room where you were most comfortable. None of us like sleeping in our own rooms without you anyway."

The idea that the three of them are so willing to lean into this group relationship without hesitation, doubt, or jealousy makes me so happy my chest literally aches. I've never been loved like this. Don't get me wrong, I know my parents loved me, as did Cece, but that love was different. It was between parents and their children. But this love, the one the four of us share, is that of choice. The three of them are *choosing* to love me, regardless of how unconventional it may seem to the outside world.

Not that the guys care much about what people think of them anyway, being leaders of the Irish mafia and all.

It's clear that the guys don't anticipate me moving back into my apartment anytime soon, if ever again. And to be honest, I really don't want to. I want to be here with them. They make me feel safe, wanted—loved. Yes, my apartment may be my own, but at the end of the day, it's nothing more than four walls holding my things, things that I can bring here. It's not like I rent my apartment; I don't have to worry about breaking any sort of contract, nor do I owe any outstanding money on it. I'll talk to the guys about putting it up for sale and moving some of my things in here. It's important that this feels like my home just as much as it does theirs. I know none of them will care if I add my own touch to the space. This can be my home, too—my family, if only I let it.

There will always be that nagging fear of losing another person that I love. But if the last few weeks have taught me anything, it's to not keep people at arm's length for fear that you will lose them. That isn't a life worth living. It's not the life my parents or Cece would have wanted for me, and it's not the life I want for myself. I would rather risk loving and losing them than never loving them at all.

I try to sit up between them so I can crawl out of bed and use the bathroom, but Ronan's arm wraps tighter around me as he nuzzles his face into the crook of my shoulder. "Ronan, I have to pee," I laugh.

"Noooo. More sleep," his raspy voice whines.

I try to untangle my legs from Finn's but meet the same resistance. "Finnnnn," I whine.

He nuzzles in on the other side of me, and if I wasn't caged in before, I am now. "Shhh, Angel."

"Unless the two of you want me to pee all over the bed, I suggest you let me up."

"I'd get over it," Ronan mumbles.

"Ew, no, not happening. Plus, the two of you are a couple of furnaces, and I'm sweating to death. Let. Me. Up." My voice sounds annoyed, but I'm all smiles. I've loved having the four of us together every night. None of them fuss about sleeping next to each other, as they seem genuinely comfortable with the arrangement, as long as nobody's hands do any unwanted traveling. Being sandwiched between them is my favorite place to be, regardless of how hot I am.

I might have to invest in some more breathable bedding; I already sleep completely naked.

Finn softly kisses my neck and mumbles, "Don't leave us."

"I'm not leaving you, you drama king. I just have to pee!" I start playfully slapping at Ronan's arm and kicking my feet under the sheets. "Mac, help me!"

When he doesn't answer, I lift my head to look behind Finn, only to find the spot he was sleeping in empty. "Where's Mac?"

"Hmmm. He went to Kings," Ronan answers.

Panic immediately courses through my body. This is the first time any of us have left the apartment in a week. I can't help but wonder if he's okay. Luca and his guys still haven't found Logan, and we haven't heard so much as a peep about any new plan from Declan. I knew the time would come when we would have to go about our business, but I just wasn't prepared to pop the little bubble we've been living in.

Ronan must feel my body go stiff. Reaching up, he hooks his finger under my chin, so I roll to face him. His sleepy blue eyes meet mine, jet-black messy curls sweeping over his forehead. Just looking at him slows my racing heart. "He's okay. He left around three to check things out after they closed up for the night. He didn't want to wake you."

I give him a soft smile and feel Finn press closer behind me, sweeping my hair off my shoulder to run his thumb across the skin. "It just makes me nervous. I wasn't ready."

"I know. But it's been a week, and as much as we hate to admit it, we have responsibilities we need to get back to." He looks as disappointed by it as I feel.

"I just want you guys to be safe."

Finn plants a soft kiss on the back of my shoulder. "It'll be okay, Angel. Kings has plenty of security and should be back in another hour or so."

"Why is he the one that went anyway? Don't you usually take care of most of the business there?" I ask, looking back at Finn. I know they all have a hand in the club, but between Ronan and Finn, they pretty much handle all of it. More often than not, Mac seems needed down at the docks or dealing with other things throughout the city. He plays the role of muscle well.

Finn's lips curl into a devious grin. "He drew the short straw."

My brows pinch in confusion. "He got laid last night, and we didn't. So he gets to suffer through work while we stay in bed with you," Ronan clarifies.

Laughing faintly, I roll my eyes. "That wasn't nice. He didn't choose it. I'm the one that jumped his bones."

"He didn't look too unhappy about it last night, Baby. Plus, I don't make the rules."

I laugh louder now. "Ummm, yes, you do. You, quite literally, make all of the rules."

"Does he now?" Finn grips my hips and pushes his growing erection into my ass.

"Hmmm, I guess not *all* the rules."

"That's what I thought." He bites at my ear, and I clench my legs as his teeth make contact with my skin.

"So sorry, Love."

"Good girl." Hell, I forgot how much I loved hearing them say that to me.

"Happy to see that still makes your panties wet," Ronan says like an absolute know-it-all.

Feigning indignation, I slap at his chest and quickly sit up before either of them can grab me, and they both laugh. The sheets pull away from their bodies as I climb from the bed, and I turn around to stare at them, not even trying to hide the fact that I'm practically eye-fucking both of them.

Jesus, they are delicious.

Finn's blonde hair is perfectly messy against his pillow, and his honey-colored eyes shine at me. His chiseled chest is dusted with a delicious amount of chest hair. My eyes trail down his abs until they meet his cock, which is standing straight up, just begging for me to lick it. My gaze moves over to find Ronan's long and thick legs crossed at the ankles, one of his legs covered in tattoos that lead all the way up and over his hip and cover his entire abdomen. I constantly find myself running my fingers over the dark ink. He's got both hands tucked behind his head, causing the muscles in his arms to flex proudly underneath even more intricate designs. I let my eyes trail the tattoos up the side of his neck until I see the cheeky grin that's spread across his face, likely from his eyes roaming my naked body as well. I never thought I would be into a man who was covered head to toe in tattoos, but Ronan has proved me wrong. *Very* wrong. The only spot he seems to have left is his other leg and the opposite side of his neck.

"Like what you see, Baby?"

Popping my shoulder, I nod, not even trying to deny it. "Yeah. I really do."

The ache in my bladder is too sharp to ignore any longer. I spin on my heels and head to the bathroom. After going about my business, I decide to rinse off my sweat from being sandwiched between two giant furnaces all night. Turning on the shower, I yell through the closed door, "Just going to take a quick shower. I'll be out in a few."

I throw my hair up in a quick bun and step into the lukewarm water. Careful not to get my curls wet, I face the shower head, letting it cool down my body. I reach for my body wash and loofah in the corner and begin scrubbing it over my skin, blissfully aware of how good it feels to not flinch from pain at the slightest touch. A few minutes pass before I hear the door to my bathroom softly open and close. I smile to myself, that didn't take long.

A strong pair of arms wrap around me, and a soft kiss lands on the back of my neck. The tickle of their facial hair sends a shiver up my spine. I look down at the pair of corded arms. Tattoos stopped carefully where the sleeve of a dress shirt would be.

Finn.

"Missed me already, Love?"

"Hmmm," he moans as he grabs the loofah from my hand and begins gently caressing it over the front of my body. I don't bother telling him I've already washed up. It feels too good. "I'll always miss you. Whether it's been days, hours, or minutes. I'm always counting down the seconds until I can have my hands on you again, Angel. I can never get enough."

Well, doesn't that just make a girl swoon.

"Well, aren't you just the charmer this morning."

"Only for my girl," he says as I feel him smile against my skin.

He continues mindlessly rubbing the loofah across my skin. I flinch a little when he rubs the bruise that still lingers on my ribs.

"Still pretty sore there?"

"Yeah. The damn thing is taking forever to heal," I answer.

Finn lifts my arm and plants a soft kiss in the center of the large bruise before he resumes washing me. "They usually do. Ronan got a baseball bat to the ribs once. Bitched about it for months. He was even more insufferable than usual, if you can imagine it."

I laugh, "How did you and Mac even survive it?"

"It was nothing short of a miracle, honestly."

I love hearing Finn joke around. He's always so serious and put together. I mean, so is Ronan, but even he isn't opposed to lighthearted banter, especially when it's at the mercy of his younger brother.

Speaking of Ronan. "He didn't want to come in and join us?"

"Asked him very nicely to stay in bed for a few minutes."

I raise a brow in suspicion. "You *asked* him?"

He runs the loofah over one of my breasts, and I inhale sharply as it passes over my nipple. "Okay, I may have offered him a small bribe."

"And what was that?"

"Hmmm, can't remember. Guess you'll have to wait and see."

Reaching around, I pinch the side of his thigh. "Finn Donovan! You are not allowed to use me as bribery."

"Oh, but I can, and I did, Angel."

Finn drops the loofah onto the shower floor and moves his bare hands through the suds covering my skin. I tilt my head back as a hand trails down the center of my stomach toward my pubic bone. "I suppose I can let it slide this one time."

His finger slides between my folds and brushes over my clit. "I figured as much."

Reaching one arm back, I wrap my hand around his neck, pulling myself as close to him as physically possible. I moan when I feel his already hard cock pressing into my ass. He's barely touched me, and it already feels so good.

It's like last night with Mac unlocked something in me. Like I was being wholly starved of them, and fucking Mac in the kitchen was like being given a single cookie. It's absolutely delicious, but I need *more*. I'm still so hungry for them.

He rubs my clit a few more times and then moves his finger down to my entrance, pushing until just the tip of it is in. "Finn."

"Shhh, if Ronan hears, there's no way he'll stay out there. I'll be damned if I don't get this pussy all to myself." His voice is low and gravelly, causing my pussy to clench around the tip of his finger, trying to pull it in deeper. "Are you sore from last night?"

"No," I answer softly. There's a dull ache between my legs, but that could quite honestly be from how much he's turning me on right now.

"Is there anything you don't want me to do?" He gently nips at the soft skin below my ear as he moves his finger deeper inside of me, and I have to force myself to focus on the question he's asking me.

"Just–just don't pin my arms down. I'm not ready for that yet. I know you like it, and I know I liked it last time, but that's what he did to me at the cabin a–and I don't think I'm ready for it yet. I'm sorry if—"

"Don't you dare apologize. There's nothing to apologize for. If you don't want me to now or ever again, then I won't. Okay?"

I nod.

"You tell me if I do anything else you don't like. Do you understand me?" His authoritative tone washes over my skin like honey.

I nod again.

"No. Say you understand. Say you'll tell me if I do something you don't like." He pushes his finger in deeper, and I gasp.

"I–I understand. I'll tell you." Finn bites at my neck hard this time.

"That's my girl." There it is, the praise I can never quite seem to get enough of. My body practically melts against his as the water continues to wash over me. Yet, his hand doesn't move, keeping his finger perfectly still inside of me. I need more.

"Finn, please. Move."

He bites at my shoulder this time, and I let out a soft yelp. "What's my name, Angel? When it's you and me, what's my name?"

A smile tugs at my lips. "Daddy."

The second the word leaves my mouth, he pulls his fingers out of me, spins me around, and slams my body against the wall. His eyes dart between mine, silently making sure I was okay with his forcefulness. I nod, and he crashes his lips into mine, kissing me so fiercely I can feel it in my toes. He brings his hands up to the sides of my face, holding it perfectly still, trying to get everything he can out of our kiss. And I let him. I let him take everything he needs from me.

When he finally pulls away, large hands still cupping my face, he stares at me, panting and virtually out of breath. "God, you are so fucking beautiful."

Tears sting at my eyes, though I'm not sure why. Maybe it's from the sincerity of his words, or maybe because this is the first time I've been with Finn since everything happened, or maybe a bit of both. I try to blink them away, but one escapes despite my best efforts. Finn's quick to brush it away with the pad of his thumb. Reaching up, I thread my fingers through his long blond hair. "So are you."

His breath hitches, almost like he can't believe someone could see him that way. But I do. He really is so beautiful. Inside and out.

Finn's lips meet mine again, and he quickly makes his way across my jaw and down my neck before closing his mouth over one of my nipples. I thread my fingers through his hair as he takes the sensitive bud between his teeth. A loud moan slips past my lips before I can stop it, and he lets my nipple go with a pop. "What did I say?"

"To be quiet," I answer sheepishly.

Finn drops to his knees in front of me and hooks one of my legs over his shoulder. "Do you want to be a good girl and come for me?"

"Yes, Daddy."

"Then do as you're told and be quiet." I know he doesn't really care if Ronan were to hear me, but that's not the point. Finn gets off on giving me orders and me obeying them. And fuck all if I don't get off on it too.

He plants kisses along the inside of my thigh as he makes his way towards my aching pussy, the hair on his jaw tickling my skin. Once his mouth reaches the apex of my thighs, he pulls his face back and gently parts my folds with his fingers. For a moment, he just stares. "I forgot how perfect this pussy is."

I can practically feel my entire body blush.

Slowly he runs his tongue from my entrance to my clit. He does this over and over again, moving his tongue so painstakingly slow it almost feels like torture. I try to use my hold on his hair to pull his face in tighter, to apply more pressure, to move faster, to do *something*. But he's a man on a mission and determined to get his fill of me. "You taste so fucking sweet, Angel. So sweet. So *perfect*."

He flicks at my clit with the tip of his tongue as he slides his finger back inside of me, immediately finding that patch of sensitive flesh. My leg tightens around his shoulder as he continues to hit all the right spots, but it's not enough to send me over the edge. "Please, please. I want to come. *Please*."

"Please . . . what?" he mumbles, not pulling his face away from my cunt.

"Please, Daddy. Make me come."

Finn lets out a deep growl, "That's my good fucking girl."

Without any further hesitation, he shoves a second finger inside of me, then a third, and begins sucking at my clit with such ferocity it's like he's a man starved. And in a way, I guess he is.

It takes no time at all for the pressure to build inside of me, and I bite my lips to keep from yelling out. I don't trust myself to say anything quietly. My hips start moving on their own accord over Finn's face as my climax reaches its peak. My pussy pulses over and over again around Finn's fingers, but he doesn't stop. His fingers begin moving inside of me at a faster pace as he pulls his mouth from my clit and looks up at me through his dark long eyelashes. "Give me another one, Angel."

His fingers continue pumping inside of me faster than before while his opposite hand finds my clit, rubbing it at a feverish pace. His eyes don't stray from mine. Much like with Mac last night, I don't come down from the first orgasm. It continues to wash over me as Finn holds my body hostage.

"That's it. You're doing so good for me, Harper."

A familiar feeling builds inside my stomach, and I know exactly what will happen if Finn doesn't let me come down from this high.

"Let it go, Angel. Scream for me now. Scream my fucking name."

"Ahhh! Daddy, yes!" I scream at the top of my lungs as Finn pulls his fingers from my pussy, still rubbing fast circles against my clit. A rush of fluid sprays out of me, hitting Finn across the chest and along his jaw. He doesn't so much flinch. His eyes stay locked on mine throughout the entire climax, pupils blown and burning with desire. I continue to shake violently against the cold tile wall, only being held up by the leg still wrapped tightly around his shoulder.

As my shakes start to subside, Finn plants a couple of soft kisses along the inside of my thigh before unwinding my leg from around him and gently setting it back on the ground. He stands up to his full height, and his mouth finds mine in a light but passionate kiss. I can taste my release on his lips as he presses his body tightly against mine, his rock-hard erection pulsing against my stomach.

"You okay?" He asks as he pulls back from my lips.

"More than okay," I answer with a satisfied smile.

"I really fucking love it when you do that."

Heat scorches my cheeks. "What? Squirt or call you Daddy?"

His eyes darken. "Hmmm, yes."

"I'll be sure to do it more often then," I say as I slide my hand between us to grab his cock, smearing the bead of precum leaking from the tip with my thumb.

Finn grabs my wrist, stopping me in my tracks. "That was about you, Angel. I wanted to taste you."

"But I want to," I say, sticking my bottom lip out.

He leans forward and plants a chaste kiss on my cheek. "Next time, I promise." I sigh and bring my hand back up his chest. "With how loud you screamed, I'm surprised Ronan's not already—"

As if summoned by the devil himself, Ronan pushes the door open, dressed now in a pair of briefs. Mac's standing next to him in black ripped jeans and a dark gray Henley. He must have just got back from Kings. They both wear deliciously devious grins as they spot Finn still pinning me against the wall through the steam-covered glass.

"Well, well, well. What have we here?" Ronan crosses his arms as he leans against the door frame.

So fucking hot.

Mac walks around him, wiping his hand across the shower glass. "Mr. Donovan. Miss Hayes. Having some fun without us, I see?"

Finn drops his forehead to my shoulder, and I point my finger at his face. "He started it."

"Thought you said you were just coming in to shower, Finny?" Ronan asks as he shoots me a mischievous wink.

Finn steps back and grabs the loofah off the ground. "Yup. Showering. Just got a little distracted."

"Sounded like you got a lot distracted. Was that you making all that noise, Mo Grá?"

I stand on my toes to kiss Finn's cheeks quickly as he goes about washing my release off his face and chest and slide out of the shower. "No idea what you're talking about, Honey."

As I reach for the towel hanging on the hook, Ronan comes up behind me and plants a firm slap on my wet ass. He plants his hands on the wall on either side of me, caging me in against him. "Good thing Finny Boy and I made a deal. Everyone's had you but me, so tonight you're sleeping in my room."

I look at him over my shoulder. "Just you and me, huh?"

"Just you and me."

"What? That's not fucking fair! I didn't make a deal. Why am I being excluded?" Mac asks in a huff.

"Sorry, brother. You snooze, you lose," Ronan answers over his shoulder. I hear Mac mumble something under his breath as Ronan's lips meet my ear again. "You're all mine tonight, Baby. Hope you're ready."

"Yes, sir."

Ronan moans and bites my ear before pulling away and walking past a pouting Mac and out of the bathroom. Wrapping my towel around myself, I walk over to Mac and thread my arms around his neck. Standing on my toes, I slant my mouth over his, kissing him deeply, relieved to see him back and in one piece. "I missed you this morning. I was worried."

"About little ol' me?" He asks as he smiles down at me.

"I didn't like you not being here when I woke up."

Mac reaches up and tucks a curl that slipped from my bun behind my ear. "I know, Mo Grá. I didn't want to go, but we have to go back to work sooner or later. We figured Kings was the safest place to start."

Finn turns off the shower and steps out. After grabbing his towel, he moves to stand behind me, rubbing his hands up and down my arms. "That's what we told her."

"I'm just not ready to pop our little bubble. As much as I've been climbing the walls, the thought of actually leaving them is terrifying."

"It'll all be okay," Mac responds. "We will keep you safe this time. No one will touch you ever again."

"We promise," Finn adds.

"I know you will."

They each give me one last kiss before stepping away. "Hey, before I forget. Ummm," I trail off as I fiddle with the hem of my towel.

"What is it, Angel?"

"I wanted to talk to the three of you about my apartment, about staying here?"

The two of them share a look, and I immediately know I'm missing something.

"I mean, if you don't want me to move in here permanently, I understand. After all of this is done, I can move back into my apartment. I just didn't know where you guys were at. Do you not want me to stay here? Is it Ronan? Oh, God. This is embarrassing. I shouldn't have assumed. Now I'm rambling." I drop my face into my hands.

"Harper." Finn's commanding voice makes me lift my face from my hands. Except when I look at his face, he looks like he's trying to hold in a laugh.

Okay, rude.

"This isn't funny!"

They look at one another again, sharing some sort of silent, apparently funny conversation. Finn runs his hand down his face as he tries to hold in his laugh. "This should be good."

"What? What should be good?" Now I'm so confused.

"Come on, Pretty Girl. Why don't you get dressed and we'll go talk to Ronan. I think you'll be interested in what he has to say."

I look back at Finn, who holds up his hands in surrender. "I'm not saying a word."

Well, this should be good.

23

Ronan

What a dickhead. I should have known not to trust him. "I just want to shower with her alone," my ass.

That's fine, though. Now I get to have her to myself all night. I feel like a sixteen-year-old kid who's about to lose his virginity, but I can't help it. My body aches for her. To touch her, to kiss her, to hold her, to be so deep inside of her she will feel me there for all of time.

Don't get me wrong, I loved this last week. It came as a shock to everyone when I willingly closed the door to my office and shut off any communication as far as our "businesses" go. I was a little surprised I was so willing to do it myself, but we needed it. *I* needed it. Since Harper got back, I've struggled to keep it together. No matter what they say, I constantly feel like what happened was my fault. Logan took her because I couldn't keep her safe. Declan planted Logan in our home, and I fucking missed it. Harper was running through the woods, practically naked because I let her down. Mac and Finn, my brothers, were broken because of me.

Me.

It's all on me.

For the first time in my life, I had no plan. I didn't know what to do. The only thing I did know was that I wanted to be here with her, where I knew she would be safe with all of us. I wanted to keep her as close to me as physically possible. So, when Finn suggested that we take a few days to rest and recover, I was all for it. I shut everything else out and focused on Harper's healing. The only time I've been on my phone was to call Mum and Pascal, to take care of a few things for Harper, and to check in with Luca. They still haven't seen or heard shit, as far as Logan and Declan go. It's too quiet, and it's making me fucking antsy. We're going to have to go on the offensive sooner rather than later. I refuse to sit around and wait for something else to happen, *again*.

Harper's healing surprised all of us. Between upping her calorie intake to put some weight back on, taking all of the recommended vitamins that Doc gave her, therapy sessions with Lisa, and loads of rest, she almost seems like she's back to her usual self. The shine is back in her hair, her delicious curves are back, she has color in her face, the sass I love to hate has returned in full force, and she's smiling.

That fucking smile.

For a man who prides himself on being afraid of absolutely nothing and no one, I was terrified that Logan stole that from her. But he didn't. Because my Baby is the strongest person I know, and she's come out the other side better than any of us ever expected.

Now, all that's left to do is finish this.

As much as I am freaking the fuck out about us all leaving this apartment again, I know we have to. I refuse to let everything we've worked so hard for fall apart just because we're hiding from Declan fuckin Whelan. Nope. Not going to bloody happen.

But first, we're going to have one last weekend for ourselves. It's Saturday morning, and none of us have anything to do until Monday when my calendar is already booked with meeting after meeting. I'm dreading it, but it has to be done.

For now, we're going to enjoy this weekend with Harper as a family. We discussed it quickly last night while she applied her skincare after our shower. We decided we wanted to take her to Kings tonight if she felt up to it. That's really why Mac went there this morning. He met with the security before they went home after the shift to ensure all the necessary precautions were in place and ready to go. Ralph and a couple of his men will drive us to and from the club in an unmarked car. Once we get there, we will enter the building from the back, where double the guards will be keeping watch inside and outside the building. We even texted Luca and his guys to see if they wanted to meet up, which they were more than happy to do as they hadn't had the chance to introduce themselves to our girl properly. I'll feel better knowing they'll be there to help keep an eye out as well. I know she needs this to get out of the apartment and regain some semblance of freedom, but I will *not* compromise her security.

Plus, I know all about their last little outing to Kings, and I'll be fucked if I miss out this time, especially after seeing her with Mac last night.

And hearing her scream in the shower with Finn this morning.

And knowing that I get her all to myself once we get back tonight.

I. Can't. Fucking. Wait.

Regardless of how worried I was when Finn told me what Harper planned on doing, I trusted her enough to know her boundaries. Not only that, but I know Mac was the right choice. He took care of her the way she needed to be taken care of.

Watching her be strong enough to take that part of herself back all on her own was one of the sexiest things I've ever seen in my life. None of us would have ever made the first move, no matter how much it was killing us. We wanted to wait until she was ready. And now that she is, all bets are off.

I'm just about to try and figure out this complicated as fuck coffee machine when I hear angry footsteps marching down the hall toward the kitchen, and I smile despite myself. I haven't been on the receiving end of one of her ass-chewings in a while. I always like it when she gets fired up.

This should be good.

Propping my hip on the counter's edge, I cross my arms over my bare chest and give her my most adorable smile. Maybe if I look good enough, I'll still come out of whatever this is with my balls.

I do have gray sweatpants on. The ladies love the gray sweatpants.

As she comes marching toward me, dressed in a pair of leggings and an oversized band T-shirt, looking absolutely fucking edible, I spot Mac and Finn walking behind her, matching grins a mile wide.

Harper stops in front of me, hands on her hips, and just stares. Clearly waiting for me to explain why I did whatever she's mad at me about. Her eyes quickly rake over my body, stopping once at my chest and then again at my half-hard dick that's starting to tent my sweatpants.

What can I say, hotheaded Harper makes me horny.

"Hey, Baby." I lean down to kiss her lips, but she puts her hand out to stop me, so I straighten. Still giving her my most panty-melting grin. "I was just about to try and figure out this spaceship so I could make us some coffee."

"Don't you fucking dare," Mac says, sneaking around us. "You'll wind up breaking it or make the worst coffee any of us have ever tasted."

He pushes a multitude of buttons before dumping some grounds in. I shoot my thumb over my shoulder in his direction, "Knew that would work."

Not a hint of a smile.

"Okay. Just tell me what I did."

"I don't know, why don't you tell me."

Finn huffs a laugh behind her, and I shoot him with a glare. "Baby, I'm gonna need some context. Nothing is coming to mind."

"I told these two," she points between Finn and Mac, "that I wanted to talk to all of you about selling my apartment and moving in here."

Oh, shit.

"They just laughed and told me to come talk to you. Laughed, Ronan!"

"Baby."

"Don't Baby me. What is it? You don't want me to stay here? I mean, that's fine. I can go back to my place when all of this is done. I just thought that with the direction this was going, you'd all want me to stay. But, if that's totally one-sided or you're not ready for it or whatever, just tell—"

"I already sold it."

Her jaw hangs open ever so slightly. A few seconds pass before she's able to form words. "Y–you what?"

"Sold it. I sold your apartment two days after we brought you home."

"You sold it?"

Christ, am I not speaking English? "Yeah, Baby."

Out of the corner of my eye, I watch Mac and Finn sit on the opposite side of the island, cups of coffee in hand, ready and waiting for the ass-reaming I'm about to receive.

Assholes.

"What did you do with all my things? My clothes, my plants, my furniture, all of my books?"

"Everything got put into storage in a unit downstairs. I got a unit with a window, so your plants would be okay. Once you were feeling better I was going to take you down there so we could go through everything and move whatever you wanted up here. We can sell whatever you don't want to keep."

She pauses a beat, digesting what I just told her. The longer she stands there, the redder her face gets. It's only a matter of time before—"YOU SOLD MY APARTMENT WITHOUT ASKING ME FIRST?!"

Pushing my hip off the counter so I can stand up straight, I look down at her and answer, very matter-of-factly, "Yes, Harper. I didn't want you to have to worry about it, and you're definitely not leaving. So I sold it."

"I-you-wha—What did you do with the money you got

from it?"

"It's already in your bank account. Got above asking, and it's already closed, in case you were wondering." Ralph's actually the one who owns it now. The apartment building he lived in was scheduled to be torn down. Not that he was necessarily upset about it. It was an absolute shithole anyway, but he was about to have nowhere to live. So, I bought Harper's apartment and told him he could have it. No strings attached. He's a good man who works hard and has served our country. He doesn't deserve to wonder where he's going to sleep at night.

"How is that even possible?"

I'm already in trouble. There's no point in lying.

"I'm the one that bought it. Ralph is going to live there."

"W-wha—I-I," Harper takes a deep breath as she starts to massage her temples. I have to use every ounce of strength not to let a smile slip. Meanwhile, the two dipshits across the counter are giggling like a couple of school girls. "How do you have my bank account information?"

Now I smile. "I know everything about you, Baby."

She takes another exaggerated breath. "Ronan, you can't do that."

"Do what?" I ask, pretending to be oblivious.

"You can't put my apartment up for sale, then buy it, then put the money in my bank account, which you shouldn't even have the information of."

"But I can."

"No, you—"

I step forward and wrap my arms around her. Keeping my voice soft, I ask, "Do you want to stay here?"

"Well, yes, but that's not—"

"Would you have sold your apartment?"

"Yes," she answers begrudgingly.

"Then why does it matter?"

"Because I don't want you to have to do that for me, Ronan."

"First of all," I reach up to cup her face, relaxed that her immediate instinct is to lean into my touch, regardless of her being mad at me. "I have more money than I even know what to do with. It wasn't a big deal." She rolls her eyes at my arrogance, but it's true. The cost of her apartment was a drop in the bucket. "Second of all, I would do anything for you. *Anything.* Haven't I proved that to you by now?"

Her green eyes stare up at me, dumbfounded by my answer. Tipping my head forward, I plant my lips on the apple of her cheeks, this time without her stopping me. "You don't want to leave. We don't want you to leave. So I took care of it for you. This is where you belong, here, with us."

She lets out a heavy sigh, and I can tell she's trying to decide whether or not she wants to be mad at me anymore. "For the record, that wasn't okay, and I'm still mad."

I huff out a laugh, "Okay, Baby."

"And I want to pay rent."

"Absolutely not."

"But—"

"No. You're not paying rent for an apartment we already own. This is your home now."

"Are you sure about this?" Her voice is no more than a timid whisper now.

"More sure than I've ever been about anything."

Harper stands up on her toes and touches her lips to mine. It's the gentlest of kisses, but it stirs my blood just the same. "Thank you," she says softly against my parted lips.

"You can bring up whatever stuff you want. Feel free to decorate or change anything here. It's all yours, Baby. You just let us know, and we'll get it done."

"I don't need to change anything. It's fine the way it is."

"Mo Grá, we could give two flying fucks about how this apartment is decorated. As long as you're here, that's all that matters," Mac pipes up. Of course, now he chooses to speak when she's no longer fuming.

Chicken shit.

Harper reaches out and points between the two of them. "Don't you try to kiss my ass, too. You knew about this and didn't tell me. You're in just as much trouble as he is."

Mac looks thoroughly offended, while Finn just smiles and takes another drink of his coffee.

"Would it make it better if I said we were going to Kings tonight?"

She whirls back on me, face beaming with excitement. "Oh my God. Really?"

"If you think you're up for it."

She's practically bouncing. "Am I up for it? Of course, I am! But wait," her face drops. "Is it a good idea? If it's not safe, we don't need to risk it."

"It'll be fine, Mo Grá. That's why I went there this morning. Met with security and secured a ride with Ralph and his team."

"Plus, Luca and his guys are meeting us there. You will be more than safe."

She hesitantly looks between us. "It's not just me I'm worried about. I don't want him to get to you, too."

"Trust me, Baby. We can handle ourselves. Let's go out and have some fun before we have to go back to the real world on Monday, Yeah?"

Her smile beams. "Okay, yeah!"

I lean down so my mouth is next to her ear and whisper darkly. "And don't forget when we get back, it's just you and me. Hope you're ready."

Her breath hitches, and she runs her hands up my bare chest. "I'm more than ready, Baby."

Fuck, I love when she calls me that.

My erection is now hard as steel beneath my pants, and judging by the way she's wiggling in place, she can feel it pressing against her.

I growl and bite the lobe of her ear. "Later."

"Promises, promises."

"So yes, we're going?" Mac asks, practically bouncing in his seat with excitement.

"Yes!" she claps. "Yes, we're going."

Mac thrusts his fist in the air. "Hell yeah!"

"Wait!" Harper's eyes go wide with panic. "I don't have anything to wear!"

Finn waves his phone in the air. "Already got it covered, Angel. Your dress should be here in an hour or so. I got it in a couple different sizes because I wasn't sure which would fit you best right now."

Harper's face softens. She walks over to Finn and slants her mouth over his. "Thank you. You're forgiven."

Mac stands abruptly from his chair. "Hey! What about me?"

She walks around Finn and wraps her arms around Mac's waist. "Make me some chocolate chip pancakes, and we'll call it even."

Mac plants a wet kiss on her lips. "You got a deal, Pretty Girl."

24

Mac

"You think she's about ready?" Ronan asks, looking at the watch on his wrist. It's about twenty minutes to nine, which is when Ralph and his men will have a car waiting for us in the parking garage. We're not risking loading her out front where anyone can see us leaving.

"Judging by how excited she's been all day, I'd be willing to bet she's still bouncing around her room." Finn laughs as he pulls his cup of whiskey to his lips. He's dressed in a navy blue suit, a white shirt with no tie, and the top button is undone. He's wearing caramel-brown brogue shoes and a matching belt. His whole look is relatively casual as far as Finn is concerned. It doesn't even look like he's applied the slightest bit of gel to his hair. I know Harper likes it when he leaves his hair like this, and I'd be willing to bet my left nut that's exactly why he left it.

Ronan downs the rest of his whiskey and aggressively sets the crystal tumbler on top of the bar where we're all standing, waiting for Harper to finish getting ready. "Are you guys sure this is a good idea?"

Finn claps his shoulder. "She needs this. We all could use a night of fun before diving back into the shit show that is our lives."

He scrubs a hand down his face. I know he's worried. We all are. But Harper deserves this. She's gone through hell and back, and a night out is just what she needs. She was so excited when Ronan suggested it this morning. I can't even imagine how happy she'll be once she actually gets out of the apartment. Our girl loves to curl up in her sweats and spend all day inside reading a good book, but she also thrives on human interaction. Harper misses working at the bookstore and interacting with customers. She misses going about her usual daily routine and smiling at passersby on the street. She misses talking to the barista when she gets her daily coffee in the morning. Since we met her, we have done nothing but keep her hidden from the life she once knew. And, while she will never fully regain that life, we can help build her a new one. One she loves.

"Kings will be locked down tighter than Fort Knox, Ronan," I say, trying to ease the tension I can practically see rolling off him in waves. "We will all be with her. We've taken all the necessary precautions, *and* Luca and his guys will be there. If, by some miracle, Declan or Logan make a move, there is no way in hell anyone will be able to get within twenty feet of her. We're good."

"You're right. I'm just starting to freak out a little."

Finn shoots me a look. It's not like Ronan to admit he's

scared. Like *ever*. But I know it's because he's terrified of something else happening to her. I know it's because he blames himself for what happened. No matter how much Harper, Finn, or I try to tell him it wasn't his fault, he will always carry that guilt. My brother isn't one who lets his failures go, and if anything were to happen to her again, I don't think he'd survive it. None of us would. But keeping her locked away in this apartment isn't a life worth living either. So, the best we can do is not let the guilt eat us alive and do anything and everything to keep Harper safe while giving her the life she deserves.

"We're all nervous too, man." Finn pours Ronan another finger of whiskey. "But, regardless of how much we would like to, we all know we can't keep her locked in here forever."

"I know."

"I'm gonna go see if she's ready." I squeeze Ronan's shoulder and down the rest of my drink.

The door to Harper's room is cracked open, and I hear her softly singing "Ruin My Life" by Zara Larson. Her voice isn't even remotely in tune with the song, but that doesn't make it any less adorable. I wrap my knuckles against the door and push it open. "Mo Grá, the car will be here soon. You almost—"

The words die on my tongue as Harper spins from her spot in front of the full-length mirror to face me. Her every movement feels like it's in slow motion as I drink her in. She's dressed in a skin-tight blood-red velvet cocktail dress that hits her just above mid-thigh. The dress has long sleeves with a dangerously low square neckline, perfectly showing off the tops of her breasts. It clings to her every curve like a second skin. For the first time since I've met her, Harper's changed her curls, which are now lying in soft waves down her back. She has on the sexiest pair of strappy black heels I've ever seen, and her lips are painted in a shade of lipstick that matches her dress. She looks stunning. But I can't help but think what the lipstick would look like smeared across my cock.

Holding her hands out, she does a little twirl. "What do you think?"

I run my fingers through my hair, unable to form words. I think she's actually broken my brain.

She stares at my face in confusion and looks down at herself. "Is it not okay? I didn't quite fill out my old size, so I had to pick the smaller one, but I was worried this one was too tight. If you don't think it's okay, I can try to find something else?"

"No," I blurt out before she even attempts to find something else to wear.

"No?" she asks, tilting her head. My eyes trail up the slope of her neck as she does so. I can feel my cock hardening in my pants from just looking at her. We're going to be lucky if we even make it out of the damn apartment once Ronan and Finn see her.

Somehow I manage to get some of the blood that's rushing to my dick back up to my brain and form words. "Harper, you look . . . you look fucking perfect. So beautiful."

"Yeah? You think so?"

I honestly don't know how she manages to do it. It doesn't matter if she's naked, wearing jeans and a band T, curled up under a pile of blankets with her glasses on while reading a book, wearing one of our shirts, dressed in the sexiest dress I could have ever imagined, or coming out of the woods after two weeks in hell, she is the most stunning woman I have ever laid eyes on. No one will compare to her. *Ever.* "I'm honestly afraid to take you out of this apartment. No one will be able to take their eyes off you. That is how perfect you look."

Her cheeks blush at my compliment, but I'm not joking. Every man and woman is going to be looking at her. It doesn't matter, though, as long as they don't touch what's ours. If one person even so much as looks like they are about to lay a hand on her, none of us will hesitate to rip it from their body.

Still standing on the other side of her room, I watch her eyes roam over my body. "You don't look so bad yourself, Mr. McDermott."

I puff out my chest in pride. Knowing tonight was a big deal, I decided to forgo my casual attire and put on something a little nicer. I'm wearing a black suit, open at the front, with a white shirt and black square-toe oxfords. I have the top two buttons undone and a couple of silver chains hanging around my neck, and I swapped out my black nose ring for a small diamond stud. "Decided to dress up for the occasion."

As she takes sultry steps towards me, I watch as her hips sway back and forth while biting my bottom lip.

Jesus Christ.

Harper runs her hands up the lapels of my suit jacket. "If Ronan and Finn look as good as you do, you won't be the only one itching for a fight," she promises.

I rest my hands on her ass and pull her tight to me, letting her feel for herself how sexy I think she looks. "There will be no fighting for you for the foreseeable future, Mo Grá." Pouting, she juts out her bottom lip, and I can't resist bending down and taking it between my teeth, giving it a playful tug, careful not to ruin her makeup. "But jealousy looks good on you."

She smiles and softly kisses me before rubbing off any of her lipstick with the pad of her thumb. Before she can pull it away, I pull it into my mouth and watch her eyes darken. She gently pulls it from my mouth, and I let out a pained sigh. "You alright there, Honey?"

"No, I'm not alright. You look so sexy. I'm going to be walking around all night with a never-ending hard-on. My dick just might explode."

Harper belts a laugh and pats the center of my chest. "I might be able to help you with that, you know?"

"Ronan has already explicitly warned me not to fuck with his plans for you tonight. Something along the lines of my balls and a blender."

"Okay, one," she holds up her pointer finger. "No matter how much he wants to be, your brother is not the boss of me. I can fuck whichever of you I want when I damn well please." I roll my lips in and try not to laugh. I love the little potty mouth she's developing. "And two," she tugs at the lapels of my suit until I bend down, my face hovering right above hers. Her voice now sultry and laced with desire, "There's an awful lot of time between now and when we get back from the club."

"Hmmm, I like where your head's at, naughty girl."

"I thought you might," she says as she winks up at me.

I give her juicy ass one more firm squeeze. As I step back, her eyes drop to my cock, which is currently tenting my suit pants, and she licks her lips.

She licks her fucking lips.

"Harper. If you don't stop looking at me like that, I'll have your dress off and on the floor in five seconds."

Her eyes pop back up to my face. "And if you don't stop looking at me like that, I'm going to let you."

Reluctantly, I step to the side and sweep my hand toward the door. "Then go give the other two their heart attacks so we can get this show on the road."

I'm not even ashamed to admit that as she steps around me, my eyes lock in on her ass. Dressed in red velvet, it looks like an apple I want to sink my teeth into. She stops in the doorway, looks over her shoulder, and catches me thoroughly checking her out. "Coming?"

I scrub my hand down my face. "Yes, ma'am."

It's what she says before winking and walking away that almost brings me to my fucking knees. "Good boy."

Ohhh, fuck me.

25

Harper

I must have been an absolute saint in a past life, because nobody gets this lucky.

As the four of us sit in the back of Ralph's car as we round the corner to Kings, I can't stop shifting in my seat. The three of them look so unbelievably sexy my pussy is practically weeping.

Finn had the nerve to look so deliciously undone that it made me want to drop to my knees right there in the kitchen. I don't know how he did it, but he looks perfectly put together while simultaneously looking like he just rolled out of bed. His hair is lying like it does after I run my fingers through it, and he's trimmed his beard so it's nothing more than a shadow of dark blonde hair covering his square jaw.

Meanwhile, Mac went and did the exact opposite. As sexy as this man usually looks in his black Henley, jeans, and black boots, Mac in a suit is on an entirely different level. When he walked into my room, I damn near swallowed my tongue.

The car slows as it turns down the alleyway in the back of Kings, and Ronan puts his hand on my thigh. His electric touch immediately setting every nerve in my body on fire. "Ready, Baby?"

I smile up at him. "Ready, Baby."

"Remember the rules. Once this door opens, you do not go anywhere without Finn, Mac, or me. You do not get your own drinks, and you don't use the bathroom besides the one in our office. If, at any time, the three of us tell you we need to leave, you do as we say. No questions asked."

Usually, I would have a snide comeback at his overbearing attitude. Not because I disagree but because it's what Ronan and I do. As toxic as it might be, we get off on pushing one another's buttons. But not tonight. Tonight, I won't argue. I know how nervous the three of them are. Finn and Mac may not be as blatant about it as Ronan, but I know they're equally worried. And I *know* the only reason we're out tonight is for me.

So, for tonight, I'll do as Ronan says without any argument.

Not that I even need to argue with him tonight for him to make my panties wet. Between his authoritative tone and his mafia boss ensemble, I might orgasm just from looking at him. Unlike Finn and Mac, Ronan's not wearing a suit, instead opting for a black button-up that's haphazardly tucked into his tight black jeans and a pair of matte black leather breaker boots. His tattooed hands are decked out in silver rings, minus the one I still wear on my thumb. His jet-black waves are slicked black, leaving an unobstructed view of his blue eyes. Not to mention his sleeves are rolled up to his elbows, which is basically porn for women in and of itself.

Too busy gawking at him to answer, he tightens his grip on my thigh. "Harper, do you understand me? I want us to have a fun night, but I will not risk your safety to do so. Please, promise me you'll listen to what we say."

My face softens. "I know, Ronan. I promise."

He leans down and kisses my cheek right next to my ear. "Good girl." Straightening, he looks between Mac and Finn. "You guys good?"

Each of them pulls open their suit jackets to show Ronan the guns holstered on their hips and nods. My eyes widen in shock, not because I'm surprised but because the sight of them with guns causes heat to pool in my lower belly.

Interesting personal development, Harp.

Looking back to Ronan, he answers my unspoken question, "Tucked in my boot, Baby," and shoots me with a devious wink.

"Let's go shake our asses, shall we?" Mac says excitedly as he throws open the door. Finn shakes his head and huffs a laugh as he climbs out behind Mac. I'm following with Ronan tucked tight behind me. Ronan and Finn each grab a hand, with Mac leading the way, leaving me sandwiched between three solid walls of muscle all the way to our VIP booth.

As soon as we're seated at our table, me next to Finn with Ronan and Mac on the opposite side, a waitress spots us from her spot at the bar and practically sprints across the dance floor to get to us before anyone else can. Once she stops in front of our table, I can't help but eye her up from head to toe. She's wearing the same black skin-tight dress that all of the other servers are wearing, yet, for some reason, hers looks even better. She has a perfectly shaped hourglass figure, legs that look like they spend every spare moment in the gym, and breasts so perky they're practically touching her chin. Not to mention, she has the longest, smoothest, and shiniest blonde hair I've ever seen. Very much unlike my dark and unruly curls.

I look at her name tag that reads "Tiffani," and couldn't be less surprised if I tried.

"Good evening, gentleman. What can I get you this evening?" Her perky voice yells over the roar of the music. Her eyes rake over Ronan, Mac, and Finn without even sparing me so much as a glance.

Yeah. Nope. Don't like her.

"Evening Tiffani," Finn answers politely. As I glance between the three of them, I notice that, while Finn's eyes are firmly locked onto Tiffani's face, not bothering to glance at the rest of her annoyingly perfect body, Mac and Ronan aren't even looking at her. Instead, their eyes are firmly locked on me from their spots across the table. I can feel my body heating under their intense stares. "The three of us will take a bottle of Jameson Bow Street and three glasses."

"Absolutely, Mr. Donovan." Tiffani flicks her blonde hair over her shoulder, and not so subtly, pushes out her breasts, practically shoving them in Finn's face.

This. Bitch.

"I'll be right back with your whiskey. Let me know if there's anything else I can get you," she smiles at the brothers. "Any of you."

Yeah, no. This isn't happening.

As Tiffani walks away, I yell calmly over the music and put my finger in the air. "Ummm, Tami."

She spins back around; the charming smile she had plastered on her face while talking to the guys is long gone and replaced by an annoyed scowl. "It's Tiffani," she says as she points to her nametag.

"Right, sorry. Tiffani. I didn't see that, much like you didn't see me sitting right here," I smile as she scoffs. Finn rubs his hand over his beard next to me, trying to hide his smile. "When you get my *boyfriends* their whiskey, could you grab me a bottle of rosé, please?"

Tiffani's jaw drops the moment the word "boyfriends" leaves my mouth. She looks between the guys, who are all doing everything they can to hold in their laughs, waiting for them to say something.

"Oh! And could you also get each of us a shot of the best tequila you have? We're trying to have a fun night, if you know what I mean?" I wink at her as I run my hand up Finn's chest. This time, Mac barks out a laugh.

Tiffani looks down at Ronan as if waiting for him to confirm or deny my requests. Little to my surprise, he does exactly what I was hoping he would. He hits her with a stony expression, and she immediately cowers in place. "Get *our girl* whatever she asks for. And Tiffani," her entire body straightens, and she smiles, excited that Ronan remembered her name, even though it's plastered right over her fake tit. "Purposefully ignore Harper again, and I'll personally escort you out of the club myself."

Shock registers across her face. "Y-yes, Mr. McDermott. I–I'll be right back with your drinks." She gives a faint smile before sprinting across the dance floor in the direction she came.

"Don't forget the salt and limes!" I yell as she runs away. Mac's got tears running down his face he's laughing so hard.

Mac wheezes as he tries to regain his composure. "God, I love you. I don't know whether to be impressed or turned the fuck on."

"That was hot as hell, Angel," Finn agrees as he wraps his arm around me, pulling me tight against his side.

"Well, I mean, come on. How dense do you have to be? I'm sitting right here."

"Jealous, Baby?"

Lifting it under the table, I run my foot along the inside of Ronan's leg. "Not jealous. Just . . ." I stretch my long leg out until the toe of my heel grazes the tip of his half-hard dick. His large hand instantly clamps down around my ankle, and I watch his baby blues darken. "Showing her what's mine."

Perfectly in sync, they all let out a low growl. Ronan's thumb rubs along the strap of my heel, still resting in his lap, as Finn drops his head, his lips grazing the skin on my neck just below my ear, all while my eyes stay firmly locked on Mac's, which are hooded with desire. Finn presses his lips against my neck, and I lean into his touch. "We're all yours, Angel. Only yours."

Yeah, this is going to be a good night.

26

Finn

Harper's been on the dance floor with Mac for the last thirty minutes, and my eyes haven't strayed from her once. She's well-beyond tipsy after downing her tequila shot and several glasses of rosé. Her face is flushed from dancing and alcohol, and she seems utterly free of any inhibitions.

"Focus" by H.E.R. is playing through the speakers, and couples are all but fucking across the dance floor, Mac and Harper included. Harper's back is plastered against Mac as she grinds her ass against him, her hips swaying in perfect rhythm with the sultry music. Mac's hands roam her body, and I watch as he periodically runs his tongue along the column of her neck.

And that dress—*fuck me*—*that dress.*

When I ordered it, I knew it would look drop-dead gorgeous on her, but I had no idea how much so. When she walked out of her bedroom, I swear my heart felt like it fell out of my asshole. I had my mouth on hers in two seconds flat, not giving a single flying fuck about her lipstick on my face.

Mac must say something funny because Harper tips her head back, and her mouth falls open in a laugh, her face radiating happiness. As much as I was worried about bringing her here after everything that's happened, I know we made the right decision.

She's happy.

Right now, she's not afraid or anxious about what's to come. She's just . . . happy. That's all I want for her.

Not to mention, watching her on the dance floor in that dress and those heels is an added bonus. I don't even care that I'm watching her pressed against Mac. I think we're well past caring about that, actually.

As much as I loved having her pussy soak my face this morning in the shower, I'm really starting to regret my little deal with Ronan. I don't think I've ever wanted to be inside of her as badly as I do right now.

"Bet you're pretty pissed at yourself now, aren't ya, Finny?" Ronan's shit-eating grin is a mile wide as he brings his glass to his lips.

"Shut the fuck up, Ronan." He's right, though. I am mildly annoyed at myself.

"Well done on the dress, by the way," he says as he licks his lips. He's been sitting at the booth with me while Mac and Harper are on the dance floor. Neither of us is much into dancing. However, he seems just as content as I am to stare at her from here.

"Our girl looks good, doesn't she?"

"Not good. Perfect. Absolutely fucking perfect." My eyes leave Harper's for the first time tonight to look at my best friend. If I didn't know it already, his face right now would give it away. He's so deeply in love with that woman it isn't even funny.

Hell, we all are.

"Yeah, she is."

Downing the rest of my drink, I slide out of the booth,."As much as I'm enjoying watching, I'm going to go dance."

He raises a brow in question. "Since when do you dance?"

"I don't. But if you're going to be a stingy asshole once we leave this club—"

"Which I am," he interjects with a smile.

I roll my eyes. "Right. If you're going to keep her locked in your room all night, then I'm taking what I can get right now. You coming?"

"Nah, you boys have fun. Luca just texted me. They should be here any minute."

Nodding, I make my way toward their spot on the dance floor. Before I even reach them, her eyes find mine, and she reaches out her hand. I clasp it in mine and let her pull me in. "Took you long enough."

"Sorry, Angel. Not much of a dancer. I was having fun watching you, though."

She runs her hands up my chest and laces them around my neck. Mac's hands are still firmly wrapped around her waist. "I forgot to say it before, but thank you for the dress. It's beautiful."

"You're welcome. But trust me, it's just as much for us as it is for you."

She tilts her back to look up at me, letting it rest against Mac's chest. "I thought as much." I bend down and slant my mouth over hers, and she lets out a loud moan, completely ignoring the stares from the people around us. Yeah, she's definitely feeling good. "I don't even know why I bothered with lipstick."

"Neither do I, Mo Grá," Mac answers as he sweeps the hair off her shoulder. "You have three boyfriends who want your mouth on theirs 24/7. Lipstick isn't bound to last long." Mac nips at the skin on her shoulder while I continue to explore her mouth with mine.

"Mmmm," she mumbles against my lips, "I suppose there are worse problems to have."

The music picks up its pace as it changes to "Don't Tell 'Em" by Jeremih. Mac and Harper's dancing automatically matches the beat of the music, forcing my hips to move in time with theirs. The faster Harper's hips roll against me, the harder my cock grows. I'd be willing to bet that by the way Mac is now feasting on Harper's neck, he's having the same problem.

Maybe if I murder Ronan . . .

The longer the three of us dance, the more people stop to stare, and for a moment, I'm worried Harper will be embarrassed. Neither Ronan, Mac, nor I give a shit what people think of us. We've shared women in the past and have never been embarrassed about it. Anyone who knows who we are knows better than to comment or pass judgment. The way our relationship works is nobody's business, and if they don't like it, they can fuck right off. But Harper isn't used to being in the spotlight. She's lived her entire life under the radar while simultaneously dreaming of the most conventional relationship possible. I know she loves and wants to be with all three of us, but doing it in the privacy of our own home is drastically different than being open about it in public.

However, as the three of us continue to dance, she doesn't give any of the onlookers a second glance. Either she's too buzzed to notice or doesn't care.

Noticing me glaring at the people staring, she grabs my face and pulls it back down to hers. "I don't care," she says, just low enough to hear her above the music. "Let them stare. Kiss me."

Not giving it a second thought, my mouth finds hers again. The taste of rosé hits my tongue as my mouth devours hers. Still swaying to the beat of the music, Mac wraps his hand around her front and slides it up until it's resting on her breasts. She bites my bottom lip as he gives one nipple a firm pinch. My hands move down Harper's sides until they reach the bare skin of her thighs. I take the hem of her dress between my fingers and slide it up ever so slightly, just enough that her pussy is barely covered.

When my pointer finger comes in contact with her bare cunt, already soaking wet for me, I rip my lips from hers. "Harper, where the hell are your panties?"

Mac laughs behind her, "Oh, hell yeah."

A devious smile takes over Harper's face. "Velvet and panty lines don't mix."

I lightly wrap my hand around her neck, and she inhales a sharp breath. "Panty lines, huh? No other reason?"

"Maybe one other reason."

Out of the corner of my eye, I watch Luca and his guys approach Ronan at our table, and he finally pulls his eyes away from us dancing. I'm normally not one for exhibitionism, especially when it comes to Harper. I don't want anyone else seeing what's mine—what's *ours*. But right now, I really am starting to not give a fuck. And with Ronan not paying attention, now is the perfect time. There is no way in hell he would let me do what I'm about to do.

"What big brother doesn't know won't hurt him," Mac says with the same sinister grin as Harper. Mac and I silently communicate and slowly move to the edge of the dance floor, where it's dark enough that no one will see what we're doing.

"Put your face against Finn's chest," Mac instructs Harper. She does as she's told and presses her face against my shirt, fisting the lapels of my jacket when Mac runs his tongue along her neck.

"You want me to play with this pretty pussy, Angel?" Slowly, I begin running my finger through her folds while Mac continues to kiss and suck along her neck. Harper nods against my chest. "You want us to make you come right here where everyone can see you?"

She lets out a wanton moan that's loud enough to hear over the music. There's no way I would let anyone else in this club see what she looks like when she comes, but fucking hell, does it only get me harder knowing that the possibility of someone seeing us turns her on.

I briefly push the tip of my index finger inside of her and feel her pussy clench around it, trying to pull it in deeper. After only a second, I pull it back out and go back to teasing her. Mac takes her earlobe between his teeth, and her knees buckle. If we weren't holding her between us, I'm sure she'd be a puddle on the floor by now. Mac looks at me through hooded eyes. "I take that as a yes."

"You want it?" I ask as I press the pad of my pointer finger firmly against her clit.

"Yes. Yes, I want it. Now." The sound of Harper's begging as she looks up at me is enough to make me come in my pants if I'm not careful.

"My needy little slut. God, you're so pretty when you beg." I sink two fingers into her pussy and immediately find the sensitive tissue, wanting her to come as fast as possible. I wrap my opposite hand around the back of her head and push her face back into my chest just in time for her to let out another loud moan. It's loud enough that Mac and I can hear, but no one else can over the music.

Mac continues pulling at her nipples over the fabric of her dress while biting the sensitive skin on her neck, leaving faint purple marks behind as he goes. There's no way Ronan won't know what we were up to now. But if he's going to spend all night with her alone, he gets to stare at the marks we leave behind.

What's a little friendly competition between brothers anyway.

Trying to make this as inconspicuous as possible, instead of pumping my fingers in and out of her, I press the heel of my hand against her clit and move the tips of my fingers against her G-spot. I grab a fistful of her hair, just the way she likes, and I can already feel her pussy start to clench around me.

"That's it, Angel. You're making a mess on my hand."

We're no longer swaying to the music. Instead, Harper has started to thrust between us rhythmically. If someone looked long enough, they would easily be able to figure out what we were doing, but I'm so far beyond caring that it isn't even funny. Now that I've tasted her again, I want more. I will never have enough.

With one hand still on Harper's breast, Mac wraps the

other around her jaw and brings her face to his. I watch as the two of them devour one another, and I'm hit with a wave of emotion so strong it tightens my chest. Here I am, with my fingers in the love of my life's pussy, watching her kiss my best friend, my brother, and I feel nothing but unwavering love for them both. What the four of us have together is considered outlandish and disgusting to many. They can't wrap their heads around a relationship like ours, but they don't need to because they don't see what we see. We see four people who would do anything for one another. Four people who would burn the world around them to keep each other safe. Four people that would kill for one another. Four people that want to build a life they could have never imagined. A life that was founded in darkness but is now filled with light.

That's what love is.

"Come," Mac demands against Harper's mouth. "Come on Finn's hand. I want to swallow every noise you make as you let go." I thrust my fingers inside of her and press the heel of my hand harder against her clit. My opposite hand tightens its hold on her curls while Mac fucks her mouth with his.

Harper wraps one arm behind her and around Mac's neck, holding his face to hers while her other hand grips my jacket so tight her knuckles turn white. Her walls tighten around my fingers as I move them a few more times before she screams into Mac's mouth. Her body violently shakes between us as she rides out her orgasm. I can hear Mac groan in reciprocation into her mouth, and I have to use every bit of restraint I have not to come in my pants.

Once Harper's body relaxes, I slowly pull my fingers out of her and pull her dress back down. Mac gives her one last soft kiss before she turns her attention back to me.

"Open," I demand.

Without question, she does as she's told, and I slide my fingers into her mouth, her tongue moving around them, licking off every last bit of her release. I slip my fingers from her mouth when I hear Mac laugh. When I look at him, I follow his eye line to find Ronan standing in front of our booth. Luca and his guys are piled into the booth behind him, each trying not to burst out laughing. There's no way they could see or hear anything from all the way over there, but they know what we were up to based on the way Ronan is glaring daggers at the three of us.

I don't regret it, not even a little.

"We should probably go say hello," Mac says between laughs. Harper looks over at the table and drops her forehead back against my chest.

"Oh, we are in so much trouble. He's never going to let us come back here again."

I tip her head with my finger under her chin and smile. "It's alright, Angel."

"Yeah. Just suck his dick real good tonight, and he'll forget all about it."

Harper whirls on Mac and smacks him in the arm. "Cormac McDermott!"

He huffs out another laugh and bends to kiss her cheek. "Come on, Pretty Girl."

Mac grabs her hand and pulls her across the dance floor toward our table. Her worried face looks back at me. I mouth "I love you" and shoot her a wink and her expression immediately softens.

The second Mac and Harper reach Ronan, he pulls her from Mac. "The three of you are really going to give me a heart attack one of these days."

"Don't know what you're talking about, brother." Mac claps him on the shoulder and climbs into the booth with the other guys.

Ronan looks over Harper's shoulder at me. "I suppose you don't know what I'm talking about either, huh?"

"Nope. No idea."

I softly kiss Harper's cheek, and she says, "Love you more."

27

Ronan

"So, how much trouble am I in?" Harper asks, bright green eyes looking up at me. Her cheeks are perfectly flushed, both from the alcohol and an orgasm. I should be furious. Finn and Mac had no right to make her fall apart like that in the middle of the club where anyone could have seen her.

Well, they weren't exactly in the middle of the club. They were tucked back in the dark, and it looked like they were just in an intense make-out session. The only reason I knew what was happening was because I know exactly what it looks like when Harper falls apart under our hands, and the only reason I saw them was because I was looking for her. I'm always looking for her. But that's all besides the point.

Nobody besides the three of us deserves to hear the noises she makes or see how beautiful she looks when she comes.

And if they do, I will gladly make it the last thing they ever see.

The only reason I'm not dragging her out of here is because, for the first time since we brought her back to us, she looks *free*. If only for a few hours, she looks like she's let her guard down and is genuinely having fun. As much as I want to throw her over my shoulder and start our night together, I won't because Harper is the only other person on this planet who can get me to shove down my temper in order to do something for someone else. I won't take this night away from her.

"So much trouble, Baby," I say, smiling down at her so she knows I'm full of shit. Leaning down so my lips brush against the shell of her ear, I whisper, "But don't worry, I'll finally make good on my threats and punish you for it later."

I lean back so I can look into her eyes, and despite just coming all over Finn's hand, they are filled with desire. "Promises, promises, *Sir.*"

"Harper," I growl, "It's taking all of my willpower not to end the night early and drag you out of here. Don't. Push. Me."

She tilts her head and bites her lower lip, eyes twinkling with mischief. "Pushing you is my favorite hobby."

"Hmmm. Don't I know it." I plant a quick but fierce kiss on her lips. "Come on, I got you another drink."

When I spin around to tuck Harper back into the booth, Luca, Enzo, Dante, and Sebastian are all standing while Mac and Finn have a fresh glass of whiskey in their hands and satisfied smiles in place.

Ignoring tweedle-dee and tweedle-dumb, I introduce them, "Dante, Enzo, you guys remember, Harper."

Dante nods, and Enzo gives her a soft smile. "Bella. So happy to see you feeling better."

I force myself to ignore the nickname Enzo gave her as Harper shyly tucks a curl behind her ear and smiles, likely remembering the condition in which Dante and Enzo first met her in. I give her hip a reassuring squeeze.

"Harper, this is Luca and Sebastian. Luca is Pascal's son. He runs Vittori Enterprises here in New York with Enzo. Dante is their security and long-time friend, and Sebastian is a genius on the computer. We never would have found you without him." Sebastian blushes at the compliment, and Luca looks at him with pure admiration.

Sebastian gives Harper an awkward wave before Luca steps forward and kisses both of her cheeks. I grit my teeth as his lips come in contact with her skin. If it were anyone else, I would have snapped their neck by now, but I know Luca is no threat to me. It doesn't stop my annoyance, though, and judging by the way Luca smirks over at me as he stands upright he knows it's getting under my skin.

Fucking smart-ass.

"So nice to officially meet you, Harper. You are every bit as beautiful as I imagined you would be."

Harper takes a small step forward, and I don't miss the water pooling in her eyes. "I just wanted to thank you all. Thank you for helping them find me. You had no reason to help, you didn't owe them anything, and you didn't know me. But you did it anyway. Without your help, who knows what would have happened to me. By no means is any of it over, but I'm alive right now because of all of you." Her voice trembles on the last sentence, and a small tear rolls down the apple of her cheek. "I don't even know how to thank you."

"No thanks necessary, Harper. My dad said a friend needed help, so we helped."

"You just focus on trying not to kill these three assholes in their sleep, and we will keep helping you all however we can," Enzo adds with a smile.

Harper wipes at her face, "Thank you."

"Alright!" Luca claps his hands together, "Enough of the heavy, let's have ourselves a fucking night, shall we?"

* * *

Have ourselves a fucking night, we did. Mac, Finn, Luca, and Sebastian got absolutely shit-faced in the span of three hours while Enzo, Dante, and I watched in both amusement and awe. I have honestly never seen four people polish off so much alcohol so fast in my life.

And I'm Irish.

Harper only had a few more glasses of rosé, and when I asked her why, she winked at me and said, "Just want to make sure I have my wits about me for my punishment later."

I have never been more ready to get home in my entire life.

"Ronan," Mac whines from his seat in Ralph's car, "You can't hog our girlfriend all to yourself all night. It's not fair."

He sounds like a petulant child. "Mac. Shut up."

"You shut up!" Harper tries to stifle a laugh from where she rests her head on my shoulder.

"Finn, I'm gonna shoot him."

I smack him on the back of the head. "One, you couldn't shoot me right now if your life depended on it, and two, I took your guns away from you both two hours ago, you fucking moron."

With Dante, Enzo, and myself not drinking, I felt more than comfortable letting Finn and Mac blow off some steam. But that doesn't mean I'm stupid enough to let them have loaded weapons when they can't even see straight.

Finn snickers, "Ronan called you a moron."

I smack him upside the head next. "You're just as big of an idiot as he is."

"How dare you! I thought I was your best friend?!" Harper's laugh finally breaks free. "Angel, tell him to be nice to us. We want attention from you, too."

"Tell you what, Love. If you can get hard right now, you're more than welcome."

Mac and Finn both get excited looks on their faces before suddenly looking like they're constipated. "What in the hell is wrong with the two of you?"

"We're focusing! Shut up!"

"Yeah, Ronan. Shut up," Mac adds. "We can't get hard with you talking."

Now, it's my turn to belt out a laugh. Their focus only lasts a few more seconds before Finn lets out a heavy sigh, "Yeah, that's not happening. You two have a fun night. Just know, I'm pissed."

"Yeah," Mac agrees. "Me too. Super pissed."

"Oh my God," Harper laughs.

Once we get to the apartment, Harper sneaks into her room to use the bathroom, and I drag the two gigantic children to bed. Once I throw them each on their beds, with trash cans next to their heads, I make a beeline down the hall toward Harper's room. She's still in the bathroom when

I push through her bedroom door.

"Harper, if you don't get out here in the next two minutes, I'm breaking down that fucking door."

My dick has been painfully hard from the moment I saw her in that tight red dress, and if I don't bury myself inside her soon, I literally might die.

I hear her laugh through the door, "Would you relax! I'll be right there. Patience is a virtue, sir."

I groan in pain as I unbutton my shirt and slide it from my shoulders, leaving me in just my black jeans. "Call me sir one more time, and the last shred of patience I have will be out the damn window."

Her laugh only grows louder. I'm glad to know she thinks torturing me is so funny. Just wait until I get my hands on her. As if her punishment for that little stunt they pulled in the club wasn't enough, now she's just trying to egg me on further. Not that I mind, though. My palm is practically itching as I grab my cock through my jeans, trying and failing to relieve the pressure.

I've imagined taking her over my knee since the day we brought her to this apartment. Her quick wit and smart attitude have been testing my willpower since day one.

And I fucking love it.

I would never do anything to really hurt her, especially after everything that has happened. I know she is just starting to feel better, but if yesterday in the kitchen with Mac showed me anything, it's that she's ready. I have to trust that she will tell me if it's too much.

"I thought you liked it when I called you that?" She calls from the bathroom.

"Oh, I really fucking like it. But only when I can have my

hands on you and not when you're hiding away in a different room where I can't get to you."

I listen as she starts shuffling around in the bathroom. What in the hell is she doing in there?

"Harper, I swear on all that is holy. If you aren't out here in ten seconds, I—"

The sentence dies in my throat as Harper opens the bathroom door, raises her arm along the door frame, and pops her hip. She's wearing a see-through, black lace and mesh thong and bra. Both pieces are decorated in small red flowers that perfectly match the lipstick she reapplied. The thin straps of the thong cut into her hips just right, and the top only accentuates her already perfect breasts. "Baby, you look . . . holy fuck."

She smiles as she pushes off the door frame and steps towards me. "You like it?"

I scrub my hand down my face. "Do I like it? There aren't enough words in the dictionary to describe how much I like what's in front of me. W–where did you even get that?"

"Finn conveniently had about a dozen pieces delivered with my dress earlier. I figured I'd give one a go. It's a shame he isn't here to see it, though. Maybe I should go wake him up." She fakes a step towards the door, and I grab her wrist.

"Don't you even think about it."

Her eyes rake over my bare chest, and she pulls her bottom lip into her mouth. With my hand still wrapped around her wrist, she takes another step forward and runs her hand up my torso until it reaches my shoulder. "What are you gonna do about it?"

My hold on her wrist tightens, and I watch as her chest heaves beneath the black lace with every breath. "You're long overdue for a punishment, Baby, and it's been too long since I've had you. I don't think you want to push me. You're already in trouble."

"Hmmm, maybe I've missed being in trouble." Her breath is nothing more than a sultry whisper.

I run my opposite hand along the string of her thong, and I can't help the moan that falls from my mouth, "So. Fucking. Sexy."

She reaches out and palms my throbbing cock through my jeans. Just her touch alone has me ready to come. I've missed the way her body feels against mine, the sounds she makes when she falls apart, the way her emerald eyes look at me when she calls out my name.

I run my hand up her side, and when I dust over the faint purple bruise along her rib cage, I watch her face closely. She doesn't flinch. My hand continues its path over her shoulder and down her arm until it connects with her hand resting on my shoulder. I grab it in mine and place a soft kiss on her palm. The metal of my signet ring on her thumb brushes my cheek.

"Are you sure you're ready for this? Because I'm not going to lie, the things I want to do to you are . . ." I shake my head, utterly unable to explain everything that's going through my head right now. But she knows. She knows me better than anyone. Better than I know myself.

"I want this, Baby." The moment the nickname leave her lips in that sultry voice, an uncontrollable shiver runs through me, and my dick twitches beneath her palm. "Remind me what it feels like to be in control of the pain. Take me. Punish me. Show me I'm yours."

I take a harsh breath and try to gain some semblance of

composure, but her words almost bring me to tears. "What do you say?"

A soft smile takes over her face, "Bubbles."

"If it's too much, if anything hurts, if I scare you, or if you just want to stop, you say it. You say it right away. Do you understand me?"

"Yes, sir."

I drop my forehead to hers and take her face in my hands, "I love you so much."

"I love you, Ronan. Now, are you going to make good on your threat or what? Because I've gotta say, I'm getting a bit bored."

I huff out a laugh, "There's my girl."

28

Harper

I reach my hand out to undo the button of Ronan's pants, eager to get my hands on him. I've missed him more than I ever could have imagined. "Did I say you could do that?"

His stern voice sends a shiver down my spine. I shake my head and drop my hands to my side.

Ronan trails his fingertips along the edge of my lace bralette over the swell of my breasts. He pulls his bottom lip into his mouth as he watches my nipples harden under the expensive lace.

"You remember the rules, Baby?" he asks, eyes not straying from my heaving chest. I nod. "Say them."

"I don't talk unless you ask a question," I answer.

His eyes snap up to mine. "Or?"

"Or I'm screaming your name."

His finger runs over my nipple and down my stomach, "You'll do exactly as I say?"

"Yes." I'm practically breathless with anticipation as his finger reaches the hemline of my panties. His finger freezes. He tilts his head and clenches his jaw. My lips curl up at the corners, "Yes, sir."

Ronan drops his hand and takes a half step back. I whimper at the loss of his touch, regardless of how light it was. Taking me in, he huffs a ragged breath and shakes his head while running his hand over the black stubble covering his square jaw. "Nothing that's mine should be so perfect."

"Ronan."

As I move to step towards him, he holds out his hand. "No. On the bed. Hands and knees."

I hesitate for a moment, but he doesn't repeat himself. Instead, he waits for me to be brave enough to either follow his directions or speak for myself. Because that's what Ronan does; he allows me to see that I'm stronger than I ever imagined I could be.

"Just . . ." I let out an exasperated sigh. Annoyed and frustrated that I have to draw a line through something I used to enjoy. Something that Logan took away from me. From *us*. "Just don't hold me down. I'm not ready."

His expression softens, but only for a moment. "Okay, Baby."

Giving him a soft smile, I move towards the bed. Once I'm on my hands and knees facing the headboard, I hear Ronan shuffle around the room. I listen to him opening drawer after drawer of my dresser, clearly looking for something. "Ronan, what are you—"

A drawer slams, and I flinch, not out of fear but in anticipation. "This will be your one warning, Harper. Do not speak unless I tell you."

"Do not speak unless I tell you," I mockingly mouth, still facing away from him.

A second later, his hand strikes my ass, and I let out a yell. "Just because I can't see you doesn't mean I don't know exactly what you just did. You just earned yourself another one, Baby."

I crane my head to look back at him, silently asking him what exactly I've earned another one of when I see what's in his hand. My eyes practically bulge out of my head when I see my bright pink rabbit vibrator firmly gripped in Ronan's tattooed hand. My eyes shoot back up to his face, "If you're about to ask how I knew you had this, we all know the kind of books you like to read, and these walls are very thin."

My mouth gapes. "Keep that mouth open like that, and I'll put it to good use."

On reflex, I instantly snap my mouth shut, and he laughs. "That's fine. We have your punishment to work out first anyway."

Ronan hits a button, and the vibrator comes to life in his hand. After running through all the settings, he settles on the constant vibration on the highest setting. Internally, I preen, knowing that's my favorite one. "Face forward, Harper."

I do as he says.

I wait anxiously for whatever my "punishment" might be. However, I'll be mildly disappointed if it's nothing but a quick round of spankings. Not that I would ever say that to him, though. Just as that thought enters my head, I feel the tip of the vibrator against my shoulder blade. The buzz of my favorite toy sends a harsh shiver through my entire body while Ronan's opposite hand plays with the string of my thong.

After letting the vibrator buzz against my shoulder blade for a moment, he turns it off and lifts it from my skin. I let out a heavy breath I didn't even realize I was holding. After a few seconds he turns it back on and places it on the middle of my lower back, right above where the black lace rests. "Do you know what your punishment is going to be?"

I shake my head. "No, sir."

"You're going to come for me." The vibrator gets lifted from my skin again, and my body tenses. Waiting to see where he's going to place it next. "You're going to come for teasing me tonight on that dance floor." Reaching around, he puts it directly on my nipple, and I shout. "For coming apart where anyone could have seen you." The buzzing is gone again, and I fist the sheets, growing more and more turned on by the second. "Then you're going to come for every day you were away from me."

I whip my head toward him. He cracks his palm against my ass once again. "I didn't tell you to turn around, Harper."

I face the headboard again as he slowly runs the head of the pink toy along the inside of my thigh. He plants a soft kiss on what, I'm sure, is my very red skin. The tender kiss is a stark contrast to the harshness in his words. Just as the vibrations are about to meet where I want them most, he pulls away again, and I whine. "You'll come for every day I couldn't touch you. Every day I wasn't able to kiss you. Every day I wasn't able to be inside of you. Every day I woke up and didn't get to see those pools of green."

Reaching around, he drags the head of the toy down my stomach. "For every day I woke absolutely terrified that you might be dead." Tears pool in my eyes. Clearly, this is about so much more than my disobedience on the dance floor. Just like I know what happened wasn't his fault, he knows it wasn't mine. He's not punishing me because he thinks I willingly ran away from him. I'm honestly not sure this is really a punishment at all.

This is a way for him to regain control over a situation he had no control over.

He needs to punish me more than I need to be punished. If this is what he needs to understand that I never want to leave him again, then I want to give this to him.

I'll give him anything.

His grip on my thong tightens. "You'll come for me, Baby. Over and over again. You'll come for me until it takes your breath away. Because that's what you did to me." Finally, *fucking finally,* he presses the vibrator against my sensitive clit, and I immediately come. His body leans forward so it's pressed against my shaking form, and I feel his lips against my ear. "That's what you did to me when you left me. Every night, I would dream of you, and when I woke up, you were still gone." Ronan's voice is nothing more than a deep growl. He pushes the vibrator harder against my clit. "You were gone. And every day, my world would crash around me. I walked through every minute of every day, feeling like I couldn't breathe. And for that," he releases my thong and wraps his hand around my jaw, forcing my face to his. "You must be punished."

His eyes never leave mine as he bites my shoulder, and the blissful pain causes me to fall apart beneath him again.

"Ronan!"

"That's it, Baby. Scream my name. Let the whole fucking world know you belong to me."

My arms give out from under me as I continue to shake

violently beneath my beast of a man. A man who would quite literally kill or be killed to make sure I'm safe. A man who loves me with every fiber of his being. A man who has built wall after wall to become the most feared man in the city. A man who would gladly knock down every single one of those walls if it means he gets to keep me.

With my ass still in the air and Ronan's body still folded over mine, my body begins to settle. Ronan pulls the vibrator away from my throbbing clit and licks the bite mark on my shoulder. I just know he broke skin again.

Fucking vampire.

He smiles against my shoulder. "That's two down. Thirteen more to go."

Oh, shit.

29

Ronan

Forty-five minutes later, my Baby Girl is completely wrung out. She's lying on her back, naked body covered in sweat. I took her lingerie off around orgasm six or seven. As sexy as it was, I wanted to be able to touch every square inch of her skin, and it was just getting in my way.

Her damp curls are spread across the white sheets, and she has tears running down her face. I don't think her body has stopped shaking since orgasm number nine. For a moment, I worried this was all too much, that I was pushing her too far too soon. But, every time I'd hesitate, giving her time to say the word, her eyes find mine, silently letting me know she's okay and that she can take it.

Because she can take anything.

My girl is strong.

So fucking strong.

This wasn't my plan for the night. I originally intended on making her ass raw and put her on her knees due to her little performance at the club. But there was a point when she recited my rules back to me. I looked at her, and I couldn't breathe. She was standing there in front of me, in that black lingerie that made her look practically edible, her cheeks rosy from our night at the club, her long curls draped over her shoulders, while calling me sir, I became so vividly aware with the fact that I almost lost it all.

My happiness, my reason for living, my perfect ray of light—it was all almost gone.

My entire life has been built on my being in control. And right now, it feels like all that control is slipping through my fingers. But there was something about that moment, and I just needed her to understand the depths of my feelings for her. The fierceness that is my need to control her. There is not a piece of her body that I do not own. Her light is mine to keep. Mine to tarnish with my darkness. Her soul calls to mine, and from now until the end of time, I simply cannot exist if she is not near.

She is mine to keep.

Now and forever.

"Baby," Her desperate whine makes my throbbing dick leak behind my pants.

"That's my girl." I curl my fingers inside of her drenched cunt, and with just the tap of the vibrator to her swollen clit she goes off like a shot. Her orgasms are like an involuntary reflex at this point. So intense they're painful. She opens her mouth to scream, but no noise even comes out anymore. "You're doing so good, Harper. So, so good."

I lean down and run my tongue along her cheek, savoring the saltiness of her tears. "Mmmm. Next to your sweet pussy, your tears are one of the best things I've ever tasted."

"Ronan, *please*. Please. I can't do it anymore."

Sitting up straight, I pull my fingers out of her pussy and wrap my hand around her throat, her hands immediately wrap around my wrist, and she whimpers. "You can and you will. Just look at you. You were made for me. Made to swim in the pain I can bring you."

She frantically nods, tears still streaming from her face.

If she wanted to stop, she'd say it, Ronan. Keep going.

"You still owe me one more. But since you've been such a good fucking girl," I turn off the overworked vibrator and throw it across the room. "Now you get to come on my big dick."

Harper sobs. She fucking sobs.

"Take my dick out, Harper."

She frantically lifts her shaking hands and unbuttons my pants. In seconds she has her hands down my briefs and pulls out my throbbing cock. The tip is covered in precum, and just the feel of her hand on the sensitive flesh is enough to tip me over the edge. The last hour hasn't exactly been easy for me either.

Okay, that's a lie, and I fucking know it.

"Wrap your hands around me." As much as I wanted to, I didn't strap her to the bed. She said she wasn't ready for that, and there was no way in hell I would force her to do something I know she truly doesn't want. With her hands not being restrained, I was worried they would get in the way, that she would try to push mine away when the sensations inevitably became too much. But she's only touched me when

I instructed her to. She's done so well.

Fisting the base of my dick with one hand, I notch it at her entrance as I wrap my other hand around her body, holding us as close together as physically possible.

I need this. I need the two of us to be so close we feel like one.

"Look at me, Harper."

Her emerald green eyes find mine, and I sink into her in one punishing thrust. With my arm still wrapped around her, I thread the hand that was holding my dick into her sweaty hair.

Holy hell, have I missed this.

I stay still inside her, memorizing how good she feels around me. So wet. So tight. So fucking perfect. "You're mine, Harper."

Harper's hand works through the back of my hair. "Yours, Ronan."

I pull out until just the tip of my dick is inside of her. "You are the light that draws me in, Baby." Slowly, I push back inside of her. "You are my reason for breathing. Every second of every day. I can't concentrate on anything else with you in my life." *Out and in.* "You have become my greatest weakness. I shouldn't want you. You make me weak, Harper." *Out and in.* "But I do want you. Because while you make me weak, you make me so strong, Baby. You are turning me into a man I never thought I would be. A man that smiles." *Out.* "A man that cares." *In.* "A man that dreams." *Out.* "A man that loves." *In.*

I drop my forehead to hers, blinking as a lone tear falls from my eye and lands on her freckled cheek. "Let me keep you. Forever."

"Keep me, Baby. Forever."

That's all it takes for me to unleash on her everything I've been holding in since we brought her home. I slam in and out of her so hard she will feel me deep inside of her for days to come. She fists the back of my hair and tightens her legs around my waist, her heels digging into the small of my back. "That's it, Baby Girl—one more. Come for me one more time. I want to feel you strangle my dick."

I give the fistful of her hair one sharp tug, craning her neck so I can bite down on it. The second my teeth meet her skin, she falls apart beneath me. It only takes two more thrusts before I'm filling her with my cum.

Staying buried inside of her, I run my fingers through her hair while softly planting kisses all over her damp face.

Once our breathing is under control, I prop myself up on my hands to get a good look at her. "You have never looked more beautiful."

After everything I've done to her the past hour, *now* she blushes.

"You okay?"

"Okay, doesn't even begin to cover it."

As if perfectly on cue, Harper lets out the most aggressive yawn I've ever seen.

Coming fifteen times in an hour will do that to you.

I gently pull out of her and look between her legs. If she wasn't so completely spent, the sight of my cum spilling out of her would be enough to get me to go again. "Stay right there."

She raises her arm and gives me a weak thumbs up. I chuckle as I go into the bathroom and run her a bath. Once I have everything set up, I head back into the room and scoop her into my arms from her spot on the bed.

Once I set her in the tub, I throw her hair into a clip and climb in behind her. With how sweaty her hair was, I'm sure it could stand to be washed, but there is no way she has enough energy to take care of her curls after a wash right now. That can be tomorrow's chore.

I move through the motions of lathering the loofa and scrubbing her body, and I can feel her relax against me. Before I know it, her head is resting against my chest, and soft snores are spilling from her lips. I kiss her forehead softly and wrap my arms around her, relaxing in the afterglow of what we just did.

My perfect, perfect girl.

When the water gets cold, I gently get us both out of the tub and manage to wake Harper enough to let me brush her teeth.

I set Harper on the chaise and quickly replace the sheets. Once I have all the bedding back in place, I tuck a sleeping Harper into bed and crawl in behind her, both of us still blissfully naked.

She pushes her body as tight against mine as she can manage as I wrap my arms around her. Her sleepy voice mumbles, "Sweet dreams, Ronan."

"Only of you, Baby."

I listen to her soft snores and the busy city below as I quickly drift off into my deepest sleep in weeks.

30

Mac

My phone vibrates in its spot on the center console. Stopping at a red light, I pick it up to see a text from Ronan in our group chat.

Ronan: Mac, are you on your way back yet?

I had to run across town to deal with some *issues*. Word got out that one of our dealers decided it would be a good idea to take some product off the top and sell it to someone else for double the price and pocket the difference, all while claiming the product was his own. We pay our dealers more than enough. Beyond being a greedy fucking asshole, there's no reason this guy would have needed to sidestep us.

In all honesty, the amount of product we lost wasn't shit in the grand scheme of things, but that's beside the point.

We can't have people thinking something like this is okay. It makes it look like we don't pay attention to what's happening right under our noses. It promotes disobedience. More than any of that, it makes us look like fools. And that can't happen.

So, with that being said, Ronan sent me to deal with the little weasel. He's now missing a couple of fingers, but I think I got my message across. And if I didn't, well, he won't make it past Friday when I have someone check on him again.

Me: Yeah. On my way back. Think the message was received.

Me: . . . After I ripped two of his fingers from his hand.

Finn: Nice.

Ronan: I need you to pull the last of the money from the bank and check on things for Harper.

A thought pops into my head.

Me: Why don't I just take her with me?

The three of us have hardly seen Harper since we woke up Monday morning. It's now Wednesday. Ronan has barely come out of his office, Finn has been running between Kings and the docks, and I've been running all over the goddamn city, cleaning up all kinds of bullshit. We haven't even eaten a single meal together since dinner Sunday, and when the three of us finally come to bed at night, we crawl into her bed, half dead with exhaustion. I don't want Harper to think we've forgotten about her or that we've forgotten about everything we need to take care of *for* her.

When Ronan doesn't answer right away, I send another text.

Me: It would be good for her to go. She hasn't been in once since we brought her to us, and I know she misses it.

The store has been closed since we took her that night. We've been supplementing her income, plus a little extra, all while making sure the building itself is maintained. Even though it's not open, I know just being within the walls of her family's store would be good for her.

Finn: He's right, Ronan. It's important to her.

Ronan: Okay, take her. But don't be gone long. And if you see anything even remotely suspicious, and I mean *anything*, Mac, you bring her back here.

Finn: I'm still catching up on a fuckload of paperwork at Kings, but I can meet you there if you want me to?

Me: Nah, man. I've got it.

Finn: Figured as much. Be careful and take care of our girl. I'll see you guys later.

Me: Ronan, I'll be there in fifteen. Send her down and have her wait with Ralph. He's out front today.

Ronan: Okay. I mean it, Mac.

Me: I know, brother. I've got her.

Pulling up in front of our building, I roll down the window and nod to Ralph. He walks inside, and a moment later, walks out with Harper holding onto his arm. He must say something charming because her whole face lights up in a smile.

I quickly climb out of my deep red Aston Martin DB12 and run around the front to open the passenger side door. Once they both reach me, Ralph pats her hand where it rests in the crook of his elbow. "Have a nice afternoon, Miss Hayes."

She squeezes his hand. "Please, Ralph, call me Harper."

He looks at me in question, and I quickly dip my chin, letting him know that's fine. "Okay, Harper. Have fun."

"Thanks, Ralph," I say before he retreats to his post at the front of the building.

Harper's arms wrap around my neck as I spin her and pin her to the side of the car with my body. "You look beautiful today, Mo Grá."

Her fingers wind through the back of my hair, and I lean into the touch. "Thank you. I really didn't have time to get ready. I hope this is okay."

She's wearing dark-washed ripped jeans with holes at each knee, a vintage Motley Crew T-shirt, black Converse, and a light gray peacoat with the buttons undone. Her brown curls are thrown into a messy bun, and her glasses are still on top of her head, letting me know her face was buried in a book.

She looks fucking perfect.

I press a soft, quick kiss to her lips. "You're perfect."

"You're pretty perfect yourself." Reluctantly, I pull from her arms and guide her into her seat. Before she can, I grab the seat belt and buckle her in. I climb into the car and return to the busy city streets.

"Where are we going anyway?" she asks, mindlessly looking out her window at the busy city around us.

I watch her out of the corner of my eye as I answer, "The bookstore."

Harper's head snaps toward me so fast I wouldn't be surprised if she pulled a muscle. The grin on my face feels so big it's borderline obnoxious.

"We-we are?"

I put my hand on her knee, feeling her soft skin poke through the ripped denim. I'm suddenly transported back in time to the day we brought her to the apartment when I sat next to her on the couch and put my hand on this very spot while trying to comfort her as everything she thought she knew came crashing down around her.

Even then, though, she felt like mine.

"Yeah, Pretty Girl, we are."

She looks a mix of excited and anxious. But I can tell by how her lips are pulled back into a megawatt smile that excitement is winning out. I knew this was a good idea.

That smile on her face—*I did that.*

"Not that I'm complaining, but why are we going there?"

"We need to pick up the last of the money that's there, and I figured it would put a smile on your face if I took you. Looks like I was right."

She reaches across the car and runs her hand along my face. "You were so right. What do you mean the last of the money, though?"

"Oh. We've slowly been pulling the money out. We didn't want to risk grabbing it all at once. Ronan has it all in a safe in our building. Honestly, it's probably more secure there than at the bookstore, anyway. We just kept it there out of habit."

"When did you start pulling it out?"

"Ronan made the call the morning after we took you to Kings the first time."

"After we slept together?"

"Yeah. He realized how important the bookstore was to you. He knew it felt like the whole thing was tainted with this giant lie. I think this was his way of showing that he knew that and he wanted to fix it. It's still not safe for you to open it back up, but at least this way, when you can go back, it will be just yours."

Harper's demeanor softens. "I-I don't even know what to say."

"You don't have to say anything, Mo Grá."

We ride the rest of the way in silence, and I know it's because she's silently digesting what I just told her. It really was a smart move on Ronan's part. The more we thought about it, the more we realized it didn't make sense to keep all that cash in a building across town anymore. Especially when the three of us are the only ones who touch any of it, well, four now, including Harper. But that's a discussion for a different day.

Once we get to the store, I park the car as close to the front door as possible. The less we're out in the open, the better. Unbuckling my seatbelt, I grab the small duffle from the back seat, and instruct her to stay put.

As I climb out of the car, my training kicks in, and I quickly assess my surroundings. Happy with not seeing anything suspicious, I open Harper's door and hold my hand out for her to grab. With her hand in mine, we walk up to the front door, and she stops. "I don't have my keys. I didn't know we were coming here." I flash her an amused smile before sliding my copy of the key into the old lock. "Oh, right. Duh."

I push the door open, and the musty, stagnant air fills my senses. Looking down at Harper, I watch as she takes a deep breath, and her face lights up. And we're only a foot inside the door. Where I smell nothing but old books, she smells page after page of stories and dreams. Romance novels about star-crossed lovers, non-fiction books that memorialize our world's history, and children's books that are such a core part of her childhood. The walls of this building, regardless of whether or not she knew what was going inside them, have helped make her who she is. They're part of her, woven into her very being.

I lock the door behind us and stand in place as I watch Harper run her hand along the dark mahogany wood that makes up the front counter. As she begins to walk down the aisles, she can't help but touch every book she passes, making sure they're tucked into their proper place.

She looks so at peace here.

The three of us need to make more of an effort to make her feel more comfortable at the apartment. More at home. More like this.

I'm sure I can speak for all of us when I say we don't give a fuck how the apartment is decorated. We hired someone to do it for us because none of us wanted to do it in the first place. The interior designer took one look at the three of us and decided dark and modern was the look we were going for. None of us disagreed, so we let her do whatever she wanted with the space. But now, with Harper there, ready and willing to build a life with us, it's important that the space also reflects her. I've seen her old apartment, and its style and feel is so far from ours that it isn't even funny.

Letting Harper get lost in the moment, I move toward the back reading rooms and into room three. It's the only one left that has any cash in the walls. I slide the oversized purple velvet couch out of the way, and tucked in the corner of the room at the bottom of the wall, is a register. Pulling the ornate gold cover off, I slip my hand inside the opening. Once my hand feels the familiar lever, I give it a good pull. The hidden passage pops open to my left. When it's closed, no one can even tell that there's anything amiss with the wall, but now there's an opening the size of a standard door.

It's not more than a foot deep, more of a shallow closet, really, but the opening is lined with shelves. Shelves that used to be filled with hundreds of thousands of dollars. And with all three rooms having one, we could keep millions tucked in these walls for a rainy day.

"All these years and I had no idea that was there." I look over my shoulder to find Harper leaning against the door frame with her arms across her chest and a curious expression across her face.

I give her a soft smile. "That was kind of the point, Pretty Girl."

Once I put the last stack of bills into the bag, I push the passage closed, replace the register cover, and slide the couch back to its rightful place.

"And here I always thought those scratches on the floor were from the cleaning crew." A genuine grin takes over her face. I knew she's somewhat made peace with the fact that this part of her life held such a blatant lie, but knowing she's able to make a small joke eases some of the tension in my chest.

"These couches are heavy as fuck," I tease.

"Cece picked them out when she took over after my parents died. I believe her exact words were, 'This is the most exquisite couch I have ever seen in my life. No other couch can possibly compare.'"

A brief moment of sadness crosses her face at the mention of the loved ones she's lost, but I catch it before she has a chance to cover it up.

I'm across the room and in front of her in two long strides. Her hands immediately find my waist as I take her face in my hand, softly stroking her freckled cheekbone with my thumb. "I'm sorry we don't ask you about them more, Mo Grá. It's clear you miss them. You were so lucky to have three people who loved you like that in your life."

Unlike Ronan and I, but much like Finn, Harper had two parents who loved her with everything they had and did everything they possibly could to keep her safe. But unlike Finn, she didn't just lose two parents. She lost three.

"It's okay," she answers softly. "Sometimes it's hard to talk about them. Especially since I remember so little about my parents." There's a moment of hesitation, like she wants to say something else but can't bring herself to.

"What is it?"

"I don't want you to think I'm a terrible person."

I can't help myself. I place a light kiss on her rosy, full lips. "First of all, never in a million years would I think you are a terrible person. You don't have a terrible bone in your deliciously perfect body." Her cheeks blush at my praise. "Second of all, I would never judge you. Out of anybody in this world, Ronan, Finn, and I are in no position to wrongly judge someone for their thoughts or actions—me, especially." Her hold on my waist tightens. "You can always tell me anything."

"It's just that, sometimes, actually most of the time, I miss Cece more than I miss my parents. I feel like–like I love her more than I loved them—my own parents. How messed up is that, Mac?" She drops her forehead to my chest.

"Harper, look at me." Like the good girl she is, she does so without any hesitation. "That does not make you a bad person. Do you understand me?"

Her only answer is the slight nod of her head.

"You were young when your parents died. The memories you made with them aren't anything you can hold onto. They're the memories of a child. Cece raised you through the most formidable years of your life. You bonded with her after your parents were taken from you, and that bond is something you'll never be able to recreate with another person. Your parents raised the child that you were, but Cece helped create the woman that you are. There is nothing wrong with your feelings for her. It doesn't mean you don't love your parents, Harper. I don't doubt for even a moment that your mom and dad would blame you for feeling that way. If anything, they would be so happy to know you had someone who could love you like they did. Your feelings are okay, and they are valid."

She's silent for a moment, her big green eyes staring up into mine."Thank you, Mac."

"For what?"

"For bringing me here today. For what you just said. For loving me."

My sweet, *sweet* girl. "From this life into the next, Mo Grá."

31

Finn

"I'll take a large brown sugar and cinnamon macchiato with caramel drizzle, extra hot, please," I say to the woman at the register.

My phone died shortly before I left Kings, and I couldn't find the spare charger. My guess is Mac used it, and the little asshole didn't put it back where it belongs, so I had to take a guess on what she would want. But if I know Harper like I think I do, I'm not worried.

The barista behind the counter is practically slack-jawed as she stares at me. It's a douchebag thing to say, but I'm used to it. I don't give her a second glance, though. She's nothing compared to my girl. "A-anything else, sir?"

I eye the pastry display next to the register. "I'll take a vanilla bean scone as well." She's still staring at me, but now she's not even moving. "That'll be all," I say deadpan.

"Right, sorry!" she says, clearly embarrassed, having been caught staring.

I give her my name, pay, and move to the other end of the counter. As I stand there, I go about the motions, straightening the cuffs of my white shirt under my suit jacket and adjusting my tie so it's center, but when I go to make sure I don't have any stray hairs hanging over my forehead, I pause. Because today, it's not slicked back and perfectly styled. No, my sandy blonde hair looks tousled and unkempt, just the way Harper likes it. I've been wearing it more and more this way, and every time I do, her stare burrows into me just a little bit harder. And I crave the way my body lights up when her eyes are on me. So, when I was getting ready this morning and finding myself missing her, I decided to leave the hair products tucked away in my neatly organized drawer.

It's not that I haven't seen her at all. The four of us have slept in Harper's giant new bed every night this week, but the last three days have been an absolute shit show. Ronan, Mac, and I have been catching up on the mountain of bullshit we missed while we were in our self-appointed bubble. With that being said, besides the occasional chaste kiss and "I love you," I've barely touched or spoken to her.

And if all that wasn't bad enough, I feel like I'm physically ill with the constant desire to be buried inside of her. I planned to steal her away from Ronan first thing Sunday morning, but, like an idiot, I let Mac, Luca, and Sebastian get me absolutely plastered at Kings. I was so hungover I could hardly move. Mac even more so.

Harper and Ronan, of course, thought the entire thing was hilarious.

I've had my taste of Harper twice now and still haven't been able to feel her pussy wrapped around my cock. I haven't been able to mark her skin with my teeth. To listen to her scream "Daddy" at the top of her lungs. To have her obey my every command and fulfill my every desire.

When I'm not buried in the job, it's all I can think about, and even then, it's a constant struggle.

She's occupying all of the space in my brain, which is why I'm here at the coffee shop on my way home from Kings, trying to hide my erection while I wait for her favorite coffee to be ready.

"Finn!" The over-eager woman who took my order is now conveniently at the other end of the counter, ready to hand me my drink. Grabbing the wrapped scone from one hand and Harper's warm drink in the other, I immediately spot a phone number on the cardboard sleeve of the drink. I set the pastry on the counter and slide the sleeve off the cup. Holding it between two fingers in her direction, and with my most serious expression, I ask, "Can I get a different sleeve, please?"

The woman's face immediately pales in horror. Before Harper, I would have probably commended the woman's efforts. I wouldn't have called her. It was few and far between I called any of them. Now, though, I won't even entertain the idea. We already have our perfect girl.

Without a word she snatches the piece of cardboard out of my hand and hands me a new one. I walk away without a backward glance.

The second I step back outside the hairs on the back of my neck stand on end. Not from the cool, late fall air but from years of my body being attuned to sensing any immediate threats. My eyes start scanning the streets around me, but I don't see anything obvious. I know something's wrong, though. I can feel it.

The stoplight at the end of the block changes, and the line of traffic starts creeping forward. The large city bus that's directly across from me moves, and it's then that I see him. Standing there on the sidewalk across the street with his hands in a wool peacoat, his smile wicked, like the devil who's finally free from the depths of hell. The man who viciously altered the course of my life. The man who took the two people who loved me most in this world. That man that's selfishly out to destroy the woman that I love.

Declan *fucking* Whelan.

Declan Whelan is in New York. In my fucking city. Standing no more than twenty yards away from me, and yet neither of us move. Both of us locked in a stare so intense it could burst the other into flames if we let it.

A city garbage truck crosses in front of my path, and just as ominously as he appeared in front of me, by the time the truck passes, he's gone.

Fear of the unknown and the intense urge to get back to my family finally makes my feet move. I have to get back to the apartment. I need to see all of them with my own eyes, see Harper. I need to make sure they're all okay.

He can't take anyone else from me.

My grip on the steering wheel is lethal as I speed toward the apartment. The elevator ride from the garage to the top floor feels like an eternity. As each floor passes, uncontrollable anger, fear, and lack of control coursing through me grows. And by the time the door opens to our penthouse, it feels like I'll explode if I don't find a way to let it out.

"Harper!" I yell at the top of my lungs as I quickly set the items from the coffee shop on the kitchen counter. She doesn't answer as I sprint down the hallway toward her room. Throwing open her door, I find the room empty. I run right into Mac's room, finding his empty as well.

They should be back by now. They should be back.

"Harper! Mac!" Silence is the only thing that follows.

Where are they? They should be back.

As I run back through the kitchen I yank the tie off from around my neck, feeling like I can't breathe.

He doesn't have her, Finn. Mac wouldn't let him touch her.

Ronan comes running out of his office on the other side of the kitchen like his ass is on fire, a panicked look in his eyes.

"Finn? What the fuck is going on?"

"Ronan. Where are they? Where are Harper and Mac? They should be back by now. Where are they?" My voice rises in volume and desperation with every word I speak.

I don't ever lose control like this. My emotions are a carefully kept mask. But right now, I couldn't hide my desperation if my life depended on it.

"They should be here any minute. Mac called just before you got here."

I start rapidly pacing in front of him, rubbing the tightness in my chest with my fist.

"Finn, what's going on?" Ronan's voice remains calm, but I can tell by the tightness in his jaw he's trying not to rise to my level of panic.

"I saw him, Ronan. He was right there." The memory of his face makes me double over. I put my hands on my knees and try to get my breathing under control.

Ronan grabs my face in his hands, forcing me to stand

upright and look him in the eyes. "Who, Finn? Who did you see?"

"Declan."

His name rings through the apartment like a gunshot. Ronan drops his hands from my face to the tops of my shoulders. "Did you just say you saw Declan Whelan?"

"Yes, Ronan. I saw him when I was leaving the coffee shop. He was standing across the street just fucking staring at me, then before I could do anything, he was just-just gone."

"Did he follow you here?"

"I don't think so. I just tried to get back here as fast as I could. I couldn't call because my goddamn phone is dead." I inhale sharply. "But Ronan, I've never been to that coffee shop before. It was just some random place I picked to get Harper a drink. That means—"

"That means he was following you." Ronan's previously calm voice is now laced with anxiety.

"And if he was following me, who's to say someone isn't following them?"

His hands fall from my shoulders as he takes a few steps back. "Jesus fuck."

"Wh-where are they, Ronan?" The shake in my voice surprises the both of us. I'm slipping, and I don't know how to fucking stop it.

Pulling his phone out of his pocket, Ronan finds Mac's contact and puts the phone to his ear. A moment later, the elevator door opens, and the ringing of Mac's phone breaks through the tense silence.

"Jesus Christ, Ronan," Mac laughs. "I know you love me, but you just called me five minutes ago."

Harper's carefree laugh almost causes a sob to break

through my lips.

The two stop dead in their tracks as they take in the panic-stricken looks on our faces. "Love, what's going on?"

Instead of answering, I share a look with Ronan, silently asking him to explain everything to Mac because I can feel them—they're screaming at me, telling me how easy it would have been for him to get to her today. They're making me feel irrevocably out of control. The demons that I keep tucked away in the deepest parts of me, doing everything in my power to keep them at bay, they're trying to swallow me whole.

I need her. I need her to slay my demons.

"Go. I'll talk to Mac."

I don't give it a second thought. Marching over, I grab Harper's hand from Mac's, set the small stack of books she has in her other hand on the counter next to her forgotten coffee, and roughly pull her behind me down the hall toward my room. In the background, I hear the low rumble of Ronan's voice as he fills Mac in on this afternoon's events.

"Finn, what's wrong? What's going on?"

I don't answer her. I can't. My mind has one sole focus right now. I need to regain control. To use her body and strip her bare. I need to watch as she submits to my every demand. I need her to fall apart beneath my touch exactly how I want her to.

Part of me worries she's not ready for this, but that won't stop me.

I shove Harper into my room and slam the door closed behind me. She spins to face me, eyes wide with panic and fear. But that's not all I see. Her thighs are clenched together in excitement, chest heaving with bated breath. She's spinning Ronan's ring around her thumb, which I've come to find is her new habit when she's anxious. She's anxious because she sees the wild look in my eyes. The look that lets her know what's in store for her.

She might be more ready for this than either of us thought.

"Strip, Angel. Now."

32

Harper

"Finn, I–I don't know if I'm—"

"You are, Harper. You're ready," he answers calmly as he moves to sit on the end of his bed. After removing his shoes and socks, he rests his elbows on his knees. His dirty blond hair falls over his forehead in the most delicious way when he looks up at me, where I'm still frozen by the door.

"Finn, what's going on?"

He scrubs a hand down his face, and for a moment, he looks *panicked*. I take a step, and he holds his hand out. "Not now, Harper. I'll explain everything later. Right now, I just . . . I just need you. I need *us*. Okay?"

Can I do this?

I don't know what's going on. I don't know if I'm ready for the way Finn pushes me. But I do know that I love him. I know that for him to be clearly displaying so much uncontrolled emotion, something has shaken him to his core. More than anything, though, I know I'm safe with him. Safe to swim in the darkest of our desires.

He won't just push me to the edge. He'll throw me over it.

But when I crash, he'll also be right there to catch me.

He needs this.

I need this.

I'm ready.

The corner of Finn's lips turn up and I realize I must have said that last part out loud. Still resting with his elbows on his knees he raises a brow, waiting for me to follow his instructions. I take my jacket off, followed by my black Converse and socks. Remembering my glasses are still tucked on top of my head from earlier, and I gently set those on top of Finn's dresser. I peel out of my jeans and vintage T-shirt and stand back in my original spot by the door in nothing but a simple black lace bra and matching underwear.

"I said, strip. That means all of it." Finn's raspy command causes heat to pool in my belly. His light accent is more present than usual. When any of them get worked up, it comes out to play, and to say it does things to me is a massive understatement. The three of them could read an instruction manual when they get like this, and I would probably be wet.

Not probably. Definitely.

I unhook the front clasp of my bra and toss it on my pile of clothes. Sliding my underwear over my ass, I let them pool on the floor around my feet. The cool air of the room tickles the wetness between my thighs. My eyes find Finn again, and he nods towards the black lace. "Pick those up."

I do as he says.

"Now, put them in your mouth."

My eyes immediately widen and my breath stills. He can't be serious? He wants me to put my dirty panties . . . in my mouth?

"Don't make me tell you twice, Harper."

You can do this, Harp."

Taking a deep breath, I part my lips and ball up the piece of lace. Shakily, I bring my hand to my mouth and slide them in. The taste of my arousal coats my tongue.

"Good girl. Now, crawl to me."

33

Finn

After only another brief moment of hesitation, Harper drops to her knees. She bends forward so she's on all fours, her breasts hanging beneath her, and she starts to crawl toward me.

My Harper.

My good fucking girl.

I sit up straight as she reaches me. Once she's between my legs, she sits back on her heels and places her palms flat on her thighs while her deep green eyes look up at me. Practically piercing my fucking soul.

I didn't even have to tell her to do that—she just did it.

Fuck. Me.

Reaching into her hair, I gently pull the silk scrunchie out, letting her curls fall free—just the way I like them.

"Open," I command.

Harper's plush pink lips open and I pull the damp lace from her mouth. Unbuttoning my suit pants, I pull my cock out. It's so hard it's painful, the veins pulsing as they try to pull all the blood from the rest of my body. I wrap the panties around my hand and rub them up and down my dick. A groan spills from my lips at the friction.

Not wanting to get carried away, I force myself to stop and drop the fabric to the floor. She looks at my cock, leaking precum like a goddamn sieve, and licks her lips.

She licks. Her. Fucking. Lips.

"Put it in your mouth, Angel."

She wraps her soft hand around the base of my shaft and whispers, "Yes, Daddy."

Slowly, she slides my cock into her mouth, taking as much of me as she can in one go. Her mouth is so wet and warm. "Your mouth was made for my cock, Harper."

She hums around me in agreement, the vibrations sending a wave of pleasure through my body as I fist her hair in both my hands. Pulling off momentarily, she licks the slit at the head of my dick, gathering a bead of precum on her tongue. She looks up at me through hooded eyes, looking perfect on her knees.

With her head between my hands, I guide her mouth back to my cock. I pull her head down until I hit the back of her throat, holding still just for a moment, testing to see how she reacts to me controlling her body. When she doesn't panic and instead swallows around me, I groan in satisfaction.

She fists the fabric of my pants on top of my legs, and I suddenly have a burning desire to feel her hands all over my body. With her mouth still working my cock we work to get my pants off in record time. The moment her palms connect with my thighs, feral and brutal desire courses through me.

She's here, right in front of me. She's safe, and I'm in control of the situation.

Taking her face between my hands again, I begin fucking her mouth without abandon. "That's it, Angel. Choke on my cock. Show me how much you missed having me inside of you."

I slide even further down her throat, and tears fill her eyes. I look down as her nails dig into my thighs, drawing tiny droplets of blood from how hard she's holding on, the pain only adding to how euphoric it feels to be back inside of her. My rhythm escalates, causing Harper to gag around me every so often. But she doesn't ask to stop, and when I look into her eyes, I don't see nervousness or fear. I see unadulterated lust and love for *me*.

My grip on her hair tightens, and I use her to suck me off. The entire thing is fast, intense, and completely unhinged. But I don't care, and neither does she. I am feral for her. For the way I feel when I'm with her. And nothing or no one—not even Declan Whelan—will take that away from me.

When I feel my balls tighten, I pull her head off my cock, and she looks at me with a mixture of confusion and disappointment. "When I come, I'm going to come inside your cunt, Angel." I grab her face in my hand hard enough that her lips purse and give her a quick but forceful kiss, tasting the saltiness of myself in her mouth. When I pull her bottom lip between my teeth, she whines.

"Get on the bed, Harper." I slide out of the way, and she crawls onto the bed. "On your stomach. Stretch your hands out and clasp them together."

She follows my directions, and my eyes immediately go to

her ass—full and round and just begging for my attention. After I finally shed my shirt, I crawl over her. Bending down, I bite her round cheek *hard*. The sound that comes out of her mouth is somewhere between a moan and a shriek. Satisfaction blooms in my chest when I pull off, and I already see a deep purple mark beginning to form. I continue to crawl over her until my legs straddle her waist and my mouth hovers above her ear. As I run my hand up one of her arms until I'm gripping both her wrists, I whisper, "Is this okay?"

She takes a deep breath, taking stock of how she feels. I know this is pushing her. Me pinning her down, especially her hands, so I want to check in. I know she's strong, stronger than any of us ever thought she was, but everyone has their limits. I just hope this isn't permanently one of hers. He doesn't have a right to take that from her.

Finally, she says, "Yes," and the last bit of tension leaves my body. For now, at least.

"That's my girl." I quickly kiss her cheek and hurry back down her body so I'm no longer caging her hips in. Slowly, I drag my hands back down her arms, through her hair, and along her spine. A trail of goosebumps follows my fingers, looking like the perfect map for me to trace with my tongue. But that's for another time. I grip her hips with my hands and lift her ass slightly off the bed.

"Tell me, Angel," I say as I trail my fingers down and over her back hole until I meet her soaking wet cunt. "Has this pussy missed me?"

I move my hand back and forth, never entering, just gathering her wetness on my fingers.

"Yes, Daddy."

Once I feel like I have enough, I remove my fingers from

her pussy and wrap them around my aching dick, coating it in her arousal. I notch the head of my cock at her entrance, pushing forward until I'm just barely inside of her. Her body momentarily relaxes as if she thinks I'm about to take her soft and slow.

How fucking wrong you are, Angel.

"Do you want me to fill you, Harper? Do you want me so deep inside of you that you don't know where I end and you begin?"

"*Fuck.*" Just a simple curse word sounds filthy coming from her sweet mouth. "Please . . . please . . . please."

"Give me your arm." She unclasps her hands and reaches one of her arms back toward me. Gripping her forearm, I pin it across her lower back, making it arch at the perfect angle. My other hand grabs the base of her neck, pinning her head to the mattress.

If she wanted to, she could get out from underneath me, but I know she won't.

"Beg for it. I want to hear you beg for Daddy's cock." She tries to push back against me, but my hold stops her. "Tell me who owns this cunt. Tell me who you belong to."

Looking back at me as best as she can with her face pressed against the bed, she pleads, "My pussy is yours. It's all yours, Daddy. Take me. Own me. Fuck me so hard I never forget you were there. *Please.*"

As soon as the word leaves her lips, I slam into her in one go. "Ahhh!" she yells at the top of her lungs. I don't pause, and I don't stop to make sure she's okay. I unleash my body on hers in a way I never have before.

Because she is mine, her body is mine to own. To do with as I please.

I. Own. Her.

"I forgot how perfect it feels when you submit to me." The sound of my thighs slapping against hers, combined with my grunts and Harper's moans, fills the room.

Fuck, they're probably filling the entire apartment.

Harper's walls start tightening around my dick. I haven't even so much as touched her clit or played with her tits, and she's ready to fall apart around me. "Fuck, your strangling my cock, Angel."

My grip on her neck and arm tightens, and I push her deeper into the mattress as I try to stave off my release. "I want to come, Daddy. Please let me come."

Was she waiting for me to give her permission? Of course, she is. Because she's my girl. And my girl doesn't come until she's told.

"Come, Angel. Come for Daddy." Harper buries her face in the mattress and lets out a scream. Her entire body shakes violently beneath my hold as I quickly pull out of her, and her release soaks the bedding beneath us. A moment later, I slam back into her, only for her pussy to tighten back up around me a second time after just a few more thrusts. I pull out again, and more of her release sprays out across the sheets. "You're doing so good for me, Harper."

My hand slides from the back of her neck to the front, and I pull her up so her back is pinned to my chest, her arm still pinned to her back between us. With my cock pounding back into her oversensitive pussy, I bring her mouth to mine. Swallowing the sobs that are leaving her lips and tasting the tears that are rolling down her cheeks.

It doesn't take long before I can't hold it off any longer. I thrust to the hilt inside of her, her tight cunt still pulsing around me, and spill my release as deep as it can get.

Once I'm sure nothing is left, I pull my mouth from hers. Only her sobs don't stop.

Fuck.

I pull out of her and gently roll her to her back, not caring about the mess she made on the bed. Harper's entire body is still shaking as she continues to cry. "Harper?"

Shit. I should have known that was too much. She wasn't ready. "I'm so sorry, Angel. Can you look at me? Please?"

Now I'm the one that's begging.

Her eyes are still pinched tight as I stroke my hand down her wet cheek. "Harper. Sweetheart, please. Let me see those gorgeous, green eyes."

Slowly, she opens them and my heart stops at how beautiful she looks.

I know that may sound strange, but it's true.

She's so beautiful. Just look at her face. Her glossy green eyes pierce my soul. Her freckles look as if they were placed by Picasso himself. The shade of pink that's covering her body is what dreams are made of. And my cum dripping from between her legs reminds me that she is my home. I couldn't dream of a more perfect picture if I tried.

After a few minutes, her ragged breath slows, and she finally speaks, "I'm okay, Finn."

"That was too much. I shouldn't have pushed you."

"No. No, it's not that. It's—"

Her eyes dance between mine. "What is it, Angel?"

"I–I feel like myself. I feel *whole*."

Jesus Christ, this woman.

I slant my mouth over hers in a gentle kiss. Pulling my lips from hers, I trail them over her cheeks, kissing away every tear. Once I've had my fill, I thread my fingers through her hair and look down at her. At the woman I love with every fiber of my being. The woman who has the power to both kill me and bring me back to life. "Thank you for trusting me."

"Always, Love."

34

Ronan

The apartment has been quiet for hours now. Where Harper's screams of pleasure floated through the apartment like my favorite song, there's now only light snoring coming from behind Finn's door. The two missed dinner, but judging by how intense whatever was going on in there sounded, Mac and I didn't want to wake them. They needed the rest, so we let them sleep.

Finn was terrified when he got home. I have never seen him so completely out of control. He's a lot like me in that way; we both need it to thrive. Yet, at the same time, he's so much different than me. Whereas I feel the constant need to control everyone and everything around me, making sure the outcome of any situation will play out exactly how I want it to, Finn has an insatiable desire to keep himself in check. To ensure that everything from the clothes he wears, to the tasks he carries out, to the feelings that course through him are all within the bounds of his control. So, when he saw Declan—the man who killed his parents and is actively threatening the love of our life—I know it turned his world upside down. That, coupled with the fact that when he got home, Harper was nowhere to be found, sent him into a tailspin of panic. One that even I couldn't bring him out of.

No, the only person that could have helped him was Harper. And based on what I heard coming from that room, she did exactly that.

Which means my girl was brave. I wasn't there, but I know that being with Finn in that state of mind and what he likely asked from her would have taken her over the edge. He would have knocked down that last wall she was keeping up, and rightfully so.

When I was with Harper after our night out at Kings, I made her feel something she'd been missing. She wanted to feel the pain and to be able to control it. To enjoy it. She wanted to take that back, and I gladly gave it to her. But, if my assumptions are correct, and they usually are, Finn made her feel *everything*.

If that's the case, they won't wake up until well into the morning.

Meanwhile, Mac and I scarfed down some pasta that he made while I filled him in on why Finn was so upset in the first place. The second the words "Declan Whelan is in New York" came out of my mouth, Mac's face paled in horror, exactly like mine did when Finn initially told me.

None of us ever thought that demented old fuck would actually stop sending lackeys to do his bidding for him, and grow a set of balls and show his face in our city.

In *our* fucking city.

But he did, and now we need to figure out how we're going to get rid of him, not just from New York but from the face of the entire goddamn planet.

Since Finn's asleep, I have the tedious and beyond annoying task of cleaning up the kitchen while Mac finishes stuffing his face. I'm about to start wiping down the counters when my phone rings on the counter next to Mac. He looks at it and drops his fork onto his plate.

"It's Sebastian."

Sebastian would only be calling me for one of two things.

"Answer it," I tell Mac anxiously as I quickly wipe my hands dry on the hand towel.

"Hey, Sebastian. It's Mac. Ronan's here, too."

"Declan's in New York." He wastes no time getting right into it.

"Yeah," I sigh, "We know. Finn saw him this afternoon. Got away before he could get to him."

"Oh, shit." Luca's voice cuts in in the background. "Is he okay?"

Luca is no stranger to Finn's story. We filled him in on our lives in the time we spent together while Harper was missing. "He wasn't. But," I look down the hallway toward his door, which I left cracked when I ducked my head in to check on them earlier. "He's better now."

"Good. Well, that's not all Seb found."

"I found Logan. Facial recognition caught him at a pharmacy in Allentown. Looks like he was there picking up some first aid supplies and antibiotics."

"Holy fuck," Mac breathes out.

"It's about a three-hour drive from here," Luca continues,

"Dante and Enzo are already on their way to grab him. Seb traced the car he was driving to the run-down motel he's staying at. You want us to bring him to the docks or straight to you?"

I look at Mac, and he nods. "Bring him here. I'll get one of the rooms in the parking garage ready."

When we moved into this apartment, we had a few "interrogation" rooms installed on our floor of the parking garage. There's nothing in them besides a drain in the center of the floor, a hook on the ceiling, and a couple of chairs. It's few and far between that we actually bring people to them, not wanting to risk more people figuring out where we live, but I want Harper to be here for this. She deserves to confront this fucker in whatever way she sees fit before the three of us rain hell down upon him for daring to touch her. And I'll be fucked if we risk taking her down to the docks.

"Alright. Enzo's driving, which means they should be there in about half the time. Based on what he was picking up at the pharmacy, I'm assuming he won't put up much of a fight. I'll let you know when they have him and are on their way back."

"Alright. Thanks guys." Without another word, they hang up.

"So much for letting them get some rest." Mac shoves an obnoxiously large forkful of pasta into his mouth, and I roll my eyes.

"Really, Mac?"

"What?" He asks with his mouthful. "It's gonna be a long night, and I don't wanna be hungry."

A couple of glasses of whiskey and two hours later, Mac and I get the call that Enzo and Dante are on their way back with a very knocked-out Logan. Which means we have two hours to get everything in the room downstairs ready, wake up our sleeping angel, and mentally prepare her for what's about to happen.

A little after eleven, Mac and I finally enter Finn's room. I move over to Finn's side to wake him up first. Before I even touch him, his eyes snap open. Good. I'd be disappointed if they didn't.

"What's wrong?" he asks as he slowly sits up, swinging his legs over the edge of the bed.

"Sebastian found Logan in Allentown. Dante and Enzo went and grabbed him. They should be here in about thirty minutes."

"Shit," he scrubs his hand over his beard. "One of the rooms downstairs?"

"Yeah. We already got it ready to go. Figured it was best not to take Harper to the docks," Mac answers from behind me.

"You want her down there? She shouldn't be in the same room as him," Finn snaps as he stands up, his voice calm but firm. As he slides on a pair of briefs, I see the panic bleeding back into his eyes, so I place my hand on his shoulder, trying to center him before he spirals back into the place he was in earlier today.

"I don't disagree, brother. I want to gouge his eyes out before he even has a chance to look at her. But we all know she needs this. And as much as I like arguing with her, she will never forgive us if we don't give her the opportunity to find closure."

"The three of us won't leave her side," Mac adds.

Finn looks between us before he turns around and looks

down at Harper's sleeping form. All three of us stand above her, drinking her in. By all intents and purposes, she looks ridiculous. Adorable, but ridiculous. Her hair is wild and tangled on the pillow beneath her, her mouth is wide open, a small trail of drool is falling from her lips down her cheek, and the faintest snore escapes with each breath. Yet, she looks completely at peace. I squeeze Finn's shoulder, knowing he helped give that to her.

Finn expels a harsh sigh and nods. "Alright."

Mac moves around to Harper's side of the bed. Bending over, he kisses the tip of her nose. "Mo Grá," he whispers.

As she starts to stir, Finn moves about his room, finding a pair of joggers and a black T-shirt to put on.

I crawl across the bed and run my hand down her arm until my fingers come in contact with my ring on her thumb. She never takes it off. I spin it around with my fingers. "Baby. You've got to wake up."

Her eyes start to flutter open. Once she recognizes that Mac and I are in the room, she sits straight up, clutching the sheet to her bare chest. "What's going on? What happened? Where's Finn?"

"I'm right here, Angel." Finn stands beside Mac.

"I'm sorry, Baby. I wanted to let you sleep, but you have to get up." Harper anxiously looks between the three of us. "Sebastian found Logan. Enzo and Dante are on their way over with him now."

Her shaky hand immediately starts spinning my ring around her thumb, and her bottom lip trembles. "He–he's coming here?"

"We have an interrogation room set up in the garage. We just wanted to give you the chance to face him. If that's something you want." I wasn't lying when I agreed with Finn. If I had it my way, she would never be near this man again. The thought of him even looking at her fills me with a blinding rage. Let alone the fact that I don't want her to see all of the things we're going to do to him. A quick death would be too easy for everything he put her through.

That said, she has earned the right to confront him. She fought back against him once, and she can do it again.

She can do anything.

"What am I supposed to do? I–I don't know if . . . I don't know if I can kill him."

I shake my head and answer, "You do whatever feels right to you. And we would never expect you to do that if it's not something you want. That's what you have us for."

"You'll all be there with me?"

Mac tucks some of her hair behind her ear. "The entire time, Pretty Girl."

Her eyes close for a moment, and when she opens them, I see nothing but fierce determination. "Okay."

35

Mac

Red.

It's creeping into the edges of my vision. Right there, ready to take hold of me. Just knowing that the man who dared take her from me, from us, the man who dared lay a hand on what's ours, is on the other side of that door. I want to rip him limb from limb. I want to crush every bone in his body, to make him feel so much pain he will scream for death.

And he will, in good time.

But right now, Harper's hand in mine as the four of us stand outside the door is the only thing stopping it from swallowing me whole *again*. She's my perfect beacon of light, standing strong on the shore amidst the sea of chaos and anger raging within me.

After we woke her, Harper quickly threw on some sweats

and one of my black T-shirts. I didn't know what would happen down here, but I didn't want Logan's blood ruining any of her clothes. Her hair is pinned up in a clip, showcasing every feature of her terrified face.

We were about to go in when Harper stopped me and said she needed a minute. None of us want to rush her, and Logan clearly isn't going anywhere, so now we're standing here, waiting.

With Ronan and Finn behind us, I squeeze Harper's hand, and she looks up at me. "I don't know what to do. I'm scared." Her voice is nothing but an anxious whisper.

"You don't have to do anything, Mo Grá. You don't have to go in there. You don't even have to look at him. We can take care of it if that's what you want."

She pulls her eyes from me and looks at the metal door in front of us. Shaking her head, she answers, "No. I said I would do this, and I will."

I look back at Finn and Ronan, and they're still wearing the same worried expression as me. None of us want her to have to do this, but at the same time, none of us want to stand in her way. Turning her to face me, I hold her face in my hands. "We will be there the entire time. He won't be able to touch you. Whatever you want to say or do within those walls is your choice. None of us will stop you. Okay?"

Her eyes fill with tears, but none of them fall. "Okay."

"I need you to know that if you stay in there, you'll see a side of us you've never seen. Remember who we are and that we would never hurt you." Her eyes widen suddenly at the realization. "And if it becomes too much at any point or you want to leave, just say the word."

She swallows hard but nods in understanding.

Ronan steps up and kisses the side of her head that's still cradled in my hands. "Let me go in first, Baby. I have some things I need to get off my chest."

Ronan steps around us, and Finn follows, but not before pressing his own kiss to the top of her head and whispering, "We've got you, Angel."

Finn steps away, and she looks up at me again. Her eyes dance between mine as her hands wrap around my wrists, and she asks, "Are you okay?"

Fucking hell, this woman. Here we are, about to confront the man who brutalized her for days on end, and she's asking if *I'm* okay. I know it's because she remembers the state I was in when we found her. She saw how I was nothing more than a shell of a human. But she's the one who brought me back, and she's the one that will keep me here.

I nod and softly kiss her quivering lips. "Let's go show him who you are."

On that note, Ronan slams the door open so hard it bounces off the wall. When we walk in, Dante and Enzo are standing against the wall to our left, arms crossed, just staring at Logan. He's hanging from the ceiling by his hands in nothing but his boxers, still passed out from whatever they gave him. His abdomen has a pretty severe-looking wound that refuses to heal from the towel rack Harper stabbed him with. And judging by the severe discoloration around it, it's got a nasty infection.

Upon seeing him, Harper's hand squeezes around mine like a vice. I squeeze right back, silently reminding her that she's not alone. "Why don't you stand over there with Enzo and Dante for a minute."

Reluctantly she lets go of my hand and takes Finn's outstretched one. "Come on, Angel."

Ronan looks over his shoulder, always ensuring he knows where our girl is. Once he spots her standing in front of Finn, caged in his arms, he looks at me, and I dip my chin. A smile crafted by the devil himself spreads across Ronan's face as he turns back to the bastard hanging from the ceiling.

In the blink of an eye, Ronan sends his fist straight into the stab wound in Logan's abdomen. Whatever barely healed skin was holding it together rips open, and blood starts slowly trickling out of the wound. Logan's eyes snap open. It takes a few moments for his groggy brain to register the amount of pain he's in and just a few longer to realize where he is. It's then I see it all play across his face. He realizes how well and truly fucked he is. Sobs of pain burst from his lips, and we've barely even begun.

Fucking pussy.

"Well, well, well. Nice of you to join us," Ronan grits out.

"Ronan, please. I was just—"

Ronan reaches up and wraps his hand around Logan's neck. "There is no point in begging for your life. Your life ended the moment you took her from me. From *us*." Logan's face begins to turn blue from lack of oxygen. "And then you had the nerve to put your hands on her. ON OUR WOMAN!" The sheer rage in Ronan's voice could bring down the entire building. "Now, now you're just on borrowed fucking time."

Walking over to Finn, he grabs Harper from his arms so Finn can *assist* me.

Don't get me wrong, Ronan is destructive, and, as we've all realized by now, when it comes to Harper, he's absolutely lethal. But Finn and I, we're a well-oiled machine. Where Ronan has spent years being a leader and building an empire, he has used Finn and I to ensure everyone is toeing the line, and when they're not, Finn and I don't just break the line. We shatter and destroy it.

For everything Liam McDermott took from me, he did give me one thing—the ability to make people fear me. And Finn, not only is his bullshit meter spot-fucking-on, but his fuse is practically zero. The moment his carefully composed exterior cracks, it's game over.

"You want to go first, or shall I?" Finn asks.

"If you don't mind . . ."

He waves his arm out. "By all means. Probably best to loosen him up a bit before I ask him some questions anyway."

I stalk toward the corner of the room where Ronan and I had set up a small table with various tools and pick up the heavy metal bat. As I move back towards Logan, I toss it around in my hand. His eyes track the movement of the heavy metal, and his entire body freezes, trying to brace for the impact he knows is coming. I swing the bat into his armpit, hitting just underneath his shoulder. A satisfying pop echoes throughout the room, letting me know I dislocated his shoulder. His feet are barely touching the ground, so I know that's got to hurt like a bitch.

I land another blow on his rib cage opposite his stab wound and watch with a psychotic smile on my face as blood continues to pour out of it. Logan's screams echo off the walls after several more methodically placed hits.

Every few minutes, I look over at Harper, terrified that every time I look at her, I'll see it on her face—that she's scared of me. Yet, every time her eyes lock with mine, I can see the only person she's afraid of is the man hanging in front of me.

And that just won't do.

He doesn't deserve her fear.

"You see, Logan," I run the tip of the bat down his sternum as he continues to cry. "We memorized every mark on Harper's body when we found her. And for every cut and bruise you left on her skin, you're about to get back ten fucking fold."

His head thrashes back and forth, and his blonde hair, which is longer now, sprays sweat across the room.

Fucking gross.

"If I had the patience to hold you down here for two weeks and starve you too, I would."

Finn walks towards me with something he grabbed off the table. When the light catches the object, I realize he picked up the scalpel. "Before this gets too carried away, why is Declan here?"

"Why would I tell you? You're just going to kill me anyway?"

I press the tip of my bat against his infected wound, and he screams out in pain. "You're right. We are going to kill you. But I can drag this out until you are literally begging for death. I don't think you quite understand who you're dealing with here."

He looks into my eyes, and I know he sees it, the uninhibited violence—the red. "When I checked in a few days ago, I told him how bad I was. He flew off the handle and told me it was time he dealt with this himself. He brought a whole team with him. He told me he would deal with it and then bring Harper and I both back with him."

"Where's your phone?"

"I have it," Enzo answers from his spot against the wall. He pulls it out of his pocket and hands it to Ronan.

I look back at Logan. "Looks like you're going to miss your

flight out of here."

Finn bends down and grabs one of Logan's feet. "Why did you do it?" Finn asks, his voice calm and controlled.

"Declan, he–he made me. I didn't have a choice."

Finn slices down the arch of Logan's foot. "She got that one running away." He stands up and walks around Logan to grab a fistful of his hair.

"Why did you do it?" Finn repeats.

"I just told you! Declan wanted me to bring her back to Ireland. I was going to marry her so Patrick couldn't take over, and I would. I was supposed to knock her up a few times and let the Whelan line live on. It's all about the power. He didn't want to give it up, and she's the only way he can keep it."

Finn pauses a moment, and Logan's face relaxes like he thinks he's about to get some sort of reprieve. Then, Finn drags the knife down the back of Logan's head. "She got that one trying to fight you off."

Reaching my hand out, Finn places the scalpel in my palm. I grab Logan's face with one hand and bring the blade to his cheekbone. "Why did *you* do it?" I repeat Finn's question.

Between broken sobs, Logan answers, "He–he caught me with a–a man. He said that after everything, he wouldn't stand for me being a faggot. He needed a way to get to Harper, and I gave him one."

The knife slides across the apple of his cheek, and blood spills down his face, "She got that one when you hit her."

I open my mouth to ask him again when Harper's soft voice beats me to it, "Why? Why didn't you just run? You didn't have to do it."

She sounds so, so fucking sad.

"Declan threatened to kill him. I—I couldn't risk it. I love him."

I don't bother asking what the other guy's name is because it doesn't fucking matter. He's better off without this cowardly piece of shit anyway. Instead, I let Harper continue, not wanting to stop her now that she's found the strength.

I move to the side, and she steps out of Ronan's arms and closer to Logan. "Yet you would have married me? Forced me to have your babies?"

"At least he would have been alive. And after you had the kids, you'd—" He cuts himself off, and I know what he was about to say deep in my bones. But Harper needs to hear it for herself.

Tilting her head to the side, she asks, "I'd what?"

Logan looks over at me, and I twirl the scalpel between my fingers, silently letting him know his options.

"After you had a couple of kids, we'd have just gotten rid of you anyway."

Everyone in the room freezes as we wait for her to process what she just heard. "So—so you were just going to steal me from my home. Ship me off to a different country, force me to marry you, use me as an incubator just to pop out some kids that share the same blood as me, then—then kill me anyway? After that man—my own grandfather—already tried to destroy my life once?"

Logan gives almost an imperceptible nod, and Harper huffs out a heavy breath. "And you-you, what, tortured and starved me for days on end because the thought of executing that plan is so disgustingly vile to *you?*"

He doesn't even nod this time.

Harper whirls around and marches toward me. "Give me

the bat, Mac."

The rage that has taken over Harper's entire being is nothing like I've ever seen. "Mo Grá, just wait a minute. Let us—"

"Cormac. Give. Me. The. Bat." I find Ronan over her shoulder, and he nods. Reluctantly, I hold the bat out, and she snatches it from my hand before moving back in front of Logan.

36

Harper

They were going to treat me as some product to be sold. Nothing more than a commodity. They were going to force me to have children and then dare take me from them. All of this because of the blood that runs through my veins?

If that's the case, then I don't fucking want it. I'll gladly take that scalpel and spill every last drop onto this floor.

But I can't do that. Because my life, my mind, body, and soul now belong to them. The three men who moved heaven and hell to save me, and I'll be damned if I repay them by giving up. I now belong to them as much as they belong to me. If I spill my blood, I may as well cut them open, too.

And that is something I refuse to do.

But I *need* to do something.

I've never felt anger quite like this. Not when my parents died. Not when Cece left me. Not the night the guys took me from the life I thought I knew. Not when I found out my own Grandfather was the one responsible for actively trying to destroy my life. Not even when this man kept me in that god-forsaken cabin, beating and starving me.

No. That was all child's play compared to the rage that's causing my body to feel like it's on fire. Every square inch of my skin feels like a raging inferno, like if I don't get control of it soon, it will burn me alive. And the only way I can think to put it out is to inflict unexplainable violence on the person in front of me.

It's the only thing that can help.

It *has* to help.

The metal handle of the bat feels like ice against my burning skin as I firmly grasp it in my hand. Finn's still standing behind Logan, and I jerk my chin up to the hook in the ceiling. "Let him down."

Finn pinches his brows, worry evident on his face. "Angel."

"Finn let him down. Please." My voice is firm but filled with desperation. Much like Mac just did, Finn looks over my shoulder to where I know Ronan is still standing against the wall. Ronan must give him permission because, after a moment, Finn turns around and unties the other end of the rope holding Logan's wrists to the hook hanging from the ceiling. He drops like a rock, crying out in pain once he hits the floor. I don't know what bones Mac broke, but I know there's no way he can stand. He can't fight me.

I'm the bigger one now.

Flexing my hand around the handle of the bat I try to come up with something to say, anything. But no words form. I can't focus on anything besides the unbridled fury. It's consumed me, and I hate it. I have to get rid of it.

Just as I'm about to move, a hand grips my shoulder firmly.

When I look down at it I see it's adorned with black ink and silver metal. *Ronan.*

"Harper. Baby girl. Listen to me." His voice is low and calm. "If this is what you want to do, none of us will stand in your way. But this isn't who you are. It won't make you feel better. Taking this piece of shit's life will eat you alive, and he doesn't deserve to haunt you any more than he already has."

Tears start streaming down my face. "I want to be strong like you."

His hand leaves my shoulder and wraps around the nape of my neck. "You are strong, Baby. So, so strong. Not doing this doesn't make you weak. You're not like us, Harper, and for that, I've never been more grateful. Don't let this man snuff out your light—our light."

"I–I have to do this, Ronan."

A heavy sigh falls from his lips before he lets go of me. "Okay, Baby."

I wait for him to step back, but he doesn't move. Looking down at Logan, curled up in a ball on the cold cement floor, I finally find the words. "I could have helped you. No one deserves to be punished for loving who they love. Had you asked for help, I would have given that to you. *We* could have given that to you. A new life. But instead, you tried to take mine, and for that, you will never know peace."

Clutching the bat in both hands, I raise it over my head, still feeling Ronan pressed against my back, ready to bring it down on Logan's head. To extinguish the fire that's burning me alive. Yet when my brain tells my arms to move, my heart stops me. No matter how hard I will it, my body doesn't move.

Come on, Harp. Be strong. Do it.

I repeat it to myself over and over, but my arms don't move a goddamn inch. So I do the only other thing I can think of.

I scream.

I scream at the top of my lungs. A scream so loud it sounds as if I'm dying. And when I can't stand anymore, I drop the bat to my side and land on my knees. Ronan follows and holds me in his arms on the floor as screams continue to pour out of me. Logan's eyes are shut tight, refusing to look at the damage he helped create as I continue trying to purge the blaze from my body.

"I can't do it. I'm not strong enough. They broke me, Ronan." My words are barely understandable as I gasp for breath. "He broke me."

I faintly feel Finn fall to the ground next to me, my body now fully cradled in Ronan's arms. He starts stroking my face as I continue to sob uncontrollably. Mac follows him but kneels before me, blocking my view of Logan.

"You are not broken, Harper. Do you hear me?" Mac's voice is uncharacteristically stern, mirroring that of his brother. "You are the strongest person in this room. You are so much stronger than him—than either of them."

He doesn't have to say their names for me to know who "them" is.

"They will never break you, Baby."

With Ronan still holding me and Finn caressing my face, Mac grabs my chin between his thumb and forefinger, forcing my cloudy eyes to look at him. "You don't need to do this, Mo Grá. Let me do this for you."

My chin quivers. "I–I thought I could do it, that I could handle it. But–but I can't, Mac. I can't do it."

"And that's okay, Harper. I can. I can do this for you. Let

me."

The three of them share a look I don't quite understand before Ronan stands with me in his arms, and Finn follows. "You two good to stay and help Mac?"

"Gladly." Dante's deep voice floats through the room. I forgot the two of them were even here.

"Where—where are we going?"

"To show you that you can handle anything." Ronan's deep voice vibrates against the side of my face.

I look back at Mac just as he's shedding his shirt. Once he pulls it over his head, he winks at me and mouths, "I love you."

Finn opens the door, and Ronan carries my shaking body from the room toward the elevator. Once the three of us step into the elevator, Ronan turns to the side so Finn can also touch me. With my body safely tucked between theirs my eyes drift shut before the elevator doors even close.

37

Harper

After what feels like only a few minutes, Finn's and Ronan's voices pull me out of a light sleep. I'm no longer in Ronan's arms and am now in what feels like a bed; judging by the rich smell of whiskey and smoke that covers the sheets, it's safe to guess I'm in his room.

My body feels completely exhausted. I'm mentally and physically wrung out, not only from my evening with Finn but because of everything that just happened in that room. So when I go to open my eyes, and everything is dark, I think it's simply because my body physically doesn't have enough energy to open them. It takes a few seconds for me to register the smooth silk fabric draped across my lids. I'm blindfolded.

The moment that realization hits, my body goes into panic mode. When I move to lift my hand to rip the blindfold off my face, my panic only intensifies. My arm won't move; neither of them will. Gasping for breath, I check my ankles to find I can't move them either. The same silk that's wrapped around my eyes is being used to tie me to the bed, and I'm completely naked.

No, no, no, no, no.

I can't breathe. I can't handle this. I'm not ready. No. *No.* This can't happen.

I'm gasping for breath when a firm hand cups my face, causing me to jump out of my skin.

"Shhh, Baby. It's just me. Finn and I are the only ones here."

"Ronan." I shake my head back and forth on the bed. "Baby, I can't do this. I'm not ready. I'm not."

"You are, Baby. You're safe. You can do this."

Finn's hand runs along my leg on the other side of the bed. "You look so beautiful, Angel. Our brave girl."

My panicked breath slows ever-so-slightly now that both of them are touching me.

"Harper, nothing is going to happen to you. It's just me and Finn. You're safe."

"I'm safe?"

"You're safe. Focus on the sound of our voices."

Deep breath in.

"The touch of our hands." Finn's hand slides over my hip and up my side.

Deep breath out.

"The feel of our lips." Ronan softly kisses my cheek.

Deep breath in.

"The taste of our kiss." Finn's lips find mine, his tongue teases the seam of my lips, and I let him quickly ravage my mouth. When he pulls away, I find myself blindly trying to follow him.

Deep breath out.

While my heart is still racing, I find that my breathing has slowed.

"That's our good girl," Finn says against my lips before quickly kissing me once more.

I listen as his feet pad about the room when Ronan's lips brush against the shell of my ear. "What's the word, Baby?"

"Bubbles," I whisper.

"You say it, and everything stops."

He and I go through this every time. And while it may be redundant, I am always grateful for it. Because in a situation where I feel like I have no control, he's reminding me that I'm the one who has it all.

"Yes, sir."

Ronan bites down on my ear, and the pain causes an unexpected but very welcome wave of pleasure to pool between my legs.

I'm ready. I can do this.

As I listen to them move around the room, I find it hard to stop my thoughts from drifting to whatever is happening downstairs. There's a heavy sense of shame and embarrassment sitting in my gut, even though I know it's completely unnecessary. While part of me knows that it's understandable why I wasn't able to kill Logan myself, nor is anyone judging me for not being able to carry out such a gruesome act, the other part of me genuinely wishes I could have done it.

My mind starts to wander to everything that could have happened to me if I hadn't gotten away, to everything that could still happen should Declan get to me. I have to force myself not to slip down that path, at least for now. Right now,

I need to be here with them.

There's no need to be afraid right now.

They'll keep me safe.

Hands pull at the ties around my ankles. "We're going to untie your legs, Angel."

When both of my ankles are free, my immediate instinct is to bring my legs together, but I don't. I keep them where they are, forcing myself to stay still until they tell me to move while doing my best to control my breathing. The sense of panic is still there, but it's not quite as loud.

I'm ready.

I'm safe.

Cold metal touches my stomach, right above my navel. The heavy object moves up my abdomen and between the valley of my breasts. When it reaches the base of my neck, Ronan says, "Open."

My lips immediately follow his command.

"Stick your tongue out."

I do as he says, and the metal object runs across it a few times before Ronan pushes it deeper into my mouth. "Close."

My lips clamp shut, and I swirl my tongue around whatever's there.

The snap of a cap opening comes from the end of the bed, and I feel the mattress dip as Finn crawls between my legs. "Bend your knees. Feet flat on the bed."

Where both of their voices were filled with love and care only minutes ago, they are now severe and unbending. I'd be lying if I said the sound didn't soothe the cracks in the deepest parts of my soul.

With my mouth still wrapped around the metal object, Finn's wet fingers find my back hole. Applying a bit of pressure, he slowly inserts one, then two fingers inside of me. "That's it, Angel."

Ronan frees my mouth of the metal object. "We're going to put this inside you, Baby."

I swallow hard and nod.

Ronan must hand Finn the plug because they stay where they are. Finn slides his fingers out and presses the plug against the ring of muscle. The fact that I can't see what's happening makes my body tense in anticipation. "Relax for me, Angel. Bare down and let me in."

"Yes—" I cut myself off, not knowing what the rules are and what I can say in front of Ronan.

"Say it, Harper," Finn snaps.

"Yes, Daddy."

Ronan moans. "Fucking hell. That shouldn't turn me on."

My lips turn up, and then Finn's pushing the plug inside of me. "Ohhh."

When the plug is all the way inside, Finn runs his hand up and down my thighs. "Damn, Angel."

"How does she look, brother?"

"Like our perfect little whore." A small whimper escapes my lips, and Ronan leans down so his lips brush against mine.

"You like that, Baby Girl? You like being stuffed full for us? Filled to the brim like a filthy slut?"

"Yes, sir." I feel like I could come right here, right now, and I know they've barely even started.

"Good. Because when Finn and I are done with you, that's what you're going to be. Fucking filthy."

38

Finn

"Eat her pussy, Finn." Don't have to ask me twice.

Firmly pressing on the jeweled base of the metal plug, I bend over and run my tongue over her dripping cunt. Pushing my tongue in and out of her every time I pass over her opening. When I look up at her as my teeth tug at her clit I see Ronan's hands pulling at both of her nipples, his mouth feasting on her neck. Harper's back bows off the bed. "Ahhh. Yes!"

I love how responsive she is to our touch.

Grabbing the inside of one of her thick thighs in a bruising grip, I pin it to the bed. Ronan follows suit, holding her other leg. Now she's spread open for me, completely at my mercy. "Fuck, Angel. You taste so fucking good. I could spend my entire life between these legs."

Harper's fists wrap around the silk, tying her hands to

either side of the bed as I dive my tongue against her. Ronan's hands continue to roam over her body, playing with her breasts and pulling at her hair.

"Oh my God," she cries out as I rapidly flick her clit with my tongue. Ronan's mouth finds hers, swallowing every moan and cry.

"I want you to come all over my tongue, Harper. Come all over my face." My tongue continues to lap up every bit of pleasure that's pouring out of her. Suddenly, her entire body goes tense, and I know her orgasm is right on the edge.

Tearing her mouth from Ronan's, she screams, "Fuck, Finn. Love . . . I'm-I'm . . . going to come. Oh, God."

She called me by my name, but I don't even care. I'm too desperate to taste her release to stop and reprimand her.

I bury my face so deep between her legs it's hard to breathe. When she's just about to come, I shove two fingers inside of her, curling them so they hit just the right spot, as Ronan bites down on her nipple.

"Ronan! Finn!" Her euphoric screams make my cock throb behind my pants as I continue licking up her sweet release. Her orgasm rips through her body, and the fact that she's unable to see or move her arms or legs only makes it drag out longer.

It's one of the most beautiful things I've ever seen.

Her tight pussy pulses around my fingers. "You better squeeze our cocks like this, Angel." I curl my fingers up against her G-spot and firmly press against the plug once more for good measure.

"Ohhh," she desperately whines.

Pulling my fingers out of her, I crawl up the bed until I'm straddling her full hips. Ronan and I share a look before he slides the blindfold off of her face. My breath catches in my throat as her glossy green eyes look between us. I'm suddenly hit with the overwhelming urge to kiss her. So I do.

My mouth devours hers, my tongue fucking her mouth as hard as it just did her cunt, letting her taste her release on my tongue. Ronan grabs my wrist, and I pull my mouth from hers. "Let me taste. I'm fucking dying."

My eyes whip to Harper, then back at Ronan, and he shrugs, as if me sticking my fingers in his mouth is no big deal.

You know what, fuck it.

If we plan to share this woman for the rest of our lives, we better get real comfortable with one another. With his hand still wrapped around my wrist, he lifts it to his mouth, and I unashamedly slide my middle and pointer fingers inside. His tongue laps up every last bit of release on my fingers, careful not to waste a drop. Ronan's eyes close and a deep rumble sounds from his chest. Harper's hips thrust below me as she moans, "Holy shit."

Ronan's eyes fly open, and I pull my fingers from his mouth. He has a satisfied smile on his face as he licks his lips. "Absolutely fucking delicious."

"She is, isn't she?"

"That—that was one of the hottest things I've ever seen."

He winks. "We aim to please, Baby."

"Can I touch you now, please?"

I look at Ronan in question since tying her up was his idea in the first place. It was never our intention to keep her tied to the bed all night. We just wanted to show her she's stronger than her fears. Just like we know she is.

"I suppose you deserve a reward for doing so well."

Leaning over, I untie one wrist while Ronan does the other.

The moment her hands are free, they wrap around me, pulling my chest to hers. Her fingers run through my hair as she kisses me as if her life depended on it.

I've never enjoyed kissing a woman as much as I enjoy kissing her. It's never been a sensual act for me, just something I did when I even bothered with the touch of a woman. It never lit my body on fire like it does with Harper. Hell, the woman just looks in my direction, and the world tilts on its axis.

Ronan lies on the bed beside us, and I force my lips from Harper's. I look over at him as he holds his hand out to find he's shed his clothes at some point and is now naked. "Come over here, Baby."

I climb off Harper's waist and move toward the end of the bed while she gets situated on top of him. With my clothes now forgotten on the floor, I grab the lube from the mattress, squirt a generous amount onto my hand and wrap it around my aching cock. I know Harper's plenty wet, but for what Ronan and I have planned, I want to be sure.

"Baby," Harper's wanton voice draws my attention back up the bed where Ronan's already buried balls deep inside of her. Harper's head is thrown back, her long chocolate curls cascading down her back, her luscious ass shaking with every slap against Ronan's thighs, her entire body glistening with a thin sheen of sweat.

Moving back up the bed, between Ronan's legs and behind Harper, I grab her hair and push it forward over her shoulder. With my hand on the center of her back, I push her down so her chest is flat against Ronan's. Ronan's thrusts slow but never stop. With her juicy ass in the air, silver plug nestled between her cheeks, I can't help myself. My hand slaps one cheek, and a loud crack fills the room.

"Oh fuck, Finn."

"Did that hurt?"

"Yes."

"Good." I bring my hand down against the other cheek. I do it again and again, alternating sides.

"Fuck, Finn. You keep doing that, and I'm not going to last. Every time you hit her, her pussy tightens around me."

"You like that, Angel?" I ask as I smooth my hand over the cherry-red skin.

"You know I do."

"Mmmm. My dirty, dirty whore."

"Finn! Jesus Christ."

I bark out a laugh, finding Ronan's torment more than funny.

I wrap my hand around my cock, giving it a few good pulls, and lean forward so my chest is now against Harper's back, leaving her sandwiched between the two of us. She has a purple mark on her neck from Ronan, so I decide to leave one of my own. My teeth clamp down on her skin, and her body shakes between us. "You know what else feels good?"

"W–what?" she mumbles against Ronan's chest.

Ronan's thrusts stop. With my dick still in my hand, I notch the head of it at her entrance right beneath Ronan's. "This."

"But I thought—the plug."

"Oh, don't you worry, Baby. The plug is staying right where it is."

Harper's breathing picks up. "It won't fit. I can't do it."

"You can and you will, Angel. You know why?"

Her body is frozen between ours. "Why?"

Ronan threads a hand through her hair and grips the back

of her head hard. "Because even though you're our dirty little slut, you're still our good girl." I push forward ever so slightly so that I'm *barely* inside of her. "So fucking good."

"And good girls do as they're told. Don't they, Baby?"

I push forward again until the entire head of my cock is inside of her, and she lets out a pained whimper. "Y-yes, sir."

"That's it. You're doing such a good job."

"I knew you could do it, Angel," I praise as I slide a few inches deeper. Harper's hands fist the sheets in a deathly grip as mine, and Ronan's hands roam her body. "I'm almost there."

"Finnnnn." The way she drags my name out makes my cock twitch inside her impossibly tight channel. Between the plug and Ronan's cock, I've never felt anything like it, and I know I never will.

It's fucking nirvana.

When it's clear I can't push forward anymore, I stop, even though I'm barely halfway in. This is our first time doing this, and I don't want to push her too far. But fuck me, do I hope it's not the last, not by a long shot. "You should see yourself, Angel. You look beautiful with your tight pussy filled with our cocks and this plug in your ass."

"You–you have to move."

"Yeah, Finn. We *have* to fucking move."

I slowly, and I mean so fucking slowly, slide out of her, and when just the tip is left inside, I push back in while Ronan pulls out.

"Holy shit . . . that feels . . ." Her words are cut off when Ronan and I pick up the pace.

"We know, Baby. We know," Ronan soothes, one hand still firmly fisting her hair, one wrapped around her back. I sit up straight so I'm able to take in the scene below me. With my hands gripping Harper's waist hard enough to bruise, I watch as mine and Ronan's cocks slide in and out of her in perfect rhythm.

"Yes. Yes. Yes . . ." Harper's chants cause my balls to draw up, and I do everything I can to stop myself from coming.

Grabbing the base of the plug, I start gently pushing it in and out of her, matching the tempo of our thrusts. The walls of her pussy start to get so tight around us that it's a miracle we can even move anymore.

"Fuck . . . me," she whispers as her body tenses between us, and she screams out in pleasure. And unlike the screams she let out in that parking garage, these are ones I could never get tired of hearing. Her cunt continues to tighten around us, so much so that the edge of my vision grows black.

I vaguely hear Ronan grunt as he comes deep inside of her, and then I finally let go.

I slam the plug back inside of her ass.

I grip both her hips.

And I thrust until bursts of pleasure rip through my body. A euphoric wave of pleasure tears through my veins at such an intensity I don't know how I'll ever be the same.

"Fuck!" I cry out as I come over and over again until it feels like she's drained me of everything I am.

Once I manage to slow my thrusts, I gently pull out of her and pull the plug from her ass. I watch as Ronan slips out of her, keeping her on top of him, and our cum spills down her thighs.

"Ronan was right. Fucking filthy." Harper giggles against his chest.

When I walk into Ronan's bathroom, wet a towel, and

return to the bed, her soft snores are already filling the room. "She passed out already?"

"Before you even made it to the bathroom."

I chuckle as Ronan gently rolls her off of him. After I'm done cleaning between her legs, Ronan and I get ourselves cleaned up, and we climb into bed on either side of her. With the covers pulled over us, she rests her head on my chest and drapes one leg over mine while Ronan curls his body around hers, burying his face in her hair.

"I knew she could do it," he mumbles into her curls.

"Never had any doubt."

He lets out a soft laugh, "Dirty fucking liar."

"Shhh," Harper grumbles against my chest, "Less talking, more sleeping."

"Yeah, Ronan. Shut up."

He reaches over her and smacks me in the forehead. "Sorry, Baby."

"I love you guys."

"Love you," Ronan and I answer in unison.

Turning my head, I place a soft kiss on the crown of her head. "More than anything."

39

Harper

The sound of pots and pans in the kitchen wakes me from my sleep. Still sandwiched between a peacefully sleeping and deliciously naked Ronan and Finn, I work to unwrap their muscular appendages from around my body without waking them. Once I manage to do so, I gently crawl over Ronan and unlock his phone on his dresser to check the time.

10:30 a.m.

I don't think I've seen any of them sleep in that long the entire time I've been here. I know Mac must have just gotten up; he can't go more than twenty minutes without eating after he wakes up in the morning. Anxious to talk to him about what happened after Ronan and Finn brought me up here, I sneak into Ronan's bathroom for a quick shower.

Turning up the temperature as hot as I can stand it, I let

the water relax my aching muscles, the soreness between my legs a pleasant reminder of what happened last night.

I don't know how they did it or how they knew that was what I needed, but they turned a night that quickly made me feel like I was so irrevocably broken into one that made me feel stronger and more whole than I could have ever imagined.

And what Mac did for me was one of the most selfless things anyone has ever done for me.

I'm sure he enjoyed the act of hurting someone who brought me so much pain—brought them so much pain—relished in it even. But the fact remains that he did that for me. He loves me so much he was willing to take someone else's life for *me*.

It isn't lost on me how big of a deal that is.

Once I'm finished in the shower, I brush my teeth using the spare I keep in Ronan's bathroom. I have one in each of theirs, actually. I run my fingers through my curls and step out of the bathroom, searching for one of Ronan's shirts I can steal. I have to smother a laugh beneath my hand when I see them still passed out in Ronan's bed. Finn's on his back, honey-blonde hair sprawled out against the pillow, one arm at his side while the other rests on his light patch of hair in the center of his chest, and his mouth is hanging wide open. Ronan's lying on his side and must have scooted over after I crawled out of bed because his arm is now draped across Finn's stomach. His dark curls hang over his forehead, and deep snores cut through the silence.

I don't have my phone; it's been sitting in my purse since Mac and I got home yesterday, not that I even use it anymore anyway. So, I pick Ronan's up from on top of his dresser, take a picture, and send it to myself before setting it as his lock screen.

He's gonna love that.

Grabbing a baby-blue button-up shirt out of Ronan's closet, the same color as his eyes, I quietly sneak out of his room. The second I open Ronan's door I hear Mac's voice floating through the apartment. He's singing along to Etta James' "A Sunday Kinda Love," his light Irish accent only adding to the sweet melody.

"Well, well, well. He sings too," I say as I sneak up behind him, wrapping my arms around his lean waist as he busies himself, flipping what looks like chocolate chip pancakes.

I seriously think we'd all starve without him. That or spend a fortune on takeout.

Considering he didn't so much as flinch when I touched him, I think it's safe to assume he heard me coming, but I like to think I caught him by surprise.

Mac flips the last pancake and sets the spatula on the counter. Spinning in my arms, he wraps one muscular arm around my waist and grabs my other hand in his. Before I know it we're slowly swaying to the beat of the music. "I'm a man of many talents, Mo Grá." Leaning down, he softly kisses my lips. "Good morning."

"Morning. It smells good in here."

"I don't know about the three of you, but I'm starving. You hungry?"

"Mmmm, for your cooking? Always." I say as my stomach growls.

"Worked yourself up an appetite last night, did ya?" He dips me in his arms and winks down at me before righting us to dance along with the rest of the song.

My cheeks heat. "Possibly."

"Shame I couldn't join."

A wave of guilt sweeps over me. "I'm sorry about last night. Wh–what happened after we left?"

His smile doesn't falter as he quickly tucks a strand of hair behind my ear. "I'll tell you all about it once they wake up. We will talk about that bastard once more and once more only. He doesn't deserve any more of our time."

"Okay, Honey."

"Okay, Pretty Girl."

As we dance in the kitchen, like a scene out of my favorite romance book, I find myself staring deep into his steel-gray eyes. "Thank you, for what you did."

Mac drops his forehead to mine. "What I did is nothing. I would give my life for you. Every second of every day, this," with my hand still in his, he rests them both over his beating heart, "beats for you. You are now the reason blood flows through my veins. You're the reason I take every breath. You are the reason this heart beats. There is no limit to what I would do for you."

This man. This beautiful, funny, loving, loyal, dangerous, violent, complex man whose soul calls to mine. He is a man who cares for the ones he loves with everything he has while still thinking that part of him is a monster. But the part of him that he calls a monster, the one he was so afraid of me seeing downstairs in that room, might be the part I love the most. It shows how loyal he is to the ones that mean the most to him. That he would bloody his hands so they don't have to.

"Cormac McDermott, I love you with everything I am."

Pulling his forehead from mine, he takes my face in his.

"Harper Hayes, I love you with everything I'm not."

Mac's mouth crashes into mine, and I sink into it. We stand in the middle of the kitchen, kissing one another so deeply it's as if we won't survive until we get our fill. It's only when the song ends and the smell of overcooked pancakes hits Mac's nose that he finally pulls away—leaving me panting and wanting more. Regardless of everything that happened between Finn, Ronan, and me last night and how sore my body feels, my body craves his.

An idea pops into my head just as Mac stacks the last chocolate chip pancake onto the plate and turns off the stove. "Are those two planning on joining us any time today?"

I laugh and pull my barely charged phone from my purse on the counter. "I don't know, they looked pretty comfortable to me," I say as I flash Mac the picture I sent from Ronan's phone, and he laughs.

"Well, don't they just look adorable? I knew they were best friends, but who knew they were so close," he says jokingly. As Mac turns around to open the fridge, memories of how close the two of them were last night flash through my mind. Finn letting Ronan suck my release off of his fingers will live forever in my memory.

If I wasn't horny before, I definitely am now.

Mac pulls a bowl of cut strawberries and another of whipped cream out of the fridge, along with some maple syrup.

I hop up on the counter as he sets everything down. "Did you make homemade whipped cream?"

He shrugs. "I know it's your favorite."

Mac's eyes roam my bare legs before stepping in between them. Reaching over, I dip my finger in the bowl of whipped cream, suck it into my mouth, and watch as Mac's eyes darken.

"How is it?" he asks.

I dip my finger back into the bowl and bring it to his lips. "See for yourself."

His lips part, and I slide my finger inside. His tongue licks around my finger, not leaving a trace of whipped cream behind. "I don't know. Might have to try again."

A devious smile spreads across my face. He takes a bit of cream on his finger and runs it down my neck. Leaning forward, he drags his tongue from the base of my neck to my jaw. "Hmmm, something's missing. Hold on. Let me try again."

Stepping back, he trails the whipped cream up the inside of my thigh, starting at my knee and reaching under Ronan's shirt until his finger brushes against my throbbing pussy. My entire body lights up as Mac runs his tongue along my leg, and when it grazes over my pussy I inhale a sharp breath.

Standing upright with a hedonistic look in his eye, he licks his lips. "That's what it was missing. Absolutely delicious."

Since he's not wearing a shirt, as per usual, I reach out and grab him by the waistband of his jeans, momentarily ignoring the erection that is begging to be touched, and pull him back to me. Taking a deep breath, I summon up the courage I know I have. The courage that Finn and Ronan reminded me I never lost in the first place. "Will you let me try something?"

The corner of Mac's mouth tips up in an adorable smirk, "You can try anything you want to with me, Pretty Girl."

Curiosity lights up his face as I push him away and hop off the counter. "Put this stuff away and meet me in your room. We'll eat later."

I sneak past him and walk out of the kitchen and back toward Ronan's room. "Yes, ma'am."

Stopping, I look at him over my shoulder. "Best remember those words." I wink at him and watch his mouth drop open before sauntering away, making sure to sway my hips just a little bit extra.

I quietly slip back into Ronan's room with a smile as I hear Mac frantically putting everything back into the fridge. Finn and Ronan are still in the same position I left them, making my smile grow. Moving to his side of the bed, I softly kiss Finn's lips, and his eyes flutter open. "Angel?"

"Shhh, I didn't want to wake you, but I just wanted to see if I could borrow some things from your room."

"You can take whatever you need. It's your home, too."

Shit, that was cute.

"Thank you."

"What do you need?"

I hesitate momentarily but remember I have nothing to be embarrassed about. "Just some things. I need to show Mac a thing or two."

A sleepy smile spreads across his face. He may be talking to me, but I can tell he's not entirely with it, especially considering Ronan's arm is still draped across him. "Mmmm, about time. Show him what I taught you, Angel."

Just like that, his eyes fall shut. Pressing one last kiss to his forehead, I whisper, "I love you," and slip back out of the room.

I run down the hall into Finn's room and grab what I need. Stopping in front of Mac's door, I quickly set the items on the floor and unbutton Ronan's shirt, leaving only the bottom two buttons done, so the shirt falls open at my breasts, the baby-blue fabric barely covering my erect nipples.

Picking the items off the floor, I take a deep breath and open Mac's door. While Finn and Ronan's rooms are neatly organized, Finn's neurotically so, Mac's is the opposite. Exactly how you imagine his room would be. While it's not dirty, it's definitely unorganized. Books are stacked sporadically throughout his room, some on top of his nightstands, some on the floor. His dark bedding lays haphazardly across his bed, and for someone who doesn't like wearing shirts, he has an awful lot of them thrown across his room.

Standing at the foot of his bed, Mac's eyes study my body, stopping once at my breasts and then again when he sees what I have in my hand.

"Still wanna try?" I ask as his eyes go comically wide.

After a beat, he looks back up at me and swallows hard before answering as he did in the kitchen, "Anything."

"Good Boy.

40

Harper

"Holy fuck."

"Pick a word, Honey," I demand as I slowly approach where he's frozen in place.

"I don't need one." The closer I get to him, the more prominent the bulge beneath his jeans becomes. "Whatever you want to do, I'm yours."

"I need one. I've never done this, and I'd feel better if you picked one. So, for me, pick a word."

His eyes track my movements as I toss everything but the black nylon rope on the bed behind me. When his stare moves back to my face, I notice the faraway look on his face. "Red."

I nod, and just like that, I watch him pull himself back to the present. "You say red, and I stop. Okay?"

His flirtatious smirk takes over his face again. "I won't, but okay."

I smile and roll my eyes despite myself. "Lose the jeans, Mac."

I watch with rapt attention as Mac makes a spectacle of slowly unbuttoning his jeans and sliding them down his muscular legs. All three of them have bodies that look like they were crafted by the gods. But even though Ronan and Finn are slightly taller and more broad than Mac, it doesn't mean he is lacking in comparison. In fact, I'd argue that his leaner form enhances his perfectly chiseled muscles. It's clear, just by looking at him, which I can't seem to look away if my life depended on it, that Mac's body was crafted for a specific set of skills. Underneath his intricate tattoos are corded arms used to inflict damage upon those that cross them, built legs used to carry the weight of his responsibilities, a narrow waist, perfect for me to wrap my legs around, and a cock that's used to bring me pleasure, unlike anything I've ever known.

Mac kicks his jeans to the side of the room, and I'm pleased to see he's gone his usual commando underneath. His dick is hard, and standing upright against his lower stomach, I have to stifle a moan when I see a bead of precum already beading at the tip. I haven't even so much as touched him yet.

I knew he would like this.

His chest heaving, he stands in front of me, waiting for my next instruction. "Lay on the bed for me."

I watch as his cock twitches before he says, "Yes, ma'am," and I swear to God, a wave of pleasure runs through my body at his words alone.

I never thought I would like being dominant, especially considering how much I love it when they boss me around. I'm a submissive by nature, and I love it. But the other day, when I fucked Mac on that kitchen chair, when I climbed on top of him and used his body to bring myself pleasure, it woke something inside of me. Judging by the way his eyes darken every time I've called him a "good boy" or the way his breath hitches when I get a little rough with him, I think it's safe to say it woke something he didn't know he wanted inside of him too.

Once Mac's laying on his bed, head resting on his pillows, I walk around the side. "Hands."

Eagerly, Mac holds his hands out, and I tie his wrists together in a simple knot. Mac, only having a low sitting platform bed, doesn't have a headboard like Finn or Ronan, so I grab the knot between his wrists and pull his hands up to rest on the bed just above his head. "I don't have anything to tie you to, so can I trust you'll leave them there?"

He nods, and I drag the tips of my fingers down his arm, along his abdomen, over his hips—careful not to touch his cock—and down his leg as I make my way back to the foot of the bed.

With his eyes glued on mine, I slowly unbutton the rest of Ronan's shirt and let it fall to the floor. Mac's eyes move over my entire body, over and over again, as if he can't get enough, and it only builds my confidence more.

I can do this.

I drag my hand up my stomach, stopping once I reach my breast. Taking my swollen nipple between my fingers, I pinch it hard while my other hand skates between my legs. As I press my fingers against my clit I feel a rush of heat drip down my thighs.

"You're so beautiful."

"So are you." He is *so* beautiful.

Unable to keep my hands off him any longer, I climb between his spread legs. Leaning forward, I run my tongue up the inside of his leg, just like he did to me in the kitchen. When my mouth reaches his upper thigh, just below his balls, he lets out a deep moan. Careful not to touch him where he wants most, I lift my mouth and repeat the same motion along his other leg. Once I reach the top of his thigh, I lift my tongue once again.

"Pretty girl," he groans.

I smile up at him as my tongue meets his stomach, and the smell of ginger and cedarwood fills my senses. Crawling up his body, careful not to lift my mouth, I drag my tongue until it finds the shell of his neck. With my legs now straddling his, I make sure I lift my hips high enough so they don't brush against him. His hips lift off the bed slightly, and I bite down against his skin. "Are you going to be a good boy and stay still?"

"For you, I'll be such a good fucking boy."

Emboldened, I move my mouth over his nipple. After lapping it with my tongue a few times, I take it between my teeth and give it a sharp tug.

"Shit . . ." he groans. I release it and work across his chest, paying the same attention to the other.

Good to know I'm not the only one who likes having my nipples played with.

"Harper, touch me, please. I'm dying here."

Pulling my mouth from his chest, I smile up at him deviously and put my finger to my lips as if I'm thinking hard about his request. "Hmmm, tempting, but I don't think I will."

His head falls back with a groan, and I have to stifle a laugh.

Sitting upright, I shuffle forward on my knees until I straddle his chest. "Think I'll take something for myself instead."

Careful not to hurt his arms, I rise up and place my knees in the space between his bent arms and the side of his face, his hands still bound together just above the top of his head. His eyes now have a full view of my pussy, and If I think too hard about how depraved this scene probably looks, my arousal might drip right onto his face.

Not that he would mind in the slightest.

"Jesus fuck, Harper." He tries to lift his head off the bed, but I thread a hand through his messy black hair and pin it to the bed.

"Want a taste, Honey?"

"Fuck yes, I do."

I pull his hair hard, and the moan he lets out is a mix of pain and pleasure. "What was that?"

"Yes, ma'am."

"That's my boy." Before he can get another word out, I lower my hips and sit on his face. Before I met the three of them, regardless of how confident I was or was not with my body, I would have hovered, afraid my weight and thick thighs would suffocate the poor guy underneath me. Not my guys.

They want everything I can give them.

41

Mac

I don't know where my sweet, submissive Harper has gone, but fucking hell. Never, and I mean *never*, has a woman taken charge of me like this. And what's more, I didn't think I'd like it this much.

No. I don't like it. I *love it*. I'm now obsessed with it. My dick has never been this hard in my entire life. I have never craved to be inside of Harper more than I do now. But she wants to come all over my face, and I'll be fucked if that's not what she's going to get.

The harder my tongue thrusts inside of her, the more she rocks back and forth. My hands are practically burning with the urge to wrap them around her and grab her full ass. Even with the ropes tied tight around my wrists, I know If I pulled hard enough, I could slip free, but I don't dare shatter the illusion.

Needing more, she reaches down with the hand that's not tightly gripping my hair and starts rubbing her clit. The moment her finger touches the sensitive bundle of nerves, a wave of her release coats my tongue.

God, she tastes fucking delicious.

Her pussy muffles my desperate moan, and I can feel precum dripping out of my cock and onto my stomach.

"Mac, don't stop."

Don't stop. Is she serious?

I keep tongue fucking her like my life depends on it, and in just a few seconds, she rocks her hips forward one more time before coming on my face. Her screams are drowned out as her thighs tighten around my head, muffling my ears. I continue to lap up every delicious ounce of her release until she lifts herself off of me.

Shuffling over my shoulders so she's back to straddling my chest, covering it in her cum, she bends down and slams her lips against mine. Harper pushes her tongue inside my mouth, and as she tastes her release, I swallow her wanton moan.

She pulls off, breathless, and just when I think she's going to grant me mercy and return the favor, she moves back down my body toward the end of the bed. With a satisfied smile on her face, she picks up the other item she brought in.

Pressing the jeweled button on the end, the small buck bullet buzzes to life. Still kneeling between my legs, she reaches out and runs the vibrator up the length of my dick. Pleasure lights up my body from my head all the way to my damn toes, and I have to clench my teeth to stop myself from blowing my load all over my stomach.

"Does that feel good?" Her sultry voice further adds to my

struggle.

"Mhmmm."

Harper runs the vibrator over the head of my dick, and when she drags it through my leaking slit, I jump. The vibrations are almost more than I can handle. "Say it, Mac. Tell me how it feels."

"It feels . . . *fuck,* so fucking good." She continues working the small black toy up and down my dick. Each pass feels like torture, yet at the same time, I never want it to fucking end.

"Mo Grá," I say through gritted teeth when I finally feel like I can't hold it anymore. "If you don't stop I'm going to come."

She gives me that devious grin again, as if she's really thinking hard about her options when we both know that's a fucking lie, before turning off the toy and throwing it on the floor behind her. I can't decide whether or not I'm relieved or immediately want it back. "Can't have that, can we."

Leaning forward, she grabs my dick with one hand. The feel of her skin finally touching me causes my eyes to roll back into my head. Then she runs her tongue over the head of my dick, tasting the obnoxious amount of precum, and I swear I'm done for. But, as if she read my mind, she reaches up and grabs my jaw in her delicate hand, forcing my eyes to open and look down at her. "No. You don't come anywhere but inside of me."

I'll say it again—*Jesus. Fucking. Christ.*

I nod frantically. "Yes, ma'am."

"Good boy." Just like the first time she said them to me the day in the kitchen when she cut my hair and trusted me with her body again, the words light a fire deep inside me. One so deep I can feel it warm the very core of who I am. They light something that only burns for *her.*

In what feels like the span of two seconds, Harper's legs are on either side of my waist, and her wet cunt is sliding down my cock. With her hands on my abs and her head thrown back, she looks like a fucking goddess. One I will gladly worship until the day I die.

"Mac, you feel so good. So. Damn. Good." Her hips rock, enunciating each word.

"Take what you need, Pretty Girl. Use my dick. Make yourself come."

Harper's nails dig into my stomach as her walls tighten around me; the urge to rip through my binds and touch her grows stronger with each passing second. My eyes bounce back and forth between her blissed-out face to where her pussy slides up and down on my cock, unable to decide which is better.

"Honey . . . Mac . . . Yes. Yes. *Yes!*" Harper begins to shake as she comes violently on top of me, using my body for nothing more than her pleasure. She hangs her head forward as her pussy continues to pulse around me, and I want nothing more than to grab her hair in my hands.

Fuck this.

With one strong, quick pull, I yank my wrists apart, and the rope falls free. Her shocked, yet not all that surprised, eyes meet mine, and the corner of my lips turn up. Grabbing a fist full of her curls, I pull her mouth down to mine and quickly flip us over so she's beneath me. "Mo Grá, please . . ."

She threads her hands through my hair and wraps her legs around my waist to connect her ankles behind my back. "Please, what?"

She wants me to beg? I don't even care.

"I need to come. Please. *Please* let me come." I slowly pull out of her, and I can feel her cunt tighten around me as if she's trying to hold me deep inside of her.

"You want to fill me, Mac?"

"Yes."

"Since you did so good—"

She doesn't even get to finish her sentence before I push my hips forward, slamming into her so hard, so desperately, that her body slides up the bed, and she cries out.

I only have to slide into her once, twice, three times before I come deep inside of her perfect fucking pussy. I come so much that when I pull out of her, I watch as it spills out of her and onto the black sheets below. Not wanting to waste a drop of her hard work, I run my fingers through her folds and push my cum back inside of her. I flop down onto the mattress next to her on my back, and we both turn our heads to look at one another. The proud look on her face warms my chest. I'm not sure whether she's proud of herself for taking control or me for letting her—hopefully, a little bit of both.

"I don't know what that was about," I say as I reach over and run my thumb across her swollen bottom lip. "But that needs to happen *waaay* more often."

"Yeah? You liked it?"

"Did I like it? Mo Grá, watching you take control was one of the hottest things I've seen in my entire life. There was not a single second of that I did not like."

Her warm giggle floats through the air. Just as I'm about to pull her into my arms, my bedroom door flies open.

Ronan shoves in, clearly feigning annoyance as he crosses his arms over his naked chest. In fact, all of him is naked. I give him a look that says, "What the fuck?" and he gestures his hand out in front of him, waving it over our naked bodies. "What, if you two get to be naked, why don't I? Morning, Baby."

I glance over at Harper and find that she's eyeing him up like she wants to eat him. Looking back at my fuckhead of a brother, I see that he's giving her the same look. Finally, he breaks eye contact with her and gives me the same devious smile that Harper had.

How much you want to bet, that's where she learned it from.

"Ronan, if you don't piss off right now—"

He holds his hands up in surrender. "Okay, okay. But if you two are done fucking in here, Finn and I would like to eat."

"We were waiting for you two to be done cuddling."

Ronan looks back at Harper, this time glaring at her like she's spilled some national secret, but we all know there's no real heat behind his stare. Relenting, I sigh, "We'll be right there."

"Good boy." Before I can jump from the bed, Ronan's naked ass sprints from the room, and Harper snorts, slapping a hand over her mouth.

"That's it, Finn's my favorite."

42

Declan

"He was supposed to check in three hours ago. Something fucking happened!" I bark at one of the guards I brought with me to this god-forsaken fucking country. I didn't bother sending one of them to tail Logan because I knew he could barely get up to take a piss, let alone run from me. Besides, he doesn't have the fucking balls. He's supposed to call me every morning at eight. It's now eleven, and not a word. Either his wound finally killed him, or they got to him. "Track his phone. Now."

It takes him only seconds to pull up the location of Logan's phone on his computer, and when he does, his entire face goes pale. His terrified expression looks up at me as if he's afraid I'll put a bullet in his head right here on the spot.

I just fucking might.

"Where?"

"His phone has been at this address in the city since last night." His shaking finger points to the screen, where a red

310

dot flashes on an address I know all too well.

Son of a fucking bitch.

"Do you think he's alive?" he asks.

"Highly unlikely." Honestly, I don't even care at this point. Logan has been nothing but disappointment after disappointment. He was one more fuckup away from me killing him myself, but that's beside the point. Because once again, those men and my disgrace of a granddaughter have fucked up my plans.

When I killed the Donovan's, shortly after Freya and Aidan fled the country, I hoped that would send the appropriate message to the McDermott syndicate. One of their men had already stolen my only child, and then they tried to take Ireland from me. They needed to understand that I was not a man to be trifled with. So, I showed them just how cruel I could be. Since then, they've steered clear of me. Even when I killed Freya and Aidan, they didn't retaliate. Years had gone by, and I remained in control; that is, until my men decided that my age and some gray hair meant I was losing it. They started thinking I was out of touch. That I was going soft. More and more frequently, they began turning to Patrick for orders. They started confiding in him and doing things his way. And before I knew it, I was nothing more than the "old man" who simply claimed he was in charge.

Then I found out about Harper. Her parents and Cece did an excellent job hiding her from me, but not good enough. When I found out about her, my first instinct was to erase her just like I did Freya and Aidan. But then I caught Logan with his dick inside of another man, and another idea came to fruition.

When Freya, my daughter, met Aidan all those years ago

and turned her back on her family, I knew I wouldn't have an heir. All I wanted was for Harper to marry Logan, create the next generation of Whelans, and stop Patrick from undoing everything I've spent years building because if I have Patrick killed in Ireland, any support I have left will go right out the window.

I didn't think that was too much to fucking ask.

But, just like her mother used to, Harper has evaded me at every turn.

No one betrays me and gets away with it. So, just like her mother, I'm about to put an end to her too.

Not the McDermotts.

Not the Donovans.

Not Logan.

Not my own daughter and her husband.

And certainly not their disgraceful daughter.

Had I known she was alive all those years ago, I would have waited until she was in the car with them.

Enough is fucking enough.

I'm Delcan fucking Whelan, for Christ's sake.

"Burn it."

It's time to show them who the hell I am. Before I destroy them, I will destroy everything they hold dear.

"Boss?"

"Hayes' Bookstore. Burn it the fuck down."

43

Ronan

"You okay, Baby?" My hand holds Harper's tight, spinning my signet ring on her thumb with mine.

Once we finished breakfast, Mac filled us in on what happened with Logan. He spared the most gruesome details, wanting to protect Harper from hearing more than she needed to, but Finn and I knew. We knew that there wasn't an inch of Logan's body that wasn't screaming in pure agony by the time Mac granted him the mercy of death.

Mac also told us he had our clean-up crew come bag up the body, which means he dismembered it, hence the purpose of the empty room with a drain in the middle of the floor, and shoved it into plastic bags before burying it in one of the dozens of abandoned lots I own on the outskirts of the city.

We're all waiting to see if the same panic that took hold of Harper last night is about to resurface, but much to my surprise and immense pleasure, she looks perfectly calm.

"Is it terrible of me if I said I'm glad he's gone?"

I lift her hand to my mouth and kiss the back of it. "Not even a little bit. He deserved everything he got and more. Nobody hurts our girl and lives."

"Then yeah, I'm okay."

As if the universe could sense that those words just came out of Harper's mouth, Trevor's name, one of the guys I have watching the bookstore, flashes on my phone as it vibrates on the counter.

Mac and Finn see his name, and their entire bodies instantly harden, preparing for what's on the other end of the phone call.

Hitting accept, I answer and bring the phone to my ear, "What's up?"

"It's on fucking fire!"

"What is?" My grip immediately tightens around Harper's hand.

"Hayes'! I don't know what happened, but the whole thing just burst into fucking flames, Boss."

Fuck.

"How bad?" My eyes are bouncing between Finn's and Mac's, trying to silently convey the severity of the situation.

"Really fucking bad. There won't be anything left. The buildings next to it are in bad shape too. The fire department is already here and working on putting it out. This is the first chance I've had to call you."

"Don't move. We'll be right there."

Mac and Finn are already moving towards their rooms to get dressed when Harper asks, "What's going on?"

I force myself to meet her eyes for the first time since the phone rang, worry etched across her face. But I know as soon as I tell her what happened, that worry will be replaced with absolute despair.

"It's the bookstore."

She's up from her chair in a flash. "What happened? Did someone break in?"

Standing from my spot, I hold her face in my hands. "Why don't you sit down, Baby."

"I don't want to sit down, Ronan. Tell me what happened. What's wrong with my store?"

I let out a regretful sigh. "There's a fire."

Harper gasps and lifts her hand to her mouth, her eyes immediately welling with tears. "No."

"I'm so, so sorry, Harper."

"How–how bad is it?"

"The fire department is working on putting it out right now, but . . ."

A small tear slides over the freckles on her cheek. "Just tell me."

"Trevor said it's—he said it's gone, Baby."

A strangled sob escapes her lips before her eyes grow wide. "Oh my God. The buildings next to me!"

That's my Baby Girl. One of the things she holds most dear in this world has been taken from her, and one of her first instincts is to think of someone else.

"He said they're in bad shape too. We'll go there right now and see how bad it is and go from there. Okay?"

She nods her head in my hands. "That was all I had left of them. That was all I had left of my parents—of Cece."

My forehead falls against hers as tears continue to fall down her face. "I know, Baby. I know."

Harper's hands wrap around my forearms like she's using me to hold herself upright. In the background, I hear Finn and Mac moving throughout the apartment. "This wasn't an accident, was it?"

Between Declan being in the city and us killing Logan last night, I would bet my right arm that this was all her grandfather's doing. By killing Logan, we took away his only plan. If he wasn't out for her blood before, he definitely will be now. He's trying to show us exactly how dangerous he is, as if we didn't know already.

Little does he know, though, he's about to learn just what *we're* capable of.

"No, I don't think it was."

In my peripheral, I see Mac and Finn waiting near the elevator. "I don't suppose there's any point in asking you to stay here?"

Harper lifts her head from mine. Her spine steels as she wipes the tears from her face; her expression morphs from sadness to anger.

My strong girl.

"No. I'm going. This is the last thing he is taking from me. I'm done crying. I'm done hiding. I'm done letting him make me afraid." I watch as sheer power and determination settle inside her deep green eyes.

Like always, as much as I want to keep her locked inside this apartment, I know she needs to see this with her own eyes. I'll call more of our guys on the way as extra backup in case Declan is hiding in the shadows, watching it all unfold. Which he probably is. Sick fuck. Reaching out, I take her wobbling chin between my thumb and forefinger. "Do as we say, and don't wander."

Her face softens ever so slightly, probably grateful that, just this once, I'm not arguing with her. "I know the rules, Baby," she answers.

"Do you want to change?" She's in sweats and a baggy sweatshirt, which barely conceals the fact that she's not wearing a bra, and her curls are thrown into a messy bun on top of her head. She looks comfy, cozy, and absolutely perfect. Like she always does.

She shakes her head. "No, I'm okay. Let's just go."

Reaching out, I take her hand and lead her toward my brothers. Mac reaches out, coffee thermos in hand, obviously just as aware that there was no way she was staying put. "Grabbed you some coffee to go, Pretty Girl."

Taking the thermos from him she stands on her toes and softly kisses his cheek. "Thank you, Honey."

While she's doing so, both dart their eyes towards me, and I mouth "Bookstore. Fire," and their expressions fall.

"I'm just going to get changed quick, I'll be right back."

Jogging across the apartment and into my room, I throw on a pair of rarely-worn dark-washed blue jeans and a gray hoodie. I quickly slide on all my rings and a pair of white trainers and head back to the elevator. I don't miss how Harper's eyes roam over my body as she pulls her bottom lip between her teeth. I fight the urge to smile, internally preening at the fact that, despite everything going on, she can't help but eye-fuck me the same way I'm always doing to her.

I give her a cheeky wink, silently promising to fulfill any fantasy running through her dirty little mind later and take her hand back in mine. "Let's go."

* * *

The firetrucks and police finally pull away as Harper stands still as a statue in front of what used to be her family's home away from home. The three of us surround her, Mac and Finn on either side of her, holding her hands, and me behind her with my arms wrapped around her waist. None of us dare say a word until Harper, the woman we love more than anything on this planet, makes the first move.

My heart breaks for her. For everything Declan has already done to her, for everything her beautifully innocent soul has had to go through in this life, and for the place she felt her parents and Cece the most that has now been burned to the ground in front of her very eyes.

I'm thankful for two things, though. One that we had the sense to move all of our money out of the walls. Not because I care if we lost it or not. Quite honestly, I couldn't give a fuck. The three of us have more money sitting in more accounts across the world than we know what to do with. But because that cash can now be anonymously donated to the two families that lost their homes alongside Harper's bookstore. I'm just waiting for it to be her idea and not mine. Two, I'm beyond thankful that she wasn't inside. Ever since we took her, I know she has felt like a piece of her was missing for not being inside her bookstore and doing what she loved. That emptiness was lessened slightly by hers and Mac's visit here yesterday, but I know that wasn't enough time. There never is. And now, there never will be.

Had we allowed her to work, though, she would have been there today, she would have been in that fire, and she would have been taken from us forever. And the three of us would have ceased to exist along with her.

"We need to help them," Harper says quietly. "My neighbors. The Stanfords just moved into that townhouse last year with their kids, and Sandra poured her heart and soul into that photography studio. This has nothing to do with them. It isn't fair."

I kiss the back of her head. "Consider it done, Baby Girl."

We stand in front of the pile of ash and smoke for as long as Harper wants, but unlike Harper, I know all three of us are keeping a strong eye out for Declan or anything else that seems nefarious. I have two dozen of my men posted up and down the street, and I haven't seen so much as Declan's shadow, but that doesn't mean it's not coming. He had already accomplished this under my men's watchful eye.

I'm not going to lie and say my first instinct wasn't to ring Trevor's neck the second we made it to the scene, but I knew this wasn't on him. Once I spoke to the fire investigator, he confirmed that there was nothing Trevor could have done. Based on what's left of Sandra's photography studio, it looks like someone broke into her building and busted through the connecting wall to get into the bookstore. All it would have taken was some fire-starter on a couple of bookshelves and a match, and the whole thing would have burst into flames. The fire investigator said he would do his best to determine the cause, but with how severely damaged everything is, it will be hard to know for sure. However, one thing he did assure me was that this fire was started by someone. He couldn't figure out a single way it would have started on its own.

My phone starts to vibrate in the front pocket of my jeans,

but I let it ring out, not wanting to draw my attention away from Harper. It stops vibrating, and a moment later Mac's goes off.

"Answer it, Mac. It could be important," Harper prompts him. He looks over his shoulder at me, and I nod. Mac quickly kisses the side of her head and steps a few feet away to answer his phone.

"This has to end. He's taken enough from me." Harper's voice isn't wobbly. Instead, she says it strong and sure. As if she knows, without a doubt, this is the last time Declan Whelan will hurt her in any way.

And she's right. Because she has us, and I know I speak for us all when I say I would rather slit my own wrists than see him hurt her ever again. She deserves everything good and beautiful in this world, and Declan Whelan has done nothing but attempt to destroy every ounce of light in her life.

It's time he pays for what he's done. To Harper and her parents, Finn and his parents, and everyone else's life he's destroyed in the name of power. I will end him, just like I did my own father. And just like I did my own father, I won't lose an ounce of fucking sleep over it.

"We'll put an end to all of this, Angel. We swear it."

"Pick us up here," Mac demands as he races over. "Thanks, Sebastian."

"What now?" Finn asks.

"Sebastian traced the vehicle that fled from the other side of the building right before the fire started. Followed it to a dive bar. The two guys that were in it are still there. You'll never guess where the bar is?" Mac's grin grows eerily wide.

"The anticipation is killing me, brother."

"Right down the block from one of our warehouses down

at the docks."

What a couple of fucking morons.

"Enzo and Luca are on their way here now to pick us up. They should be here any minute."

I nod my head at Finn. "Go with Mac. I'll stay with Harper."

I watch as both of them hesitate, likely remembering the last time I was left alone in the penthouse with Harper while they took care of business. It takes everything in me not to take it personally, but I get it. Thankfully, Harper speaks up, "We'll talk to Ralph when we get there. We'll be okay. Go."

She swipes a stray hair off of Mac's forehead before standing on her toes to kiss his lips. "Be careful." Turning, she does the same to Finn. "Come back to me."

The sound of Luca's red '74 Chevelle cuts through the noise of the city as he rounds the corner onto our street. I see he's not trying to fly under the radar today. That car is his pride and joy, but it sticks out like a sore thumb, and I swear to God you could hear it from Staten Island.

Luca slides to a stop just beyond the caution tape, not bothering to get out of the car, knowing time is of the essence. Enzo rolls down the passenger side window and gives Harper a wink. "Hey, Bella."

"Love you, Pretty Girl. Be back soon." With one last kiss, Mac moves toward Luca's car and climbs in the back seat.

"We'll make them pay, Angel. I love you."

"I love you," she says before he follows my brother. The moment Finn's door closes Luca peels off down the street.

"Come on, Baby, let's get you home."

44

Mac

"Correct me if I'm wrong," Luca says from the driver's seat. "But isn't that one of your warehouses we just passed?"

I don't bother asking him how or why he knows that because I know the answer.

Sebastian.

"Sure is," Finn answers from his seat next to me. "Fucking idiots didn't even bother to do their homework before they started drinking themselves into a stupor."

For as smart of a man as Declan is, or at least portrays himself to be, he puts his trust into some real lackluster individuals.

Enzo turns in the front passenger seat to face us with the same sinister grin I had when I found out where the bar was, "So, grabbing them from the bar and bringing them back there?"

Seeing that we're pulling up to the bar, I pull my gun from the waistband of my jeans, chamber a round, and put it back. I don't plan on using a gun in a bar full of civilians, but it's wise to be prepared. "That was my plan."

"Want to fill us in on the rest of your plan?" Luca asks as he pulls his car to a curb a block from the bar so they don't hear us pull up. I'd be lying if I said I wasn't insanely jealous of Luca's car. As much as I love my Aston Martin, there's something about classic American muscle.

Luca puts the Chevelle in park, and he and Enzo face me and Finn. I look at Finn, and he raises his brows. "This is all you, brother."

"Any chance you have any extra gas in your trunk?" I ask Luca.

"Just an extra gallon."

Looking at Enzo, I can tell he knows exactly what I'm thinking. Dante might be their muscle, but I have a hunch Enzo's their crazy. "That'll work. We'll get them out of the bar and back to the warehouse. We need to keep them alive long enough to talk. I doubt they'll tell us where Declan is, but we need to at least try."

"Then?" Enzo asks, grin still intact.

I look over at my best friend and he answers for me, "We use them to send a message. He hurt our girl for the last time."

"He wanted shit to burn, so it'll fucking burn," I say as red starts to creep around the edge of my vision.

"Any idea on how to get them out here without drawing a shitload of attention to us?" Luca questions.

"I'm on it," his best friend says as he flings his door open. "Go wait by their car and get ready to grab them. Luca, stay here with the car running. They can follow us in that car back to the warehouse."

Before we can question him, he's out of the car, down the block, and heading towards the back of the building.

"Should we be concerned?" Finn asks Luca, who simply waves him off.

"He does this kind of shit all the time. It'll be fine."

I chuckle as I open my door while tapping Finn on the arm with my opposite hand. "Come on."

We're just reaching their shitbox Dodge Neon when a loud bang sounds from the other side of the building. Moments later, I already see Enzo rounding the building and heading back to Luca's car. Another minute goes by when the double doors slam open with a smoke cloud. Patrons of the bar start pouring out, coughing and covering their eyes. Finn and I back up and wait against the side of the bar until we see two men stumble towards the tiny white car. Just as they move to open their doors, Finn and I use the fact that they can barely see from the smoke stinging their eyes to our advantage and ambush them.

Everyone else is too worried about running away from the building to see what's happening right next to the doors.

Neither of the men put up much of a fight due to their disoriented and inebriated state, and with each of them in our well-practiced choke holds, they are knocked out in under a minute. Finn and I throw them into the back seat before we climb into the front. Finn slowly backs out of the parking stall so as not to draw any extra attention and rounds the block back in the direction of our warehouse.

In no time at all, we're pulling up to the back side of our building where we usually park. It's the side that faces the

Hudson and is out of sight of the street and cars driving by. Unless someone's looking, no one will know we're here. Luca's Chevelle pulls up next to us, and we climb out.

Luca's fighting a laugh, and Enzo's smile is a mile wide. This is the most excitement I've seen from him since we met.

"What was that?" I ask him, also trying not to laugh.

"May or not have turned up the temp on the grease baskets cooking fries in the kitchen."

Any other day, I'd ask him exactly how he managed that, but these two won't be passed out for long, and I want to get them hung up before they're able to put up much of a fight.

"Grab the gas can. Luca, help us get them inside."

We get the two guys tied to chairs side-by-side in the middle of the warehouse just in time for them to come too. As soon as they realize the position they're in, both of them start thrashing violently against the binds, but it's no use. We're all well-versed in rope tying. Those knots aren't going anywhere.

"Who the fuck are you?! Where are we?" The first guy with an ugly blonde bowl cut yells.

"Do you have any idea who we are?! Who we work for?" The moron with the beer gut carries on.

"I don't know who you are or what your names are, and frankly, I don't give a flying fuck." As I move toward them, they both tense up in their seats. "But I know what you've done and who you work for." Leaning forward, I put my hands on my knees to be at eye level with them. "And as for your first two questions, if you don't know who we are, you haven't done your fucking homework. Which is obvious since you've been holed up in a bar just a few blocks from this warehouse, which we own, since you set the love of our life's bookstore on fire this morning."

It takes a few seconds for what I just said to register in their idiotic brains, but once it does, they know how royally fucked they both are. "Shit," bowl cut groans as he hangs his head.

"Shit is right, you fucking idiots." Luca laughs behind me as Finn walks up next to me. "Should have ditched the car and crawled back into whatever hole you came from."

Standing up straight, I cross my arms over my chest as Finn asks, "Don't suppose there's any chance you'll tell us where Declan is?"

The two of them are silent for a moment before beer gut spits in our direction. "The lot of you can fuck right off."

I watch Finn as he watches them, looking for any indication on their faces that they might tell us where Declan is. After a few seconds, he looks over at me. "Fuck it. We'll find Declan without them. I don't have the patience for them today."

"Couldn't agree more, brother." As much as I'd love to spend hours on end making them feel pain they've never felt before until they pray to whatever God they believe in for death, hoping they'll eventually tell us where Declan is, I'd rather be home with our girl.

They're only here to send a message, after all.

"Enzo, you're up."

Enzo approaches from behind and begins pouring the gallon of gasoline over things one and two, who are back to flailing around like a couple of fish. It's too little too late, buddies. You're about to pay for what you did to my Pretty Girl.

I take bowl cut's phone from my pocket, which I grabbed before we tied them up. I scroll through the contacts until I find Declan's name and hold the screen over my shoulder.

"Can you call Sebastian and see if he can trace this number?" I ask Luca.

"Yeah, one sec." A few seconds later, Sebastian picks up, and Luca speaks softly, "No, we're fine. I just need you to see if you can trace this number." Luca gives Sebastian the number, and we wait while Enzo continues soaking them in gasoline. "It's alright. We'll be done soon."

"Nothing?" I ask.

"No. He said the phone has some kind of software that makes it look like the signal is coming from fifty different locations. He said he could get it eventually, but it would take him a couple of days."

I let out a heavy sigh. We'll just have to figure out something else. In the meantime, I hit the video chat icon next to Declan's name. It only takes a few rings for him to answer, and his ugly fucking face fills the screen.

"Cormac. I'd ask what you're doing with Jarod's phone, but I'm sure I already know the answer."

I chance a glance at Finn, who's gone catatonically still at the sound of Declan's voice. "Much like Logan, the men you sent to do your dirty work today are absolute wastes of oxygen."

"They burned down Harper's precious store, did they not?"

The sound of her name spilling from his mouth makes me clench my jaw, but I force myself to maintain my composure. "They then proceeded to drive to the closest bar and celebrate their hard day's work instead of dumping their car. Which, by the way, is right next door to one of our most *well-used* buildings. Like I said, waste of fucking oxygen."

"Is there a purpose to this phone call?" His voice remains calm, but judging by the muscle ticking in his jaw and the redness of his face, I can tell he's anything but.

"We just wanted to make something clear."

"And what is that? That you killed my men? I have a dozen more where they came from. If they were stupid enough to get caught, then they deserve to die."

"I haven't killed them *yet.* I wanted you to see firsthand that I'm just as deranged as you are." I bring the phone closer to my face. "But what makes me even more of a threat is that I'm willing to risk *everything* for her. We all are. You risk your life for no one and nothing. You're nothing but an old, weak coward. You've messed with my family for the last time. You better treat these last few days on this earth as a dream come true. Because when I find you, I'll be your worst nightmare."

"Fuck me. That gave me goosebumps." Enzo whispers wide-eyed next to Finn, who's now staring right at me instead of off into space.

"Finn, do it." Finn blinks, and the fog clears. He reaches into his pocket and pulls out a lighter Luca had in his glove box.

"No, no, no!" Beer gut screams. "We'll tell you whatever you want to know!"

My best friend turns to face them. " I don't give a fuck. You wanted to play with fire, so play with fucking fire." He throws the lighter into the pool of gas at their feet, and I flip the camera so Declan can watch his men go up in flames.

I can't hear anything else Declan's saying over the men's agonizing screams, so I prop the phone up against the discarded gas can on the ground. He can watch them burn for all I care.

"God, that always smells fucking awful." Luca throws his suit jacket over his nose.

The four of us walk toward the door, and the screams have stopped by the time we reach it. We'll call our clean-up crew to take care of what's left of the bodies and their car, but now I just want to go home and see Harper.

Mo Grá.

Enzo opens the door of Luca's Chevelle and props his arm against the roof. "Since we have to drop you off, do you feel like ordering some pizza for lunch since we were such a great help today?"

I huff out a laugh and notice the red has cleared. "Tell Sebastian and Dante to meet us there. We can strategize while we eat."

Luca and Enzo climb in the car, but I grab his arm before Finn can walk to the other side. "You good?"

"That's the second time, Mac. When I saw him outside the coffee, I couldn't move, and today I just heard his voice through a phone, and I fucking froze. What am I going to do when the time comes? When it matters?"

"You won't freeze, Finn. When it matters, you won't freeze."

"How do you know?"

"Because when it matters most, it'll be for her. For Harper. Your Angel." Finn lets out a harsh breath, and I know what I said sank in. I mean every word. "Come on, let's get these assholes some food."

45

Finn

When the four of us return to the apartment, Sebastian and Dante are already there and working on polishing off the first of four pizzas. On instinct, my eyes scan the room for Harper, and I look over to find Mac doing the same thing. Ronan must pick up on it. "She's in her room. She's been sleeping most of the afternoon."

Luca follows Enzo, who's bitching that they already finished the Meat Lover's pizza, and rubs a hand down the back of Sebastian's hair. Sebastian doesn't say anything but looks up at him the way Harper does me.

Feeling like I'm intruding on a moment, I look at Mac and nod in the direction of Harper's room. We can eat after we see her. There will never be a time again, for as long as I live, when my first instinct isn't to go to her.

Mac and I quietly shuffle into her room and move toward her bed. She's sprawled out on her stomach in the middle of the king-sized mattress. Her hair is spread across her pillow, with both hands tucked underneath. The white duvet is pulled down to her waist, leaving her bare back exposed, just begging me to run my fingers along her spine, so I do. As my finger trails up the curve of her back, Mac bends down and places a soft kiss against her cheek. She begins to stir but doesn't open her eyes. "Mac? Finn?"

Without even looking at us, she knew we were here. "Shhh, Mo Grá," Mac whispers, "Go back to sleep. We just wanted to see you."

"Did you find them?" she mumbles into her pillow.

"We found them, Angel. We made them pay, I promise."

She doesn't so much as flinch at the menacing undertone of my words and instead snuggles further into her pillow. "Hmmm, thank you. I love you."

"We love you, Pretty Girl."

I softly kiss her shoulder blade, and Mac and I move toward the door before I stop. "Harper."

"Mmmm." Her grumble sounding annoyed that I'm still talking.

"Luca and the guys are here. So when you wake up, please put some clothes on."

I expect her to mumble something incoherent, but what she says makes Mac bark out a laugh and me palm my dick through my jeans. "Yes, Daddy."

This fucking woman.

Softly I close the door and turn around to face Mac, who's still laughing his ass off. "If you don't shut the hell up." He continues, so I jet my fist out and punch him in the stomach;

he doubles over, and his childish laughing stops. And just to be an asshole right back, I say, "That's a good boy," before stepping around him.

I hear him rumbling something about not being his favorite anymore as he rights himself and follows me back toward the kitchen.

"How's our girl?" Ronan asks as I stand next to him and grab a slice of Margherita.

"Sassy as ever."

He huffs a laugh, and a smile takes over his face. "Good."

After giving everyone time to stuff their faces, Mac, Luca, Enzo, and I fill the rest of the guys in on what happened.

Ronan clears his throat and wipes his hands on a napkin. "You already called the cleanup crew?"

"Yeah," Mac says as he shoves his last bite of pizza into his mouth. "Woo alweady get da cash tawken caw of?"

His older brother rolls his eyes but answers, "Yeah. Harper wrote a card to each of them as soon as we got back and put them each in a duffle bag full of cash. Had one of our men come by to grab it and drop it off at a hotel I put them up in. Anonymously, of course."

Of course. God forbid anyone knows that Ronan isn't made of ice.

"Happy to hear someone else got to experience Enzo's crazy," Dante says, leaning back in his chair and crossing his corded arms across his barrel of a chest. The man is fucking huge.

"Hey!" Enzo reaches next to him and backhands Dante on said chest. Dante doesn't so much as flinch. Something tells me, though, that few people could get away with putting their hands on Dante DeLuca. Besides being the group's muscle,

I'm not entirely sure what his role is. But what I do know is that they trust him fully, as he does them. "Don't act like you don't like it," Enzo adds with a cheeky grin.

I watch as Dante fights a smile and rolls his eyes.

"So how do you want to fuck this pig? The pig being Declan, of course." Luca, as per usual, looks more than willing to help us. I don't know how we're ever going to repay him, or his father for that matter. He didn't have to ask his son to help us, but he did anyway. Pascal didn't have to take in Emma either, but something tells me the two of them aren't that hard up at his house in Saint-Jean-de-Luz in France. And from the sounds of Emma's giggles in the background on our last phone call with them, I think it's safe to assume they have, well, *bonded.* But I won't tease my best friends about that yet.

"Actually," Ronan braces his arms on the counter, his rarely worn sweatshirt covering all his tattoos but the ones on his hands and neck. "Sebastian, how easy would it be for you to get into one of Declan's bank accounts and transfer all the money to someone else?"

I look over at Ronan. "To who?"

"I was thinking about giving our new friend Patrick a call."

Sebastian mirrors Ronan's movements, resting his surprisingly muscular arms on the kitchen island. "It might take me a couple of days, but consider it done."

"Dante, can we get some of that tactical gear?"

Dante nods.

"Good. It's time to show this fucker who the hell we are. And it's about to be the last lesson he'll ever learn."

46

Harper

As much as I wanted to thank Luca and his guys for their help today, I want this more. For the first time since I got back, I feel ready.

After what happened this morning, I know they've been sitting out there developing some sort of plan all afternoon. If I know my guys, which I do, whatever plan they've concocted isn't going to wait long, and after what they did for me today, hell, what they continue to do *for me* over and over again, I'll be damned if I waste another minute. So, when I hear the guys say their goodbyes, I slide out from under the covers, tousle the roots of my curls, pinch my cheeks for some color, and spritz a bit of their favorite perfume along my collarbone. I open my bedroom door with nothing on but a pair of burgundy lace panties. "Are they still here?"

"No, Angel, you just missed them."

"You want me to call them back up?" Mac asks.

Pulling the door open all the way, I answer, "No, that's fine. I was just checking."

Sauntering down the hall, I watch as the three of them go about cleaning up the kitchen. "Checking for wha—" Ronan's question dies on his lips once he sees me. I watch the muscles in his jaw clench as his eyes roam my body from head to toe and back again. "Baaaaby," he groans. It's then that Finn and Mac stop what they're doing to look at me.

"Fuck me." Mac runs his hand through his permanently tousled hair.

"That was the plan," I say as I make my way over to the bar and pour myself a finger of whiskey.

"You want to play, Angel?" Finn moves around the island, his bottom lip pulled between his teeth and his hands fisted at his sides, letting me know he's more than willing to participate in my game.

With the crystal glass of whiskey between my fingers at my side, I sashay back down the hall. Once I get to my door, I look over my shoulder. "Coming boys?"

47

Harper

Ilaugh as the three of them race across the apartment toward me. Taking a few steps into my room, I spin to face them as they move through the doorway. Holding my finger up, they all stop in their tracks. With the opposite hand, I bring the glass of whiskey to my lips and tip it into my mouth. Without swallowing, I stretch out my finger and point it at Finn.

I know having to deal with Declan has brought a lot of emotions to the surface for him. Emotions that he will never let see the light of day if he has anything to do with it. So, if only for a minute, I want him to have my undivided attention. Plus, I'm curious to see if he'll get on his knees for me—just once.

Finn takes a step forward, and I turn my hand and move my finger in a "come here" motion. He raises his brows and tilts his head to the side, his expression saying, "You sure this is a game you want to play?"

Ohhh, but I do.

I give him the same look back, and he relents, moving until he's standing in front of me. Once we're toe to toe, I point my finger at the ground. Knowing what I'm asking of him, he stills. His jaw clenches and I listen to him inhale and exhale a sharp breath. For a moment, I wonder if he'll deny me. But my doubts are pushed to the side when he drops to his knees.

A wave of pleasure pools at my core, and my chest heats at the gesture. This isn't a small feat, not when it comes to Finn. Especially considering Mac and Ronan are in the same room. I cup his bearded jaw in my hand and bend forward until my closed lips brush against his. Knowing that the whiskey is still in my mouth and because they all can read my thoughts clear as day, he opens his mouth. Slowly, I let the whiskey spill from my mouth and into his.

"Jesus fucking Christ." I'm not sure which one of the brother's deep Irish accents that was, but their groans of approval send shivers down my spine. My eyes don't stray from Finn's, though, as the last of the whiskey falls from my mouth. When it does, he doesn't move, and he doesn't close his mouth.

Holy shit. He's actually waiting for me to tell him what to do.

"Swallow," I tell him, my tone soft yet commanding.

Finn's mouth closes, and he swallows the mouthful of whiskey. Once he does, his tongue licks his full lips. "Fucking delicious."

"You lucky fuck," Mac says from his spot behind Finn.

"You know what else is delicious?" Finn reaches up and fists the front of my lace panties.

I shake my head, already knowing what he's going to do. "Finn, no. These are one of my favorite pairs."

"Yeah. You're done telling me what to do, Angel." With one hard yank, he rips the delicate lace right off my body. He then grabs the glass from my hand and hands it over the shoulder to Ronan, who doesn't even set it down anywhere and instead just throws it across the room.

"I think that's the first time I've seen you break one of those glasses without wanting to wrap your hand around someone's neck," his brother mocks.

Ronan's bright blue eyes stare into mine. "Who said that wasn't my plan?"

While I'm distracted by Ronan's devious threat, Finn's tongue touches my pussy. He drags it through my folds, and my head tips back, loving the feeling of his mouth on me. Entirely too soon, he pulls away. "Tastes even better than the alcohol."

Just as I'm about to reach out and grab a handful of his blonde hair to guide his head back, his hands grip my waist. In one fluid motion, he stands, lifts me from the ground, and throws me back onto my bed.

Finn crawls between my legs and plasters his body against mine. I melt into the bed, reveling in the weight of him on top of me. Finn kisses me hard. My mouth opens immediately for him, and I lap up the taste of whiskey on his tongue.

The moment is over all too soon when Finn tears his lips from mine. "Tell us what you want, Angel."

"I thought you said I was done telling you what to do."

Finn grips my jaw in his hand. "You are. But even though you aren't in charge here, it doesn't mean we won't give you what you want. So, I can either take my sweet time finding out, or you can be a good girl and just tell me right now."

"I want you all to make me come. Then I want you to come."

Mac walks along the side of his bed, now naked, trailing his hand from my ankle, past my waist, along my stomach, and over my breast. The featherlight touch makes me lift my hips against Finn. "Where do you want our come, Mo Grá?"

"Inside me. I want all of your come inside me." I moan when Mac pinches my nipple.

Ronan, also beautifully naked, walks along the other side of the bed, his touch identical to his brothers. "You like that, Baby? You like when we all come inside you? When we mark that pretty skin with our mouths and hands? When you're so full of us, there isn't an inch of you that isn't ours?"

"Fuuuuck. Yes. Yes. Fuck yes."

Finn kisses me again, pulling my bottom lip between his teeth hard enough that the spark of pain pools into a wave of pleasure. "Such a good fucking girl."

Finn sits back on his knees, and Ronan's mouth takes his place. Where Finn's kiss is sure and ruthless, Ronan's is commanding and intense. And when Mac takes over, his are slow and steady. Each kiss is so different, but they all light my body on fire. One isn't better than the other, and I could never live without each of them. "You all make me so happy."

Finn stands at the foot of the bed while Ronan lays on his back beside me. "Come here, Baby."

Without hesitation, I roll over and straddle his waist. Ronan reaches up and sweeps my hair across my back so it's all hanging off to one side. He cups the other side of my face and strokes my cheek with his thumb. Mirroring him, I do the same. He slides his hand down my arm, grabs my wrist, and brings my palm to his lips. He places one kiss after another over the signet ring on my thumb. "I love you, Baby."

"And I love you, Baby."

"Now, sit that pretty pussy on my cock." Lifting my hips, Ronan places the head of his cock at my throbbing entrance. I'm so wet that I seat him fully inside of me in one go. "God fucking damn it," he groans. "So perfect."

As I start moving on top of Ronan, a strong body climbs onto the bed behind me. When the comforting scent of cedarwood and ginger hits my nose, I know it's my Mac.

He grabs my waist just above where his brother is holding me. "You trust us."

For once, it's not a question. They know I trust them with everything I am. They're not going anywhere. I know this now. As long as the four of us remain breathing, we belong to one another.

The head of Ronan's cock grazes along the perfect spot inside of me, and I let out a moan as I tip my head back against Mac's shoulder. "Always, Honey."

Reaching back, I wrap my arm around Mac's neck as I slowly ride Ronan. Having him buried inside of me feels like it's exactly where he's meant to be. But I want more.

I need more.

I need them all.

Ronan and Mac share a look I don't quite understand. Before I can question what they're thinking, both their grips on me tighten. Effectively stopping my movements. A small whine slips past my lips, and Ronan chuckles. "You can move again in just a minute, Baby, but for now, lean forward."

"Mac, if you're sticking your dick in my ass, you don't have to make such a big deal about it. We've done this plenty of times at this point."

Ronan's laugh grows louder now. "Fuck, I love the mouth you've had on you lately."

"Such a dirty girl." I listen as Mac uncaps the lube and flinch when the cold liquid lands on my ass. He drags two fingers through the lube until he gets to my back hole. Without any further teasing, he pushes two fingers deep inside me, all while Ronan bites and kisses the skin of my neck. The sudden stretch burns only for a moment before it morphs into pleasure. Mac moves his fingers in and out of me a few times before I can't take it anymore.

"Mac, please. *Please.* Fuck me, please."

"You want my brother and I to fuck you, Baby?"

I nod frantically while Mac slides his fingers from me. "Yes. So bad. I want you both to make me come. Now."

"Your wish is my command, Pretty Girl." Slowly and carefully, Mac slides inside of me. "So fucking tight."

Ronan moves one hand from my waist and threads it through my hair, pulling it to give me just the right amount of pain he knows I now need.

"You should see yourself, Angel. Taking both their cocks like the queen you are."

Once Mac is all the way seated inside of me, I beg, "Move. Fuck me. I'm okay. Move now."

Completely in sync, Mac and Ronan begin moving in and out of me at the perfect pace, gradually bringing me closer and closer to the edge I'm so desperate to fall over.

"Finn . . ." I reach out to the side of the bed, wanting to touch him too.

"I'm here, Angel."

Ronan lets go of my hair, and I sit up slightly, resting my

palms flat on his tattooed chest. Finn begins fiercely fucking my mouth with his tongue while Ronan grabs one of my breasts and squeezes it in his hand.

"You feel so fucking good, Baby." Mac cracks his hand down on my ass, taking me completely by surprise, but in the best way. "Jesus, Mac. Do that again. She just got so tight around me."

"I fucking felt it, too." He does the same on the other cheek, and I moan into Finn's mouth.

"I'm not going to last," Ronan moans from below me.

I dig my nails into Ronan's chest hard enough to draw a couple of droplets of blood, and that's enough for him to let go. He calls out my name, and the feeling of him spilling inside of me finally sends me over the edge.

Before I even have the chance to process what's happening, Mac's slowly pulling out of me and lifting me off of his brother. I can't help the blush that crawls up my face as I feel Ronan's cum slide down my thighs.

Ronan follows my gaze to my legs, drags a finger through the mess, and brings it to my panting mouth. He wipes the mess across my lips and slams his mouth against mine. Between his kiss and the aftershocks of my orgasm, I feel my legs start to wobble as I kneel on the bed in front of Mac.

Ronan pulls away, and his burning eyes stare deep into mine before he climbs off the bed, and Finn takes his place. Without him having to instruct me to do so, I straddle his narrow waist and sink down onto him. He wraps his hand around my throat and pulls me down against him so his lips brush the shell of my ear and whispers, "That's my good little girl. Now ride Daddy's cock."

A wanton whine leaves my lips just as Mac sinks back inside

of me. "Ride his cock, Harper."

It takes me a minute to figure out how to move in a way that feels good. I usually let them do all the moving when there's more than one of them, but it's unlike anything I've ever felt when I do it. I feel more powerful than I ever could have imagined. While I trust these three men with every bone inside my body, with my safety, body, and heart, they trust me just the same. They trust me to give myself to them in a way I never could with anyone else. They trust me to take care of each of their souls and own them just like they do mine.

Mac reaches around and starts rubbing my clit just the way I like it. "Oh-oh yes, Mac. Right there."

"You fuck us so good, Angel. You were made for us. Made to take our cocks. Made to be our queen."

Finn tilts his hips slightly, and his cock rubs back and forth over my G-spot. "Don't stop. You both feel so good."

Finn's still holding me by the neck, and Mac has a bruising grip on my hips when I hear Ronan moan beside us. I look over to find his hand around his dick, which is now fully hard—*again.*

I don't know what it is, but watching a man stroke his cock is beyond erotic.

"You look so damn sexy, Baby. Watching you fuck yourself on their dicks is one of the hottest things I've ever seen."

I lick my lips as I watch a bead of cum form at the tip of his cock.

Ronan looks between it and my lips and smiles. Tilting his head, he asks, "You want it?"

I stop my movements between Finn and Mac, silently signaling for them to take over, and nod eagerly. Ronan shuffles back onto the bed until the head of his dick is in front of my mouth. With Finn's hand still around my neck, I dart my tongue out and lick the droplet of cum from the crown.

"Our perfect fucking girl," he says lovingly as he strokes my hair.

I open my mouth and take him as far as I can while Finn and Mac fuck me. But unlike how Ronan and Mac were alternating strokes before, Finn and Mac are sliding in and out of me simultaneously. Leaving me feeling completely empty and deliciously full over and over again.

I'm left floating between them. Each of them using my body to bring them pleasure while feeling like their most prized treasure. It's Ronan who falls first, still sensitive from his first climax, and I swallow every last bit of his release down my throat, not wanting to miss a drop.

"Feeling you swallow his cum beneath my hand, fuck, Harper." I pull my mouth off of Ronan's dick just in time to moan Finn's name as he pinches my nipple with his other hand. "Yes, Angel. You're doing such a good job. Come for us."

Mac slams in and out of my ass so hard slapping noises fill the room. I look over my shoulder at him. His face is consumed by pure unadulterated passion, and I swear to God, it's the sexiest he's ever looked.

My orgasm comes out of nowhere. So strong and fierce, I know what's coming. Finn quickly pulls out of me as my release sprays him and my bed beneath us. I scream all of their names into the room I once thought would be my prison.

"You're fucking gorgeous coming for us like that, Mo Grá." Finn slams back into me as Mac growls, "You're ours."

"We get to keep you all to ourselves," Finn moans.

Ronan reaches out and cups my chin in his hand, quickly swiping away a tear I didn't even know was falling with his thumb. "In this life and the next."

My pussy continues to pulse around him as Finn comes with a roar, filling me so entirely with his cum that I feel it spill out between us. Finn doesn't pull out as Mac wraps one arm around my chest and pulls me upright so my back is tight against his front. "Come with me, Pretty Girl. Come with me now and forever."

"Mac," I half moan, half sob as another soul-shattering orgasm wreaks havoc on my body. Mac's words of adoration continue to float through the room as he spills his release deep inside of my ass.

With ragged breaths, we all sprawl out onto the mattress before cleaning up and tucking ourselves into my bed in one of our usual positions. Ronan and Finn on either side of me, and Mac between my legs, resting his head on my stomach. While Mac doesn't usually fall asleep here and ends up crawling to either side of the bed, it's one of my favorite places for him to be. And as I run my fingers through his unruly black hair, every few seconds, he lets out a deep sigh of contentment; I know it's one of his favorites, too.

As each of their breaths begins to slow, I whisper into the room, knowing that whatever is about to happen over the next couple of days has a chance of taking them away from me. Of taking all of this away from me. "Don't ever leave me."

In unison, each of them says one simple word. "Never."

My entire body is theirs. Theirs to love. Theirs to cherish. Theirs to keep.

48

Mac

The sun has barely started to rise when I wake Ronan and Finn up. The three of us leave a comatose Harper in her room, grab a cup of coffee, and shut ourselves into Ronan's office. I don't want to risk her hearing if she wakes up, which is highly unlikely. That woman is practically dead to the world right now.

Instead of sitting across his desk from us in his chair, Ronan takes a seat on the small couch he has in his office. He kicks his feet out, crosses his ankles, and drapes one arm across the back while sipping his coffee. Finn and I quickly spin the two armchairs to sit in somewhat of a circle. "What's with the early wake-up call, brother?"

I look between my brother and my best friend. The two men that I would die for, without question. Two men I know would do the same for me without blinking an eye. Two men who continuously keep me grounded when the demons of my past, of who I was made to be, constantly threaten to pull me under. Two men that mean more to me than any earthly possession I could possibly imagine. And if my life weren't already wholly dedicated to them, what I'm about to suggest would solidify that notion. "Two things,"

Ronan and Finn look at one another and then back at me. "Okaaaay. What's the first thing?" Finn asks as he absentmindedly picks one of Harper's hairs off his sweatpants with a small smile. He'd be far more annoyed if it were anyone's but hers.

I take a deep breath. Here goes nothing. "I think we should ask Harper to marry us. I mean, I know we can't all marry her legally, but the law was never really our friend anyway. I'm in this with her, with you guys." Finn pauses, cup of coffee halfway to his mouth, while my brother's eyes widen. "If that's not what you guys would want, I totally get it. Long-term, I know it isn't the most conventional relationship, but I just thought, I just love her so much, and I know you both do, too. After everything that's happened, everything that could still happen, I just—"

Finn lowers his cup and puts his hand on my knee. "Mac, you don't have to explain yourself."

"No?"

"No, man. I think I speak for both of us when I say that's what we want."

I look at my brother, whose small smile is filled with agreement and understanding. "Yeah?"

"I just wasn't expecting that to be what came out of your mouth. But hell yes I want to fucking marry her."

"All of us?" I ask, wanting to clarify that I'm not bowing

out, not in this life and not in any life after.

Finn squeezes my knee. "Yeah, Mac. All of us."

"She deserves everything good in this life," Ronan adds, "And if it takes all three of us to make sure she gets it, then that's what she'll get."

"So we're doing this then? We're asking Harper to marry us?"

"We're asking Harper to marry us. Once all of this bullshit is taken care of, we'll set it all up." Not *if,* but *when.* Like Finn and I, my brother knows this can't and won't go on any longer.

Finn slaps my leg before sitting back in his chair. "What was the second thing?"

I'd be lying if I said I wasn't equally as excited about this proposition. "In the meantime, how would the two of you feel about a new tattoo?"

49

Harper

When I wake up, the guys aren't in bed anymore, but my panic is short-lived when I hear them milling about the apartment. I tie my curls up in a messy bun and throw on an oversized T-shirt. Before I leave my room to find them, I turn around and put on a pair of fuzzy socks. The late fall temperatures have definitely hit the city, and being this high up in the building, I've started to notice the floors have a bit of a chill.

All the guys are relaxing in the den, each with a cup of coffee. Ronan's sitting in his armchair, Finn in the one across from him, and Mac on the leather couch. "Morning," I greet, and all of their attention is redirected to me. Suddenly, the chill I felt when I rolled out of bed is long gone.

Mac stands from his spot and shuffles over to me. "Morning, Mo Grá. Coffee?"

I smile at him, noticing he changed his nose ring for a diamond stud today. "Please."

He places a quick kiss on my lips and heads to the kitchen.

Ronan reaches out and grabs my hand, pulling me onto his lap. "Sleep good, Baby?"

"Like a log. How long have you guys been up?" My hand runs down the lapel of Ronan's black suit jacket before slipping into his black dress shirt with the top two buttons undone and grazing the warm skin along his chest.

"Only a couple hours. We had a few things we needed to get done before we started the day."

"You guys eat breakfast yet?"

"Yeah, but Mac has a plate ready for you in the microwave. You can warm it up whenever you're ready."

Sliding my hand from his shirt, I cup his face in my hands and give him a deep kiss. I feel his cock twitch beneath me and smile against his lips. Much to his reluctance, he lets me go, and I walk over to Finn.

"Saving the best for last, Angel?" He asks as I straddle his lap.

I push a wayward clock of honey-blonde hair from his face and lean forward so my mouth is next to his ear, "Don't tell the others."

He knows I'm kidding, but it earns me a rare and beautiful smile all the same. One he seems to only reserve for me.

"Here's your coffee, Pretty Girl," Mac says as he rejoins us and sets my cup on the table. Just as I'm about to lean in to give Finn his good morning kiss and join Mac on the couch, something abnormal catches my eye on Finn's neck. It looks like a tattoo. That can't be right. He doesn't have a single tattoo that shows beyond his collar or wrists. But as I look a little closer, I realize it's definitely a tattoo, the skin around it red and raised.

"What is that?"

Feigning ignorance, he asks, "What's what?"

I raise my brows and sternly prompt, "Love—"

"Angel." Firmly gripping his bearded jaw, I turn his head to the side.

Holy shit.

In a thick old English font, from just below his ear down toward his collarbone, reads "Harper." My name is on Finn's neck.

"Finn . . ."

"Angel . . ."

"What did you do?"

"You mean, what did we do?" Ronan asks from behind me.

Quickly standing from Finn's lap, I look between Mac and Ronan to find the same exact tattoo along the side of both their necks. I didn't notice it right away on either of them, so used to their tattoos constantly being on display, both with Ronan already having one on the opposite side of his neck and Mac's showing through the open buttons of his Henley's or just not having a shirt on at all.

"Y-you got my name tattooed on you?"

"Yeah, Baby. We did."

"On your neck?! Everyone will see it all the time."

The three of them chuckle in unison. "That's kind of the point," Mac answers with a cheeks-splitting grin.

"When?"

"This morning while you were asleep. Ronan's pretty good with a tattoo gun."

My head snaps to Ronan, who shrugs. "I don't do super big

pieces, but I did a lot of our smaller ones."

"What is even happening right now?" I massage my temples with my fingers.

"Don't look so surprised, Baby. You know I'm good with my hands." He shoots me a menacing wink.

I look back at Mac. "Why would you do that?"

Standing from the couch, he walks around the coffee table so he's directly in front of me. Grabbing both my hands in his, he says, calm and sure, "It's simple, Harper. We want you with us every minute of every day. And now, even when you can't be, you *will* be. Just as your soul belongs with ours, your name belongs on our skin. In every sense of the word, you are *ours,* and we are *yours.* We wanted everyone to know it."

"This—this will last forever." I reach up and drag my finger along my name.

"Because that's what we are. Forever."

This isn't a marriage proposal, but it sure as hell feels like one. I look between the three of them. "Forever."

With my hands still in his, Mac brings my hands up to his lips and kisses my knuckles.

"Can I have my good morning kiss now, please?"

Finn fakes a pout as Mac gently pats my ass. "Go. Then come have your coffee."

Standing above him, I slant my mouth over Finn's and kiss him fiercely. Sitting on the couch next to Mac, I look at his brother. "So, can I get one too?"

Leaning forward, he picks my mug off the coffee table and hands it to me. "I'll give you as many tattoos as you want, Baby Girl, but first, we have a few things to go over."

50

Ronan

"I need three of you down at the docks tonight to pick up a delivery," I say to one of my men on the phone from the office at Kings. It's early evening, and the club won't be open for a few hours, but I needed to come down to take a look at our books. Usually, Finn takes care of most of the Kings' business, but I hadn't been here in a while and wanted to check-in. So, like the excellent boss and best friend I am, I suggested he stay home, curled up on the couch with Harper. "They'll be there at 11:15 in a dark blue Honda Civic." The phone dings, signaling another incoming call, and I pull the phone from my ear to see that it's Sebastian calling. It's been two days since we set our plan in motion the day Declan burnt Hayes' Bookstore. He'd only be calling for one thing. "Get it done. Text me or the guys if you have any problems," I bite out, quickly ending the call to answer Sebastian's.

"Got him?"

"Yeah, Ronan. I fucking got him."

"Text me the address. I'll run home to grab Finn and Mac and meet Luca and Dante there."

"Seb and I will meet you at the apartment," Enzo says in the background. I hear the sound of a car starting, letting me know they're already on the move.

"See you in a few." Pocketing my phone, I grab my suit jacket off the back of my chair and race out of the club, to my car, and back to the apartment. Once I pull into our parking garage level, I find Enzo and Sebastian waiting with several duffle bags in hand. We gave them clearance to the entire building when Harper was missing, which has come in handy on more than one occasion. I come to a screeching halt in my stall and barrel out of the car towards them. Enzo throws a black duffle at me. "Your guys' clothes are in there."

"And those?" I ask, nodding towards the remaining bags in their hands. "Seb brought some of his equipment to help keep an eye on things, but this one," he holds it up, a maniacal twinkle dancing in his eyes, "Just some extra toys in case you guys need it."

"Thanks, man. Let's go upstairs."

As the elevator takes us to our floor, Enzo asks, "Bella know about this part of the plan?"

Side-eyeing him, I answer, "Stop calling her that. And no, not yet."

"Good luck with that one," he mumbles under his breath.

When the elevator doors open on our floor I find Finn, Mac, and Harper sitting in the den watching *Dirty Dancing*. Finn spots me out of the corner of his eye and immediately reaches for the remote to turn off the TV. He looks over my shoulder at Enzo and Sebastian, then down at all the bags in our hands. "You found him." It's not a question. He knows.

Nodding my head, I throw the duffle at him, and he catches it. "You and Mac go get changed."

Without another word, he quickly kisses Harper on his way past her. Mac stands from the couch and does the same. Harper looks over the back of the couch at me, her green eyes wide. "Hey, Bella," Enzo greets her, then winks at me. They break off and head toward the dining room. Walking around the couch, I squat in front of Harper and rub my hands up and down the tops of her thighs.

"It's time?"

"Yeah, Baby. It is."

Harper bites her lip, clearly nervous but not trying to let it show. "What do you need me to do?"

I look into her eyes and squeeze her legs in my hands. "Harper,"

I watch as it only takes a moment to process. She looks over her shoulder to see Enzo and Sebastian unloading their equipment onto the table. Taking a deep breath, she looks back at me; the nervousness she was just trying so hard to hide has now taken over her face. But that's not the only thing I see. She looks sad. Frightened. Because she knows what I'm about to ask her. "That's why Enzo and Sebastian are here, isn't it?"

I nod. "I know you want to go. I know you want to face the man who has single-handedly tried to destroy your life at every turn. I'd be lying if I said I didn't think you deserved that much. But I'd also be lying if I said you being there wouldn't be a distraction. Because you would be, Baby. We have no idea what exactly we're walking into, but we do know that he's hell-bent on destroying you, no matter what. I know we let you come with us that night at the docks, but that was different. Liam had no idea you were there, and we were in control of the situation. Tonight, we won't be. If you're there, we won't be able to focus. We won't be able to do our job. And if we can't do our job, you won't be safe." Tears start to well in her eyes. "We need you safe, Baby. Please stay here with Enzo and Sebastian. Please be safe."

My thumb finds hers, and I spin my ring that she still has there. When I look back up at her face, I see it. For once, she's not going to argue with me—she understands.

After a moment, she nods and whispers, "Okay."

"Okay?"

She untucks one hand from mine and drags the tip of her pointer finger along her name on my neck. Besides asking her to marry us, this tattoo is one of the best ideas my brother has ever had. It's a badge of honor, inked on my skin for the rest of time. And even though she won't be there, Declan Whelan will see her name on our skin as we put an end to his miserable fucking existence. "I'll stay here."

I let out a harsh breath, hearing her say the words out loud. Leaning forward, I kiss her quick but fierce. "Ralph is downstairs, and once we leave, he's going to shut down that elevator. He's got extra men posted all over the building. Enzo and Sebastian will be here the entire time. Do not leave until we get back under any circumstances. If anything happens, you do exactly as Enzo tells you. Okay?"

Her chin wobbles as she nods.

"Tell me you understand."

"I understand."

My strong girl.

I give her one last deep kiss and force myself to pull away, needing to get changed. Sliding into the tactical gear Dante sent, I quickly get dressed and meet Mac and Finn, who are saying their goodbyes to Harper by the elevator. Looking over at Enzo, I raise my brow in silent question, and he nods. "We've got her man. I'll protect her with my life."

Harper pulls away from Finn and moves toward me like a magnet. Always drawn toward one another. I take her face in my hands. "We'll be back before you know it. Everything will be better. I promise."

She nods, blinking back the tears slowly slipping from her eyes. "I love you, Baby."

My mouth crashes to hers. She immediately opens for me. I take in every touch taste, and moan like it might be the last time I ever get to experience it. Pulling away, I take one of her curls between my fingers and look deep into her eyes. "I love you, Harper Hayes."

She grabs one of my wrists and turns my hand over between us. Sliding my signet ring off her thumb, she places it in the palm of my hand. "No," I shake my head and put it right back on her thumb with more force than necessary. "That is yours. Keep it with you always. We have you with us, remember?" Her wide eyes stare up at me. "Here," I tap her name on my neck. "And here." My finger moves to my chest. Harper places her hand on my chest, feeling the rhythm of my beating heart under her palm.

A moment later I turn and pick up the duffle of weapons Enzo brought, and join Mac and Finn in the waiting elevator.

Standing in the elevator, I stare at the love of our lives, barefoot, wearing a pair of jeans and one of her favorite vintage T-shirts, her arms crossed in front of her. Her messy curls hang over her shoulders, and her reading glasses are perched on her head. Her freckled cheeks are the perfect shade of pink, and her emerald eyes shine with unshed tears. I spare a look at my brother and best friend to find them staring at her the same way I just was. Like this is the way we want to hold her in our memory forever.

Our perfect girl.

"I'll see you soon then?"

"See you soon, Baby."

51

Finn

With a stroke of luck, it only takes us twenty minutes to drive through the city to the address Sebastian gave us. And with an even greater stroke of luck, the sun has just set by the time we pull up in front of the giant pre-war building in Bowery. A group of giant men in matching tactical gear walking around the city streets in broad daylight isn't exactly inconspicuous.

While the neighborhood is now considered one of the wealthiest in the city and is filled with a beautiful roster of architecture, like the rest of the city, there is no shortage of abandoned buildings. The ones in Bowery just happen to be a little nicer than the rest.

As we pull up, Luca and Dante emerge from an alleyway, dressed in the same dark clothing as us. The three of us climb out, and Ronan slaps the duffle bag onto the car's roof. He opens it, and we quickly pull the weapons out of the bag.

"Nice to see you enjoying your gifts," Dante's deep voice rumbles.

"They in there?" Ronan asks, not wasting any more time.

"Yeah. Seb just called and said he's already tapped into the cameras around the block. Nobody else has come or gone since they showed up. He'll keep an eye out and call if they do."

We all look at Mac, including Ronan. Regardless of being the boss and the one we turn to for direction, he knows that this is where Mac excels and that our best chance lies in doing what he says.

"Alright. Finn, Ronan, and Dante, you take the front door. Luca and I will take the back. On my signal, we move as one. We all know who the target is. Anyone else in there dies. Nobody leaves this building." The four of us nod in agreement. "Alright, turn your coms on and get your weapons ready." We all follow his instructions, and once everyone is ready, Mac looks between us. "Let's move."

Luca and Mac get a head start so they can run down the alley that leads to the back of the giant brick building. Once they reach the back door, Mac's voice sounds through our earpieces, "We're ready."

Ronan and I file behind Dante and move toward the front door, guns at the ready. "Ready," Dante's deep voice rumbles through the coms.

"On my count . . . 3 . . . 2 . . . 1" I listen as Mac busts down the back door at the same time as Dante raises his giant boot and crashes through the large wooden front door with minimal effort. Like a well-oiled machine, Ronan and I break off on either side of him. Shots go off around me as I drop a man who emerges from a doorway in front of me before he can so much as raise his gun.

Too slow motherfucker.

I turn around just in time to see Dante bash a man's skull against the tile floor hard enough that he goes limp with just one hit. Ronan and I converge on Dante, and the three of us move through the grand first floor, killing a dozen more men until we meet Luca and Mac at the base of the staircase leading to the second floor.

"They've got to be upstairs. We cleared that half," Luca says, breath ragged.

"This half is clear, too," answers Ronan.

Floorboards creak above us, and we all look at the terrified man pointing a gun at us at the top of the old wooden staircase. Ronan's quick on the trigger, raising his handgun and shooting him square between the eyes. Dead before his body even hits the top step, we watch as his lifeless form tumbles down the stairs.

Without missing a beat, Mac orders, "File in behind me. Dante, you take the rear." He looks right at Ronan and I. "Let's end this. For us. For our girl." With light and quick footwork, Mac steps over the lifeless body and moves up the stairs with the stealth of a trained killer, each of us following his every move.

Once we reach the top of the stairs, Mac clears the bathroom to our immediate left while Luca and I do the same to the small room on the right. Dante and Ronan make quick work of the following two bedrooms and come up empty, leaving the room at the end of the hall. Eyeing Mac, I can't help but state the obvious because if they're not there, Sebastian must have missed something. "That's the only room left."

Swallowing hard, Mac slowly moves down the narrow hallway, the rest of us behind him. Turning the knob, Mac slowly pushes the door open to find Declan Whelan standing across the empty room in front of a set of glass double doors leading out to a patio, staring out into the night. Our eyes scan the room as Patrick and eight of his men step out of the shadows. Each of them pointing weapons at the five of us.

"You didn't think this plan would actually work, did you?" Declan asks, not bothering to face us.

"What plan is that exactly?" Ronan asks, lowering his weapon and stepping around Mac and me.

"You thought stealing my money and putting it into Patrick's account would force my hand? You didn't think I'd know that you were behind this? He and I may not see eye to eye, but I still have something that he wants. *Power.*" All of our eyes snap to Patrick's. "I know Patrick wants to take over, and I'm willing to give that to him. In exchange for a few things, of course."

"And what exactly is that?" Ronan asks as he takes a few steps forward.

Patrick aims his gun right at Ronan's forehead. "You stay right there, boy-o."

"I'm able to use him, his men, his money, and resources for anything that I need done," Declan clarifies.

"And?" I prompt.

At the sound of my voice he turns and looks right at me. "Well, hello, Finn. My, my, my, you look just like your father. I bet the face you make when you take your last breath will be just like his, too." Against every instinct in my body, I fight the urge to freeze. This is when it matters most, and I won't let them down. I won't let Harper down.

"What else is Patrick offering you, Whelan?" Ronan bites.

"To help me kill every last one of you. Why the hell do you think I flew him and his men all the way here? I'll start with all of you and finish with my bitch of a granddaughter." Ronan jerks forward, but I reach out and grab his arm, silently begging him not to do anything rash, as much as we all want to. "I knew you'd be keeping tabs on Patrick. He arrived not more than two hours ago, and low and behold, here you all are."

Mac speaks next, "You expect us to believe that you're more than willing to hand everything over to Patrick? Everything you've built and have been fighting so hard to get back, you're willing to give away just to have us killed."

Declan unbuttons his suit jacket and expels a heavy breath. "Yeah, you're right. He's just as dead as the rest of you." In a split second, two of Patrick's men move their guns from us and train them on Patrick. "Sorry about this, Patrick. But when you called, telling me all of my money had been moved from my account to yours, I knew I had the perfect opportunity." He looks back at Ronan, Mac, and I. "Your father's efforts were less than impressive. Logan was one of my greatest disappointments, and I know I'll never get Harper to do as I ask, she'll only continue to get in my way." He looks at Patrick. "And you, you thought you could just stay tucked in the shadows and watch as everyone turned their backs on me until you could take over."

"Boss, that's not what I—"

"Shut the fuck up, Patrick. I couldn't put an end to you in Ireland; not a single one of my men would respect me if they knew I had you killed. But now"— he sweeps his hand out, gesturing to the situation in front of him—"it will just look like you died helping put an end to this horrendous fucking family."

"You'll never get to Harper." My voice is strong and sure. There isn't a chance in hell he's getting into that penthouse, but we're not stupid enough to know he isn't going to try.

Declan laughs, "You know, it was surprisingly easy to figure out the food delivery schedule for your building. I wouldn't be surprised if there were one of their trucks full of my men by the loading dock as we speak, just waiting for my signal."

There it is.

Right on cue, Mac lowers his gun, pulls his phone out of his pocket, and brings it to his ear. "Ralph. Catering truck at the loading dock. Move on it. Now." The moment he hangs up the phone, every single gun in the room is aimed at Declan. The man's arrogance made him believe he was still five steps ahead.

"Jokes on you motherfucker." Ronan backsteps until he's standing between me and Mac.

"What are you all doing?" Declan shouts to the men he thought were so loyal to him. "Shoot them!"

"Nah, *Boss.* I don't think they will."

"I don't think so either," Ronan adds. "You see, Patrick is a new friend of ours. As a matter of fact, he helped us deal with a little issue by the name of Liam McDermott."

"Sure did."

"And when you sent your little lackey, Logan, to take our girl, he's the one who helped us put all the pieces together. What was the matter, Declan? Couldn't handle the fact that your pet project liked sleeping with men?"

"You don't know what the hell yo—"

Ronan holds out his hand. "It was a rhetorical question. I could give less of a fuck why you did what you did. But the fact of the matter remains—you did it. And now you're going to die for it."

Declan looks at Patrick with pleading eyes as if he wasn't about to have him killed. "After everything I've done for you? Everything I've given you?"

"You know why these men are willing to follow me and not you? Why each one of them is more than willing to put a bullet in your demented fucking head?" Declan's visibly sweating now, regardless of the chilled fall air in the abandoned house. "I'm not here to chase power or to reclaim some sense of psychotic familial dictatorship. I want what's best for them. For our people. For the syndicate. If Harper wanted it all, I'd gladly let her have it. I'd step aside and help her lead our people. But she doesn't, and we deserve better than a piece of shit like you."

"Don't talk to me like you're some fucking saint. I've seen the things you've done. Hell, I taught most of it to you!" Declan spits.

"I didn't say I was a saint. None of us are good men, but the things you've done, Declan. You're not a man to be trusted. You have no code. You have no morals. The only person and the only thing that matters to you is *you*. That makes you the most dangerous person in this room."

"How?" Declan's attention is back on Ronan.

"As much as Patrick despises you, he can read you like a book. He knew that if he called you and admitted he had your money, you'd be willing to fake some sort of deal. We just had to wait and see what your play was. So when you told him you wanted him to fly to New York to help take us down, he knew exactly what you had in mind. You may have been one step ahead of us in the past, Delcan, but you never knew who was on your side. We used that to our advantage."

"So that's it then? You're going to kill me?" He looks over at Patrick, who shakes his head, and then at Ronan.

"Not me. Him." Ronan sticks his thumb in my direction.

"Me?" My heart speeds up in my chest.

Ronan leans in, so I'm the only one who can hear him. "You, Finn. You know better than anyone what it feels like to be at the mercy of this man's wrath. You deserve this. We want this for you. Your parents would want this for you. Harper would want this for you."

This matters most.

My eyes are trained on Declan's. The human succubus who takes from everyone and gives to no one. Declan opens his mouth, likely to spew more utter bullshit. And in the span of half a second I decide I no longer care. I don't want to hear another word from his useless mouth. I don't want another breath of air to be wasted on him. I don't want to see life in his eyes for a second longer. His lips part; I raise my gun from my side, aim it at his chest, and pull the trigger.

His hands go to his chest, trying to stop the blood as it pours from his body. I take a few steps forward until I'm a couple of feet from him. Just far enough that he can't reach out and touch me. I watch as he gasps for air, his lungs likely filling with blood. Another shot rings through the room as I shoot him in the thigh, and he drops to the floor. "That was for my parents."

They matter most.

Another shot lands in his shoulder. "That was for my childhood."

I matter most.

Blood sprays as another bullet rips through his stomach. "That's for fucking with my brothers."

They matter most.

"And this," I step forward and grab a handful of his gray hair, pressing the barrel of the gun underneath his chin. "This is for Harper and everything you've done to her."

She. Matters. Most.

I squeeze the trigger, instantly feeling his body go limp as I hold him by the hair. A sweet sense of satisfaction washes over me when I look up and see his brains sprayed all over the double glass doors.

"Well, that was satisfying." Patrick's voice cuts through the silence.

Mac comes up behind me and claps me on the shoulder. "You did it, man. When it mattered most, you didn't freeze."

I take a deep breath, reveling in the fact that both of them knew I could do this. That they trusted me with something so important. That, regardless of what Liam said to me that night on the dock, I matter.

I release my hold on his hair and watch his body fall to the ground. It feels like the weight of everything I've lost has been lifted. Like, before I was only living, and now I can learn what it feels like to be truly alive.

With my brothers. With Harper.

A family.

Teaghlach.

* * *

Luca and Dante offered to help Patrick and his guys clean up the scene and dispose of the bodies so we could get back home to Harper. All three of us are more than ready to have her in our arms without Declan's threats hanging over our heads.

When we asked Patrick what his plan was when he returned to Ireland, he simply shrugged and said, "I guarantee no one but his usual old cronies will question, or care, where he is or what happened to him. And if any of his friends decide they want to cause a disturbance, they'll be easy enough to take care of."

We thanked him, his men, and Luca's team for their help. Reassuring them that we would have never been able to do *any* of this without them. We are indebted to them for the rest of their lives. Patrick smiled and told us to come visit him in Ireland any time. Luca nodded and said, "I'm sure we'll ask you to return the favor sooner than later."

For some reason, I didn't doubt that for a second.

Ralph also called Mac back, letting him know our visitors in the food truck had been taken care of and "relocated."

Ronan pulls away from the curb before hitting a button on the steering wheel, dialing Harper's number. She answers on the first ring, "Is it done?"

"It's done, Baby."

"You're safe now, Pretty Girl."

"Finn? Love . . ." My name sounds like the most perfect song as it falls from her mouth.

"I did it, Angel. I did it for you."

Harper's harsh breath fills the car, "Come home to me."

"Always." Harper is my home. She's *our* home. And we'll always come back to her.

52

Harper

"Okay, I'll see you guys soon, Honey. Love you." Hanging up the phone, I finish applying a light coat of brown mascara to my lashes as I stand in front of my bathroom mirror in nothing but a matching bra and panty set. With the mascara wand still in my hand and my mouth hanging open in that stupid "I'm putting my mascara on my face," my eyes stray to the small tattoo where my thigh meets my hip. Just like it always does when the skin is visible. And just like it always does, an unmistakable warmth spreads through my chest at the sight of it.

Love.

The day after they killed Declan, I told Ronan I wanted a tattoo that represented them as well. I had each guy write the first letter in their name, which Ronan tattooed in small font. The entire tattoo isn't any bigger than a silver dollar, yet somehow, it feels so much larger.

Just like when they put my name on their necks, this is a symbol of my commitment to them. That they'll always be with me.

Not to mention, any time they see it, they can't help but place a soft kiss on the black ink. And without fail, it always takes my breath away. Every. Single. Time.

Feeling satisfied with my hair and makeup, I exit the bathroom and move toward the walk-in closet. Staring at the wide array of clothes I've accrued since I "officially" moved in, thanks to Finn, who has a box of clothes, shoes, and jewelry being delivered practically every other day, I have no idea what to wear.

Mac just called to let me know they were all on their way home from meeting with the contractor at the brownstone they bought last week. The brownstone that's going to be a bookstore. My new bookstore.

As hard as I fought them on it, saying over and over again that it was *entirely* too much, they told me, over and over again, that it wasn't nearly enough. However, as much as I protested, I'm also beyond excited. Though it won't be the store I fell in love with reading in, the one my parents started after fleeing Ireland in hopes of a better life, or the one I created hundreds of memories in with Cece, it will be *mine*. They took me to at least two dozen locations and told me to pick whichever one I wanted. The moment we pulled up outside of the old brownstone, I knew it was the one without even having to step inside. It's a few blocks from the one I lost in Greenwich Village, but just close enough that my previous customers will know I'm there. I'll be involved with the later remodel and design plans. Still, they assured me I didn't need to come today as they were simply discussing the logistics of completely gutting the inside of the beautiful building versus restoring it.

Mac told me they'd fill me in on the meeting later tonight, but they had somewhere they wanted to take me first. He told me to wear whatever I wanted as long as it was reasonably warm.

So, that definitely rules out any club dresses, yet still leaves endless options.

Ugh, what I would give for another one of Finn's outfits to show up right about now.

Looking through my dresses, I find one of my favorites. A taupe sweater shift dress that hugs me just right. It hits me mid-thigh and has a turtleneck to keep me warm. Rifling through my underwear drawer, I pull out a pair of sheer black stockings and slide them on underneath a pair of over-the-knee black Saint Laurent suede boots. I pick out a rose gold watch and a matching black purse with rose gold hardware. I'm surprisingly pleased when I step up to the full-length mirror to assess my outfit. It's casual enough that I won't stick out like a sore thumb but just dressy enough that I won't look like a hobo. Grabbing one of the perfumes I know all three of them love, I give myself a few good sprays.

Up until after everything went down with Declan, the four of us hadn't had a chance to go on any actual dates besides the few times we went to Kings. So, once the dust settled, the three of them have been taking me out whenever they get the chance. Whether it be all together, with two of them, or just one-on-one. When we do go out together, I don't miss the strange looks people give us, whether it's because they know who Ronan, Mac, and Finn are or because I'm not afraid to give them *all* affection when we're in public—or maybe it's a little bit of both. Regardless, the guys don't give a single fuck, and neither do I. I've spent too much of my life afraid to love and live a life worth living, content with just living each day as if it were another to check off the list. But they make me brave. They make me strong. And after everything I've been through—everything we've been through—I'll be damned if I don't love them as loud as they love me.

The guys also called Emma within a few days of Declan being gone to let her know she could come home. However, much to my amusement and much to Ronan and Mac's horror, she said she was more than willing to extend her stay with Pascal for the foreseeable future. I make sure I poke at that whenever I get the chance.

It's been two months of perfection.

I'm not naive enough to think that this will be how it will always be. I haven't forgotten who the men I love are. There will be other wars to be won, enemies to be beaten, knocks at death's door, not to mention all of the trials and tribulations regular relationships go through times three. I know this. But I also know that while it's okay to be afraid, it's even better to take a risk. Because without taking risks, I wouldn't have let myself love them.

Knowing I still have a few more minutes before they get here, I leave my room and walk toward the bar to pour myself a quick glass of wine.

Glass of wine in hand, I sit in Ronan's usual spot and look around the apartment. Over the course of the last two months, I've been making trips down to the storage unit where Ronan put my things from my old apartment and brought them up here, along with buying a few new things here and there. They even let me add some fun wallpaper to a few of the walls. On the built-in bookshelves next to the TV, I smile when I see, between stacks of my favorite books, the framed photo of my parents, Cece, and me when I was little, a black and white photo of my parents from the day they got married, and one a customer captured of Cece and I laughing behind the front desk of the bookstore a few weeks before she died.

I changed out the large black rug in the den for one with a dark green and tan Persian rug I found at one of my favorite flea markets. A wide variety of my plants sit throughout the apartment, along with some of my favorite throw pillows and blankets in the den and each of the bedrooms. My eclectic coffee mugs fill the cabinet above Mac's precious coffee machine, and some of my favorite pieces of art hang on the walls.

While it is still, very clearly, an apartment belonging to three men with expensive taste, you can now see me here as well.

The elevator dings, and I down my last sip of wine. "Honey, we're home!" Mac's cheerful voice booms through the apartment, and I can't help but let out a laugh.

Ronan spots me and raises a brow as they make their way over. "Pretty sure that's my spot, Baby."

I shrug. "Felt like being naughty." His eyes darken, but even the terrifying mafia boss can't fight the smile that tugs at his lips. I stand from the chair and make my way toward them, giving them each a kiss hello.

As I pull away from Finn, he grabs my hand, holding me still in front of him. "You look beautiful, Angel, and those boots," he groans as he hones in on my stocking-covered leg between the top of my boots and the bottom of my dress.

I kick out one of my toes. "Pretty nice, right? One of my boyfriends picked them out for me." The three of them share a look I don't quite understand before Finn looks back at me.

"Hmmm, bet they'd look even better wrapped around me."

No matter how many times I'm at the receiving end of their filthy mouths, I can't stop the blush that crawls across my cheeks. "I could probably make that happen."

"Later," he promises.

"You ready, Pretty Girl?" I stare at the men I love with my entire being, butterflies in my belly and heat pooling even lower. I'll never get over how damn sexy each of them are. And I'm the lucky bitch that gets them all to herself.

Mac's dressed in his usual all-black ensemble, except he's dressed it up with a pair of black slacks and sweater, and a dark brown pair of leather boots. His smile is beaming as his gray eyes dance across my face. Finn's wearing black dress pants and button-up with a caramel-brown wool coat open at the front. His beard is trimmed, and his blonde hair is perfectly undone, just the way I like it and how he now wears it daily. When my eyes land on his black leather boots, I smile at the scuff on the toe. Just last week, I was feeling particularly bratty, and when I sassed off a little too much, he chased me through the apartment. Once he caught me, my Converse scuffed the tip of his right shoe. My *punishment* made it all worth it, though. Judging by the look on his face, he's thinking about the same thing I am. Ronan's got on a dark green suit, black dress shirt, and black shoes. A midnight curl hangs over his forehead, pointing to his pools of blue. His hands are adorned in his usual jewelry, including the signet ring I bought to replace the one he refused to let me give back. At the thought of it, I instinctively twirl the one on my thumb. The top two buttons of his dress shirt are undone, and my mouth salivates at the site of his chest tattoos.

Like I said, so damn sexy.

They each smile at me, fully aware I'm gawking at them. Swallowing hard, I answer, "Just need my jacket." I quickly grab my black peacoat off my bed and throw it on, leaving the buttons undone until we get to the lobby. The elevator always feels like it's a hundred degrees. Then again, it might just be me. Considering I'm usually sandwiched between three giants who constantly do everything they can to turn me on.

Like breathing.

How dare they.

Ronan and Finn are waiting by the open elevator, but my sweet, sweet Mac is still waiting where I left him, hand outstretched and ready for me to grab.

When we get into the elevator, Ronan hits the button for the rooftop instead of pressing one for the lobby. I look up at them in confusion. And, of course, like the smart-asses they are, they all say nothing and simply smile down at me.

I roll my eyes at Ronan, who pulls his lip between his teeth before growling, "Keep sassing me, Baby. It turns me on."

Mac reaches around me and smacks his brother in the head. "Focus."

"Fight nice boys," Finn jokes from the other side of Mac.

Before I can ask them what exactly is going on, the elevator stops, and the doors open. My jaw drops as I step away from the guys and out of the elevator. Where there were a few sets of string lights, there are now dozens, and across the entirety of the snow-covered rooftop are red and white rose petals along with at least fifty lit candles. Snowflakes fall from the sky as I take a few more steps forward and listen as the soft melody of Hozier's "Work Song" floats through the air.

When I turn around, my breath stalls in my lungs, my heart stops beating in my chest, and every thought in my brain ceases to exist. Tears fill my eyes, and I don't even bother stopping them.

All three are on their knees, velvet ring boxes in their hands. *Holy shit.*

Mac lets out a laugh. "So, not quite speechless, but pretty close."

I must have said that out loud.

"Wha–wh . . ." I know what's happening, but my brain can't seem to comprehend it.

"Harper," My eyes find Ronan's. "You've branded my fucking soul, Baby. I never thought I'd find someone who captivates me the way you do every minute of every day. I thought I was destined to spend my life alone. Then, that night at the bookstore changed everything. You made my life worth living. You make me wake up every day wanting to be a better person." A sob catches in my throat as I watch a tear fall down his cheek. "I love you more than I ever thought I could love another."

"From the moment I sat next to you in the back seat of that car," Finn says from the other side of Mac. "I knew I was lost to you. I wouldn't change it for the world. You dance in the dark with me, Angel. You're the piece that's made a man who hasn't felt whole for as long as he can remember finally feel complete. I'll never be able to thank you enough for that." Ignoring the cold, I drop to my knees right there in the snow in front of them. "You have given me everything I could have ever wanted and then some. A second chance at happiness.

At a family. I love you."

My eyes find Mac's, who's a sobbing mess between Ronan and Finn. "My Pretty Girl. You saved my life. You have opened your heart to me and fully embraced me for who I am. Every part of me. Even the part I try to hide from myself. When we kissed in that elevator, I knew right then and there, my soul was meant to find yours. I love you so damn much, Mo Grá. Now and always."

I'm a full-on sobbing mess now. There's no way this is cute, yet I can't find it in myself to stop.

"We know we can't really do this legally, but we're yours in every way that matters," Mac says as he opens the box in his hand. "Marry us, Harper Hayes. Be our wife."

He doesn't ask because it's not even a question. "Of course, I'll marry you." I look between them with tear-filled eyes. "Yes, yes, yes."

Finn's up off his knee first. He lifts me off the ground and swings me through the air. Gently setting me down, he pulls the ring from his box. It's a gold band with five black diamonds. "For the darkness in us that you crave."

Ronan walks forward and crashes his mouth to mine. When he pulls away, he opens his box. It's the same as Finn's, but instead, it has five white diamonds. "For the light inside of you that has filled the cracks of our souls."

Mac's in front of me next, and I can now see the giant pear-shaped emerald ring in the box he's holding. It sits on a gold band with a halo of diamonds around the deep green center stone. "We don't deserve you, but we're keeping you anyway."

Mac kisses me fiercely, both of us crying tears of joy.

Finn slides his ring on first, followed by Mac's, and then Ronan's, creating the most beautiful stack of jewelry I have ever seen in my life.

The four of us eventually make our way back down to the apartment after deciding to skip dinner entirely. I spent the entire night being loved and worshiped by each of them. We made love, knowing it was the start of our new lives together. And once our bodies were fully spent, I laid back in bed, listening as they bickered back and forth.

It was at that moment that I felt the last piece of my heart fully heal. The one that I didn't even know was still broken. I now know what it feels like to be at peace.

Because these three men—these dangerous men—will always be here to keep me safe.

THE END.

Epilogue

Four Months Later

Ronan

"You really think he'll go for this?" I ask Mac while nervously adjusting my tie in the reflection of the full-length mirror Harper put in my room for today.

"I think it's perfect. Hell, we might even make him cry," he answers from behind me.

I huff out a laugh. "He's going to cry today anyway."

Shit, I'm *going to cry today.*

"Yeah, but we're not going to make him cry. She is."

Mac looks over my shoulder and finishes tying his matching tie just as Finn pushes through my door. "You guys about ready to head upstairs? Pascal just came down to let me know everything's all set. Emma went to check on Harper."

Mac pats me on the ass like a tool. "All you champ."

Turning to face Finn, I answer, "Yeah, we just wanted to talk to you about something quick."

His eyes widen. "What? What happened?"

"Nothing happened, man." He walks over to my dresser and grabs the large manila envelope before returning to stand next to me. "Here, open this."

Finn slowly opens the envelope and pulls out four large pieces of paper accompanied by four social security cards. His brow pinches in confusion. "What are these for?"

"Would you just read the damn papers, Finny," I answer.

"Application for a name change?" he mumbles under his breath. Mac and I look at one another with smiles on our faces as he flips through each application. Only when he sees the name on the first social security card does it seem to register on his face. The papers start to shake in his hold as he rapidly flips through each card. When he reaches the last one, I watch as a tear falls from his eye and lands on the piece of paper.

Looking up at us with tears in his eyes, he says the most beautiful name I ever could have imagined. "Harper Donovan-McDermott."

Mac claps him on the shoulder. "Yeah, man. Harper Donovan-McDermott."

My hand reaches out to grab his other shoulder. "And you're looking at Ronan and Cormac Donovan-McDermott."

He looks between us in disbelief. "You—you guys changed your name? For me?"

After we proposed to Harper, our original plan was to each keep our own last names, but then Harper came to Mac and me a few days later and suggested this idea. She told us that while she valued her last name, she was more than comfortable giving it up.

"Hayes isn't my parent's real name. It's nothing more than an identity they created to hide from the evil that was after them. I know it's who I've been since I was born, but this is who I am now. Who I want to be for the rest of my life. I can't legally marry all

of you, but I can change my name. We can change our name."

Mac and I were on board immediately. Finn was our brother, and we knew how important it was for him to keep his last name. We wanted to do this for him. For *us.*

"Yeah, Finny. We did."

"D—does Harper know about this?"

"Who's idea do you think it was?"

A strangled sob leaves Finn's lips. "Told you we'd make him cry," Mac says as he elbows me in the ribs.

Finn smiles so wide it damn near breaks his face. "I can't believe you guys did this for me."

"We'd do anything for you. You're our brother, and this is our family."

"Don't ever spend another moment questioning it," Mac adds.

Finn doesn't say anything else. He just nods, holding the papers in his hand as if they were his most prized possession. And as the three of us stand there in our matching suits, I can't help but feel like this is where I was always meant to be.

Here, with my brothers, about to marry the love of our lives.

Harper Donovan-McDermott.

She is my home.

My peace. My life. My heart. My Baby.

Every moment in my life has led me to her. In this life and every life after, wherever she is is where I'm meant to be—where *we* are meant to be.

"Let's go marry our girl. Shall we, boys."

Harper

"Harper, Honey, you look so beautiful." Emma closes my door and stands in front of me, eyes full of tears and hands clasped over her heart.

I would give anything to be able to have my mom and Cece here with me today, helping me get ready, zipping up my dress, clasping my necklace, and sneaking me a glass of wine to calm my racing heart. But even though they aren't with me physically, I know they're here. And they would be so happy that I have a woman like Emma here to watch over me.

I wave my hands in front of my face. "Stop. You're going to make me cry."

"Oh, please. I've been crying all day. Just ask Pascal."

My chest warms at the thought of Emma finally finding the man she deserves. One that will move heaven and hell to give her everything she wants and to keep her safe, rather than one she needed to find safety from. She's an amazing woman who's raised three amazing men. She deserves everything good in life, and I'm so happy she's found that in Pascal.

While Mac and Ronan still act as if they are horrified at the very notion of their mother falling in love, I know they're secretly happy for her. Luca constantly teases them about being step-brothers now—much to their dismay.

Emma has now officially moved to Saint-Jean-de-Luz, and I think it's safe to say I am more than excited to visit her new home in France.

Emma spins me so I'm facing the mirror. Pulling my hair to the side, she places a necklace around my neck. Looking down, I take it between my thumb and forefinger. It's a dainty oval-shaped diamond on a thin gold chain that sits right in between my collarbones.

Her hands rub up and down my arms, as she says, "It was my mother's. She gave it to me when I was a girl before she died. I always knew I was going to give it to one of the boys' brides. I just didn't know who would be first."

I was originally so nervous to meet Emma when she and Pascal flew home a few weeks ago to help prepare for the wedding. I didn't know how she would react to all of them being with one woman, regardless of how much they all assured me she wouldn't care. I'm happy to say I was worried for no reason. The moment she laid eyes on me, she embraced me in the kind of hug only a mother knows how to give. She has been nothing but loving and accepting of our relationship.

"Emma, I don't know what to say. It—It's perfect."

Now I'm definitely going to cry.

"I'm so, so happy the three of them found love in a woman like you. It's all a mother could hope for."

"I'll take care of them. I promise," I whisper as I look at her in the eye through the mirror.

She gently kisses my cheek. "I know you will."

Taking a deep breath she releases my arms and steps back. "Alright. No more crying!" I laugh as she wipes at her cheeks. "The boys should be upstairs by now. I'll give you a minute to yourself, and you can meet me by the elevator when you're ready."

"Okay," I smile, still looking at her through the mirror. She softly closes the door, leaving me to myself.

Knowing we weren't going to have a large wedding, we decided to have it right upstairs on the roof. The only guests we invited were Emma and Pascal, Luca and his team, Ralph, and Patrick.

Ronan brought a company in to put glass flooring over the pool to use as a dance floor, and I had the rooftop decorated just like the night they proposed to me. Nothing but twinkling lights, candles, and white roses. It's perfect.

Standing in front of the mirror, I take one last look at myself before officially becoming Harper Donovan-McDermott. My usually unruly hair lies in soft waves down my back, with my bangs slicked back and pinned behind my ears.

I chose a strapless, ivory A-line gown with a sweetheart neckline that flares out just above my waist. It's made of the most delectable satin fabric and has a slit up to the middle of my thigh. Something I know the guys won't be able to take their eyes off of. I also have on a pair of white strappy heels that are adorned with pearls.

I've never felt more beautiful.

"Alright, Harp. Time to get yourself married."

Gathering the short train of my dress, I open my door and head toward Emma, who's practically bouncing with excitement as she holds my bouquet of eucalyptus and white roses.

As we take the short trip up to the roof, I can feel my heart beating out of my chest, not out of nerves but of excitement.

Legal or not, I just want to be married to them. To be theirs for the rest of my life.

As the elevator stops on the roof and the doors open, Emma steps out, and the music starts to play. "Marry Me" by Train floats through the evening air, and as the guys turn around from their spot at the makeshift alter, my once-racing heart stalls in my chest.

There in front of me are the three most beautifully dangerous men I have ever known. Three men who are unequivocally and irrevocably mine.

Each of them is dressed in a deliciously tailored black tuxedo. They all match from head to toe, except for the cuff links I gifted them each last night. One's with the nickname I gave each of them engraved into the silver metal.

As I walk down the short aisle, I watch a tear roll down Mac's cheek first. His steel gray eyes lovingly stare into mine before giving me a cheeky wink. Next to him, Finn holds one hand over his heart and mouths, "Beautiful." Finally, my eyes move to Ronan, who I catch looking me over from head to toe, stopping at the spot where the satin splits at my thigh. *Knew it.* When his eyes meet mine, I momentarily get lost in the deep pools of blue, shining with the tears he's trying so hard not to let fall.

As the four of us stand in front of our closest friends, the people I now call family, I know that in the deepest depths of my soul, with them, I. Am. Home.

Acknowledgments

First, I want to thank everyone who supported me through the release of book one, *Dangerously Safe*. There would have been no book two if it had been for all of you. Because of all of you, I had the courage to not only write this book but to do so without fear of being judged.

I'm fully aware of how uncommon it is for someone to write a book where I am from—especially one of this nature. And I'm even more aware of how fast word spreads in a small town. So, to those of you who did nothing except support me every step of the way, I am forever grateful.

Amber, I would have been totally lost without you over the course of the last few months. I am so glad BookTok brought me you. Your crazy ideas and constant cheering from the sidelines have brought me more confidence than you know. No matter what crazy idea, question, or TikTok thirst trap video I throw at you, the answer is always a resounding "Fuck yes, bitch!" Because of you, I have learned, laughed, and learned some more. You didn't *have* become one of my biggest cheerleaders, but I am so so glad you did.

To Samantha and Emily, I said it after the first book, and I'll say it after this one too. Thank you, thank you, thank you. You both listen to me when I need to complain and cheer me on when I need a pep talk. I couldn't have done any of this without you. I love you both x a million.

Next up, my betas! This was my first round of beta reading, and with a team like you, I can't wait to do it all over again! Abigail, Sadie, Lilah, Tilly, and Yolanda, you guys are truly amazing. I think it's safe to say that this book would be a mess if it weren't for you ladies. Thank you from the bottom of my heart.

My love, thank you for being my number-one fan, now and always.

Mom, when I'm wrong, I say I'm wrong (most of the time). Much to my immediate horror, you dove head first into *Dangerously Safe*, and I gotta say . . . I'm so glad you did. Thanks for being a cool mom. Dad, the answer is still no . . . please don't read this one either. But thank you for cheering me on regardless!

Last but not least, my readers. You took the time to read an indie author's book and made her little dream come true. Thank you for all of the encouragement, praise, recommendations to other readers, and reviews. I hope you fell in love with Harper, Ronan, Mac, and Finn right along with me and are as sad to see them go as I am. But I can't wait for you to see what I have in store next. I love you all!

Also by S.R. Clark

McDermott Empire Duet
Dangerously Safe
Dangerously Kept
Reverse Harem Mafia Romance

Vittori Enterprises Duet
The Prices We Pay
Reverse Harem/Polyamorous Billionaire Romance
Preorder here

About the Author

S.R. Clark is an indie author who lives in West Virginia with her husband, toddler, and hound dog. She writes reverse harem/dark romance books. She has a soft spot for characters who live unapologetically for themselves and who will lay down their lives for the ones they love. When she's not writing, she loves getting lost in a good book, cooking/baking, and exploring with her family.